THE SPRINGS OF
AFFECTION

Also by
Maeve Brennan

In and Out of Never-Never Land
Stories

The Long-Winded Lady
Notes from "The New Yorker"

Christmas Eve
Stories

The Springs of Affection

Stories of Dublin

Maeve Brennan

INTRODUCTION BY

William Maxwell

HOUGHTON MIFFLIN COMPANY

Boston   New York

1997

For information about permission to reproduce selections from
this book, write to Permissions, Houghton Mifflin Company,
215 Park Avenue South, New York, New York 10003.

Library of Congress Cataloging-in-Publication Data

Brennan, Maeve.
Springs of affection : stories of Dublin / Maeve Brennan ;
introduction by William Maxwell.
p. cm.
ISBN 0-395-87046-1
1. Dublin (Ireland) — Social life and customs — Fiction.   I. Title.
PS3552.R38s67 1997
813'.54 — dc21   97-18296   CIP

Book design by Anne Chalmers
Typeface: Granjon (Adobe PostScript™)

Printed in the United States of America
QUM 10 9 8 7 6 5 4 3 2 1

With the exception of "The Poor Men and Women," which appeared originally in *Harper's Bazaar*, all of these stories were first published in *The New Yorker*.

The stories were collected by the author in her previous books of short fiction. Sixteen are from *In and Out of Never-Never Land*, published by Charles Scribner's Sons in 1969. "The Poor Men and Women," "An Attack of Hunger," "Family Walls," "Christmas Eve," and "The Springs of Affection" are from *Christmas Eve*, published by Scribner's in 1974.

The contents of the present volume were selected and arranged by Christopher Carduff of Houghton Mifflin Company.

CONTENTS

THE SPRINGS OF
AFFECTION

INTRODUCTION

BY WILLIAM MAXWELL

Because I had been her editor I was asked to write the obituary notice that appears in the November 15, 1993, issue of *The New Yorker*. It begins: "Maeve Brennan died a few days ago, at the age of seventy-six. She was a small, charming, effortlessly witty, generous woman with green eyes, hugely oversized horn-rimmed glasses, and chestnut hair worn in a vast beehive."

In 1934 her father, Robert Brennan, was appointed the Republic of Ireland's first envoy to Washington, and he brought his family with him. Maeve was seventeen. At the end of her father's term he and the others went back to Dublin, and she stayed on in this country through the rest of her life. I don't know whether in Ireland she is considered an Irish writer or an American. In fact, she is both, and both countries ought to be proud to claim her.

Before she came to *The New Yorker* she wrote copy for *Harper's Bazaar*. She was hired by William Shawn, *The New Yorker*'s managing editor (and editor in chief after Harold Ross died), to write about women's fashions. She then moved on to doing short notices of novels and whodunits and an occasional lead review. The unsigned fashion and book notes are untraceable at this point. The lead reviews are so original and well done that they raise the question, Why wasn't she asked to do more? The answer perhaps is that W. H. Auden was also reviewing books for *The New Yorker* during this period.

For a while her office was next to mine, on the twentieth floor of 25 West Forty-third Street. I was aware of the quick sound of her heels and her beautiful Dublin accent before I caught a glimpse of her disappearing down the hall. She was in her early thirties and wore her hair in a ponytail, which made her look younger than she was.

I think we became friends because we both liked Tolstoy's *The Death of Ivan Ilyich* and Turgenev's *The Sportsman's Notebook* and the novels and music-hall reminiscences of Colette. A story she submitted, about a Lady Bountiful rather too pleased with the idea of her own kindness toward the unfortunate, was taken, and for the next twenty-one years her fiction passed through my hands on its way to Mr. Shawn or the printer.

She would wander into my office, sit down, and say thoughtfully, "*Time* magazine is all a dream." Or talk about Oliver Goldsmith, whom she was so fond of it was almost as if she had known him. She used as a kind of talisman a sentence of his: "Innocently to amuse the imagination in this dream of life is wisdom."

She had a large framed photograph by Louise Dahl-Wolfe of Colette in old age, looking as if nothing in the way of human behavior, no matter how odd or perverse, would surprise her. One morning when I walked into my office it was hanging on the wall above my desk. It remained there for a month or so and then it was gone. I knew I had said or done something Maeve didn't approve of. After a short while the picture was back. It came and went, like a cloud shadow. I never knew why and thought it would be a poor idea to ask. The only bone of contention between us I was aware of was that she refused to read the novels of Elizabeth Bowen because Bowen was Anglo-Irish. On the other hand, she venerated Yeats, who was also Anglo-Irish, and she knew a good deal of his poetry by heart.

One day I found a quotation from Yeats written in pencil on the plaster wall where I could read it sitting at my desk: "Only that which does not teach, which does not cry out, which does not persuade, which does not condescend, which does not explain, is irresistible." In time there were other such statements for my mind to be caught by in moments of abstraction. One of them was "It is dangerous to mock a fool. God." Even so, she did frequently.

All but one of the stories in this book originally appeared in *The New Yorker* and then were published in two collections, *In and Out of Never-Never Land* (1969) and *Christmas Eve* (1974), both long out of print. Her best stories are always set in Ireland and have no characters that are not Irish.

The group of stories that are written in the first person are, I assume, autobiographical since the narrator is called Maeve and the narrator's brother and sisters have the same names as Maeve's brother and sisters. They live in a small brick family house on a dead-end street in a suburb of Dublin. It is where she lived as a child and it is her imagination's home. Also, these stories do not read as if they were fictitious. Though slight, they are definitely stories, written with great care and radiant with the safety and comfort of home. Even when the house is brutally ransacked by plainclothesmen—the father is for the Republic and against the Irish Free State and was at the time on the run—nothing really bad happens. The house is protected by love.

Over a period of fifteen years Maeve published, in "The Talk of the Town," what were presented as "communications from our friend the long-winded lady." They were anything but long-

winded—two to four printed columns. Half descriptive, half re-
flective, they are visually as true to nature as the prints of Hoku-
sai. They are always about New York City—about a rainstorm
watched through the window of a borrowed apartment, about a
man she sometimes sees who is always combing his hair, about a
bad-mannered dog, about invisibility, about self-service elevators
that creak and carry on as if they were unsafe and frequently stop
at the wrong floor, about the light from the sky at a certain time
of day, about a part of town where the atmosphere is of shabby
transience, about the states of mind of people seen only once or
who are imaginary, about a cageful of tiny birds for sale in the
basement of a five-and-ten-cent store, about apprehension that
has no known cause, about a young man waiting for his date in
the bar of what turns out to be the wrong hotel, about what lies
behind the curiosity that leads her to turn first to the obituary
pages of the morning paper. Forty-seven of these pieces were
published as a book under the title of *The Long-Winded Lady*
(1969).

One of the long-winded lady's observations is that "the impulse toward good involves choice, and is complicated, and the
impulse toward bad is hideously simple and easy." After holding
back from marrying anyone for a long time, in 1954 Maeve became the fourth wife of St. Clair McKelway. It may not have
been the worst of all possible marriages but it wasn't something
you could be hopeful about. He was one of the most gifted of the
New Yorker reporters, and if there was anyone who disliked him
I never heard of it, but he was a heavy drinker and a manic de-
pressive and subject to what he called "blank-outs," during
which he did not always know who he was and his behavior was
sometimes highly bizarre. What money he had he spent as fast as
possible and it was against his principles to pay any bill. His wives
were all beautiful and charming women, and his marriages

tended to be brief. He courted women ardently until the vows were said and then his interest in them faded.

He and Maeve lived together for a number of years, mostly in Sneden's Landing, north of the city on the west bank of the Hudson River, and then parted amicably. During this period she wrote a series of stories about a bohemian enclave, which she called Herbert's Retreat. They are satirical in tone, and seem to me to be heavy-handed and lack the breath of life.

Brendan Gill's office was next to Maeve's and there was so much slipping of notes under his door, and hers, and mine, and so many explosions of laughter as a result of our reading them that — we learned through the grapevine — Mr. Shawn decided it wasn't good for the office morale, and Maeve was moved down the hall to the other side of the building.

Who bothers to preserve funny remarks? If they survive in the memory it is usually by accident. Recently, between the pages of my copy of *In and Out of Never-Never Land,* I came across a carbon of a *New Yorker* form letter addressed to a Mr. Boyce, who had written to the editors expressing a hope that they would print more of Maeve Brennan's Herbert's Retreat stories. This carbon was sent to Maeve as a matter of office procedure. Across the bottom on the reverse side she had written a second, corrective letter:

Dear Mr. Boyce:

I am terribly sorry to have to be the first to tell you that our poor Miss Brennan died. We have her head here in the office, at the top of the stairs, where she was always to be found smiling right and left and drinking water out of her own little paper cup. She shot herself in the back with the aid of a small handmirror at the foot of the main altar in St. Patrick's Cathedral on Shrove Tuesday. Frank O'Connor was where he usually is in the afternoons, sitting in a confession box pretending to be a priest and giving penance to some poor old woman and he heard the shot and he ran out and saw our poor late author stretched out flat and he picked her up and fearing a scandal ran up to the front of the church and slipped her in the poor box. She was very small. He said she went in easy. Imagine the feelings of the young curate who unlocked the box that same evening and found the deceased curled up in what appeared to be and later turned out truly to be her final slumber. It took six strong parish priests to get her out of the box and then they called us and we all went and got her and carried her back here on the door of her office. We will never know why she did what she did (shooting herself) but we think it was because she was drunk and heartsick. She was a very fine person, a very real person, two feet, hands, everything. But it's too late to do much about that now.

I have a lot of live authors, Mr. Boyce, if you would like to ask about any of them, if there is anything you would like to know about any of them, I'll be happy to oblige. Most of them have studio portraits, ready for framing, some life size, some even en famille, as we say around here in our amiable but decidedly spirited, even brisk, New Yorker Magazine Way. And thank you for your kind interest in the unfortunate Miss Brennan. I am glad to know that someone remembers her. As for her, I'm afraid she would only spit in your eye. She was ever ungrateful. One might say of her that nothing in her life became her.

Sincerely,
William (Bill) Maxwell

After she was living alone again, Maeve began to write what are clearly her finest stories. They are about a couple named Rose and Hubert Derdon, and they live in that very same small house in a suburb of Dublin. It has a bow window, and there is a tiny grass plot in front, a walled garden in back with flowers and a yellow laburnum. The front door leads into a narrow hall. Past the stairs, down three steps, is the kitchen. The front and back sitting rooms are separated by folding doors. One room is heated by a coal-burning fireplace, the other by a gas fire. Upstairs, there is linoleum on the floor of the back bedroom, none in the front one. The tone of these stories, however, is entirely different.

At the beginning of their married life the Derdons lived in a flat in Dublin, and Hubert had a friend named Frank who was given to fits of merriment that were contagious. But then they moved to this house, and Frank dropped out of their lives, and there is no more laughter. They are now in their fifties. They have only one child, a son named John, who has left home to study for the priesthood. Leaving Rose a prey to fantasies.

At times... she would become terribly excited and run to the front windows knowing that John was coming home, that he was at this exact moment walking along the street carrying his suitcase, and that she would have to wait only a minute or so to get her first sight of him, coming around the corner from the main road. But of course he wasn't coming, and he wouldn't be coming, and the excitement inside her would flatten out and stupefy her with its weight, and her disappointment and humiliation at being made a fool of would be as cruel as though what she had felt had really been hope and not what it was, the delirium of loss.

Hubert goes off every morning to the center of town—he is a sales clerk in a men's outfitters in Grafton Street—and comes home again in the evening. The reader is not allowed past the front gate and can count on the fingers of one hand the times the two characters in these stories are seen going to Mass or walking down O'Connell Street or wandering among the flower beds of

St. Stephen's Green. Totally forlorn without her son to look after, Rose becomes obsessed with her husband's remoteness. His mind is to the same degree fixed on what he considers her shortcomings—her country ways, her insecurity with strangers, her possessiveness with her son. As a study of one kind of unhappy marriage these stories are surely definitive. When Hubert dresses in the morning the last thing he puts on is a garment of lies, which do not, even so, conceal the fact that where there should have been feeling there is none—only the desire for privacy and solitude. Because he is too clever for her, her anger turns against herself. She is also afraid of him, of what he might say or do if she drives him too far. This in turn increases his anger against her. Their moments of understanding do not bring them closer but instead only serve to drive them farther apart. They try unsuccessfully to deceive each other in very small matters. They both want it to appear that nothing is amiss. Their hatred and anger are almost palpable.

There is much to admire in these ferocious stories—the storytelling art; the prose, which is plain and exquisitely precise, at times passing over into poetry without ever becoming "poetic"; the gift for dramatic confrontations; the ability to suggest something devastating while seeming to be making an innocuous statement; the at times almost clinical descriptions of states of mind. For example:

"When Rose appeared in the doorway Hubert felt such dislike that he smiled."

And "how could he grieve for what he could not define, or mourn for what had vanished without a trace?"

While Maeve continued to write stories about Rose and Hubert Derdon, she began to write stories about another couple, Delia and Martin Bagot. These stories are gentler, though the marriage is again unsatisfactory and is in some ways similar. The Bagots have two little girls, born two years apart, and some cats and a dog — a stray that Delia rescued from boys who were tormenting him. Martin hates animals. He also longs to be free of his family, which he regards as an encumbrance; he is by temperament a bachelor and should have remained one. There was a little boy, who died when he was three days old, and Delia has never recovered from the shock of his death. It has made her vague, ineffectual, given to falling asleep in the daytime. What keeps her from slipping over the edge into insanity is the children's need for her. She was brought up on a beautiful farm in County Wexford and has a way with flowers. There are moments of happiness, when she introduces a new piece of furniture into the house or when, in "Stories of Africa," a retired bishop of the South African Missions, who was a close friend of Delia's father, comes to tea and by his saintliness and the sweetness of his nature and his memories of her childhood home restores to Delia a sense of who she is. So far as the Bagots' marriage is concerned, the bishop's visit does not alter the situation or provide a way out. There is no way out.

Maeve had a fondness for the rundown neighborhood bordering on Times Square — the visible remains of past grandeur, the crowded colorful untidy fly-by-night air of its inhabitants, the mixture of tourists and transients of every kind all appealed to her imagination, and she sometimes lived there in one small hotel or another. She also lived in the Wellfleet woods and in Amagansett. Fortune had up its sleeve one last great pleasure for her: she formed an intimate friendship with Gerald and Sara Murphy. The Murphys were old enough to have been Maeve's parents, and they had lived in France during the twenties and known everyone of any importance among the expatriate writers and artists. It is said that Gerald served as the model for Dick

Diver, the hero of Scott Fitzgerald's novel *Tender Is the Night*. While living in France he painted six or eight large cubist paintings and then stopped because after the death of his two young sons he had no more heart for painting. His canvases are now highly valued by museums. He too had a gift for aphorisms, one of which Maeve was given to quoting: "As we grow older we must guard against a feeling of lowered consequence." He had a Yeats letter, which he promised Maeve would have when he died, but he neglected to put this in writing.

One of the last stories Maeve wrote about the Bagots, "The Springs of Affection," is in form, if not quite in length, a novella and far outdoes anything she had previously written. It belongs with the great short stories of this century. Both Delia and Martin are dead and the whole sweep of their lives is dealt with in a masterly fashion by moving in and out of the mind of Martin's twin sister, Min, who kept house for him after Delia died and who is now a very old woman. She hated Delia. She wears Martin's wedding ring on her finger. She has brought back to Wexford as much of the Bagots' books and furniture as she can crowd into her small flat and sits in happy possession of it. What in the earlier stories was an at times almost unbearable sadness is now an unfaltering irony. Dominated by false pride, ungenerous, unreachable, unkind, the old woman is the embodiment of that side of the Irish temperament that delights in mockery and rejoices in the downfall of those whom life has smiled on.

Many men and women found Maeve enchanting, and she was a true friend, but there wasn't much you could do to save her from herself. Though she lived in the country from time to time, she never learned to drive a car; when she wanted to shop for groceries she called a taxi. She put parquet floors in a city apartment she did not own and then found she preferred living in the Hotel Algonquin, leaving the apartment empty until the lease expired. Then she rented a little house near Rindge, New Hampshire. Inevitably she got into debt. She had a valuable library of books by Irish writers, which she would hock when there was no other way she could lay her hands on some money. The books were rescued a number of times by a colleague who was given to anonymous acts of benevolence, and then they disappeared forever. When she returned to the city, *The New Yorker* stepped between her and destitution by seeing to it that there was a place she could go to when she chose, and be fed and sheltered. There is no way of knowing how often she took advantage of this. She had begun to have psychotic episodes, and she settled down in the ladies' room at *The New Yorker* as if it were her only home. Nobody did anything about it, and the secretaries nervously accommodated themselves to her sometimes hallucinated behavior, which could turn violent. During the last decade of her life she moved in and out of reality in a way that was heartbreaking to watch and that only hospitals could deal with. Long long before this she wrote on my wall, under the quotation from Yeats: "A certain degree of self-esteem is necessary even in the mad. Conrad."

For a while her letters to me went into the office files and then, because *The New Yorker* was rather absent-minded about its archives, I decided to keep them in a drawer in my desk, and so I still have them. They tended to be about animals — her cats, a black Labrador retriever who figures in some of her stories, a baby skunk she rescued from the cold; or unexplained ruminations that could have been lifted from her journal; or descriptions of some natural phenomenon like an ice storm; or about people, or about something imaginary; or about money: "I think I feel as Goldsmith must have done, that any money I get is spending money, and the grownups ought to pay the big ugly bills"; or

The Morning
after the Big Fire

From the time I was almost five until I was almost eighteen, we lived in a small house in a part of Dublin called Ranelagh. On our street, all of the houses were of red brick and had small back gardens, part cement and part grass, separated from one another by low stone walls over which, when we first moved in, I was unable to peer, although in later years I seem to remember looking over them quite easily, so I suppose they were about five feet high. All of the gardens had a common end wall, which was, of course, very long, since it stretched the whole length of our street. Our street was called an avenue, because it was blind at one end, the farthest end from us. It was a short avenue, twenty-six houses on one side and twenty-six on the other. We were No. 48, and only four houses from the main road, Ranelagh Road, on which trams and buses and all kinds of cars ran, making a good deal of noisy traffic.

Beyond the end wall of our garden lay a large tennis club, and sometimes in the summer, especially when the tournaments were on, my little sister and I used to perch in an upstairs back window and watch the players in their white dresses and white flannels, and hear their voices calling the scores. There was a clubhouse, but we couldn't see it. Our view was partly obstructed by a large garage building that leaned against the end wall of our garden and the four other gardens between us and Ranelagh Road. A number of people who lived on our avenue kept their cars in the garage, and the people who came to play tennis parked their cars there. It was a very busy place, the garage, and I had never been in there, although we bought our groceries in a shop that was connected with it. The shop fronted on Ranelagh Road, and the shop and the garage were the property of a red-faced, gangling man and his fat, pink-haired wife, the McRorys. On summer afternoons, when my sister and I went around to the shop to buy little paper cups of yellow water ice, some of the players would be there, refreshing themselves with ices and also with bottles of lemonade.

Early one summer morning, while it was still dark, I heard my father's voice, sounding very excited, outside the door of the room in which I slept. I was about eight. My little sister slept in the same room with me. "McRory's is on fire!" my father was saying. He had been awakened by the red glare of the flames against his window. He threw on some clothes and hurried off to see what was going on, and my mother let us look at the fire from a back window, the same window from which we were accustomed to view the tennis matches. It was a really satisfactory fire, with leaping flames, thick, pouring smoke, and a steady roar of destruction, broken by crashes as parts of the roof collapsed. My mother wondered if they had managed to save the cars, and this made us all look at the burning building with new interest and with enormous awe as we imagined the big shining cars being eaten up by the galloping fire. It was very exciting. My mother hurried us back to our front bedroom, but even there the excitement could be felt, with men calling to one another on the street and banging their front doors after them as they raced off to see the fun. Since she had decided there was no danger to our house, my mother tucked us firmly back into bed, but I could not sleep, and as soon as it grew light, I dressed myself and trotted downstairs. My father had many stories to tell. The garage was a ruin, he said, but the shop was safe. Many cars had been destroyed. No one knew how the fire had started. Some of the fellows connected with the garage had been very brave, dashing in to rescue as many cars as they could reach. The part of the building that overlooked our garden appeared charred, frail, and empty because it no longer had much in the way of a roof and its insides were gone. The air smelled very burnt.

I wandered quietly out onto the avenue, which was deserted because the children had not come out to play and it was still too early for the men to be going to work. I walked up the avenue in the direction of the blind end. The people living there were too far from the garage to have been disturbed by the blaze. A woman whose little boy was a friend of mine came to her door to take in the milk.

"McRory's was burnt down last night!" I cried to her.

"What's that?" she said, very startled.

"Burnt to the ground," I said. "Hardly a wall left standing. A whole lot of people's cars burnt up, too."

She looked back over her shoulder in the direction of her kitchen, which, since all the houses were identical, was in the same position as our kitchen. "Jim!" she cried. "Do you hear this? McRory's was burnt down last night. The whole place. Not a stick left... We slept right through it," she said to me, looking as though just the thought of that heavy sleep puzzled and unsettled her.

Her husband hurried out to stand beside her, and I had to tell the whole story again. He said he would run around to McRory's and take a look, and this enraged me, because I wasn't allowed around there and I knew that when he came back he would be a greater authority than I. However, there was no time to lose. Other people were opening their front doors by now, and I wanted everyone to hear the news from me.

"Did you hear the news?" I shouted, to as many as I could catch up with, and, of course, once I had their ear, they were fascinated by what I had to tell. One or two of the men, hurrying away to work, charged past me with such forbiddingly closed faces that I was afraid to approach them, and they continued in their ignorance down toward Ranelagh Road, causing me dreadful anguish, because I knew that before they could board their tram or their bus, some officious busybody would be sure to treat them to my news. Then one woman, to whom I always afterward felt friendly, called down to me from her front bedroom window. "What's that you were telling Mrs. Pearce?" she asked me, in a loud whisper.

"Oh, just that McRory's was burnt to the ground last night. Nearly all the cars burnt up, too. Hardly anything left, my father says." By this time I was being very offhand.

"You don't tell me," she said, making a delighted face, and the next thing I knew, she was opening her front door, more eager for news than anybody.

However, my hour of glory was short. The other children came out — some of them were actually allowed to go around and view the wreckage — and soon the fire was mine no longer, because there were others walking around who knew more about it than I did. I pretended to lose interest, although I was glad when someone — not my father — gave me a lump of twisted, blackened tin off one of the cars.

The tennis clubhouse had been untouched, and that afternoon the players appeared, as bright and immaculate in their snowy flannels and linens as though the smoking garage yard and the lines of charred cars through which they had picked their way to the courts could never interfere with them or impress them. It was nearing tournament time, and a man was painting the platform on which the judge was to sit and from which a lady in a wide hat and a flowered chiffon dress would present cups and medals to the victors among the players. Now, in the sunshine, they lifted their rackets and started to play, and their intent and formal cries mingled with the hoarse shouts of the men at work in the dark shambles of the garage. My little sister and I, watching from our window, could imagine that the rhythmical thud of the ball against the rackets coincided with the unidentifiable sounds we heard from the wreckage, which might have been groans or shrieks as the building, unable to recover from the fire, succumbed under it.

It was not long before the McRorys put up another garage, made of silvery corrugated-metal stuff that looked garish and glaring against our garden wall; it cut off more of our view than the old building had. The new garage looked very hard and lasting, as unlikely to burn as a pot or a kettle. The beautiful green courts that had always seemed from our window to roll comfortably in the direction of the old wooden building now seemed to have turned and to be rolling away into the distance, as though they did not like the unsightly new structure and would have nothing to do with it.

My father said the odds were all against another fire there, but I remembered that fine dark morning, with all the excitement and my own importance, and I longed for another just like it. This time, however, I was determined to discover the blaze before my father did, and I watched the garage closely, as much of it as I could see, for signs that it might be getting ready to go up in flames, but I was disappointed. It stood, and still was standing, ugly as ever, when we left the house years later. Still, for a long time I used to think that if some child should steal around there with a match one night and set it all blazing again, I would never blame her, as long as she let me be the first with the news.

The Old Man
of the Sea

ONE THURSDAY AFTERNOON, an ancient man selling apples knocked at the door of our house in Dublin. He appeared to me to be about ninety. His hair was thin and white. His back was stooped, his expression was vague and humble, and he held his hat in one of his hands. His other hand rested on the handle of an enormous basket of apples that stood beside him. My mother, who had opened the door at his knock, stood staring at him. I peered out past her. I was nine. The first question that came into my mind was how did that thin old man carry that big basket of apples—because there was no one in the vicinity, as far as I could see, who might have given him a hand. The second question was how far had he come with his burden. I am sure the same dismayed speculations were in my mother's head, but she had no chance to ask him anything, because as soon as the door began to open he began to talk—to describe his apples and to praise them and to say how cheap they were. After every few words he paused, not so much to catch his breath, it seemed, as to collect his wits and to assure himself that the door was still open and that we were still listening, and, perhaps, to make certain that he himself was still standing where he thought he was. As soon as my mother could with politeness interrupt him, she said hastily that she would take a dozen apples for eating and a dozen for cooking. She got two large bowls from the kitchen, filled them with apples, and paid the old man. She left me to close the door. I watched him shuffle down the tiny tiled path that led to the sidewalk. He closed our gate carefully behind him and started to open the gate next door, but I was quick to tell him that our neighbors were away. He nodded without looking at me, and continued on his way. I hurried into the front sitting room. From the window there, I could see what luck he had at the four other houses that remained for him to visit. By the rapidity with which he retreated from each door, and by the abrupt manner in which he pulled the gates to after him, I judged that he had sold no more apples.

I charged off down to the kitchen. My mother was already peeling the cooking apples. My Uncle Matt, my mother's brother, was standing in the door to the garden, smoking a cigarette. My little sister, Derry, was sitting on a chair and trying to clasp her hands behind its back.

"I suppose you took every apple he had in the basket," my uncle said to my mother.

"Oh, no," I said quickly. "He had most of them left, and he didn't sell any more. We must have been the only people who bought any."

"What did I tell you?" my mother said, not taking her eyes from the apples. "God help him, it would break your heart to see him standing there with his old hat in his hand."

"A half a dozen would have been enough," my uncle said amiably. "Now you've encouraged him, he'll be on your back the rest of your life. Isn't that so, Maeve?"

"Like the Old Man of the Sea," I said, but they paid no attention to me.

"You ought to be ashamed of yourself," my mother said to

my uncle, "always thinking the worst of everybody. This is the first time I ever laid eyes on him, and I'd be very much surprised if he ever turns up here again. It's not worth it to him, dragging that big basket around from door to door." I was thinking of the old man who had attached himself to Sindbad the Sailor. I was thinking how helpless and frail the old man had looked when Sindbad first encountered him, and how, after Sindbad took him on his back to carry him, the old man grew heavier and heavier and stronger and stronger, until, when it was too late, Sindbad began to hate him. It was a story that had fascinated me, especially the description of the old man's cruel, talonlike hands and the way they dug into Sindbad's shoulders.

On the following Thursday, the old apple man again appeared at our door, at the same time in the afternoon. When my mother opened the door, he was standing as before, with his battered hat in his hand and his thin shoulders stooped and the basket of apples beside him, but this time on top of the basket were balanced two large brown paper bags, full of apples. He bent over painfully, lifted the bags, and offered them to my mother, saying something we did not understand. He had to repeat it twice before we caught it. "A dozen of each," he was saying.

My mother started to speak but changed her mind, turned away, got the money, paid him, and took the apples. I stood at the door and stared at him, hoping to catch in his faded eyes a glimpse of the villainy that had possessed the old sinner Sindbad found on the beach, but this old man seemed to have no sight at all. Again I watched him from the front sitting-room window, and then I joined my mother in the kitchen.

"He didn't go near any of the other houses," I announced. "I suppose he was afraid they wouldn't buy any."

"I suppose he was," my mother said dismally. "But I didn't

want two dozen apples today. The most I would have taken was a half a dozen. And I didn't want to say it the other day with your Uncle Matt here, but he charges more than McRory's." McRory's was the store around the corner where we bought our groceries. "Oh, well," said my mother, "maybe they're better apples." But she left the bags unopened on the kitchen table.

"He was depending on us," I said.

"Oh, I know that very well," my mother said. "I was a fool in the first place, and now I'll never get rid of him. If he turns up next Thursday, I'll take a half a dozen and no more. I'll have the exact money ready."

This resolution cheered her, and she spilled the apples out on the table.

"They are very good apples," she said. "I wonder where he gets them."

"I wonder where he comes from," I said.

"Oh, the poor old Christian," she said. "And he probably has to walk all the way."

"Unless he could find someone to carry him," I said.

"Not with all those apples," she said in surprise.

"He looks very tired," I said, trying to remember if his fingers were talonlike.

"Why wouldn't he look tired?" my mother said. "He's a very old man."

The next Thursday, she had the money ready in her hand when she answered the old man's knock. She hardly had the door open before she spoke.

"I only want a half a dozen apples today," she said clearly, smiling at him. I smiled, too, to show that we meant no harm. He already had the bags in his arms and was lifting them up to her. It was a step down from our front door to the path, so that, although she is a small woman, he appeared smaller than she. She gravely repeated what she had said and shook her head at the bags.

"Just give me a half a dozen," she said, and I could not have told if she was still smiling, because I was staring at the old man. He seemed about to cry. My mother suddenly reached and took the two bags, and hurried away, calling to me to get the money and pay him.

"Now what'll we do?" I asked her when he had gone.

"Oh, it isn't that I mind the apples so much," she said, "but I don't like feeling I *have* to buy them."

"Did you see that his basket is always full up, except for the apples we take?" I said.

"Oh, I suppose he only goes to the ones he's sure of," she said bitterly, "and you can't blame him for that. He's only trying to get along, like everybody else in the world."

The following few Thursdays, we put up no fight, but I did notice that the old man's fingers were not at all talonlike. They were short and stubby, with bulging knuckles.

Then one Thursday afternoon about three months after we had bought the first, fatal two dozen, my mother decided, everything having gone wrong that day, that she would put her foot down once and for all.

"Now look here," she said, "I'm buying no apples from that old fellow today. Even if I wanted them, I wouldn't buy them. Even if he breaks the door down, I won't answer it."

Derry and I exchanged a glance of anticipation. We were going to pretend we weren't in. We had done that before when unwanted callers came, and we enjoyed it very much. We liked keeping rigidly quiet, listening to the futile knocking at the front door, and we especially enjoyed having our mother at our mercy for those few minutes, because we all felt sure that the least squeak we made, no matter where we were in the house, would betray us to the straining ears outside. Then there was always the sense of triumph when at last we heard our little gate clang shut again and knew that we had defeated our enemy. This time, however, there was an extra suspense that we could not have explained. We were all in the kitchen when the old man's knock came. Our kitchen was separated from our front door only by the length of a small, narrow hall, so we shut the kitchen door. We heard the first knock, and then the second, and then the third. Finally, the old man knocked several times more in rapid succession. Derry and I began to reel around, giggling helplessly, and my mother gave us a reproachful look. She was distressed anyway.

A familiar scratching noise came to our ears, and we gazed at one another, aghast.

"He must have got in somehow," my mother said in a fearful whisper.

I opened the kitchen door very gradually. "He's got his hand in the letter box," I whispered over my shoulder to the others.

In the middle of the front door there was a wide slot through which the postman pushed letters and papers so that they fell inside on the hall floor. On the outside, the slot was protected by a brass flap, and the old man had lifted this and was trying to peer into the hall. We knew very well that the slot gave only a limited and indistinct view of the hall, but we were unreasonably startled to realize that he had found an opening in the house. Suddenly he began to shout through the slot.

"He's roaring mad!" Derry whispered. "He'll kill us all."

"Can you make out what he's saying?" asked my mother, who was appalled.

"He's saying, 'Apple, apple, apple,'" I said.

Derry and I collapsed into hysterical mirth. My mother bundled us out into the garden and came out herself.

"Have you no heart?" she said. "To laugh at an unfortunate old man who probably never gets enough to eat!"

"Now we're really not in," I said, "because we're out in the garden."

Derry joined me in screeches of laughter.

"If I thought he could hear you," my mother said fiercely to us, "I'd murder you both."

"Well, it's too late to answer the door now," she added. "I couldn't face him after this. I'll make it up to him next week."

There was sudden silence—no knocking, no shouting.

"He's gone away," my mother said, in a tone of guilty relief.

At that moment, the tousled head and avid eyes of the woman next door appeared over the wall that separated our garden from hers. "Mrs. Brennan!" she shouted. She had a powerful voice. "There's an old fellow outside with apples for you. He says he's been at your door for a half an hour. He says he comes regularly and he knows you're depending on him. I told him you were in the garden. He must be back around at your door by now. There he is."

There he was. The knocking had started again.

"Oh, God forgive me!" my mother cried. "That old villain! He must have known I was hiding from him."

"What are you hiding for?" our neighbor shrieked. "Do you owe him?"

"Oh, no," my mother said indignantly, "but I don't want any apples."

"Well, why don't you just tell him to go about his business?"

"I will, of course. That's what I'm going to do."

"Just give him a piece of your mind for making a nuisance

of himself and shut the door in his face," commanded our neighbor, with relish.

My mother went into our kitchen, took her purse in her hand, and marched to the door, with Derry and me following. The old man was a pitiful sight. He had forgotten to take off his hat, and his eyes glittered, whether with anguish or with anger it would have been hard to say. He pushed the two bags of apples rudely into my mother's arms without looking at her. She opened her purse to pay him and gave a cry of distress: "Didn't I go and pay the grocer only an hour ago, and I'm fourpence short!" She handed him the money and showed him that it left her purse empty. "It's all I have in the house at the minute," she said.

He grabbed the money, counted it, and gave her back a dreadful look of contempt. Then he lifted his enormous basket, which was, as always, full to the brim, and turned his back on us. This time, we all stood in the front sitting-room window and watched him. He didn't close our gate, and he scuttled slowly off down the street as though he couldn't get away from us fast enough.

"First, he thought we were making fun of him," my mother said, "and now he thinks I was trying to bargain with him. He might have known I'd make it up to him the next time."

She, who never tried to bargain with anybody in her life, was filled with shame.

"Next week, we'll have the door open for him before he knocks," I said.

But the following week there was no sign of the old man, and he never came near us again, although, filled with remorse, we watched for him. One afternoon, my Uncle Matt dropped around to see us, and my mother, in a confiding mood, told him the whole story.

"Well, I could have told you," he said, grinning.

"It wasn't so much the apples, you know," my mother said.

"Oh, no," said my uncle. "You'd have liked him to come to your door and ask straight out for money, like the rest of your beggars."

My mother was noted for her inability to refuse food, clothes, or money to anybody who came to the door.

"How many times must I tell you not to call them beggars," she said angrily now to my uncle. "They're just unfortunate, and I wouldn't be so quick to laugh at them if I were you."

"Well, you're well rid of *him,*" my uncle said. "And I may as well tell you now that I saw him strolling down O'Connell Street the other morning wearing a suit of clothes that I couldn't afford to buy, and not an apple in sight. There's your poor old man for you."

"Now how did you know it was him?" my mother cried skeptically. "You never saw him at all."

"Wasn't I here the first time he came to the door? I was standing in the middle of the kitchen, and you had the hall door wide open. Of course I saw him."

"Well, you're making all that up about seeing him on O'Connell Street."

"I saw him, and I passed close enough to touch him. He had his married daughter from Drumcondra with him."

"And how do you know she was his married daughter from Drumcondra, may I ask?"

"Oh, you couldn't mistake *her,*" my uncle said airily. "I knew her by the way she was wearing her hat."

"That tongue of yours, Matt," my mother said. "I never know whether to believe you or not."

For my part, I believed every word my uncle said.

The Barrel
of Rumors

IN DUBLIN, my mother used to take parcels of food to a community of Poor Clare nuns who had their convent a long walk from our house in Ranelagh. Sometimes she used to send my sister and me with the parcels. The Poor Clares are silent. They never speak, to each other or to anyone, and they are a closed order, which means that they never see outsiders and no one ever sees them. These Dublin Poor Clares had no food except what their friends — women, mostly, people like my mother — brought to them. They were forbidden to ask for anything, but we heard that if their food supply got dangerously low, the Reverend Mother was allowed to signal their distress by ringing the bell in the steeple of their chapel. To my regret, our house was too far from the convent to let us hear the bell, but my mother assured me that there was no need to worry; the nuns had never yet been driven to ring for help.

One hall in the convent was open to visitors for a part of every day, and it was there we used to call with our offerings of food. A huge revolving barrel with an open section had been built upright into the narrow end wall that sealed the public hall away from the rest of the convent. We used to place our parcels on the floor of the barrel and then turn it around so that the open section faced the nun on the other side of the wall. The nun would immediately turn it back to us, always sending us a present of a few holy pictures or some medals.

The nun who attended the barrel was named Sister Bridget. She was the only member of the community who had permission to talk to visitors. A tiny square waiting room opened off the hall, and we used to go in there and hold conversations with her through a blind grille in the wall. One of my names is Bridget, and she had the idea that I would someday develop a vocation and maybe become a Poor Clare like herself. She used to offer many prayers for my vocation, and I enjoyed talking with her about it. I was about twelve then.

I had heard that the Poor Clares slept in their coffins, with stones under their heads. I had been told that they were measured for their coffins the first day they entered the convent and that they never knew any other bed afterward. My mother liked to throw cold water on this story, but I could not forget it. I used to wonder if they had separate cells for sleeping, with a coffin in each cell, or if they slept in a dormitory, and if they had sheets and blankets and pillowcases, and, if so, how they made their beds in the morning. Also, I wondered, what about the coffin lids? Where were they kept? On the floor alongside the coffin? Or leaning, like hockey sticks and bicycles, against the wall? I knew that the nuns never slept more than a couple of hours at a time and that they arose at intervals during the night, even in the dead of winter, to go to their chapel and pray. It was a picture to dwell upon.

I asked my mother many questions about the nuns, but her answers were never satisfactory. One time that I remember asking her about them, her younger brother, my Uncle Matt, was lounging about the room. We were in the front sitting room, and she was trying to coax one of her precious ferns to twine itself around a long bamboo cane that she had stuck into its pot.

Q: Do the Poor Clare nuns have any other convent besides the one here in Dublin?

A: I think they have another convent somewhere in Ireland, and I believe they have one in England.

Q: If nobody is allowed to see them, what happens when they're moved from one convent to another?

A: How would I know? I suppose a car, a little van, maybe, backs up to the convent door, and the nun gets in and shuts herself in.

Q: Would she bring her coffin with her?

A: I wish you'd stop all this nonsense about the nuns sleeping in their coffins.

(UNCLE MATT: Of course she'd bring her coffin with her. Doesn't she have to get her sleep, like anybody else? She'd carry it under her arm like a music roll. Do you mean to tell me you've never seen a nun walking along the street with her coffin under her arm?)

Q: What if a Poor Clare gets sick and has to have the doctor?

A: I don't know.

Q: What about if they're dying, and the priest has to come?

A: I don't know. Besides, that would be different. A priest would be different.

Q: What about if they talk in their sleep? Would that be a sin for them?

(UNCLE MATT: Well, of course, it would depend what they said.)

A: That's enough of that, now. I don't want to hear another word out of either of you.

Lentils, dried peas, eggs, and flour were chiefly what my mother used to bring to the nuns. Sometimes she baked a cake for them.

Once, she brought salt, and Sister Bridget thanked her particularly, telling her that the community had been without salt for two weeks. Although the walk to the convent was long, it was not lonely. We had to cross at least two busy main streets, full of traffic as we walked along, and the way was very pleasant, with trees lining the sidewalks in front of the houses, and benches to sit on in case we got tired.

The convent and its chapel formed three sides of a square court, which was carefully tended and had a small, smooth grass lawn and bright flower beds. The fourth side of the court was on the public road and was walled off, with an iron gate through which visitors entered. The wall was very high and you couldn't see through the gate. To the right of the gate was the gate lodge, where an old woman lived and attended to visitors who called during off hours.

Although the convent had fixed visiting hours, the chapel was always open, and people could go in there and pray any time. People who lived near the chapel used to attend Mass and Benediction there. It was a beautiful little chapel, the plainest I have ever seen, with a small, almost bare main altar flanked by two tall statues of nuns—Saint Clare on the left as you knelt facing the altar, and Saint Camillus on the right. Both saints wore the brown habit of the Poor Clares. To the right of the altar, a great grille was set into the wall, and through this grille the nuns used to witness Mass and receive Benediction, and through the grille people kneeling in the chapel could hear their voices answering the prayers and singing the Benediction hymns.

One Sunday afternoon, my mother took me to Benediction there. I watched the altar and listened to the voices of the nuns, but my real attention was given to a small old woman kneeling in the seat ahead of me. This old woman, dressed in black, had her head half turned, so that I could see her face, and she was listening to the voices from behind the grille with such concentration that she appeared desperate, her eyes wide open and her mouth working along with the words.

My mother saw me watching her, and as we left the chapel, she said, "That poor old woman comes here every chance she gets. Her daughter has been in there fourteen years, and she's got so she imagines she can hear her daughter's voice out of all the others. We came out together one day, and she told me she can't hear any of the other voices anymore, only her daughter's voice. It's like as if her daughter was in there alone, she says. It's sad to see her straining like that, to hear every word."

"Was it her oldest daughter or the youngest?" I asked. Being the middle one, I was concerned with such things.

"I don't know that," my mother said.

"Do you suppose the daughter thinks about her mother out there and doesn't think of anybody else?" I asked.

"She could hardly help thinking of her," my mother said. "After all, she's still her daughter. But, of course, once they're in there, they're in there," she added, "and they're not supposed to think about what they've left behind. It's hard to know what goes on in their heads. Maybe they try to forget about the outside world altogether."

"Except for our sins," I said. "They have to pray for us."

"That's true," my mother said. "They have to think about all the sins we commit."

If this thought amused her, she gave no sign of it.

One sunny morning late in the summer, my mother called me into the kitchen, where she was packing a parcel for the Poor Clares.

"I was wondering if you would like to take Robert with you," she said. "It's a long walk, but you could go slow. Then you could put him in the barrel and send him around to see the nuns."

"Put Robert in the barrel?" I cried.

Robert, my brother, was at this time about two years old.

"Certainly," my mother said. "Children are allowed in the barrel until they're three years old. After that they're too old. You can take him if you like. I'll put his blue suit on him."

A few minutes later, I started off, pushing Robert in his pram. He sat back placidly against his pillow and stared at me. The nun's parcel made a comfortable prop for his feet. He was very pink and cheerful. My mother had dressed him in a suit of pale blue wool that she had knitted herself and that fitted him very tightly all over and left his fat legs bare. He wore short white cotton socks and brown sandals. His hair, of which he did not have much, was brushed into a golden crest on top of his head, and he shone with health, contentment, and cleanliness. I was in a great hurry to get him into the barrel, and I sped along, almost skating behind the pram.

When I got to the convent, I rushed into the waiting room and told Sister Bridget I had brought Robert to see her. She was delighted and said she would call the other nuns. I didn't know, and didn't like to ask, whether she meant that she would call all the nuns or just a few of them. I imagined them, silent and swift, of all ages, descending upon Robert from every part of the convent. I hoped none of them would be in the chapel, because surely they would never be allowed to interrupt their prayers.

I went back to the hall and lifted Robert into the barrel, making sure he had his back against the wall. He sat very solidly where I placed him, a good deal larger than the parcels I was in the habit of bringing. As soon as I heard Sister Bridget's voice, I revolved him out of sight. He didn't seem to mind disappearing. There was silence on the other side of the barrel. I couldn't hear a rustle — not even the suspicion of a whisper. Even Robert made no sound. I stared at the blank side of the barrel and wondered what was going on on the other side.

After a minute or two, the barrel began to move, and Robert gradually came into view, sitting exactly as I had placed him, looking very matter-of-fact and friendly. I lifted him out and put the parcel on the warmed-up spot where he had been sitting. When the barrel came back the second time, Sister Bridget had sent us more presents than usual. There were extra holy pictures and extra medals and a special present for Robert, a holy picture sewn by some nun to a square of white satin and embroidered with white-satin thread. I went back into the conversation room and received Sister Bridget's compliments about Robert and acknowledged the hopes she expressed for him, which I took to be blessings, considering their source. Then I heard a few words, perfunctory this time, about my vocation, and left.

As I trundled Robert home, I was exasperated to think that he had been where I might never go and that he didn't even realize his luck. He was in great good humor. He waved his arms and pointed at people and objects that interested him and even talked a little, but I could make no sense of his language, and anyway none of his remarks seemed to have to do with the barrel, which he had apparently forgotten. He was unable to tell me what he had seen, and by the time he got old enough to express himself, it would all have passed from his memory. Not from him would I ever learn how the nuns looked, if they were young or old, if they were pretty or ugly, if they smiled at him, or nodded to him, or tried to take his hand or stroke his head, as other strangers did. He never would be able to tell me what the inside of the convent looked like. Worst of all, I realized that no matter what I heard, I would never really know for sure if the nuns slept in their coffins, with stones for pillows.

The Day We
Got Our Own Back

ONE AFTERNOON some unfriendly men dressed in civilian clothes and carrying revolvers came to our house searching for my father, or for information about him. This was in Dublin, in 1922. The treaty with England, turning Ireland into the Irish Free State, had just been signed. Those Irish who were in favor of the treaty, the Free Staters, were governing the country. Those who had held out for a republic, like my father, were in revolt. My father was wanted by the new government, and so he had gone into hiding. He was on the run, sleeping one night in one house and the next night in another and sometimes stealing home to see us. I suppose my mother must have taken us to see him several times, but I only remember visiting him once, and I know I found it very odd to meet him sitting in a strange person's house and to leave him there when we were ready to go home. Anyway, these men had been sent to find him. They crowded into our narrow little hall and tramped around the house, upstairs and downstairs, looking everywhere and asking questions. There was no one at home except my mother, my little sister, Derry, and me. Emer, my elder sister and my mother's chief prop, was out doing errands. Derry was upstairs in bed with a cold. I was settled comfortably on a low chair in our front sitting room, threading a necklace. I was five.

After the men had searched the house, they crowded into the room where I sat, from which they could watch the street. They brought my mother in with them. They camped around the room, talking idly among themselves and waiting. My mother stood against the wall farthest from the windows, watching them. She was very tense. She feared that my father would risk a visit home and that he would be trapped, and that we would see him trapped. One of the men came and stood over me. He pointed out a blue glass bead for me to add to my necklace, but I explained to him that the bead was too small to slip over my needle and that I had already discarded it. This exchange with this strange man made me feel very clever. He leaned closer to me then.

"Tell us do you know where your Daddy is," he whispered.

I stopped threading and began to think, but my mother flew across the room at him. She is a very small, thin woman with a pointed face and straight brown hair that she has always worn in a bun at the back of her head.

"Aren't you ashamed of yourself?" she cried. "Asking the child questions."

The man drew away from me, and she went back to her place against the wall. At that time, in 1922, she had been through a good many years of trouble and anxiety. All the first years of her marriage were dominated by the preparations for the Rebellion of Easter, 1916, and she had seen my father captured and condemned first to death and then to penal servitude for life. At the time that I was born, he was in jail in England and she was alone in Dublin, not knowing when, if ever, she would see him again. Actually, he was released less than a year later, and in 1921 we moved into our house in Ranelagh, where we now waited to see what was going to happen.

Suddenly my mother, thinking of Derry, alone in the room

above, abandoned her wall and darted to the door leading to the stairs, but one of the men was before her, with his revolver raised against her. She stood with both hands against the doorjamb, staring up at him, half smiling. I have often seen her smiling like that when she is agitated.

"You can't open that door," the man said.

"Didn't you see the little one sick upstairs?" my mother said. "She'll be frightened by herself."

"Never mind about that," the man said. "You're not getting out of this room."

Again my mother retreated to her wall, and I returned to my necklace, and the men continued their talk. After a while, they abruptly got up and went away. My mother remained anxious, suspecting that they might be watching the end of the street for my father's arrival. She went upstairs to speak to Derry, and when she came back, I followed her down the three steps into the kitchen, which was small and squarish, with a red tile floor and a door that gave out onto the garden. She sat down at the kitchen table. I asked her if she would like a cup of tea and she said yes, she would like a cup. I filled the kettle, splashing water all over the floor, but she wouldn't trust me to light the gas, and in the end she had to make the tea herself. Some time later, Emer came home, and my mother gave her tea and told her everything that had happened and all that had been said, not forgetting the question that had been put to me. Listening to her, I was once again spellbound with gratitude, excitement, and astonishment that the strange man had included me in the raid.

The only other raid I remember took place about a year after that, and the men were rougher. Again there were in the house only my mother, my little sister, and I. This time, the men came in the morning. My mother was getting along with her housework, and she had an apron tied about her waist. She had shined the brass rods that held our red stair carpet in place, and now she was polishing the oilcloth on the dining-room floor. The men crowded in as before, with their revolvers, but this time they searched in earnest. They pulled all the beds apart, looking for papers and letters, and they took all my father's books out of the shelves and shook them, and they looked in all the drawers and in the wardrobe and in the kitchen stove. There was not an inch of the house they did not touch. They turned every room inside out. The newly polished oilcloth was scarred by their impatient feet, and the bedrooms upstairs were torn apart, with sheets and blankets on the floor, and the mattresses all humped up on the bare beds. In the end, they went back to the kitchen, and they took down the tins of flour and tea and sugar and salt and whatever else there was, and plunged their hands into them, and emptied them on the table and on the floor. They took all the cups and saucers and plates down. Still they had found nothing, but the house looked as though it had suffered an explosion without bursting its walls. At last, they got ready to leave, but as they were on the point of going, one of them, a very keen fellow, rushed over to the fireplace in the front sitting room and put his hands up the chimney and shoved his face as far into the grate as it would go, trying to look up and see what might be there. A great soft shower of soot came down around him, covering his shoulders and his face. He pulled hastily back into the room, with black hands and a black-mottled face. Some of the soot had gone up his sleeves. Some of it was still drifting out over the carpet. He glanced at his companions and pawed at himself, and then they went away.

When they had gone, my mother gazed about her at all the work they had made. It would be a long time before she had the house neat again. We all trailed down into the kitchen and surveyed the mess there. This time, there was no question of making tea, because the tea was on the floor, along with the flour and the sugar.

We had seldom heard my mother's voice raised in laughter. She has a very quiet, almost secret manner in amusement. Now, however, she began to tremble and to smile.

"Oh," she cried, "to see the look on his face when he came back out of the chimney!"

My little sister and I began to jump around, cackling.

"Oh," cried my mother, "what warned me not to have the chimney cleaned? Oh, thanks be to God I forgot to have the chimney cleaned!"

And with us chattering a delighted, incredulous accompaniment, she laughed as though her heart might break.

The Lie

THERE WAS A JOKE between my mother and me about the first time I went to confession. She took me to see the priest herself, but we were late leaving home, and by the time we got to the chapel there were two long rows of women kneeling outside the confession box, waiting to be heard. My mother said later that she could tell by the expression on their faces that they all had a great deal to confess and that they would take their time about it. She was worried, fearing we had a couple of hours to wait, and knowing that I was only seven and restless and nervous because this was the first time I was going to get into the box. However, we knelt together at the end of one line and settled down to wait. The priest had not yet arrived, but when we had been kneeling there a couple of minutes, we saw him hurrying down the aisle from the altar. He was a fat old man, and I stared at him in terror. As he came toward us, he glanced around at all the waiting women, and then he saw me. He stopped and spoke to my mother.

"Is this the first time she's going to confession?" he asked.

When he heard that it was, he took my arm and pulled me gently to my feet and along past all the knees of all the waiting and greatly surprised women and pushed me into the box ahead of the first woman in line. There I was, kneeling in the dark, when the shutter just above my face was pulled back and I saw the priest's profile.

"Start now, child," he said impatiently. "Don't be afraid."

After I had stumbled through the first prayer and come to the telling of the sins, I stopped, because I couldn't remember any sins.

"All right now, child," the priest said, "were you disobedient?"

"Yes, Father."

"And did you lose your temper a couple of times?"

"Yes, Father."

"That's right. For your penance say three Hail Marys. Now make a good Act of Contrition."

A minute later I was again stumbling past all the knees and all the irritated faces, and my mother took me to the altar rail, where I said my penance, and we left the chapel.

"What penance did he give you?" she asked as we were walking home.

"Three Hail Marys."

"You must have had more sins than I thought," she said, laughing. "Didn't he give that crowd the surprise of their lives! Some of them must have been kneeling there an hour or more."

After that, whenever I went to confession, I got the same penance — three Hail Marys — and my mother always asked me what the priest had given me, and when she heard, she would laugh again, thinking of the angry faces of the women the first time. Sometimes she told other people about it, and I always liked to hear the story. Although everyone knew about it, I still felt it to be a private joke between the two of us, and I loved that. Then one day, sometime in my ninth year, I spoiled it all. I saw the little joke die, and I knew that I had killed it.

It happened in a very simple way. My younger sister, Deirdre, had a toy sewing machine that she loved. She was seven then. The machine actually made stitches, and she used to work with it for hours, turning the little handwheel that made it go. I had no interest in sewing and never touched the machine, but it was her favorite toy.

One day, I wandered into the front sitting room, where I found my mother in her usual chair, with a pile of mending on a table at her side. She was busy with a sock. I hurled myself across the room and into her lap. Under this onslaught, she pricked her finger with the needle, gave a cry of irritation, and pushed me away. I tumbled deliberately down on the floor and sat there, glaring at her in outrage.

"What's the matter with you?" she cried, putting her punctured finger in her mouth.

"I wanted to sit on your lap."

"Well, you can't. You're too big, for one thing."

"Derry sits on your lap," I said.

"Derry only weighs about a half a pound."

That was true.

"And," continued my mother, "you must weigh almost as much as I do myself."

It was all too true. I rushed upstairs in a fury, and into the room I shared with Derry. There was the little sewing machine, sitting on the window ledge, where she had left it. I took it up and gazed at it in hatred. Then I tugged the little wheel off. After that, I wrestled with the machine until it was ruined. When it was all broken, I regarded it, first with satisfaction and then, very quickly, with dismay and regret. I was very sorry I had broken Derry's toy, and I was afraid of what would happen to me. I did the only thing I could think of. I leaned out of the window and dropped all the pieces down onto the cement path outside our kitchen door. Then I went thundering back down the stairs again.

"Derry, Derry!" I shouted. "I was trying to work your sewing machine, and it fell out through the window, and I'm sure it's all broken."

My mother and Derry came running, and we all dashed into the garden and surveyed the pitiful remains of the little machine. Derry began to cry. I was very much upset. After all, it was my first murder.

My mother stooped down and gathered up the pieces. "How did it happen to fall out of the window, Maeve?" she asked.

"I don't know, I was only holding it in my hand and out it went. Isn't it a good thing I didn't fall out, too?"

My mother refused to be diverted by the picture of me following the machine down onto the cement.

"Are you sure you did nothing to *make* it fall out, Maeve?"

"Oh, no!" I cried. "No, I didn't!" and tears of real grief filled my eyes, to think that she would believe me capable of such an act.

My mother looked perplexed and sad, but she promised Derry a new machine, and we all went back into the house, where peace soon descended on us. As a matter of fact, Derry got very much interested in the workings of the machine, which had been somewhat mysterious to her till then, and she spent a good deal of time examining the broken parts. I tried to forget about the whole incident, and succeeded until the following Saturday, when I had to go to confession.

I told the priest that I had flown into a bad temper, and he nodded. Then I told him that I had been envious of my younger sister.

"Envy is a serious sin, my child," he said. "You must beware of that."

I told him I had smashed my sister's sewing machine.

"Deliberately?" he asked.

"Yes, Father."

"You broke one of her toys because you were envious of her?"

"Yes, Father."

"That is a very serious matter, to do a thing like that," the priest said. "If you don't learn to curb yourself, you may do some-thing you'll be very sorry for, one of these days. Did you tell her you were sorry?"

"Yes, Father."

I then told him I had lied to my mother.

"You told a lie to your *mother?*" He went on to say that lying is a serious sin in itself, but that one who told a lie to her mother had taken a very bad turn on life's road.

"For a penance," he concluded, "you can say five Our Fathers and five Hail Marys."

Much shaken, I left the confession box, said my penance, and went home, feeling very free and glad it was all over, and full of love and contrition and good resolutions.

I arrived home just as tea was being put on the table, and we all sat down and started to talk.

"And where were you this afternoon?" my father asked me.

"I went to confession, Daddy."

"And what penance did you get this time?"

"Five Our Fathers and five Hail Marys, this time," I said.

"Well," remarked my father, "you're going up in the world. I wonder what you had to tell, to get that size of a penance."

I hardly heard him. The minute the words were out of my mouth, I knew I had made a terrible mistake. Burning with guilt and shame, I stared at my mother. She was looking back at me in a way that confounded me still further, because although her ex-pression was serious, I knew she was not angry. I was very sorry and very sad. I was ready to yell with anguish.

"Oh, Maeve," she said at last, "my poor child, why couldn't you have kept your mouth shut?"

"What's going on around here *now?*" my father asked, bewil-dered.

He got no answer.

The Devil
in Us

I WAS PEACEFULLY APPROACHING the end of my thirteenth year when I was startled out of all placidity by an unanswerable question that still returns sometimes to puzzle my mind. I was at a convent boarding school in Kilcullen, a village in the County Kildare. There were sixty or more girls at the school, and we used to be taken for long crocodile walks into the flat and spiritless countryside that surrounds the village. There were several shops in Kilcullen, but the only building I ever entered there was the church, where we occasionally went to confession. Most of the time, we went to confession in the convent chapel, which we approached on tiptoe through the darkened main hall of the nuns' quarters. We wore navy blue uniforms, with long black wool stockings and black slippers, and before entering the chapel for confession, or for morning Mass or Sunday-afternoon Benediction, we covered our heads with white net veils. By the end of my first term, my veil was so full of the chapel's dark and musky fragrance—of incense and flowers and snuffed-out candles— that I was afraid to wash it, for fear of committing sacrilege.

My first year at school went off fairly smoothly. I was not an outstanding success, but neither was I a failure. There was nothing to read, because the tiny school library was kept locked up behind the doors of a tall, glass-fronted bookcase, and I detested hockey and basketball and all the other sports we were expected to practice, but I was a cheerful enough scholar. It was at the beginning of the second year that things began to change, but the change was so gradual that I was never able to decide which day, or even which week, I began to recognize it and to grow accustomed to it. I did feel, however, that it all started one fine September afternoon in singing class. It was the only class for which the entire school was brought together. We met in the biggest classroom, which had a piano. We used to stand in a great, sweeping semicircle, with the choir girls on the right and the rest of us arranged roughly according to height. I was in the middle of the curve and felt myself to be directly under Sister Veronica's eye, although actually, of course, I was no more conspicuous than any of the others. And in any case I knew from experience that a girl who tried to remain hidden was often the first one to attract attention to herself.

That afternoon, with all the other girls, I was rendering "The Mountains o' Mourne" at the top of my voice and keeping my eyes fastened on the pale, protruding eyes of Sister Veronica, who kept time for us with one of her long, limp hands. Sister Veronica believed that a girl who can look you straight in the eye is a good girl, and I was hoping she would notice my honest gaze.

The door opened, and Sister Hildegarde, the Sister Superior in charge of the school, walked in, portentous and unsmiling. She was a short, wide woman with a large white face on which moles grew. She and Sister Veronica together ruled us, with the help of three young lay teachers and two or three lesser nuns. We were afraid of the two head nuns. We were afraid of them separately, but our fear increased threefold when they were both present, because they seemed to set each other off, and the decisions they made when their eyes met were always to our disadvantage, and there was no appeal from them. They were unpredictable and deadly in their accusations and in their judgments, and we never knew where we were with them. This time, however, the occasion seemed peaceful enough, and we continued to sing with all our hearts. Sister Hildegarde took up her position behind Sister Veronica and a little to the side, so she could see us all.

When the song was finished, we started in on "Who Is Sylvia?" which we had learned to sing in parts. Halfway through, Sister Veronica, at a word from Sister Hildegarde, waved abruptly to us to stop.

Sister Hildegarde stepped forward. "I have a suspicion that all of the girls are not doing their best," she said. "You know, Sister, that there are certain girls here who are only too glad to let the others do the work for them. If it were not for your work, and Maggie Harrington's voice, I don't know where the choir would be this year."

Maggie Harrington was the star singer of the school. She led the choir in singing for Benediction every Sunday, and she was also head girl. She was eighteen years old, with wiry brown hair that she wore in a queue down her solid back, and a broad red face on which rimless spectacles rode and flashed in triumph. Sister Veronica smiled at Maggie, and at the other members of the choir, who were grouped around her. They were very important girls, although some of them were only twelve, and the rest of us looked at them enviously, because they were in everybody's good graces and always knew the right thing to do.

"I am going to watch very closely this time," Sister Hildegarde said. "I think I know which girls are shirking. I think you know, too, don't you, Sister?"

Sister Veronica agreed that she was pretty sure which girls were holding back their voices, and added meaningfully that it was usually the girls who gave the most trouble, in and out of class, who did the least work. "I've never seen it to fail, Sister," she said, staring us all down. "Laziness and troublemaking go hand in hand. A busy girl is a good girl. The Devil can always find work for idle hands."

Sister Hildegarde nodded agreement. "Give them a note, Sister," she said.

Sister Veronica gave us a very loud note on the piano, not taking her eyes from us. "'The Spinning Wheel,'" she said.

This was one of my favorite songs. During the chorus, we were supposed to whir like spinning wheels, and I was whirring with every ounce of breath when, to my astonishment and dismay, I saw that Sister Hildegarde was beckoning me to come forward. My conscience was clear. I knew that I had been making a great deal of noise, and the thought went through my mind that perhaps the best girls were now going to be brought forward, to give an example to the rest of the school. I stood in the spot she indicated, facing the piano, and was immediately joined by three other girls who had been summoned from the ranks. We stood together, not singing, until the song was finished.

"Now we know who the culprits are," Sister Hildegarde said.

"I suspected it all along, Sister," Sister Veronica said. "In fact, I think I could have given you the names of these four girls without ever coming into this room."

"Girls, why?" asked Sister Hildegarde intensely. "*Why* are you not singing along with the rest of the school? Do you think you're too good to sing with the other girls? Do you think it's beneath you to take advantage of Sister Veronica's instruction?"

We knew enough not to attempt to answer; in a case like this, to answer meant to answer back, a very grave offense. Also, we kept our eyes on the floorboards; a direct gaze when one is in the wrong is evidence not of goodness but of boldness.

"You see, Sister," said Sister Hildegarde, "they have nothing to say."

"That is how they sounded when they were singing, no doubt," said Sister Veronica.

Maggie Harrington gave a musical laugh and smothered it decorously.

"Well may you laugh, Maggie," Sister Hildegarde said.

"Now let's hear what these four can do by themselves. Give them a note, Sister."

We took the note and set up a self-conscious but passable version of "The Spinning Wheel."

"They sound more like Singer sewing machines than spinning wheels," Sister Hildegarde said coldly when we had finished.

"A pity you can't feel inclined to sing like that in class," said Sister Veronica. She turned to Sister Hildegarde. "You see they *have* voices, Sister. It's sheer stubbornness that keeps them from doing their part."

"Now that they know they're being watched, perhaps they'll do a little better," Sister Hildegarde said in a discouraging voice.

A week later, singing class came around again, and this time the four of us got into trouble over "The Rose of Tralee." We grew a little desperate, trying to give the impression that we were singing as loudly as the others, but by now Sister Veronica was convinced that we were defying her, and no matter how red we got in the face, or how hard we breathed, she would not believe that we were not cheating. The others watched us with amusement and some scorn. They wondered why we wouldn't sing or, if we *were* singing, why the nuns insisted we weren't.

That is what puzzled me. I could hear and feel I was singing, and I thought my three companions in guilt could hear and feel they were singing, too. I couldn't ask them, because we had been forbidden to talk to each other, on the theory that we were less harmful to the general tone of the school apart than together, and we were too cowardly to break the rule. The worst of it was that once we had been proclaimed black sheep in singing class, our disgrace gradually spread out and discolored all of our school life. In a short while, everything we did seemed to be wrong. I learned very little that term, because I spent most of the time either standing in banishment outside this or that classroom door or marching around to Sister Hildegarde's office to inform her of some new sin. The three other black sheep were just as badly off. Those three weren't very close friends of mine. As a matter of fact, Sister Hildegarde's mysterious accusation was the first bond we had in common. One of the girls, Sally Lynch, a tiny black-haired girl with a fringe across her forehead, was only twelve. The two others, Mary Anne Rorke and Cecilia Delaney, were fifteen. Cecilia was fat, but Mary Anne was very ordinary in appearance. We were all in different classes. It puzzled me then, and it still puzzles me, to know why we were chosen to play this role. It was an unexciting, quiet school. No great crises arose, and no great crimes were committed. It seems to me now that, far from making trouble, we four simply attracted what little trouble there was, and perhaps it all looked the same to the nuns. After having been judged guilty, of course, we began to look very guilty in our efforts to reinstate ourselves, and that didn't help us at all. Also, I grew quite nervous, partly from importance.

Finally, one Saturday night, Sister Hildegarde walked into the recreation hall during the desultory hour that preceded bed, and raised her hand for silence. "Girls," she said, "you know that a few among you have given us a great deal of anxiety this term. The four to whom I refer have caused a great deal of discontent and bad feeling this term. We call them the Devil's walking sticks. He couldn't get along without them. But now they are going to have a chance to redeem themselves. Tomorrow afternoon, they are going to have a chance to show Our Blessed Lord that they are sorry for their bad behavior and want to make amends. Maggie Harrington and the rest of the choir will not sing for Benediction. Instead, these four girls will go up into the choir loft and sing the hymns alone. They have had as much practice as anyone else in the school. If they don't know the hymns now, they'll never know them."

I had never even imagined such a severe trial. All the girls looked at us with sympathy. No one smiled. We four went to bed and had nightmares, and woke next morning to face the worse nightmare that was waiting for us. When the moment finally arrived, near four o'clock, we ascended the stairs to the choir loft as though we were mounting the scaffold. We could hear the girls shifting about down in the well of the chapel, and we could see the white-veiled heads of the smallest girls, who knelt in the front rows. Immediately behind the students, the postulants, in their first year of religious life, would be taking their places, and behind them the novices, and at the back the black-veiled nuns. To add to our distress, we knew that five or six pairs of parents had come visiting that Sunday and that they were down there, too, waiting for us to begin. No doubt their daughters had told them that we were up here to vindicate ourselves.

The priest, Father O'Connor, came in, followed by the altar boy, and Sister Angela, a very young, pretty nun who taught piano and who had been sitting at the organ with her head bent in meditation, struck up the first hymn of the service, the "O Salutaris Hostia." Staring at her, we opened our mouths to sing, but we could only caw. Again she began, and again we cawed, this time so pitifully that even we were not sure we were making any sound at all. A third time, smiling wildly to encourage us, she tried, and we gave up altogether, and made no sound, and stopped looking at her, and looked at the floor instead. She raised both hands from the organ and tried to conduct us back into the hymn, without the music, when suddenly, from below, arose the heroic voice of Maggie Harrington, and she was joined almost at once by all the voices of the regular choir. They sang the Benediction right through, hymn after hymn, without faltering, and Sister Angela accompanied them but kept her eyes charitably averted from our faces. Later, we heard that they had begun singing where they knelt, and I have often thought of how they must have looked, kneeling up straight with their hands joined and their white-veiled heads raised to the altar, while they sang and saved the day. We four, far above them, had no courage for anything. We didn't even have the courage to pray.

When the Benediction was over, Sister Angela rose and went swiftly down out of the loft. Almost at once, the terrible face of Sister Veronica appeared at the head of the stairs. "You made a fine show of yourselves," she said calmly. "I hope you're pleased with yourselves. You may come on down now."

We trooped down, relieved that we were not to be abandoned forever in the loft but very unwilling to face the immediate future. Sister Veronica remained on the narrow stairs, and we had to press past her, touching her heavy black robes. At the door of the chapel, Father O'Connor was congratulating the heroines. He was still in his vestments, and he looked over their heads at us with a glance that was incomprehensible to me then, but that now seems to me to have borne a glimmer of amusement.

Nothing happened the rest of that Sunday. We went in to tea along with the rest of the school. I felt mournfully elevated — I did not yet know why — and I ate a great deal of bread and butter, and marked the glances of fearful speculation thrown at me by the other girls at my table. Anything might happen to me now. I might even be expelled.

Several relatively peaceful days went by, and then we had

singing class again. Sister Veronica and Sister Hildegarde entered the room together. They nodded to the four of us to come to the front of the room and stand before the school. When we had been isolated in this manner, Sister Hildegarde, whose face was filled with severity and grief, said, "We all heard these girls try to sing last Sunday. We know what a shameful exhibition they made of themselves and of the school. I am not going to punish them and I am not going to scold them. Their case is too grave for that. Not only did they let us down but they deliberately let Our Blessed Lord down. I am only going to say that they need all the prayers they can get. Will every girl who is willing to give an extra minute each day to say a prayer for these misguided and stubborn girls raise her hand?"

We four continued to look where we had been looking, at the floor. Cecilia, the fat girl, began to sob. I was relieved to know where we stood. We had been given our chance, and the Devil in us had defeated us. The reason for our guilt was still hidden from us, but in a dim but comforting way we were now convinced of its existence. We had not seen the shape of the Devil, but we had felt his power, in our dry throats and thumping hearts. The thing was now clear to us that had always been clear to the nuns, because we realized as well as they did that if God had been on our side, surely He would have given us the voice to sing His praises.

The
Clever One

NOT LONG AGO, I was staying in Washington, D.C., with my younger sister, Deirdre, who is married and has four young children. It was spring. We sat in her large, pleasant living room, with the trees all fresh and green outside on Garfield Street, and the shrubs bursting into bloom—white, pink, blue, yellow—in her garden, where the children were giving themselves whole-heartedly to some raucous game, and we began to speak, as we often do, of the time when we two were small together. There is less than two years between us. Our childhood was spent in Dublin, most of it in a small house in Ranelagh.

"The first time I remember seeing you," I said, "was before we went to live in Ranelagh. It was when we were living in the house on Belgrave Road. You must have been about eighteen months old, I suppose. Someone was holding you in their arms, and you snatched Emer's cap off her head and threw it in the fire, and she cried. It was a new woolen cap she had." Emer is our older sister.

"I don't remember that," Derry said, but she looked pleased at the thought of the burning cap. "I don't remember Belgrave Road at all."

"The next time I have a clear memory of you," I continued, "you must have been about three. We were living in Ranelagh. I went into the front bedroom and found you wandering around in your skin, crying for someone to dress you, and I dressed you."

"I don't remember *that*," Derry said.

"Well, do you remember when you were six or seven and almost got St. Vitus's dance? You kept shaking and dropping things all over the house."

"Oh, I remember that, all right," Derry said, smiling.

All the time we were talking, she was hemming a pink cotton dress for her older daughter. I looked at her hands, so steady and sure with the needle, and I thought of how we had all feared she would lose the use of them.

"You were never able to help with the washing up," I said, "for fear you'd break all the cups and saucers. When you weren't dropping things, you lay on the bed with your eyes wide open, not able to wake up. You looked awful. You gave Mother a terrible fright. She got the woman from next door in to look at you."

"I *remember* all that," Derry said impatiently.

"But you were asleep," I said.

"I was no more asleep than you are now," she said. "And I was no nearer getting St. Vitus's dance than you are now, either," she added, this time with a touch of defiance.

I stared, or glared, at her. "What do you mean?" I cried.

She looked me straight in the eye, but the color began to rise in her face.

"Do you mean to tell me you were putting it all on?" I cried, sounding almost as thunderstruck as I felt. Derry's delicate health had loomed as importantly in my childhood as the Catholic Church and the fight for Irish freedom. The first word I ever remember hearing about Derry was that she had been underweight when she was born and that her health was precarious. My mother always dressed us exactly alike, and people used to call us Mrs. Brennan's twins, but I was the large, hardy twin and she was the thin, pale one, always with me, and always silent, while I talked endlessly. Remembering how strongly all this had shaped our childhood, and the way it had determined everything between us and around us, I naturally was aghast to hear her now, more than twenty years later, calmly tearing it all away. I decided that she was joking.

"You're joking, aren't you?" I said.

"I am not," she said.

"But why did you do it?" I asked.

"Well, for one thing, I always got out of doing the washing up," she said. "And I was always too delicate to go to school much, if you remember."

"All those washing ups I did," I said. "And do you mean to say you never told anyone at all about it?"

She gave me an exasperated look. "That would have been pretty silly, wouldn't it? The whole point was that no one knew."

"And you've kept it a secret all these years," I said.

"To tell you the truth, I hadn't thought about it for years, till you brought it up just now. Of course, I really did have colds sometimes, and I did have those terrible chilblains in the wintertime." She began to laugh, and so did I, but not very heartily.

Just then, two of her children began a battle under the windows, and she ran out to investigate them, leaving me to think about her duplicity all those years ago, when she was so small and frail it would have taken a strange-minded person to accuse her of the least offense, let alone of keeping the house in an uproar over her health for years on end. I was more admiring than anything else, because I hadn't really minded doing the washing up alone, since I always received high praise from my mother for doing it, but I was stunned to think that Derry had been capable, so young, of thinking up and carrying through such a black and complicated plot, and of not speaking about it to anyone — not even to me.

It was then I remembered that this was not the first time she had set me back.

The first time it happened, she was not more than seven and I was almost nine. In those years, as I say, I was larger than she was, and I won't say I bullied her, but I did boss her around. All her life, I bossed her unmercifully until the moment of which I am about to speak, and I suppose that even after that things did not really change very much between us. I remember I had a favorite game called "sitting on Derry." I used to make her lie flat on the floor while I sat on her stomach and stared into her face, grimacing in a manner that we both considered terrifying. It was a simple game, but I suppose she must sometimes have grown weary of it.

I felt superior to her and protective toward her because she was so tiny, and because she hated school and never did well in her lessons, and because she got ugly, painful chilblains in the cold weather and I never did, and most of all because she was shy. As a matter of fact, I never gave her a chance to say a word. People were always told that I had the brains in the family. "Derry has the beauty," they used to say, "but Maeve has all the brains." I believed every word of this. I used to look at Derry and think solemnly about my brains and about how I never had any trouble in school and always got good marks. In games, I always hammered myself into the lead, while Derry played off by herself somewhere, and I was always first to enter myself in singing competitions, although I had no voice, and in reciting contests, although I had no eloquence. I had even made up my mind to become an actress, but I had not spoken to anyone at school or in the family about my ambition, for fear of being laughed at.

However, one day Derry and I were sitting together in the back garden of our house in Ranelagh. It must have been summertime, because we were sitting on the grass and there were forget-me-nots and London pride in bloom in my mother's flower beds. We had a bead box on the grass between us, and we were stringing necklaces and enjoying my conversation.

"When I grow up," I said to Derry, "I'm going to be a famous actress. I'll act in the Abbey Theatre, and I'll be in the pictures, and I'll go around to all the schools and teach all the teachers how to recite."

I was about to continue, because I never expected her to have anything to say, but she spoke up, without raising her head from her necklace. "Don't go getting any notions into your head," she said clearly.

I was astounded. Where had little Derry picked up such a remark? I had never said it, and I was not sure I had ever even heard it. Who had said it to her? I was astounded, and I was silent. I had nothing to say. For the first time, it had occurred to me that little Derry had *brains*. More brains than I had, maybe, even?

A Young Girl
Can Spoil Her Chances

Upstairs in the bedroom that he had shared with his wife for more than thirty years, Mr. Derdon stood erect before the chest of drawers that was his alone and worked placidly on the knot of his navy blue bow tie. Mr. Derdon was wearing his waistcoat and his trousers. Both of these garments, which had been made for him at a discount by one of the tailors in the men's outfitting shop where he worked, were of a smooth navy blue wool material that had a faint gray line running through it. The coat of this suit hung ready to put on, over the back of a straight chair on his side of the bed. The companion chair stood on Mrs. Derdon's side of the bed, but there were no clothes hanging on it or laid across it. As usual, Mrs. Derdon had got up and dressed herself and got out of the room before her husband was properly awake.

If this were an ordinary morning, she would have finished her breakfast by this time. Already, on an ordinary morning, she would have begun on her housework, and when he arrived downstairs she would leave whatever it was she was doing and go back to the kitchen to wait on him while he had his breakfast. But this was not an ordinary morning. It was a nuisance of a morning. Today was the forty-third anniversary of Mrs. Derdon's father's death. She was having a Mass said for the repose of his soul, as she did every year, and, as she did every year on this day, she was going to attend the Mass, which meant that Mr. Derdon's morning was going to be upset — he had awakened annoyed, thinking about it — because she was not going to be on hand to give him his breakfast and see him off to work.

Mr. Derdon was taking his time over the arrangement of his tie. He was watching himself in the mirror that hung over his chest of drawers, but although his hands and his eyes were on his tie, his attention was downstairs in the hall, and he was listening for the sound of the front door closing, which would tell him that Mrs. Derdon had gone out of the house and that he was alone and could go downstairs without fear of her seeing him. If she was going to go off like this, go off leaving him to have his breakfast alone, she was not going to have the satisfaction of seeing him settled at the kitchen table before she left. He had his mind made up. He was not going to go downstairs until he was sure she was out of the house. Time was on his side. He could hurry over his breakfast once he got down, but she should have been out of the house and gone minutes ago. She should have walked half of the way to the church by now, if she was to be kneeling in her place before the priest ascended the altar to start the Mass. He could afford to take his time. She would get tired of standing around down there waiting for him.

At last he heard the front door close. She was gone. Within the space of the minute that followed, he had his tie right, and he had slipped into his coat, and he had put his glasses and his clean handkerchief and his change and his pen-and-pencil set and the other objects that lay through each night on top of his chest of drawers into his pockets, and he was standing at the head of the stairs that led down to their narrow hall.

It gave him a fright, to see her standing below him in the hall dressed in her outdoor clothes, wearing her gray coat and her black Sunday shoes. Her head was bent, her face shadowed by the brim of her hat, and she was looking at something in her prayer book and standing very still, so that for an instant he thought he was seeing things, but she looked up at him and closed the prayer book.

"I thought you'd gone," he said.

"I had to come back. I forgot something," she said, and he continued on down the stairs and turned sharply at the foot and went straight down the three steps that led to the kitchen. She followed him. Of course, he knew very well what had happened. Trust her. Each of them had tried to play a trick on the other, and she had won. She had known all the last ten minutes what he was up to, delaying up there. She wouldn't call up to him, or come up, as another woman would have done. She would have called that "bothering" him. Doing the direct thing was "bothering" him. For some reason, she had been just as determined to see him as he had been not to see her.

"I suppose you know you're going to be late for Mass," he said, and he took the teapot off the stove and brought it to the table and sat down and reached for a piece of bread.

"I've left everything ready," she said.

She was standing uncertainly in the doorway. She even had her gloves on. In a minute she would have the gloves off and be fussing around putting more things on the table and asking him did he want anything.

"Are you going to Mass or not?" he said.

"Hubert," she said. "I thought of something very funny this morning. Do you know, I'm exactly the same age today that my mother was the day I was married."

"It was bound to happen sooner or later," Hubert said.

"Two days from today I'll be fifty-three, and it was two days before my mother's fifty-third birthday that I was married."

"I was married that day, too, you know," Hubert said. "She seemed a lot older than fifty-three," he added.

She hesitated, looking at his face, and at the table, and at his face again.

"Well, I just thought I'd tell you," she said. "It seems funny, when you think of it. I'm going now. Don't forget to give the front door a good bang. Be sure it shuts itself."

"All right, all right, all right," he said, but he heard the front door close, banging this time, and he didn't know whether or not she had heard him.

She had heard his voice, but not his words. She was satisfied. She had wanted to see him, and she had seen him. She didn't like to have to go off and leave him in the house by himself.

This day, the anniversary of her father's death, was always a queer day, and even now, after forty-three years, she was upset by it. Today it fell on a Tuesday. Tuesday, the ninth of September. He had died two days before her tenth birthday. Every year, when his anniversary came around, she was reminded that in two days it would be her birthday, and then, on her birthday, she would be reminded that on her tenth birthday he had been only two days dead. Not even two days, not officially, because he had died sometime between half past six and half past seven in the evening, and she had been born sometime after three in the morning. A few minutes after three, her mother had told her. So that at the moment when she became exactly ten years old, her father, not yet buried, was not quite two days dead.

Every year, on her birthday, she would count her own increasing years, and she would also think of the lengthening span of time that separated her from her father, but most of all she would think and think of those two incomplete days, and she always woke up on the morning of her birthday with a terrible feeling of apprehension, as though she had forgotten to do something important and was going to be found out. The feeling of apprehension that she had, at the thought of the incompleteness of those two days, was terribly painful, and she could never get over the idea that something had been left undone in connection with her father's death — that he had failed to see somebody he might very much have wanted to see once again, or that there had been a carelessness about his wake or his funeral, or a lack of respect in the handling of his coffin or at his grave. She had been too small to see that everything was done the right way. She had been bundled next door to a neighbor's house with her little brother. From minute to minute she had not known what was happening to her father, or who was looking at him. But the neighbor's oldest girl had known; she had been watching, and when the coffin was carried in she had called to Rose to come and look at it.

Mrs. Derdon knew perfectly well that the incompleteness of the two days' interval between the hour of her father's death and the hour of her own birth was accident pure and simple and only accident, but there it was, the apprehension lived, and that—the sense of accident—was what it lived on.

But he need not have died. He had not been old and he had not been sick. He had been frail—he often lay down on the bed for a rest—but he had not been sick. If he had only managed to hold on for that little bit of time till he got to her birthday, he might not have died at all. He would have been safe. It would have been her birthday. It would have been the Big Day, and he would have been so watchful all day long, thinking about what an important day it was, that he might not have lain down for a rest when he came home in the evening, and if he had not lain down, he might not have died. They had both been so busy thinking of the Big Day, and talking about it, that they had paid no attention at all to the days that went before it, except to cross them off the calendar with a pencil. The father had drawn a bright red star around the Big Day, but he had paid no attention at all to the days that went before it, and neither had she, except that they were both glad, every evening, that another day could be crossed off to show them that they were that much nearer to the day they were both looking forward to. All the days before her birthday had been ordinary days, dull workaday days, not to be valued but only to be pushed out of the way, and then one of the ordinary days had turned around and made itself into the most important day of all.

If he had been sitting with her that night in his old armchair in the kitchen, as he often was in the evenings, he would have caught back the breath he lost and then he would have been all right. She had often seen him catch back his breath. He always looked at her, and she would look at him and see the tears come into his eyes while he caught his breath, and then they would both smile because he was himself again.

He used to hold her on his lap. That annoyed her mother. Her mother used to say that she was too big and heavy to hold, but he always said that she was no weight at all. When he went up to lie down on the bed, after he came in from work, Rose used to like to go up and lie down with him and talk to him until he was rested, but her mother put a stop to that.

He had come in from work as usual that evening, and Rose had stood beside him while he crossed off that day on the calendar. Then he had said, "Will I sit down there by the fire, or will I go up and take a little rest?"

Rose had said, "Whatever you like," and she couldn't help laughing when she looked at him, because she was always so glad to see him.

"Oh, I don't know, I think a little rest," he said, and he put his hand around the back of her neck, under her hair, and gave her a little shake. "Only one more day now, Rose," he said, "and then we'll see what we will see."

She was delighted, because she knew he was referring to the present he had promised her, which was to be a surprise. And Jimmy, who was only five then, was sitting by himself on the floor in front of the fire, and got up and came over to them, because he knew that there was to be something for him as well, even though it was Rose's birthday. And the father had bent down and said, "Yes, Jimmy, there'll be something nice for you, too." Then he had started up the stairs, and she had stood at the bottom with Jimmy beside her and watched him go up. He had not looked back, but then, of course, he had not known they had come to the foot of the stairs and were looking after him.

Her mother had not gone upstairs to see him as she usually did when she came back to the kitchen from the little shop that she kept in what had once been the front sitting room of the house. First the mother had been busy getting the tea, and then, when it was ready, she said she would let him sleep on awhile. And then the woman next door had come in and had begun talking. He had died alone. He must have been terribly frightened, but he had been very brave. He had not cried out or called anybody's name. They had all been downstairs and they had heard nothing. But her mother and the woman next door had been laughing and talking. He could have called out and they might not have heard him. Maybe he had tried to call, "Rose, Rosie!" "Rose" meant that he was calling her, and "Rosie" meant that he was smiling, calling her name for the second time. There had never been any need for him to call her twice. She had always run to the sound of his voice. He had always come into the house calling her.

She had been restless that night, sitting at the kitchen table with no one paying any attention to her. Her mother and the woman next door had been sitting facing each other across the fire. Jimmy was on his mother's lap and she was holding him close to her, with one arm along his leg and the other arm around him and around his neck, her hand on his neck cuddling him while she talked over the top of his head to the woman next door. Jimmy had been wearing the short trousers that his mother had made for him from an old skirt of her own, and the red jersey that his mother had knitted for him. The mother had taken off his boots and stockings when Rose brought him home from school, and his little feet shone in the light from the fire.

Rose had sat there wanting to hold Jimmy but afraid to ask, and at last she had said that she thought she would just run upstairs and see how her daddy was. But her mother, who was different in her ways when they had visitors, had given her a look that Rose knew was put on for the benefit of the woman next door and had said, "You stay where you are, Miss, and let your daddy have his rest. I'll be the one to decide when it's time to wake him. Do you hear me?" And the mother had given a significant nod at the woman next door and said, "Rose is the greatest little busybody you ever saw."

And the woman next door had smiled, not very nicely, and said, "She's just looking for notice. Isn't that it, Rose?"

"Oh, she wants notice, all right," the mother had said. "But sure, he spoils her. No matter what I say, he spoils her. And it's only going to make it harder for her in the long run."

"Nothing worse than a spoiled child," the woman next door had said, and then they had gone on to talk of something else, and Rose had sat patiently on until her mother had seen fit to go upstairs to where the father lay.

Rose had never found out what it was her father had intended to give her for her birthday, or what he had intended to give Jimmy. There had been times—once or twice, anyway—that he had made a deposit on whatever it was he wanted and then the people in the shop would put the present, the toy or the doll, away until he had the money to pay for it in full. Rose could not believe that he had not put down a deposit on something for her someplace; not on the present for Jimmy, perhaps, because that would have been smaller, but on something for her. And she went in and out of Miss Greene's shop several times, and in and out of O'Malley's, loitering a minute and looking around and hoping that one or another of the people behind the counter would say to her that her father had made a deposit on something for her and that they had it there, keeping it for her, but nobody ever said anything to her about a deposit being made, and she was afraid to ask.

But it was not the loss of the present or the loss of the birthday or even the loss of her father that afflicted Rose so much as the knowledge, which she alone possessed, of that lost fragment of time between the moment of his death and the moment that had marked her birth. A big piece of time had been broken off, and it had gone down, and maybe it had taken others besides him with it, but if it had she did not know of them. The terrible thing was that no one besides herself seemed to notice that a piece of time, a fragment, had been shattered off their lives, and that nothing had happened during that time—no minutes or hours or anything like that. It was on that uneven fragment of time that Rose concentrated her attention, trying to guess its shape (not exactly like a day, and not exactly like a night) and trying to imagine what accident had caused it to slip away when it might have held firm until she and her father had gained the safe ground of her birthday. It was her knowledge of the power of accident, and her natural, confused apprehension, as much as the desire to see that he got something to eat, that had caused her to trick Hubert into coming downstairs this morning, when she knew perfectly well that he was enjoying his sulk.

She was just in time for Mass. As she walked into the church she held herself very straight, and her face wore a self-conscious, almost disdainful look, the look of one who has found nothing to criticize so far but who fears that at any moment she may find herself among people who are beneath her and who will try to be too familiar with her.

Hubert knew that look. She only wore it outside the house. Hubert disliked having the order of his day disturbed. He didn't like to have his breakfast all topsy-turvy, and he didn't like seeing his wife running around the house at that early hour of a weekday morning with her hat and her gloves on, and her big bulging prayer book in her hand, but what he disliked most of all was to see her go out to face the world wearing the face that she showed to the world, the face that she imagined impressed people—as if anybody ever noticed her. Her pretensions, the pitiful air she wore of being a certain sort of person, irritated him so much that he could hardly bear to look at her on the rare occasions—rare these days, anyway—when they went out together. They had been living in Dublin for over thirty years and she was still the same simple girl from her simple country town, and that was all right, in its way, if she would be content with that, but the minute she got out of the house she started imagining things about herself, as though by imagining, and pretending, she could deceive people into thinking that she was the sort of woman she was not. And what was more, thinking that she could deceive people into thinking that she was a sort of woman that had never existed anywhere, any time, except in her head.

Hubert thought it was a very bad way to start the day, thinking about all that. But, once he started thinking about all that, he kept on thinking about it, and the end of it was that he arrived at work seven minutes later than usual, but still well ahead of most of the other men, and in a bad mood. He did not mention the dislocation of his morning to anyone. He did not like to give confidences or to receive them, and he disliked being asked questions, and almost never asked anyone a question. His department, staffed all by men, was at the back of the big main floor of the shop, behind the wide, carpeted stairs that led up to the second floor. The ceiling of the main floor was over two stories high, and a balcony had been run around the walls of the men's outfitting department to create extra room for storing stock and for doing such work as making and checking sample books and checking orders. Today Hubert was to spend his time on the balcony, to begin checking the samples in the books against the amount of material they had in stock. The department did a lot of work with priests, and as he arranged what he wanted to get through in the course of the day, Hubert put clerical samples well out of his way, so that he might not come upon them until tomorrow, or even the day after tomorrow. Hubert's only son, his only child, was a priest, and Hubert disliked being reminded of the fact that John was now Father John Derdon.

He had been disappointed when John joined the priesthood, but, to tell the truth, at the same time he had been relieved. John was a poor example of a fellow, weak and timid and with no aptitude for anything and no inclination toward anything, and Hubert had never been able to imagine what he would do or could do with himself in the way of earning a living and making a life for himself. For a fellow like that, becoming a priest was as good an answer as any. He would be taken care of, and he would always be told what to do and what not to do. He would be safe all his life. In time, as he grew older, he would probably get to walking and talking with as much authority as any of them, in his black clothes. What had happened to John, his fate, could all be laid at Rose's door. She had ruined the boy. She had kept him all to herself all his life, and she had ended up by ruining him. It was a pity about John. Hubert did not like to think about John. There was something very meager and lost about him the last time he had come to see them, with his stiff new manners and his collar back to front and his carefulness about himself and about everything he said. Very uneasy John was that day, as if he was trying to set a good example to himself, watching himself and then looking at his parents as if he was hoping they would tell him that everything was all right.

The morning that had begun badly for Hubert went on badly. The two boiled eggs that Rose had left ready for him, and that he had decided to swallow at the last minute, after having decided earlier to punish her by leaving them where they were, sat coldly on his stomach. He wanted nothing to eat when midday came, and he decided to take a stroll and maybe have a glass of milk or something.

It was a cool day with bright sun, but there had been showers in the morning, and Hubert wore his raincoat when he left the shop.

He was an unremarkable, decent-looking man, not very tall. His face was pale and thin and he had blue eyes. He wore the expression of a friend, but of a friend who is making no promises. He walked as he worked, methodically, and made his way slowly along the narrow, crowded length of Grafton Street, sidestepping the prams and watching where he was going, not glancing in any of the shop windows. Grafton Street was bedlam, he thought, and he was glad when he emerged into the wider and freer and quieter spaces of Stephen's Green. One of the high park gates, open, faced him diagonally across the green from the corner where he was standing.

It had been years since he was in the park, many years, but when he and Rose first came to Dublin it had been their favorite place, the favorite place of all. They were always in there on Sunday afternoons — they spent all their time there. They never minded the rain then, never minded anything; they walked through the park in all weathers. There was a hat Rose had then, a little hat with a brim, very like the hat she had worn this morning. She loved the park. She was always wanting to go in there. She used to like to feed the ducks, and she never was finished exclaiming over the beauty of the flowers, and over the ingenious arrangements of the flower beds, and over the convenience of the benches and chairs that were placed along the edges of the paths for people to sit on, and over the care that was taken of the grass and of the borders and of the shrubs. She was always in the park during those first weeks — months, it had been — before they found the house they could afford and moved out to Ranelagh.

During those first weeks together they lived in a house on Somerville Street, in two small rooms at the top of the house — a long walk up to get to them — and Rose had grown very fond of those rooms. The day they left Somerville Street, Rose cried. They were moving out into their own place and all she could do was cry. All she would say, when he asked her what was wrong with her, was, "Nothing. I can't help it. I can't help it."

She had seemed all pleased and contented with the house, and he could not understand what had suddenly overcome her. He had been worried himself, worried about money, wondering if they were going to too much expense, and her tears had unnerved him.

Then, their first Sunday in the house, they were at their dinner when she suddenly put her head down into her hand and began to cry again. "Oh, I wish we had stayed where we were. It was so nice there. I wish we could have stayed there."

He had lost his temper. He had said to her that there had been nothing but mistakes ever since their marriage and that maybe everything had been a mistake, the marriage, too, the marriage most of all, and what did she mean by saying that she wished they had stayed where they were, what was going on in her mind, she was better off now than she had ever been in her life before.

That was a miserable day, that first Sunday in the house. The place had looked so cold and bare and hard to deal with, even after they had the bedroom set arranged, and the rest of the furniture they had then—part of a sitting-room set and the yellow table and chairs in the kitchen. The place had still looked poor and bare, and even to him it had seemed a long and not a happy way from Stephen's Green. He had begun to wonder again if maybe they had gone in over their heads, but he had recovered himself, after his outburst, and when they were finished with the dinner, he had suggested that they get on the tram and take a ride into town to Stephen's Green, and walk in the park as they had been doing. But it was not the same thing at all, having to take the tram in and the tram back—it was as though they were now visitors in what had formerly belonged to them.

But the worst thing Hubert remembered about that unhappy day was the look of terror that had crossed Rose's face when he had spoken roughly to her. He had been shocked by the terror and hurt on her face. He had only struck out at her in natural annoyance and impatience—that is what he told himself—but the effect on her had been that she was trampled. It took nothing and she was beaten to her knees. Her plate was full in front of her, but she ate only a little of it, bowed toward it all the time like a punished child or a punished, furtive dog. And then he left her to do the washing up, and when he came back down to the kitchen, having recovered his temper, to suggest that they go to the park, there she was standing by the sink finishing up what was left on her plate, and when he appeared in the door of the kitchen she had turned in a panic to hide the plate, to hide what she was eating, and he had turned and gone back upstairs, pretending that he had noticed nothing.

He never could understand her — her secrecy, her furtiveness, her way of stopping what she was doing and running to do something else the minute he came into the room, as though what she was doing was forbidden to her. She was afraid of him, and she never made any attempt to control the fear, no matter what he said to her. All he ever said to her was that she ought to try to take things easy, try to take life easier — things like that, that would reassure her. But she was afraid of him, and that was the whole of the difficulty, and that is what defeated him at every turn, and that is why he gradually, or finally — he could not have told how it happened — gave up any attempt to get on any kind of terms with her.

Anyone who saw them together could see that she was afraid of him — or Hubert thought he was justified in thinking that anyone who saw them together could see her fear — and it wasn't fair, because he wasn't the sort of man a person need be afraid of. She behaved sometimes like a person who was trapped in a place where she did not want to be, with a person she was deathly afraid of and who did not want her there. There were times when her face was not the face of a normal person. He shut it out of his mind after a time — her fear, or whatever it was that was the matter with her.

When the child was born she was much happier and she seemed easier in her mind, but then she became completely wrapped up in the child. It was unhealthy and wrong, the way she came to depend on John even before he was big enough to walk. Then she made John afraid of him, too. He would hear the two of them chattering away, but when he would open the door and go into the room where they were, they would both fall silent. He would catch them exchanging glances that excluded him. And when she wanted to reprove the child she made a habit of saying, "Your daddy doesn't like that, Johnny," or "Your father won't put up with that from you, Johnny." As though he, Hubert, the silent father, who never spoke an unkind word to the child, and who never had a chance to say much more than "Good morning" and "Good night" and "Happy Christmas"—as though he was the only one who didn't like what the child was doing.

Hubert had an idea that she knew perfectly well the power it gave her, her being afraid of him and his being always afraid that he was going to hurt her feelings, but he never went so far as to challenge her with that, with the power it gave her, or with his other suspicion, that she got a certain enjoyment out of irritating him. He never could bring himself to say, "You're afraid of me. I don't know why you're afraid of me. I think you ought to make an effort to get over it. It's not fair to me nor to yourself nor to the child. And I think you get a satisfaction out of being afraid of me. I think you know very well what you're doing—getting the child to side with you when there's no need for anybody to take sides at all. I don't like these games. I don't like them a bit. I wish you would make up your mind to stop all this nonsense. I wish you would stop it. All this cringing and running out of the room whenever I walk in will have to stop. It will have to stop. It will have to stop."

But when he got to that point in his thoughts Hubert would have to stop himself, because he would begin to feel his anger against her getting out of hand. The anger was dreadful because there seemed to be no way of working it off. It was an anger that called for pushing over high walls, or kicking over great tower-ing, valuable things that would go down with a shocking crash. The thing he really wanted to smash was out of his reach and he did not even know what it was, but when he thought of things that were out of his reach but that he could smash if he could reach them, he felt better. But there was no way of talking to her. She took the least word as a rebuke, and when he made an attempt to talk to her, to talk sense to her, he only ended up feeling ashamed of himself and sick of himself and sick of her. But it was a long time now since he had made any effort to find out what was the matter with her or why she was so unhappy. Obedient, yielding, and gentle, she outwitted him at every turn. She gave in to him. She gave in to him on everything. It seemed there was no limit to her capacity to yield, and he thought there was no if or but about it — she would go on forever giving in and make no move to assert herself. There was something in her that he could not fight, or there was something in her that he could not find, and he did not know what it was or what was wrong.

It was her eyes that gave her away, or didn't give her away — whichever way you looked at it. She had her father's eyes and her father's features. That is what her mother had told him. The first time he saw Rose she was behind the counter in the little bit of a shop her mother kept in what had been at one time the front sitting room of their house. You went in through the hall door and you turned right and you were in the shop. Rose was twenty years old then, and her hair was a very light, sunny brown. He noticed her hair that day, because she had her head bent over a scrap of crochet she was working on, and the sun shone directly on her hair through the square window behind her. Her hair was fastened back into a bun, in a style that was too old for her and that gave her a very plain, quiet look. She had a piece of cloth in her lap, a big handkerchief or a piece of a pillowcase or something like that, and when she saw him she dropped the crochet into the cloth and folded the cloth, making a little bag of it, and stood up and smiled at him, all at the one time. She seemed to be very glad to see him. He thought she was a nice-looking girl, very open-faced, like a child. With that open face and her obedient nature she should have had blue eyes, clear blue eyes, but her eyes were green, the color of seaweed, a deep green, not dark but full of clouds.

He asked her for a small packet of cigarettes. She reached to a shelf at her side and took them and put them on the counter, and then immediately she took them up again and opened the packet and counted the cigarettes inside. She counted under her breath and then "Six," she said, and showed him the open box.

"Isn't that what there usually is?" he said.

"I have to count them," she said apologetically, "or my mother will eat me. A man came in here the other day and took a packet of cigarettes like that, and the next thing I knew he was back complaining that there were only four cigarettes in the packet. And I didn't know what to do. I gave him another instead, and when I told my mother about it she was angry and she said he'd played a trick on me. So I have to count them now."

Hubert smiled at her but he was thinking that it was not surprising that someone had taken advantage of her. He was thinking of her as he walked down the street, when he heard her calling after him ("Wait a minute, wait a minute"), and by the time he turned she had already caught up with him, running after him.

"I only wanted to tell you that I have to open the cigarettes for everybody," she said, "not just you."

"I know that," he said. "You told me that."

"I was afraid I had hurt your feelings," she said.

"Oh, no, no. It's not that easy to hurt my feelings," he said, and he thought she seemed too excitable. He didn't like her running after him down the street like that, calling attention to him.

Rose and her mother and her little brother Jimmy spent their evenings in the room that was down the hall from the shop—a big dark kitchen that seemed to be all doors and that only had one window opening out onto their small, high-walled yard. The mother always sat in a wooden armchair beside the fire. Rose sat on a straight chair alongside a table in the center of the room, and Jimmy lounged on a wooden bench under the window. Jimmy was fifteen then, a silent boy who smiled every time you looked at him. Like Rose, he was constantly watching his mother. Rose used to sit there in that kitchen like a good child, hardly speaking. The night they decided to get married, he was sitting at the table across from Rose, and even then Rose hardly spoke, but she watched him. Even when she was pretending to look down at the table or at the fire, he knew she was watching him.

Rose's mother was a woman who knew what she was about. She knew the difference between right and wrong, and she spoke her mind. She took no nonsense from anybody, and when they were all there that night she said to him, "I hope you know what you're about, Hubert. It's no joke, getting married. It's not just a matter of putting the ring on a girl's finger. They say a young girl can spoil her chances, but a young man can spoil his chances just as easy and just as much. I don't know if you and Rose know each other well enough. You want to think a bit, you and Rose both. You want to wait a while and not rush in without thinking. You don't want to be in a hurry about this. You want to give yourself time in case you want to change your mind. Better to change it now before it's too late. Rose is flighty. She changes her mind from minute to minute. She never knows what she thinks one minute to the next. She thinks according to whoever is talking to her. She's only a child. You want to be sure you're on firm ground before you take a long step. Now, I know what you're thinking, Rose. That I'm hard. I'm not hard at all. But I know you. You're a young fellow, Hubert, with no one to advise you, and I'm older and wiser, and even if Rose is my daughter I want you to know that I have your welfare at heart just as much as I have hers. And she is changeable. She can't help that. It's her nature. I think you should think about this awhile."

"Oh, Mother, don't be talking like that to him," Rose cried. "It's not fair. You'll be giving him a bad picture of me. It's not a bit fair."

"I don't want any of your back answers, Rose," her mother said. "And now, to prove that I'm right, I'm going to give Hubert an example of what I mean."

"Oh, well, then, there's nothing I can do," Rose whispered.

"Here's what I mean," her mother went on. "And I'm telling you, Hubert, so that you'll know and so that nobody can be laughing at you behind your back. Do you know the lane that runs alongside the Children's School over on Patrick Street? Well, you wouldn't know it, being a stranger here, but it's there, and there's nothing at the end of it but a disused stable with a broken door. The door got broken about a year ago when some young hooligans got in there one night, for what reason nobody knows and nobody likes to think, and they were never found, although we all have our ideas as to who they were. No decent girl would go down that lane by herself, and at night no girl would go down there with anybody if she had any respect at all for herself, but the tenth of June last, Rose slipped out of here when my back was turned and waited there at that stable for over two hours at night, from half past eight until nearly eleven, waiting for a young fellow down the street, a young fellow, a young rascal that's not good enough for Rose to wipe her boots on, or wasn't good enough until she let him wipe his boots on her."

"Oh, Mother!" Rose cried.

"That's what he did," the mother said. "And the reason she went there and waited was this. He came in here to the shop and told her he'd made a bet with some of his chums that she would meet him there, and he told her that if she didn't meet him he'd lose his week's wages and be a laughingstock besides. And, of course, without thinking twice or asking me, off she went in her best shoes and stood there for two hours. Stood there. Waiting for him. Any other girl in the world would have known what to do, but not this poor soft thing. So he won his bet and she'll never live it down. They broke their hearts laughing at her. And I'll never live it down, and poor Jimmy had his heart broken with the way they made fun of him in school. That's what she did. She did it out of softheartedness, and I know that, and I know she meant no harm, but it's not right for a girl to be so soft and so careless and to have that little respect for herself and her family. I've been meaning to tell you about this. I never intended to let her conceal it from you."

"There was no need for you to tell him, Mother," Rose said. She was crying quietly, with her head bent, and he wanted to reach across the table and take her hand, but he was afraid that her mother might guess that the touch of Rose's hand was already familiar to him. He was afraid of her mother.

"There was every need for me to tell him, Rose," her mother said. "And there is no need for you to cry like that. You're not a baby anymore. You're talking about getting married, and you want to prove that you're sensible enough to get married. And that's why I say that you ought to think this over, both of you, a bit longer, before you make any promises. Think it over for a while. A month, or a week, maybe. Maybe it would be a good thing if you stayed away from here for a week or so, Hubert, and gave it thought. And Rose can be thinking, too."

"I'll be back in Dublin in a week," Hubert said.

Rose turned and looked at him and he looked across the table at her. He knew she wanted him to say that his mind was made up and that he would never change it. Her eyes were timid and afraid, but they met his eyes with certainty and she looked ready to smile. She was sure that he would say to her mother that his mind was made up and that the fellow who had played that trick on her deserved to be kicked, and that there was no doubt at all in his mind as to what he wanted to do and that they would go together to the priest at the first possible opportunity and arrange to be married as soon as possible. He couldn't be coming down here from Dublin all the time. And he wanted her, but Rose didn't expect him to say that out loud.

But Hubert was thinking that she was there for the taking. She would walk out of her mother's house with him, or she would stay there and wait for him. She would do whatever he said. No matter what he said or did, she would not complain against him or disagree with him. And there was time. And he wanted her mother to think him a responsible man who weighed and lived by reason and not by whim or impulse. He took his eyes from Rose and looked at her mother.

"Twenty-four hours," he said. "Either I'll come back tomorrow night or I won't. I'll sleep on it."

He looked then at Rose with a grin of complicity, but her face was not the same. It had been spoiled and blurred by astonishment and she looked stupid and cruel. She looked quickly at her mother, who regarded her with calm triumph.

"So be it," the mother said. "It's not long enough, but I can see that you know what you're doing. I was beside myself that night she went out, wondering what had become of her, and when she got back and I heard what she'd done I got onto her. I was ready to kill her. I finally asked her if there was any excuse she wanted to make for herself, and do you know what she said to me? She said, 'But, Ma,' she said, 'they would all have been laughing at him if I hadn't turned up.' Did you ever hear the like of that in your life? They would all have been laughing at *him,* and of course she couldn't have that, oh, no, they mustn't laugh at him, even though she hardly knew the fellow, except to say hello to, and so to save his face she must go and put herself in the way of being laughed at and worse—laughed at and talked about. I don't know what they didn't say about her. I had to force her out to Mass the next Sunday, and the Sunday after that. But she didn't want *him* to be laughed at. And she thought that was a good enough reason for what she did."

Stephen's Green Park is enclosed behind high iron railings and it is surrounded on all four sides by broad, busy streets. Mr. Derdon had walked along the west side of the green, keeping on the far side of the street from the park, and along the south side, past the massive-fronted city houses that had so impressed Rose when she first saw them. Now he made his way along the east side, past St. Vincent's Hospital and the college, and he found himself on the corner of Somerville Street. He stopped on the corner and gazed along the narrow, gray street, which was closed at its far end by three houses. It was in one of the houses along the side where he stood that Rose and he had had their first home. He couldn't remember the number of the house, and he was not inclined to walk along and look to see if he could remember the house when he came to it, but he knew it was one along toward the end of the row.

A friend of his, a man who had been a great friend of his at that time, had helped him to find the rooms. Frank Guiney, a very good-hearted fellow. He and Frank had been great chums, but Frank had gone to try his luck in England. Hubert wondered if Frank had ever come home again. There had never been any word from him after a couple of postcards in the weeks that followed his departure. Frank had been a great friend. The night Hubert and Rose arrived at Westland Row Station, Frank met them at the station and they all walked back to Somerville Street together, Hubert and Frank carrying the luggage and Rose carrying only a basket filled with bits of food — tea, sugar, things like that — that her mother had gone and got from the shop at the last minute before they left. There was even a bottle of milk, because the mother had said there would be no milk to compare with in Dublin. Rose hadn't wanted to take the basket of food. She had been embarrassed about carrying it, and in the train she had put her coat over it, covering the little bags and parcels it was filled with, but when they had left Westland Row and were walking along the street she carried it easily, smiling as she went along between himself and Frank. Frank complained that Hubert must have married an heiress, he had so much to carry. Frank was very funny that evening. He said the case he was carrying must be full of ornaments, it was so heavy.

"China ornaments," Frank cried. "China cats and china dogs and great big china horses. What do you want with so many ornaments, Rose? Eh?? Isn't Hubert ornament enough for you? Mind you don't put him on the mantelpiece by mistake, now."

Rose had been all doubled up with giggling. Then when they were along Somerville Street Rose said, "Which of the houses are we going to live in?" And Frank gave a flourish of one of the parcels he was carrying and nearly dropped everything with his nonsense, and he said, "The *best* house." When they came to the house, stone steps in front and a dark green door, scratched and dented and with a crack in the fanlight, Frank put everything he was carrying on the ground and stretched to rest himself before starting the long climb to the top of the stairs.

Frank looked at Rose and he said, "She smiles and smiles and smiles." Rose was obviously longing to go into the house and straight up to see the rooms, but she stood obedient and pleased while they both looked at her.

"She smiles and smiles and *smiles,*" Frank shouted, and then he said to Hubert, "Does she never stop smiling?" And Hubert said, "Never."

Now, as Hubert stood at the corner of Somerville Street, looking along the fronts of the houses to try to see which one might have belonged to him and Rose, he was seeing the three of them as they had stood there that evening, but the word in his mind was agony. Agony agony agony was in his mind while he watched the three figures that stood a few houses and over thirty years away from him, and he watched until the vision dazzled and his eyes filled with tears. He turned quickly away from Somerville Street and continued along in the direction of the Shelbourne Hotel. Terrible the things you remember, he thought; it's a long time since I have walked around here. It does no good to remember those times, he thought, but at the same time he was thinking that it did no harm to remember them. They had been blessed that evening, Rose and himself, and Frank, too. They stood in the state of grace. And then Frank had collected himself and his ornaments, and the three of them had marched into the house together and up the stairs with all flags flying.

And today Rose was the same age as her mother had been on that evening. Hubert glanced across at the park, and quickly glanced again, with curiosity. How many years since he had been in there? Ten, or more? He couldn't remember. He might go across and go inside for a minute, find out if there were any changes. He was enjoying his walk. The exercise was doing him good, but he wished he had a newspaper to carry in one of his hands. Hands always seemed to get in the way when they were empty. His hands were in his pockets. He ought to have a stick, if he was going to start walking as much as this. A stick was natural, if you were walking. A stick or a newspaper. Anything more was a nuisance.

After John had gone away, left home, Rose had fallen into

such despair that one night he had bought a hyacinth and brought it home to her in an attempt to distract her from herself, and he had never felt so silly or so conspicuous in his life as he had felt walking out of the shop and along the street with the plant between his hands. They had wrapped it around with pink paper and folded the paper into a high cone, making it look much bigger than it need have looked, and much too festive. He had tried carrying it in one hand but it wouldn't balance. He had chosen a blue hyacinth in full bloom, and he was very anxious not to let it get bruised or broken. He had an awkward time in the tram, with both hands on the plant, and, as luck would have it, he had to stand the whole way home that evening, of all evenings. By the time he got home he was nearly angry. He had taken the pink paper off when he got into the house, and he had put it standing in the middle of the dining-room table where she would see it first thing when she came to the door to call him to his tea. She had come in and he had pretended not to notice that there was anything out of the way, and she had said, "What on earth?" and she had lifted the hyacinth off the table and put one arm around it to hold it, while with her free hand she patted the spot on the table where the damp plant had been sitting all bare with no saucer under it. "Oh, Hubert," she said, "a lovely hyacinth. Isn't that a lovely color of blue. But it needs water. And I'll put it in a bigger pot. I have a big one out in the shed, the pot the poor rose geraniums died in. I'll get it out after tea. I'll have to find a good place for it, where it'll have all the sun." While she was talking, there was, in spite of the sadness that lived all over her face at that time, a little smile on her lips, a faint smile that was closed, secretive, half satisfied, you might almost say, and almost triumphant, as she talked about the hyacinth and what she would do for it. Then, of course, later on she had slipped back into the perpetual attention she paid to John's absence from their life. The fact that he had gone to serve the Church that she was so devoted to make no difference at all in her feelings, and did not console her.

Hubert wondered what had become of that blue hyacinth, whether it had flourished or withered away in the new pot she had put it in, if she had transplanted it into the garden later on, or what. He had seen hyacinths growing out in the open, he was sure of that. Perhaps that same hyacinth was in her front garden now, or in a sunny place at the back. If it was there, would it have grown bigger, and would it bloom every year, or what? He would ask her about the hyacinth tonight, just out of curiosity.

For a girl brought up in a town, Rose had an unusual interest in gardening and a great feeling for flowers. Her two gardens, the little one in the front of the house and the bigger one behind it, were always lovely. Even in the wintertime she managed to have something out there that would catch your attention. Even in the wintertime the beds had an appearance of order and form, and looked as though they were keeping to a pattern that had been devised for them, for those particular beds, and never for any other beds in any other garden. Rose had gone mad over the gardens in Stephen's Green Park. She said she had never imagined anything like the park. He had a memory of her walking there in a navy blue skirt and a long-sleeved white blouse and no coat. It must have been a very warm day. The navy blue skirt had a matching coat that went with it. She called this outfit her costume, and it had been her wedding dress.

The park was full of mothers and nursemaids and children that afternoon. The women sat along on the benches that lined the paths, and they talked to one another and watched the children and admired them and scolded them and called to them. The children were running all over the place. He and Rose strolled along. They were not yet used to being together.

Rose said, "I was just thinking, it's nice being married."

Hubert looked at her, but she was not looking at him.

She said, "I can't see how a married person could ever commit a sin. I don't know what kind of a sin it would be that a married person could commit. There isn't a single thing I can think of that I would have to tell the priest if I went to confession this minute. Nothing is a sin anymore. Isn't that funny?"

Hubert's eyes were on the path. Children's legs raced into his vision and disappeared as the small boys and girls chased one another across the path and around the benches. He dodged to avoid knocking down a very small girl in a white dress and white boots who stamped slowly and unsteadily along by herself and kept herself upright by embracing the empty air in front of her with open arms. As he stepped aside to avoid the child, Hubert saw Rose's skirt move as she walked along beside him. In the sunlight, in the navy blue skirt, her slender hips appeared commanding and alien, and she was his, and if Hubert had been told at that moment that Helen of Troy had come back to earth and was called Rose he would not have denied it. Behind him a woman screamed, "Come back here, Paddy Mernagh, till I wring your neck!" Hubert thought of Rose and the future, and his thought was all of innocence and of the necessity of earning enough to enable them to hold their heads up and never have to give thanks to anybody for anything as long as they lived.

Hubert was approaching the corner of Grafton Street from which he had begun his walk around the square, and he thought that if he had time he might run across and take a look into the park to see what changes might have been made in there. All these years, and he had not been in there. He wondered why he had never taken John into the park when John was little. Maybe Rose had taken John in there. She might have, when they were in town to buy things. It would be a shame if John had never played there, and he was nearly certain that John never had. He wouldn't ask Rose about that. If John had never been taken to play in the park, Hubert didn't want to know of it. He was sorry now that he had made the effort to remember the exact number of years it had been since he had been in the park. It was thirty-three years since he had been in there. He had not been in there since the last Sunday he had gone there with Rose, their first Sunday in the house. It didn't seem possible that anyone could spend thirty years in Dublin without once going in and out of Stephen's Green Park, but he was a man of habit, and he always went straight home after work. Thirty-three years ago. He was twenty-eight then. He decided to cross the street at once and go into the park at the next entrance.

He paused at the curb to look up and down the street, and then he saw, at the far end of the square, a funeral approaching him on his side of the street. The hearse was drawn by two black horses that had black plumes on their heads, and he had the impression that the line of black mourning cars behind it would be a long one. Hubert liked to follow the custom of paying respect to the dead by walking a few steps along with the funeral, even if it meant turning around and walking back a few steps. He had plenty of time to cross over to the park before the funeral drew alongside him, but he didn't mind the delay. He wanted to see the funeral pass, and as soon as he had the chance he would look in the paper and guess which funeral it had been. The funeral was still a good distance away, and he began to stroll idly toward it. He was measuring the distance between himself and the hearse, trying to guess the point where they would be abreast, and at the same time he saw, without looking, the figure of a woman who stood motionless in the gutter with her back to the street. She was there begging. He could tell that without looking at her. All his life he had denied beggars. He detested and despised them. He passed her by. The coffin was covered with rich wreaths of flowers, banked with flowers like an Easter altar. It was a coffin that spoke, even now, of the rewards of wealth and of the beauty and satisfaction of ceremony and order. Hubert turned to walk with it, and as he turned he admired it. He took one two three four steps, and five and six. Six steps were enough, and he had taken his eyes from the coffin and was about to glance discreetly into the first car of mourners when he found that his gesture of respect had brought him nearly face to face with the begging woman, and that she was looking at him and had pulled her hand out from under her shawl to take whatever he would give her. Her shawl was wrapped tightly around her shoulders and around the child she had, whose head was just visible against her shoulder, and it was the hand that supported the lower part of the child's back that was now extended to him, not in demand but expectantly, while she still kept her elbow close against the child, holding it safe. She thought he had passed her by and then changed his mind and turned back to her.

He turned his back on her and walked quickly away from her, but not before he had seen her hand tighten and draw back to the child, and not before he had seen the look of expectancy on her face turn to a hatred so forlorn that for a moment it looked as though her face had been cut off. She thought he had done it on purpose. She thought he had turned back on purpose to disappoint her. But she must have known the funeral was passing. She had not been looking at the funeral at all. She had been looking at him and thinking of what she was going to get. She had seen him pass her and she had seen him turn back to her. She thought he would do a thing like that. She thought he was the sort of man who would do a thing like that. He thought he would turn back again, and this time quickly give her something, but shame kept him going and he walked more and more quickly away from her. A woman passing glanced at him, and he realized he had been walking along muttering and rubbing his eyes, and what he had been saying was "I wouldn't do the like of that. I wouldn't do the like of that." All the mourners must have seen him, hurrying along making faces like a lunatic. He wished he had given the woman something; it would have been easy enough to give her something. There was no need for her to beg, there were plenty of places she could go to, where she would get help, but all the same she was pitiable standing there, and she had said nothing to him and she had not called names after him, as many others would have done in her place. But how could she think he was the kind of man who would play a trick like that? He should have explained to her that he was looking at the funeral, but she would still not have understood why he gave her nothing. To pass her by and not give her anything, all right, but to turn back to look at her and still give her nothing. It must have seemed that he was mocking her or that he had something worse in mind. How could she have thought that of him? She held the child as if it was threatened. She had both arms around the child the way Rose used to hold John, as if there was nothing in the world but that one baby. The way she held the child against her body was a reproach and a warning to everyone who came near it. Women like that were impossible to deal with. They would give themselves heart and soul to what they knew must go. There was no reasoning with them. All the mathematicians in the world could kill themselves working, and those women would not even look over their shoulders to see what was happening. They would learn nothing and they would see nothing and they would care for nothing as long as they had the child. If you told them they were ignorant and reckless, risking themselves, they would not hear you. They would not be able to hear you. All the history and she kept always on the floor beside her. She had brought the basket from her mother's the day she was married, and it had lasted as long as it had because it was too cumbersome for daily marketing and so she kept her work in it — her knitting and crocheting and the mending. She was making an afghan, square by square. As she worked, her lips moved, and every time she finished a row of stitches she lifted her head up as though she had suddenly come to a decision that had been difficult to reach but that was now pleasant to reach. From time to time she glanced appraisingly around the room and she watched the clock. The clock was mahogany, and it had been a wedding present from an old friend of Hubert's, Frank Guiney, and it had a place of honor in the center of the mantelpiece. When she heard the boy leave the evening newspaper she got up and fetched the paper and sat down and began to read it, but when she heard Hubert's key in the lock she quickly closed the paper and folded it to look as though it had not been opened at all.

Hubert hung his raincoat and his hat in the hall and went up to the bedroom and changed his coat for an old three-button cardigan of tan wool. When he got down into the back sitting room Rose was sitting in her chair working on her crochet.

"I put the paper in your chair," she said.

"Is there anything in it?" he asked.

"No," she said doubtfully. "Oh, I don't know. Maybe there is."

He walked over to the window, where he stood looking out at her garden. It was only a patch of grass, edged with flower beds and bounded by gray cement walls that she had disguised with ivy and another creeper that had a red pointed leaf. It was just a patch, and she had spent a good part of her life trying to make it nice, and his son had spent his childhood in it, and he himself had spent all his summer holidays sitting out there in a deck chair. They never went away anywhere for a holiday because it cost money to go away, and in any case they did not like to leave the house alone.

"I'm going down to put the kettle on now," she said.

He turned and looked at her. She was getting up out of her chair. She did not get out of the chair gracefully but she got out of it easily, without helping herself with her hands, and when she stood up she stood up straight.

"Tell me something," he said. "You remember the hyacinth I brought you one time. What became of it?"

"The blue hyacinth," she said. "It did very well after I put it in the big pot. I showed it to you. It had a lovely bloom."

"And where is it now?" he asked. "Did you put it out in the garden?"

"Oh, no. Hyacinths *go,* Hubert. They only have one season. You have to get new bulbs every year."

"I'll get you another one," he said. "I'll get it for you tomorrow. I'll bring it home with me tomorrow night."

"Oh, you'd never find a hyacinth this time of the year," she said. "Only in the spring you get hyacinths, and this is September."

"Oh," he said. "I see. I forgot for a minute."

"I'm sorry, Hubert," she said.

He said, "It's all right."

"What put the hyacinth into your mind?" she asked.

"Nothing. I just happened to think of it," he said.

She went to the door.

"Will you light the fire for me?" she asked. "And I'll go on down." She hesitated, as though he might say no.

"I'll light it," he said. "Go on, go on, do whatever you have to do."

There was a box of wooden matches on the mantelpiece next to a framed photograph of John on the day of his ordination. Hubert avoided looking at the photograph. It was her morbid insistence on unhappiness that had caused her to put it there when she had another copy of it in a similar frame upstairs in the bedroom, and it wasn't a good likeness anyway and he intended one day to take it down and hide it. He struck a match and bent down and lighted the gas with great care and adjusted it by turning the tap slowly and pressing his lips together with the effort. Then he went to his chair and took up the newspaper and sat down. He did not open the newspaper. He sat quietly and watched the pale rose of warmth spread over the ashen grill in the grate. He sat like that until Rose called him to tea, and then he stood up out of his chair and buttoned his cardigan and pulled it down around his body and went to join her in the kitchen. As he went, the words of their conversation about the hyacinth came back to him, and he smiled, thinking that in spite of the habitual apology in her voice she had been half smiling as she explained to him about the difficulty of getting spring flowers when it was not spring. Even poor Rose could not shoulder all the blame for the change in the seasons.

In the kitchen the tea was laid out on the table and Rose was standing up pouring the tea. He used to try to get her to leave the teapot on the table so that she wouldn't be jumping up and down every five minutes, but she insisted on leaving it on the stove where the tea would keep hot. He pulled out one of the old yellow chairs and sat down, and in a minute she joined him, taking the chair across from him. In the middle of the meal he remembered the funeral and he told Rose about it, and she went up to the sitting room to get the newspaper to see if they could discover who it was had been buried with such pomp. While she was about it she collected the morning newspaper and the newspapers of the last three mornings in case they would have more information. She had a fairly good idea of whose funeral Hubert had seen—a wholesale grocer named Kinsella, whose father had come from Cork with nothing and built up a good business—but she didn't want to say the name aloud to Hubert until she was certain.

All the time she was going to get the papers and getting them, looking at the dates to be sure she had the right ones, and bringing them down to the kitchen, she was thinking how thoughtless Hubert was to bring up the subject of a funeral and not remember that this was the anniversary of her father's death. But she was interested herself and she stole a look at the papers while she was carrying them down and it was John Patrick Kinsella, it was his funeral Hubert had seen.

Rose left Hubert to read the full account of Mr. Kinsella's life and circumstances, which he had read earlier with less attention, because it had been in yesterday morning's news, and she herself looked idly through the back pages of the old Sunday paper, and found several items that she had missed on her first reading. When she remarked on this to Hubert, he observed that she had never learned to read properly, that she was a careless reader who skipped too often and did not concentrate on what she was reading, and it was a pity, because it was hard to form a good habit when you were older, and just as hard to break a bad habit once it had taken hold of you.

A Free Choice

Rose stood waiting for the dance, a waltz, to end. She felt ill at ease, being stranded like this without a partner. She wondered why Hubert Derdon had not come in search of her, to ask her for a dance or to ask her if she would like to go into the dining room and find something to eat. A lot of them were in there in the dining room, she knew, but she did not want to go in there alone. She would rather have been sitting down, more out of sight, but there were no chairs along the sides of the room but only at the ends. Mrs. Ramsay's drawing room, cleared for dancing, seemed enormous, and from where Rose stood, the ends of the room seemed not only far away but impassable, with sofas and chairs crowded together and people sitting there together, people who knew each other well but who did not know her very well, and she was younger than any of them and anxious not to appear to push herself upon them. Her mother had warned her not to be forward. It was only an accident that she was at the party at all. Father Kane had arranged for her to be there. The party was being given for the people who worked at Ramsay's shop, where Rose's father had worked before his death. Father Kane was very good. He had even arranged for Rose to get a ride in the car that brought a crowd of the girls from Ramsay's.

Rose thought the room was lovely. She was standing in front of long sweeping curtains of blue velvet. The blue of the curtains put the blue of her dress in the shade, and her dress was velvet, too. Rose felt that the dress she had made for herself, that had seemed so grand at home, could never compete with the splendor of the curtains, and since she was not competing with the curtains, she felt that they protected her, falling from the top of the tall windows to the floor behind her as they might well have fallen in front of her. She had been looking forward to seeing this room, which was famous in the town, although not many people had had the privilege of visiting the house and seeing it for themselves. She recognized the velvet curtains the minute she walked into the room, and she turned at once to speak to Hubert Derdon about them, but just as she turned, Mr. Lord, who had been a very old friend of her father's, came up and asked her for a dance, and she danced off with him, feeling very nervous and shy, and when the dance was over, Hubert had disappeared, and she had not had the chance since to speak to him and tell him what she knew about the curtains.

She had first glimpsed the curtains as she walked through the front door into the big hall outside, and she had been astonished, as though she had caught a glimpse of an old friend from long ago, someone she had worshiped and had never dreamed of seeing again. There were the curtains her father had told her about, and they were exactly as he had told her they would be. And he had never seen them finished. During the months before his death, Rose's life had been full of talk about velvet, and he had brought home bits of velvet to show her — rose velvet and red velvet, several different colors of green velvet, a yellow velvet that was called amber but that he said was old gold, mouse-colored velvet and orange velvet and blue, his favorite color, every shade of it. Many of the other men and women who had been working the two men who had brought it began to take it out of its box. They walked all around the box, looking at it and tapping it before they found the right place where they would begin to open it. They didn't take the top off the box and lift the table out, they took the box away from the table a bit at a time. First they took the top off and laid it on the grass and then they pried the sides off, and the way they worked at it you'd think they were afraid of it. Then the table was out in the open and they cut away the paper it was wrapped in and you should have seen it there, all glass with the sun shining down on it. She has an arch there over the path, covered with roses, and the table caught the roses and made the most of them. A looking-glass table, that's what it is. Mrs. Ramsay will be able to see all around herself but I wish you could have seen the way the roses looked in it. It sparkled in the sun and all the roses sparkled. It made a fairyland out of the garden. I felt that I was dreaming. I looked up. The sky was blue. It was a lovely day. Rose, you should have been there. I was standing in the drawing room, no curtains on the windows and no carpet on the floor yet, all bare, but I like the wood under my feet, the bare wood—the floors are lovely in that house—and I was looking through the window at the table standing there in the sun and I was thinking about you and making wishes for you. I was wishing... I don't know what I didn't wish for. Then they picked the table up and began carrying it into the house. They set it down for a minute in the hall and it looked as if the sun was still shining on it. Then they began carrying it up the stairs. They watched each other's feet and they never spoke a word all the time they were going up the stairs and they went very slowly, one step at a time. The table tilted a bit and I could see myself in it, all different ways. There is a prism in the Protestant Library—I will take you there to see it. I won't tell you what it is—it is called a prism, prism—and then you won't know what to expect and you will be surprised. And Mrs. Ramsay has a big diamond that she wears on her marriage finger. There are a lot of things that catch the light. I watched myself all the way up the stairs. That is a very big enormous square hall she has there, with as many windows in it as if it was a room, but I was standing as quiet as if the table depended on me as much as on the two that were carrying it, and I began to feel as if I was at the bottom of a well watching myself go away from myself. I was standing there looking up. It is very funny to see yourself looking up the stairs. I suppose that is the way we appear to God—always looking up when we want something. Then they got up on the landing and the table went away out of my sight. I suppose I won't see it again."

The curtains comforted Rose because, although she had not remembered them all these years, she recognized them the minute she saw them. All these years they had been here, looking just as he had imagined them and as he had described them. The curtains had been here, looking like this, on the day she had not come with her father—on all the days she had not come here with him or gone anywhere with him, days and weeks and months that had followed him into eternity. She began to believe that she had been remembered at some time far back, at some moment when she had thought herself down and out and forgotten and derided. It had all been only in her imagination, that she had been forgotten. She had not been forgotten at all. She felt she had as much right in the room as any of the others who were dancing around and talking together in little familiar groups. Even though she had no job at Ramsay's—they were hiring very up-and-coming girls there now, one or two even from Dublin— she had been in on the plans for this room, she had known as much about it as anybody, long ago; before the wallpaper was on the walls, she had known about this room, the furniture that was waiting to go into it and the carpets that had been bought for it. The two little marble-topped tables near the fireplace there — she remembered them now, although she had never seen them before. And the big sofa was against the end wall, under the landscape picture from France, as he had told her it would be. It was all as he had told her it would be. They had rejoiced together over the beautiful room that was growing in their minds. There were two small white plaster portraits on the wall, one on each side of the door that led into the dining room, and he had never been able to remember the names of the people they represented. He called them "masks." Rose looked at them now and thought them very dull, very religious-looking, very out of place in this brilliant rich room. She thought of her father looking at them and wondering who they were. He could have asked, but everybody seemed to know, and he had not wanted to appear less well informed than the rest of them.

He had been very pleased that Mrs. Ramsay had called him in on the planning of the house, and that she had trusted him to find the right stuff for the curtains. She had asked his advice on other matters connected with the decorating and painting, and even on the placing of the pictures. He told Rose that this extra work provided him with a great chance, the first real chance he had ever had, and that it might mean great things for him. He and Rose both knew that he was fitted for something better than unrolling and rolling bolts of linen and cotton and serge over the counter all day long. He told Rose that miracles would never cease, because it was just at the moment when he was feeling himself to be of no importance to anybody at all in the world that Mrs. Ramsay had sent for him and started to talk to him about the way she wanted her new house to be.

It got on her mother's nerves, the way they covered the kitchen table with scraps of velvet every evening and sat there together going over the scraps as though they were counting gold and diamonds. Her mother said it was getting to be too much of a good thing and that it was bad for Rose to sit there dreaming over things she could never have. Rose and her father were like two misers sitting at the table over their treasure while her mother stood and confronted them. At that time of the evening, after tea, Rose and her father generally had the kitchen to themselves. They had a small shop in what had once been a front sitting room, and Rose's mother went in there after tea and sat there talking with anyone who cared to drop in and occasionally selling something—bread or cigarettes. She became more and more annoyed about the samples as the weeks wore on and still the color of the curtains had not been settled on by Mrs. Ramsay and still Rose's father talked about them and about what Mrs. Ramsay had said to him.

"Mrs. Ramsay is making a fool of you and picking your brains for nothing," Rose's mother said. "And you are making a fool out of the child, giving her notions about herself and what she knows. What does that child know and what good would it do her if she did know anything? What chance has she got, and why can't you leave her alone and let her learn her lessons? She has a bag of homework there, hasn't she? She won't thank you later on in life. Giving her ideas is all you are doing."

When she spoke like that, Rose's father used to take his hands off the table and put them in his lap and stare down at them and say nothing. When she left them and went back to the shop he always sighed, but he did not look at Rose, and then he always said, without raising his head, "No use provoking her. Let her have her say. She means no harm."

Rose looked at the masks and pretended to be so interested in them, far away as they were, that she could not look into the faces of any of the dancers as they went by. She felt that she had been stranded there in front of everybody. She blamed Jim Nolan, who had been her partner in the last dance. He had given her to understand that he would be back, and so she had waited for him and he had not come back at all. At first she imagined he had been delayed, but now she realized he had never had the slightest intention of coming back. If she had only known, she could have found her way out of the room and then she would not be standing here making a show of herself. It was not fair. There was a chance he might have been annoyed at what she said to him, but he had not seemed annoyed, and he must have known she meant no harm.

She had been delighted when Jim asked her for a dance. He had worked at the same counter with her father years ago, but he was not more than ten years older than she was, and he was very handsome and tall. The other men who had asked her to dance were quite old men, all of them married and old enough to be her father. She was surprised that Jim took any notice at all of her, because he was popular and she knew that every girl in the room was watching him. He had a lovely friendly smile. She had always seen him, all her life, in Ramsay's and around the town, walking with somebody, usually a man; he was great with the girls, but the women laughed when his name came up and said he would be hard to catch. He was different from the other men, very dark; there was something foreign about him, like an actor.

Before dancing with Jim, Rose had believed that she was having a lovely time at the party. All of her father's old friends had come one by one to ask her for a dance, and one time there were two men competing for her hand—Mr. Cleary, who was fat and nearly bald, and Mr. Fagan, who was thin and always smiling—and they asked her to choose between them, and she could not, and they all stood there laughing and she felt very much at home. Mrs. Cleary came up to them and took Rose's hand and asked her how had she learned to be such a good dancer, and she told them about the way her father used to always dance her around and make her keep time, and Mr. Cleary said, "Your father was a great dancer. I can see him now." And Mr. Fagan said, "When he danced, he was enjoying himself. You could see that." Then Mrs. Cleary squeezed Rose's hand and said she was a good girl and that it was a pity her mother hadn't come tonight, to see how popular she was.

But when Jim asked her to dance—from the moment when he appeared before her to her astonishment—she remained in astonishment. The brilliance of that moment when she had first looked into his face and said she was free remained around them, and made them both free from the rest of the people in the room so that she understood at once that it was not the velvet curtains or the masks that had made the room familiar to her but the impression that remained on it of her father's hand. Somehow, however he had done it, her father had managed to make the room ready for this moment when she and Jim would dance together. Her father had loved her. This room could never have been his. And as it was now, he had only dreamed it. He had never seen it at all, but he had known how it was going to be.

She looked up at Jim and told him it was her first big party. He said nothing, but he smiled down into her eyes as though he knew what it was she really meant to say. How could Jim know what she really meant to say, when she did not know it herself? She was filled with gratitude and with the assurance that whatever she said next did not matter very much, because she was saying it to him, and he would not mind what she said, because it was Rose who was speaking. "I am afraid I am not a very good dancer," she said. The truth was that she felt she was dancing quite well—splendidly, in fact, although she was a little worried for fear she might not be able to stop gracefully at the end. But

Jim continued to smile at her and seemed to hold her more closely to him, and he told her she was much lighter than a feather, lighter than a swan's feather, lighter even than a thrush's feather. Then he began laughing and he asked her if she had ever danced with a feather bed, and without giving her time to say no he told her to look over her shoulder and she found herself staring straight at Mrs. Fleming, who was in charge of the hat counter, and whose extravagantly towering hair arrangement was designed to draw attention away from her fatness, which was alarming, seeming to flow solidly not down to the floor but away from her and around in all directions, as though she grew larger while you watched. But Mrs. Fleming had been on the floor all evening. She had not missed a step, dancing around like a young girl with all the younger men, smiling brightly on everyone, like an empress.

Now when Rose found that Jim was inviting her to laugh with him at Mrs. Fleming she was exhilarated, as though she had won a great trophy she had not known existed. She felt that her new dress was as good as any dress in the room, and that she was a natural dancer and could dance with anyone. There was no doubt about it, people would say that she and Jim were meant for each other. He had only been acting with all those other girls. He had only been playing for time. He had not been himself, and it was perfectly possible that he had never been himself all his life until this moment. She would be a very good influence in his life. He would see that her heart was true and that she was not like the other girls, who were only out for a husband.

It was clear to her, as she laughed up at him, that all the stories she had heard about him were lies, or at least that he was misunderstood by those who envied him. He was not wild and a flirt and a drinker and a loud talker, as people said — he was not any of those things, he was something else entirely, and she wanted to confide her understanding to him and to show him that he could trust her, but he was making it obvious that he could trust her, and they were dancing too fast for conversation, so she contented herself with saying to him, boldly, that she thought he was a funny man. He looked at her sharply and he looked very pleased, so that for a moment she thought he was going to stop right there on the floor, and he squeezed her hand tightly—that is why she thought they had stopped dancing—and he said, "You're going to have some explaining to do, young lady. You're going to have to explain that remark."

And then they seemed to dance faster than ever, and when the dance ended he swung her around in a half circle so that for the moment she lost her balance, and when she righted herself she laughed very loudly, taking it all in her stride, as though she were accustomed to occasions like this and to the world, and some of the older women nearby turned and glanced at her and then at Jim, and looked away. She knew they thought she was making a show of herself but she did not care. She turned smiling to Jim, thinking he would take her arm and lead her off to sit down where they could have their talk, but instead he smiled affectionately at her and thanked her and walked quickly away. He would be back, she knew, and she began to wait for him. Mr. Lord, with whom she had had the first dance, came up and asked her to be his partner again now, but she told him she was engaged and he smiled and said, "Oh, so that's the way it is, is it?" and went away.

That was the moment, if she had only known it, when she could have made her way out of the room and to a place where she would not have been so conspicuous. But how could she go, when there was a chance that Jim might come back? And now she had been standing here for a long while, hardly noticing the time, and she would have to go on standing until the dance was over. If she walked in one direction, to the dining room, and made her way through the crowd of people gathered at the end of the room, all of them talking together, sitting and standing, all familiar together, she might find Hubert Derdon among them, and he would imagine she had come looking for him. And then again, in the opposite direction, toward the hall and the stairs that led up to the ladies' cloakroom, she might find him in that crowd there at the end of the room or in the hall itself, and she did not want to find him.

Not for one minute would she want Hubert Derdon to think she, Rose, would try to find him or that she would ask him for anything or expect anything from him. Only last night he had asked her if he might see her home from this party. She had been very pleased. That was only last night. She had thought of him all day and of the way he had looked at her when he turned at her door and spoke about the party. And here she was, and except for that one minute when she had seen him in the hall just after she arrived with the other girls, he had not spoken to her. It was a shame. She had imagined herself walking around here with him, and that everyone would see them together. She could have told him about the velvet curtains and all the rest. There was a lot to tell him that she had imagined he would like to hear. She and Hubert had never been alone together. Her mother had always come in and sat in the kitchen with them when he came to visit, and then her mother had done nearly all the talking, with Hubert occasionally making a sharp remark. That was one of the things Rose had against him — his tongue was too sharp. He was too sure of himself. But he was very nice, or at least he had seemed to be nice until tonight.

Perhaps Hubert had found one of those smart girls from Ramsay's; Father Kane would have introduced him around. This was

Hubert's first visit to Wexford. He had come down from Dublin on a holiday with a nephew of Father Kane's, and Father Kane had been taking the two of them, Hubert and the nephew, all around everywhere in his car and showing them all the sights. But Hubert was a quiet sort, and he liked to walk by himself and to look around by himself, and one afternoon, walking like that, he had come into the shop and Rose had been behind the counter and so they had met each other, and for the last week he had been dropping in for an hour or so every evening. He was a stranger still, and it was clear now that he would always be a stranger. There was no use hoping for anything from anybody. She wondered if by chance Father Kane had said anything against her. Father Kane might have said that she was not quite good enough or something like that. Father Kane was fond of her and he had arranged for her to come to this party, but perhaps he had his doubts about her. There was no way of telling. And Hubert might have changed his mind about seeing her home. Perhaps Hubert was reluctant to be seen in public with her. And there was always the chance Jim Nolan might ask to see her home, and if he did, she wanted to be free to go with him. Hubert was a stranger and he would be going away soon, and she could never feel as much at home with someone like him as she could with someone like Jim Nolan. She wished she were whirling around the floor with him again, being told that she was as light as a feather and that she was going to have to explain herself because she was so interesting. She should have offered to go with him when he walked away from her. It was what any of the other girls would have done.

She wondered where the music was coming from. She knew it was coming out of a piano, but she was certain she remembered hearing a violin during the time she had been dancing with Jim Nolan. She had wanted to ask some of the other men she was dancing with where the music was coming from, but she had not wanted to betray her ignorance of a house like this. In a house like this there would be a special room for the music, she was sure of that, although she did not know what the room might be called, or where it might be placed in the house. She had heard there was a cellar here with wine in it, but perhaps that was only a story.

People were always talking about the Ramsay family, and everyone had been surprised when Mrs. Ramsay invited all the ordinary people who worked in the shop to a party. It was nice of Mrs. Ramsay, but it was not like her to be all that familiar with those who worked for her. Mrs. Ramsay was very stately. She had been standing in the drawing room here holding court when Rose had arrived, and Rose had wondered if she should go up and greet her, but she had decided not to call attention to herself, and then the music had started, and the dancing. Father Kane had been standing at Mrs. Ramsay's elbow then, and he had waved at Rose but he had not beckoned to her to come and be introduced. Even so, Rose had hoped that Mrs. Ramsay would notice her, but Mrs. Ramsay had not noticed her. Mrs. Ramsay's youngest daughter had just come home from a year at school in Paris. Everyone said that the Ramsay girls were spoiled but that the youngest was the worst of the lot and that she had to have her own way in everything. Her name was Iris. Iris Ramsay. There was no sign of Iris Ramsay here tonight, but then it was not likely that she would bother with an affair like this when she had seen so much of the world and knew what was what.

Now she was sure that the music was coming from the dining room, and she looked in that direction and there was Jim Nolan walking out of the dining room and toward the dancers in the company of two women Rose did not know except by sight—they both worked at Ramsay's. They were much older than Rose and she had admired their dresses earlier—they were both very smart. Jim had not so much as looked in her direction, although he must have known she was still standing there and that she was waiting for him. All the time she had been standing here he had been in the dining room talking with his real friends. Rose began to tremble.

The people dancing around on the floor seemed very noisy all of a sudden, and very much occupied with themselves, and selfish, and their talk and laughter sounded ill-humored and at the same time intimate, as though they rejoiced in a private joke at the expense of some person who might, at any moment, be at their mercy. Surely someone had turned up the lights; the room was too bright, and in the brightness, which was hard on her eyes, Rose felt that her face was burning, and her body felt confined and tired in the dress she had made for herself. She believed that she had made the dress well, and that she had even made it very well. She had dreamed that Mrs. Ramsay might notice her appearance and might compliment her, and then she would be able to tell Mrs. Ramsay that she had made the dress herself, and from a pattern bought at Ramsay's, but that the choice of velvet had been her own—the pattern-maker had recommended taffeta. She had even gone so far as to imagine that she had made the dress better than she knew, and that Mrs. Ramsay, with her practiced eye for style, would notice how nicely it was cut, and that she would recognize in Rose what she had recognized years ago in Rose's father—the extra touch of imagination that she had told him he possessed, and the unusual instinct for color.

The room was too hot. She felt in the short sleeve of her dress for her lace handkerchief, so that she could pat her forehead with it, but the handkerchief was not there. She remembered taking it out of her raincoat pocket out there in the hall and fitting it carefully, all folded into a triangle as it was, into the sleeve, but now it was gone. But it couldn't be gone. It was real Irish linen, edged with real lace, and it had been a present from her mother four Christmases ago, and from the day she received it until tonight it had lain in its tissue paper in its original complicated pointed folds. She had never so much as shaken it out. She had barely touched it. It had stayed in its box, lying like a treasure at the bottom of the drawer where she kept her clothes, until tonight. It couldn't be gone, but it was gone. It must have slipped from her sleeve when she was dancing around so gaily, making a show of herself. If she hadn't been so taken with herself she might have felt it go. Now it was down there on the floor under someone's feet. It would be a rag by this time. Even if it was a rag, she would be glad to have it back. Her mother had hesitated a long time before buying it, and then she had asked that it be wrapped in white paper, because it was a present, and she had carried it home and walked in smiling and saying to Rose, "I have something lovely for you." It was the best handkerchief money could buy. Her mother had gone out to buy a woolen vest for herself, and she had seen the handkerchief, and instead of buying the vest for herself she had bought the handkerchief for Rose. The lace on it was real and there was a great deal of lace on it. When Rose first opened the box and lifted up the handkerchief, she and her mother looked at it very carefully, tracing the shells and roses and daisies and shamrocks and ivy leaves that covered it like the ornamentation on a wedding cake; and not funereal anyway, because they were so small and so white — not a cold or an icy white but a radiant white, like rose petals.

Rose knew that when a thing is gone it is gone. She tried not to think about the handkerchief, but she could not forget that it had been, was being, kicked around the room like a rag. There was no use thinking about it, and there was no use wondering who those plaster casts that he had called masks represented, or what names those faces had been called by when they were alive. If he were alive now, she would ask the names and tell him when she went home tonight. She would not mind asking. He had always said that she was very brave. But if he were alive now, he would be here tonight with all the rest of them, and her mother would be here and the three of them would be the center of attention, because her father would have got along so fast and gone so high in Ramsay's after the curtains were up.

Rose had carefully not been staring at the dancers as they went by, but now she looked and saw, quite close, a tall dark girl with a pearly forehead. The girl was Dr. Malloy's wife, his bride, and she was dancing with her husband. They had been dancing together during most of the evening, and once Rose had seen them talking and laughing with Mrs. Ramsay. They had not been married long. They had met in Dublin and been married there and Mrs. Malloy was still very much of a stranger. Rose had heard her mother say that they were only children. And the woman next door had said they were children who did not know how well off they were and that some people went through life being spoiled. The woman next door had gone on to say that it was only an accident they had married at all, because Dr. Malloy had been interested in another girl altogether, and he had only married this one on the rebound. Rose's mother had said, "Oh, everyone knows she was not his first choice, and she knows it, too, poor girl." The Malloys were dancing smoothly in time with the music, which had grown faster, but they were not smiling or talking. They were looking at each other and their faces reflected a common memory that was still too new to be familiar and too brilliant to be believed in. Rose thought, They cannot take their eyes off each other.

Oh, why could everything not have been different? She

looked away from the Malloys and tried to measure the distance, the great distance, between her and the door that would provide her with escape. Why could everything not have been different, but if everything had been different, everything would still have seemed exactly as strange to her. Her mother said, "Rose simply does not know the difference." Another time, her mother said, "Rose, you don't know the difference and you will not learn." But why could everything not have been different? Why could Hubert Derdon not have asked her to dance at least once? From time to time during the evening, she had seen him watching her and she thought he had even nodded at her once in a while as she danced around, but he had never made a move to come near her and now there was no sign of him at all. Why had Jim Nolan asked her to dance if he was only going to make a fool of her? Why had Mrs. Ramsay not made some sign of recognition, and why had Father Kane not even taken the trouble to speak to her? Why were the ceilings so high in this house, and why were all the girls so sure of themselves, and why had nobody taken the trouble to see that she, Rose, got something to eat, or a glass of lemonade at least? She was not going to walk into that dining room by herself and walk up to the table, or tables, or whatever they had, and ask for something as if she were a beggar.

The only thing to do now was to get out of the room as quickly as she could. It did not matter who saw her or what they said about her. It could not be helped if Hubert was around the hall and saw her. She did not care what he thought or what anybody thought. She longed to be at home and out of sight. She would make her way out of the room and go upstairs and take her raincoat off the big rack that was set along on the landing up there. Then she would slip out of the house and go home by herself. It was a very long way and she was afraid of the dark, but she had to get home. Her mother would want to know what sort of a feast Mrs. Ramsay had provided and she would not be able to tell her. And where was the music coming from? She knew nothing. She felt she knew nothing.

She hurried toward the end of the room, keeping so carefully out of the way of the dancers that she scraped the shoulder of her dress twice against the wall. Her dress would be marked from the wall, but that did not matter now. And after all, it turned out to be quite easy to make her way through the throng that was collected at the end of the room. None of them looked at her, and no one seemed to think that there was anything at all remarkable in her appearance, alone and hurrying as she was. She need never have feared that they would imagine she was trying to push herself upon them.

The big square hall was deserted, but someone had opened the front door to let the cold air in and Rose began to shiver as she ran up the stairs. It would serve them all right if she caught a bad cold. One blessing—the landing was deserted, and the bathroom door by the coat rack was open to show, in the wall inside, a square window of red and green glass. It would be very dark out. She turned to the big rack that was crowded with ladies' coats and scarves and began to rummage for her raincoat. A sound from the long dim hall behind her made her turn, and she saw a girl in a bright blue uniform coming out of one of the rooms. It was Mary Lacey, who had gone to school with her.

"Oh, Mary," Rose said, "I never saw you in your uniform before."

"And you in your silks and satins," Mary said, in a disagreeable tone, but her face was forlorn.

"Oh, Mary, I made it myself, every stitch," Rose said, "and it's only the cheapest velvet—nothing like as good as the curtains on the windows downstairs. I bet your uniform cost a lot more than this, Mary, and better made, too."

"Oh, the same old Rose," Mary said. "You haven't changed a bit. I remember the day after your poor father's funeral. You came to school, we were at our desks waiting for the nun to come in, and you said to me, 'Oh, Mary,' you said, 'it was a lovely funeral, only for the coffin.'"

She opened her hand and they both looked at the key that lay there on her palm.

"I had to lock all the rooms up here earlier, before anybody got here," she said. "She's that afraid somebody might try to steal something from her. And then she told me to come from time to time and see if everything was all right. I don't mind. I'm glad enough to get out of the kitchen. They left the door open between the kitchen and the pantry, and every time the dining-room door opened I kept looking along to see what I could see. I couldn't help myself."

"I'd forgotten about the coffin," Rose said. "My mother said, 'It's time to close the coffin.'"

"With all they have in this house," Mary said, "all their belongings and all their money and all, you'd think they'd have different keys for the rooms, but no, it's the same key for all the rooms. The kitchen used to be in the basement but they brought it upstairs. They can do anything they like."

"Is it very hard work, Mary?" Rose asked.

"Oh, it's more tedious than anything," Mary said. "Not hard. But look, there's someone on the stairs. Come on back in here with me."

She pushed open the door of the room she had just left and went in there, with Rose following her, and closed the door softly behind them. The room was dark except for the faint red light cast by an altar lamp that burned low under a large picture of the Sacred Heart. The picture was hung between two windows, and the lamp was set on top of a glass-fronted cabinet that stood against the wall there. Rose could see the shine of the glass panels and through the glass small white shapes, of little ornaments, perhaps, precious china ornaments that were too good to be left out where they might be touched. The curtains were drawn across the windows; she could see only tall dark forms where the light would enter in the daytime. And where the darkness became impenetrable she knew the bed was, by the outline and the bulk she sensed there. But Mary was pulling her by the arm.

"Look, Rose. Look at that. Did you ever see the like of that? It's her dressing table. I'll never forget the first time I saw it. It's all glass. Even the little knobs on the drawers are glass. Only the legs are wooden. Isn't it lovely?"

"It's lovely," Rose said, and as she approached it, walking only a few steps to it, she began to see her own shadow and then her face in the large oval mirror that made its center, and then she saw Mary, who was standing behind her, and the two girls stood and watched themselves.

"We look very mysterious," Mary said. "Don't you think we look mysterious — as if we weren't here at all. I wish I looked like this always. I'm fatter than you are."

"It's the uniform," Rose said. "It's too big for you."

Mary giggled. "I knew you'd say that," she said. "The minute you said it, before you said it, I knew that was what you'd say. I wish I could always look mysterious, this way. I don't look like myself at all. I could float up and down the main street and I wouldn't care what anyone said about me. I'd go to Dublin and then to London and I wouldn't say anything to anybody. And if anybody said anything to me I'd say, 'I'm Miss Iris Ramsay and I don't like *anything*.' ... She makes me sick, that one, the way she goes around the house pretending to talk French. And there's nothing anybody can do to please her. Her mother is going to do the whole house over for her. That's why she's having this party, to get all the good they can out of the place before they start to do it up. They would have had to move everything anyway — the carpets and the furniture and everything. They're going to get all new curtains and new paint and new wallpaper everywhere, and a new carpet for Miss Iris's room."

"They're going to take down all the curtains?" Rose said.

"All the curtains, downstairs and up here. She says the place is too heavy and old-fashioned. She wants all light colors. And she wants this dressing table for herself. She says it's not suitable for an older lady. She says it's suitable for her room. She's to have it. She means to have it and she will have it. When could I ever put out my hand and see a thing I wanted and say that it was mine? Oh, what difference does it make to me? I have to laugh. What difference does it make where it is? Not a particle of difference. What do I care what room it's in? Whatever room it's in, it's still not mine. This room or that room or her room or some other room, I'll see it just as much and want it just as much. Tell me something, Rose. I want to know—is Jim Nolan down there?"

"Yes. I saw him. He's down there," Rose said.

"I thought I heard him," Mary said. "First I thought I heard him talking and then I thought I heard him laughing and then— I was in the kitchen; he must have come into the dining room— and just before I came up here I heard him again."

"I saw him," Rose said. "Here and there. He was talking to two women from Ramsay's—Miss Martin, I think her name is, and another one."

"I knew he'd be here," Mary said. "Oh, what's the use. I knew he was here. He always goes around with the same gang of fellows, and when I saw one of them, Tommy Rice, I knew he was here."

"He fancies himself," Rose said angrily.

"You're right there," Mary said. "He fancies himself. Oh, yes, he fancies himself. No doubt about that. He fancies himself. More and more he fancies himself. But I knew that."

(These were the words she said, but her voice, helpless, went on its own way. *He is perfect,* her voice said. *He is perfect. He is perfect. Yes, he is. Perfect.*)

"I was great with him once," she said. "Well, I suppose I can say I was great with him. It was only for a couple of weeks, a little over two weeks, last summer. He thought I was great. I believed him. It must have been a poor sort of greatness that I had, but I didn't know the difference then. Oh, I don't care. It's over and done with. When a person doesn't want you he doesn't want you. Oh, I wish I could go away. Even a few miles, but I wish I could go to Dublin."

"Oh, Mary, I wish there was something I could say to you," Rose said. "I would like to kill him. He is not good enough for you. It's awful. Everything is all wrong. You are worth ten of him."

Mary looked at her as though she might say something, and then she looked as though she had decided not to say what she really wanted to say but to say something else instead. "Oh, it doesn't matter," she said. She sat down in the easy chair that stood not far from the dressing table and she put her head back and sighed.

Rose took a step toward her and would have touched her, but she was afraid of making the pain worse. She tried to think of the word that would mean comfort to Mary, but either she could think of no words at all or all the words she thought of were wrong. It was useless. "When a person does not want you, he does not want you." That is what Mary had said, and Rose knew it for the truth, but how she knew she did not know.

She thought of Hubert Derdon, and of how he had looked at her last night, when he had asked to see her home, and of how he had looked at her tonight, when he had not asked her to dance. She felt she was between the devil and the deep blue sea. The last few evenings, when Hubert had been coming to the house every evening, she had been glad to see him walk in, and happy and excited as long as he was there, but every evening, the minute he stood up to leave, she had wanted to tell him not to bother to come back again, and to tell him that she was not depending on his visits. Every time he walked out away from her into the night, without even a hint that he might come back, she felt like telling him that it meant nothing to her whether he came back or not; but he always went without a word, smiling at her but never giving her a chance to tell him that if he never appeared in the house again she did not care, and that she would rather he never came back at all than to come back and go off again, leaving her with what was worse than emptiness.

She would rather have no hope at all, and know there was no chance for her, than to have to contend with this little hope she had, that she was ashamed of, because it was so little and so timid. She felt that Hubert knew about this hope—that it was little and that it was timid—and that he was amused by it and that he was playing with her and hoping she would betray herself and then, for some reason unknown to anyone, he would laugh at her. And her mother would laugh, too. And her mother's reason for laughter was not unknown to her but familiar. Her mother would laugh out of despair, because once again Rose had let the side down. Her mother would laugh because her mother knew that sooner or later somebody would let the side down, because that is the way it was in their family. It was bad enough to be not good enough, but to invite laughter was a crime against the family. And everybody outside the house was ready to laugh. Her mother had told her again and again that they were all only waiting to see somebody make a false step.

Rose did not want to turn away from Hubert, because to turn away would be to admit that she had been turned toward him and had been disappointed. It was very important to keep hope secret, because then the disappointment that followed would also be secret. A girl who let herself in for being laughed at deserved what she got. Rose did not want to turn away from Hubert and tell him never to darken her door again, but she wanted to turn away from him before he had the chance to turn away from her. But she did not really want to turn away from him at all, because without him before her eyes she would have to look again at what did not exist—except in darkness, where it could not be seen, although she knew it saw, and in sleep, where it could not be heard, although she knew it cried out to her. She did not want her father to see her sad.

The red flame under the picture of the Sacred Heart flickered wildly, and sank, and went out. Rose put her hands to her face to keep herself quiet and then she put both hands out and caught Mary by the shoulder and felt her start from sleep to wakefulness. "Oh, Mary," she said, "wake up quick! The Sacred Heart lamp has gone out! Please wake up."

Mary sighed, and then she jumped to her feet. "Oh, Rose," she said. "How long was I asleep? Was it long?"

"Only two or three minutes, Mary. I wouldn't have wakened you only that the lights—the light in the lamp there went out. I'd better be getting on downstairs. I shouldn't be in this room at all."

"You'd better be getting downstairs and I'd better get back down to the kitchen. I'll get another light for the lamp. I'm going to open the door now, Rose, but don't you go out till I see if there's anyone on the landing."

There was no one on the landing, and as Mary bent to lock the door behind her she smiled up at Rose. "I don't know what's the matter with me, falling asleep," she said. "I keep falling asleep. Every time I sit down, I fall asleep."

She walked quickly away from Rose toward the back stairs

and she must have heard Rose call her name, but she did not turn around or look back. Even after she had disappeared, Rose continued to look after her. She had remembered a hundred things to say to Mary, but she had not been able to remember the right thing to say. She knew that if she had been able to take away all the wrong words she would certainly have found, underneath them all, the one word that would kill pain, and kill it, and make it never come back anymore. There was such a word. She had known it once, and she knew it still, but she could not translate it for Mary. *Father.*

What Rose wanted was a word for Father. She wanted a word that she could *say*. There was a simpler word for Father now, but she did not know what it was. In his new form, he was formless and would not answer to Father. There was a word for him now, as he was now, but she did not know what it was, only that it was a common word, and that she ought to know it so that she could say it to herself in a whisper. Once, he took her to the abandoned quarry outside the town, and they stood together near the edge, and saw the glitter of water on the bottom far below them, and he had thrown a penny in, and they had watched it drop down, and he had told her that the penny would fall forever and that it would never stop falling, because the quarry was bottomless and the water they could see was only the beginning of a drop so deep that no man could imagine it. He said that for all he knew, and for all anyone knew, the penny might continue to fall through all eternity. And then he had laughed at her and told her that if she wanted to save money she should throw it in the quarry, because no one would ever find it there, and only she would know where it was. Only she, and only he.

In the hall below, Hubert waited alone and watched for Rose to come down the stairs. He held her lace handkerchief in his hand.

He had seen it slip from her sleeve as she entered the drawing room, and he had picked it up and put it in his pocket to keep for her. He would have told her he had it, but she had given him no chance to speak to her. She had danced off, and then she had gone on dancing, round and round the room, and finally she had begun dancing with that Nolan fellow, and he had gone off in a rage to the dining room and eaten ham sandwiches one after another so that he would not have to watch her smiling in the arms of that glorified corner boy, that ladies' delight, that actor at love.

Hubert was angry and anxious. She had slipped away. He had lost her forever. He was sure of it. He had looked for her everywhere. He did not want to ask one of the girls to go up and find out if she was all right. He did not know Rose very well and he did not want to annoy her. And he did not want to ask anyone to go up anyway, for fear that she might not be up there at all. All these past nights it had been the same thing every night. Every night he had gone to her house to make sure she was still there and had not vanished, and every night, when she saw him to the door, she turned that face to him that said she was seeing him for the last time and did not care — that face of indifference and of downright cruelty. Because she knew very well why he came back, night after night, without being asked, and without any hope of being asked, apparently. She must have known why he continued to appear at her door, making a fool of himself, and not caring that he was making a fool of himself. And he didn't care that he was making a fool of himself now, standing right out in the middle of the hall with her little handkerchief in his hand. He had begun his vigil by leaning carelessly over there against the open front door, with his hand and her handkerchief in his pocket, and a careless eye on the stairs, but his anxiety had got the better of him and he had moved near and nearer to the foot of the stairs until now it was all he could do to restrain himself from going up the stairs two at a time and calling out to her to come to him and stop her nonsense. But what if she wasn't up there? She might have vanished, flown, slipped away home by herself. It was only to be expected. She would do whatever came into her head. She had no sense. She was like a child. She often appeared to him like a child who walks through a madhouse and is not afraid because she does not know the difference between inside and out. But she had every right to be afraid. Anything might happen to her. What if she had taken it into her head to go off home alone? He might never see her again, because she was as good as invisible with that mother of hers always there in the kitchen with them every night, always there and always talking.

Then Rose appeared, coming around the curve of the banisters from the landing above. Hubert thought, Lord, what a beautiful house this is. Look at the wonderful staircase they have. And he watched Rose. He thought, She is immortal, with that fair hair … She made him think of the Forest of Arden. She had her coat over her arm and she was coming down slowly one step at a time, like a child. He thought she looked discontented, but then she glanced up and saw him watching her and she gave him a con-spiratorial smile, as though he had seen her at a disadvantage and she did not mind. He thought, She is not very big, and he won-dered admiringly what size shoe she wore. When she reached the third step from the bottom she stood still and looked at him.

"I am afraid of the stairs," she said, and then she said, "You look very polite, standing there."

"I was thinking I would like to take a bite out of you," he said, and he grinned foolishly as she stepped down three more times and came to stand before him.

He gave her the handkerchief, relinquishing it as though he were giving up his passport, or his ticket of passage, or, as it was, his one and only hope of refuge in her country. She took the handkerchief without surprise, but he saw how her fingers closed around it once she had it in her hand. She looked at him and he thought, She is the only one in the world who can see me... Her eyes were green, the color of seaweed, and in their depths he found the light that would define him and enclose him in constancy. He thought, She is my own true self, and he wanted to tell her all his troubles.

"I can't dance," he said. "I would have told you before, but I was ashamed."

"Hubert," she said, "there were a whole lot of things I wanted to tell you. I wanted to tell you about my handkerchief, that it was lost, but it wasn't lost at all, but I didn't know that. There were a whole lot of other things I wanted to tell you about, about the curtains and so on—a whole lot of things. But first I want to know—there is no one else I can ask, but please don't laugh at me—I've been wanting to know, where is the music coming from?"

"Oh, wait till I show you," he said. "It's as good as an orchestra. You'd never find it unless you were looking for it. The house is bigger than you would think. We have to go through the drawing room. Wait till you see. I'd never have found it only that I was looking for you."

He took her coat and folded it over the back of a chair. "That will be safe there," he said.

He took her hand and led her toward the drawing room as though they were about to dance, like the others. At the entrance he felt her hesitate before the confusion in the room, and he smiled at her to encourage her.

"Come along now, Rose," he said, "chin up and step together. If we're not careful, some of these lunatics will trample us under."

The Poor
Men and Women

THE PRIEST'S MOTHER was distracted with herself, wakeful, impenitent, heated in every part by a wearisome discontent that had begun in her spirit very young. She wore herself out cleaning her house, going over her rooms with her dry violent hands, scraping and plucking and picking and rubbing the walls and floors and furniture, and stopping in the middle to clench her fingers tight, tight, tight, but not tight enough, never enough for her, there was no tightness hard and fast enough to satisfy her. Therefore she continued in want.

She was forty-seven, with a gaunt body and a long soft face. Her hair, brown, was done up at the back into a kind of bun or loaf. Her hands were large and hard, like a boy's. By comparison her husband's hands seemed small, because although about the same size they were narrower and better shaped, with soft scrubbed tips. He, Hubert, worked in a men's outfitting shop and wore a hard black hat to work. His mouth, smiling and placid in youth, still smiled, but it had withered and darkened, and he wore no mustache over it.

Every Friday morning he gave her the housekeeping money. She would waylay him as he came down the stairs buttoning his waistcoat, ready to leave for the office, and ask him for the money. She would hurry up the three steps from the kitchen, where the dirty breakfast things were, to catch him on the way out. One morning she closed the kitchen door and waited behind it to see what he would do. He put on his hat and took his umbrella and went out of the house without a pause. She thought he might have left the money on the hall table, but he had not done that, and she had to ask him for it point-blank in the evening. He smiled pleasantly and took it out of an inner pocket where he had it all folded and ready.

"I thought maybe you didn't need any money this week," he said. "You weren't in the hall this morning."

"I was in the back hanging out the clothes and I mistook the time."

She would not give him the satisfaction of knowing he had scored. Still, her spite broke out.

"I might have run short," she cried. "For all you cared there might not have been a penny in the house."

He was sitting reading the evening paper and he bent it backward to look at her.

"Always the martyr, Rose," he said, and she knew he had seen through her trick.

"Is that the only word you know!" she cried. "Martyr, martyr."

"Wife and martyr," he said, without interest. It was an old joke of his.

They were Mr. and Mrs. Derdon, and they had been married to each other for twenty-seven years. He was the senior by five years. They slept in the back bedroom upstairs, and their window looked over their little walled garden, not much different from the other gardens in the terrace, and beyond that over a strip, gray and corrugated, of garage roofs. Beyond the garage yard and off to one side of it were the velvety, emerald green courts of a private tennis club, that were shaded on their most distant side by a dense, irregularly placed wall of strong old trees.

Mr. and Mrs. Derdon shared a double bed made of brass and fitted with a long bolster and a heavy patchwork quilt. The quilt she had made during her school days. The foot of their bed was to the window, which had a cream-colored pull-down blind and white net curtains.

Hubert went to bed about ten every night, she a little later. She got up at seven, he at seven-thirty. On Sundays she got up and went to eight o'clock Mass, and came back and got the breakfast in time for him to be at the chapel door by ten.

In bed he wore flannel pajamas, and she wore a flannel night-gown. Their bodies were about the same length, lying down. Neither of them snored, but they both breathed heavily. He huddled himself up into his shoulders and slept on his right side, with his face to the wall. She slept on her back. He slept calmly. She slept desperately, looking as exhausted in sleep as though she had been very sick. Sometimes he would turn the blankets down off him in the night. Then her neck and shoulders would be uncovered, and she would wake up stiff in the morning and frown painfully, first thing. At bedtime she let her hair down into a loose plait. In the morning she pinned it up into its bun without ever looking in the mirror.

She liked to see the changing daytime sky. The night sky had less interest for her; she wanted no mystery, no blackness, no stars, no soft darkness, no curtains, no comfort, no promise of rest. The daytime sky, impassive gray, impassive blue, had won her. That endless offhand gaze occupied her, and when she raised her eyes and met it, it was in contention, returning stare for stare. She felt she was proud.

The gathering of the clouds enthralled her, whether they were lumped together in little balls or rolls, or separated into great soft masses, or dragged out in streaks. She relished the black congestion of the rain clouds, as they sank helplessly down on their swollen stomachs before bursting. The water poured over her roof, over her soft grass, and over the spindly frame of her laburnum tree. It could not touch her. She stayed inside, near a closed window, and watched the glass run down. She said the rain had a smell. To prove it, she opened her kitchen door after a storm and tasted without pleasure the cool steam rising up from her relaxed garden earth. She raised her eyes at the same time to see how the sky drew back relieved and clean.

As long as the light of day lasted, she kept looking up as often as she got the chance. She was ashamed to be seen standing in her garden or in the street looking up. She thought the others might think her queer.

At times, more when she was a young woman than later on, she took a bus out to the country, where she could sit on a wall or lie down on the grass and give herself up to her stare. More often she took a ride on the top of an open tram, and watched the sky slyly from under the brim of her hat, and imagined that she was ploughing a soft furrow in it with the top of her head as the tram rushed her along.

She could see the clouds easily from the windows of her house, but then she considered the neighbors. It disgusted her to think they might see her standing looking out, and perhaps imagine she had some interest in what they did, so she kept away from the windows except when she had to clean them.

One time she was recovering from the flu. She got out of bed for the first time on a Sunday afternoon, and Hubert brought up a comfortable chair from downstairs and put it near the bedroom window, with a low stool before it for her feet. She lay back in the cushions there, lying low in her shawl and in her loose brown hair, and passively watched the sky. The next day she felt strong enough to go downstairs, and she never sat there like that again;

but years later, all the same, she could recall every line of the sky on that evening when she lay there weak from her sickness.

That evening the clouds met and parted and rose and descended in a way that she never forgot. Their deliberations were delightful, as they touched back to back and front to front, and slid alongside each other, and melted slowly into each other and slowly drew apart, and folded each other with blind white stretchings and opened themselves freely into long uneasy yawns. At last the light behind them grew very strong and seemed about to break through, but to her satisfaction, because she did not trust the brash pure light, it began its final retreat, a long slow fading, until she realized with surprise that she had witnessed the full twilight and that night had arrived before her eyes.

She roused herself unwillingly in the silent room, and a moment later Hubert came in with a tray of tea and toast, and exclaimed to find her awake there in the darkness, with the blind up.

"I should have come sooner," he said reproachfully.

When he snapped on the light, balancing the tray awkwardly on his arm, crouching over it as though anxiety would save it from falling to the floor, she gazed at him with such heavy eyes that he was startled, thinking she had a return of her fever, but it was luxury that lay on her eyelids and wetted her eyes, and she pressed her untidy invalid's hair back with her flat hands and tried to say something; but then her joy, too vague, too large, unshared and already lost, turned to weak tears, and he shook his head in despair and put the tray down on her knees.

"Don't cry till you've tasted it anyway," he said, watching her for a sign of a smile. "Maybe it's not as bad as you think."

"Oh, it's not the tea," she said. "Thanks very much, Hubert. The tray looks lovely."

He pulled the shawl up around her shoulders and sat down on

the side of the bed, watching her to encourage her, with his hands between his knees. She touched the teapot with the point of her finger, feeling the hotness of it, and could find nothing to say to him.

He said reluctantly, "What are you worrying about now, honey? You shouldn't be worrying your head about things that don't matter."

"The things that matter to me might not be the things that matter to you. Has that ever crossed your mind?" she cried at once.

The tears ran slowly down her cheeks. She might cry like that for an hour, he knew.

He sighed and got up.

"Well, is the tea all right, at least?" he asked.

"Oh yes. The tea is all right, thanks. You shouldn't have gone to the trouble. I hate to put you to any trouble."

She turned her eyes to the window and looked resentfully out at the darkness, putting her hand against her mouth as though she were appalled.

"In the name of God, Rose, why don't you make an effort to pull yourself together. Come on now, and I'll wrap you up and you can sit downstairs all comfortable till it's time to get back into bed. It'll be a change for you, to get out of this old room."

"You're very nice all of a sudden, Hubert. All concerned about me."

When she looked directly at him her eyes were wild and afraid with malice.

"What ails you? Now what's ailing you?" he cried.

"Nothing ails me, except that I'm sick and tired of being made an excuse of. I hate a hypocrite. If you want to go back downstairs, go on."

"Are you gone mad, or what?"

"Oh yes. The first minute I go against you, I'm gone mad. All I want is to be left in peace."

"Look, bang on the floor or if you want anything. I'll be down there if you want anything. I declare to God, I don't know who'd have patience with you."

"I won't want anything," she said dispiritedly.

She was lying back as passive and stricken as though she had not spoken for hours. She did not look up when he went out of the room, but she listened to his steps going down the stairs, and knew a moment later, by a stealthy settling of the house, that he was buried in his armchair by the fire again, with his pipe and the Sunday crossword. She drew a difficult breath of relief and exhaustion and eagerly poured herself a cup of tea.

It was not often that she was sick. She had a strong constitution. She was originally from a country district. She liked to work around in her little back garden, keeping the grass bright and whole, and growing lupine, London pride, wallflowers, freesia, snowdrops, lilies of the valley, forget-me-nots, pansies, nasturtiums, marigolds, and roses. She had other flowers, too. In one corner she had grown ambitious and made a rock garden. In front of the house, in the tiny plot of ground, hardly bigger than a tablecloth, she had peonies, poppies, and crocuses, and a diamond of frail new grass. In the window of her front sitting room she had an array of ferns, and in the spring hyacinths and tulips in red pots.

She was drawn to the poor. There was a constant stream of poor men and women, beggars, coming to her door to ask for food or money. She had never been known to refuse anybody at the door. This annoyed Hubert. He said too many came begging, and that they had got to know her, and that they took advantage. He was often known to give money himself, but he protested that with her it was too much of a good thing. She continued to give to whoever came to the door. Two or three came regularly, some came once in a while, and there were some who only came once. There were some who offered needles, pins, shoelaces, or pencils for sale. One man brought his wife and a large family of young children and stood in the street singing heartily before he came to the door. His wife carried a baby in her arms. She took up her stand, glanced at her husband, and murmured timidly along with him as he sang, while the children gazed hopefully about at the blank windows up and down the terrace.

There was one man who had been coming to the door longer than any of the others. This was the man with the crooked hand. He always came at a certain time on Thursday afternoon. Mrs. Derdon took an interest in this poor man because she suspected that like herself he came from the country. He wore a countryman's soft cloth cap and a navy blue serge suit, with the collar of the coat turned up around a scarf in the winter, and in the summer around a shirt that was not clean and that had neither collar nor tie. His left hand hung down at his side. It was sound. His right hand he carried high against his chest, like a treasure, with the shoulder hunched protectively behind it. This hand was deformed, or rather it had been maimed, crushed into a hard veiny lump, the skin of it cured a tender red, a boiled color, very sore-looking. Only the stumps of the fingers were left, and the thumb had folded over into the palm. His eyes, blue, seemed weary enough to die, but still the poor natural mouth, obedient to its end, a mouth so lonely it appeared to have no tongue, opened itself to her in a thin, bashful smile of recognition and supplication. Never mind, never mind, never mind, no blame to you nor to me nor to anybody, the mouth said, only fill me.

This man's humanity, the sin he got with it and its daily punishment, lay so plain on his cheeks that he looked hammered and chilly, like a corpse. From the very beginning he looked to be on his last legs. Once Hubert, glimpsing him from behind the sitting-room curtains, said, "God help us, if he doesn't look like every poor unfortunate man you ever saw."

There must have been a time when he knocked on all the doors of the terrace to find out who was open to him, but for years now he had come straight to her. His feet slapped the pavement inoffensively as he went along. He begged in silence. She kept thinking he might say something to her, but he never did. One time she threw a friendly remark after him, and he turned back so confused that she was ashamed. It was a long time before she tried to speak to him again. No matter what the weather was like, he appeared at the door on the dot. Even on the worst days of winter he did not spare her, but stood before her, shivering, dripping, shrinking, and smiling, with his cap and his shoulders black from the rain, and his upraised hand turned to flaming glass by the wet and cold.

She often thought of asking him in for a cup of tea, but she had not the courage. Besides, if by an odd chance he accepted, and came down into the kitchen, what would they talk about? Of course she could give him the tea and leave him to drink it, there were plenty of little jobs she could find to do to keep her busy, but that would be uncivil, and in any case she knew very well that what she wanted was to talk to him. What she did not know, and could not imagine, was what in the name of God they would talk *about*. She could not be sure of more than a yes or a no out of him, and the idea of asking him in for a cup of tea and then firing a list of questions at him was even more uncivil than to keep herself silent and busy while he drank it. And she wanted to hear what he had to say. She was curious about what had happened to him in his life, but over and above the ordinary recounting of events and changes, there were things she wanted to hear him talk about that she could not accurately put a name to. There was a lot went through her mind while she worked around the house and garden, alone all day.

Mr. and Mrs. Derdon had one son. Father John Derdon, the priest. He never let her know when he was coming to see her, because he said she made too much fuss getting ready for him. As a rule he came to the house when both his father and his mother would be likely to be at home, but one afternoon he dropped in and found her alone, it being the middle of the week. She shouted joyfully at the sight of him, and began to unbutton his raincoat with her accustomed rough anxiety. He let her pull him out of it, and he struck lightly at her, laughing. She still had not grown accustomed to the black priest's clothes on him. The black cloth gave him a bad air, as though he had stolen in from another century, or out of a bad dream. He was not the same.

He was fair-haired and fair-skinned. His head was long, and he brushed his limp fair hair very smooth around it, making a point of the high square forehead he had. His eyes were light blue, troubled, even aghast light blue. His clothes were the clothes of any priest, and yet there was something thin and jaunty about him, in the tilt of his head, or in one of the conscious, unnecessary gestures he was always making, that belonged more to an actor than to a priest.

"It's long enough since you came near us," she said. "I'll get something for you to eat. Thanks be to God, I have a nice little bit of chicken down there."

He went upstairs to wash his hands and look about his old room. He had the front bedroom, the best. There was everything just the same as ever. There were photographs of him, alone, and with other boys, and other seminarians, and on his ordination day. His mother had got frames for them and placed them on the chest of drawers, on the desk, on the mantelpiece, and around the walls. He heard her come into the room, and he turned, rolling up his shirtsleeves, to smile at her. He turned from her eyes to the gardens outside.

"Look at all the flowers," he said foolishly.

She was close behind him and had taken his hand. She had strong, dry hands; it was impossible to forget their grasp. She captured his limp hand and fell down on her knees to kiss it and force it with her mouth. She petted it along her cheeks, along the hard curve of her jaw, and into her neck, so that he could feel that warm hair springing stiff and strong above it, and the soft hollow of her flesh below. Out of this dream he snatched away and hurled on her, half in laughter.

"Mother, Mother, how often must I caution you. My hands. Mother, my hands."

"Ah, Glory be to God, the consecrated hands," she cried, covering her mouth with her fingers, mocking him with her dismay. She screamed with laughter, squaring back on the floor with her knees spread out and her eyes staring up from under a scalding water of pain and rage.

"I forgot about your hands, son. Wasn't it naughty of me. Wasn't it *naughty*. Such impertinence, touching the almighty hands of a priest. I know you dislike me to touch your precious hands. Oh, I know it very well."

"Not only you, Mother. Anyone, you know very well. A priest's hands, as you know very well—"

"Oh, I know, I know. I knew it before you were born. Don't harp on it now. All I wanted was your blessing, John. That's all, that's all I wanted."

She snapped at him pettishly, scrambling to her feet, very much exerted, brushing off her dress.

"I'll give you my blessing, Mother, a hundred blessings.

There's nothing I wouldn't give you, if I had it to give. Do you want me to give you a blessing?"

She straightened like a housekeeper, with her hands under her chest.

"Never mind about that, now," she said sharply. "But hurry yourself and come on down to the table."

She came a step toward him.

She said, "Oh, love, what's the matter with me. I'm all nerves. Don't mind what I say."

"I'm all to blame, Mother," he said hurriedly. "I'll be down before you have the cloth on the table."

From the dining-room window she saw, as she had earlier in the day, that the laburnum tree in the back garden had come to full bloom. She smiled hardly to see it, the generous little tree, a furious yellow, a million blossoms, lifting itself as near to glory as color could bring it. That spindly trunk, thin as a leg, was glorious for them every summer, boiling in the sun with smell and color. She had to smile, knowing the look of the shapely little blossoms, each one as yellow as the next, the petals of them unusually smooth, to see and to rub. Her fingertips tingled, and she caressed the complicated lace of her best cloth, spread on the table for John.

She could remember years ago, sitting in this room with John, or sitting above in his own room, talking to him for hours, deriding his father to him, and repeating tales about the shopkeepers she had to deal with and about the neighbors. Night after night she had followed him upstairs when he went to do his homework. She was constantly being insulted by shopkeepers and hawkers at the door and by people she came up against in the street, or in the park when she went for a walk. She couldn't measure up to them, she often said, but she wouldn't let them have the satisfaction of getting away with it. Hubert had grown weary of listening and said she would do better to forget these things. Hubert said there was no sense dredging things up, and that if a person as much as looked crooked at her, she felt she had been dealt a mortal injury. He said she was only punishing herself, and that if she wanted to, all right, but she could leave him out of it.

But John was a very sympathetic little boy, always. From his earliest years there had been an understanding between him and her. They used to go together to the park, and they would sit on a bench and stare the people down. If a woman they didn't like looked at them, he would pipe up and ask the woman what she thought she was staring at. That was when he was a child. Later, when he got to be twelve or so, he became very conscious of his dignity, and he used to like to go off and spend long hours in the library. On the day he left to study for the priesthood, she went to the parish church and posted a slip of paper in the petition box, and on the paper she had scribbled with her indelible grocery-list pencil, *I want my own back, I want my own back.*

The seasons of the year made little difference to the poor men and women. They came winter and summer, but in the cold weather they looked worse off. A young woman came knocking at the door, a day that was very cold. She had a child with her, a little girl. The woman was bedraggled, servile, and not far from witless. The little girl was eight, very small for her age, with a sly, worn face that had great spirit in it. She wore heavy boy's boots on her little feet, and no stockings. When the door was opened she smiled ingratiatingly, chin out like a monkey. She jumped up and down and rubbed her knees together for warmth. She examined Mrs. Derdon's dress with bright envious eyes and tried to see past her into the hall.

"What's up there?" she asked rudely, pointing straight up to the bow window that belonged to Father Derdon's room. "Is that a room up there?"

Her mother turned and slapped her sharply in the face.

"She's too forward altogether, ma'am," she said, with an anxious smile. She gave the child a shake. "Tell the lady you're sorry," she demanded.

The child, whose face was blotched with the marks of her mother's hand, grinned and waved her arms. She seemed to be daring her mother to give her another slap. Mrs. Derdon stepped back into the hall.

"It's my son's room up there," she said. "I'll let you see into it, but you have to come down to the kitchen first of all and let your mother have a cup of tea."

The child refused milk and drank tea with the two women. When she had eaten everything on the table, she got up and began to wander around the kitchen.

"This is mine," she said, touching the chair on which she had been sitting.

She touched the gas stove. "This is mine," she said.

"She's always acting around," her mother said indifferently, keeping a tight grip on the handle of her teacup as it sat in the saucer. "I'm grateful for the tea, ma'am," she added. Since sitting down at the table she had gone sleepy, basking in the warmth of the range.

"This is mine," said the little girl, putting her hand up to the checked curtain at the window.

"Now," said Mrs. Derdon, seeing that the tea was all finished, "would you like to see the room upstairs?"

"I want to see in there," the child said pertly, as they ascended the three steps to the hall. She pointed at the sitting-room door and darted to open it.

"This is mine," she shrieked. "This is mine, this is mine."

She touched the sofa, and the two upholstered chairs, and the table of ferns, and the mantelpiece vases, and the china figures standing neatly spaced on the piano, where they were safe since it was never opened.

"This is mine," she screeched, squatting on the carpet like a big bedraggled frog.

"A lovely place you have, ma'am," the mother said.

"Now we'll go upstairs and see what's there," said Mrs. Derdon, with an awkward, encouraging smile. The child slipped adroitly past her, dodging her hand, and streaked up the stairs as though she knew the house.

When they reached Father Derdon's room, she was standing at the window with her face pressed to the glass and the white curtain bunched out of her way.

"There's the gate we came in at," she cried to her mother, beckoning excitedly. She tugged at her mother's hand. "And there we are, Mam, coming up the street. Look at us out there."

A little girl with long shining ringlets and a pink coat walked up the terrace, and with her a lady wearing a fur scarf on her shoulders.

The child took her eyes from the window to stare at her mother. "The lady there is you, Mam, and that's me with the coat and the curly hair."

The mother gave her a derisive push.

"Go on with you," she said, smiling sheepishly at Mrs. Derdon.

The child pulled violently and cried out with temper.

"There we are!" she screamed. "Look at us out there."

"Shut up your mouth. I'm getting sick and tired of your lies," the mother cried, giving her a hard slap. The child grinned quickly up at them before the tears had gone back into her eyes.

"You slap her too often altogether," Mrs. Derdon protested.

"Ah, you know yourself it's the only way to get any sense into

them, ma'am. This one's got into the habit of telling lies and trying to show off every minute. She's got too impudent."

The child left the window and bounced on the bed.

"This is mine," she said, a trifle subdued, winding her long
dirty fingers over the end rail. Her fingers were like twigs, her
eyes were sharp as thorns; there was neither love nor shame in
her smile. She lay back on the bed and stretched her ragged arms
across the white quilt.

"That's a brooch you have on you," she said inquisitively.

Mrs. Derdon was wearing an elaborate brooch of gold and
blue enamel. She put her hand up and touched it.

"I'll tell you what I'll do. I'll give it to you for a present," she
said quickly, and she leaned over the end of the bed and pinned
the brooch to the child's dress, where it lay heavily among the
rags as though it had been thrown away. The child glanced triumphantly at her mother who, observing Mrs. Derdon for the
first time, wore a startled and distrustful air. The poor woman
grew jumpy, fearful that the gift might be regretted before they
had time to get out of the house. She urged the child to get up off
the clean quilt, and to stop annoying the lady, and to say thanks
for the lovely brooch. The child, an experienced conspirator,
hopped obediently off the bed and was downstairs in the hall before her mother had finished blessing their benefactor.

Mrs. Derdon regretted her brooch before she had the door
well shut on the two hastening backs. It was a brooch that had
come to her at her mother's death. Her mother had worn it day
and night, and used to leave it lying among her hairpins when
she went to bed. It had been familiar to the eyes of her long-dead
father. Some of her own earliest memories depended on it, and
now she had set it adrift. The only thing remaining to her out of
the past was the patchwork quilt on the bed above.

It was not the first time she had given in haste like that and regretted it. John's baptismal shawl, that she had spent long months making, had gone the same way, to a poor woman at the door, and a pair of new gloves of her own, another time. Sometimes she wondered if she hadn't spent her whole life giving away the things she valued the most, and never getting any thanks for them. There seemed to be no limit to what people would take. She had often said to John that if you gave people an inch they'd take an ell. Hubert, hearing her, remarked that she had only herself to blame since she forced the ell down people's necks. Hubert then asked John if he could tell him what an ell was, and they both laughed.

Out of all the poor men and women who had come to the door all the years she had been living in the house, there was not one she had ever run across in the street up to the time she met the man with the crooked hand on O'Connell Street bridge, on her way to buy new sheets.

The suburb in which she lived was about a twenty-minute bus ride from the center of the city, but she seldom made the journey except for a special reason. The bus run came to an end at the near side of the Liffey, and she was glad of that, because it gave her an excuse to walk across the bridge and get a look at the river. There were crowds of people about. Mrs. Derdon was wearing black laced shoes that she had polished before leaving the house, and the soles were so thin that she was made aware of the hard pavement at every step. Being still a countrywoman, she was accustomed to clearer streams, but she still was anxious for a sight of the dark forceful Liffey in her high bed. As she walked across, feeling the cold push of the wind on her face, she spotted the man with the crooked hand, stealing along near the parapet, guarding his hand before him. As they came face to face, he raised his eyes and saw her. At the sight of her, his face expressed such surprise and welcome that she put out her hand and began to speak to him, but he recovered himself and touched his cap and passed her by. She continued on, and a few seconds later turned to look for his back in the crowd, but he had disappeared. She stepped out of the stream of people and looked searchingly all the length of the bridge, but he had really gone. She thought he must have been in an extraordinary hurry, to get out of sight so fast.

Going home on the bus, she thought with satisfaction that the encounter on the bridge would give her the chance she had been looking for, to strike up a conversation with him. She made up a dialogue between them:

s h e : I saw you on the bridge the other day.

h e : Yes. I saw you, too. I would have spoken, but you seemed to be in a hurry. How strange that we should meet.

s h e : Not at all. It's a small world.

Or she might say:

"You've been coming to the door a good many years now."

No, that would never do. He might think it was a hint to stay away. She might take a joking tone, asking him what was the great hurry he was in on the bridge. Well, the words would present themselves when the time came.

That Thursday, when he did not turn up at the door at the usual time, she became uneasy and spent the rest of the afternoon waiting for him in the front sitting room. At five past six Hubert turned the corner of the terrace and walked slowly up to the house, as he did every night. When she saw Hubert she realized that the man with the crooked hand would not be coming at all. She went and took his money off the hall table, where she had left it early in the day, and put it into a cup on the kitchen dresser. Hubert let himself in with his key, and finding the tea not ready, not even started, he inquired in surprise if he was early. He compared his watch with the clock on the sitting-room mantelpiece, and called cheerfully down to the kitchen that he would like a boiled egg.

When they were sitting at the table having their tea, she told him about meeting the poor man on the bridge and about him not turning up at the door.

"You probably frightened the life out of him," Hubert said placidly. "Running up to him like that with your hand out, especially since there was nothing in it."

"But I was only going to say a word to him; there's no harm in that."

"All you have to do is look at that man's face, for God's sake. A man like that has no use for your fuss and talk, Rose. Give him whatever you want to give him, but let him alone."

"But he looked so glad to see me, Hubert. I never saw anybody in my life so glad to see me."

"He'll know better next time. How was he to know you'd want to embrace him."

"Hubert, the way you always put me in the wrong."

"Rose, honey, you bring it on yourself. You will not get it through your head that in this life you have to learn to leave well enough alone."

After a moment of silence, to give him time to take the top off his egg, he said consolingly that he was sure the man with the crooked hand would be back, as soon as he got over his fright. He added that if the man *didn't* come back, it might be just as well, since it would save them a little money. He was only joking, saying that. He meant no harm.

On the following Thursday the man with the crooked hand appeared at the door as he always had, in the middle of the afternoon. As soon as she saw him she knew that he would not say anything. She had made up her mind that she would leave him alone unless he said something of his own accord. He held up his sore hand and gazed at her without a sign of the radiance that she had seen in his face on the bridge. If he felt ashamed that he had given himself away, there was no sign of that either. He was too far gone in want. He was gone out of reach. It gave her great comfort to see him at the door again. She never afterward thought of getting him into conversation, and after a while she forgot the curiosity that had devoured her concerning him, although she continued to watch for him, and for the others who came.

An Attack
of Hunger

MRS. DERDON had the face of a woman who had a good deal to put up with. At this moment, she was in the kitchen, putting up with getting the tea ready for herself and her husband. Her husband's name was Hubert. She was putting up with setting out the two cups and the two plates and the two saucers and so on, two of everything. There was no need now to set the table for more than two people. The third place was empty, and the third face was missing. John, her son, had left the house and he would not be back, because he had vanished forever into the commonest crevasse in Irish family life—the priesthood. John had gone away to become a priest.

The thought that Mrs. Derdon was not putting up with (because she had never faced it) was, Oh, if only Hubert had died, John would never have left me, never, never, never. He would never have left me alone.... But she was putting up with the secret presence of this thought in her spirit, where it lived hidden, nourishing itself on her energy and on her will and on her dwindling capacity for hope.

She had never made up her mind about anything. Decision was unknown to her. Her decisions, the decisions she made about the food she put on the table and about various matters about the house, were dictated by habit and by the amount of housekeeping money Hubert allowed her. Hubert was a frugal man. It was not that he meant to be unkind, but he was careful. He had calculated that the household could be run on such and such a sum, and that was the sum he produced every Friday morning. He always had it ready in his hand, counted out to the penny, when he came downstairs on his way to work. Every Friday morning she waited at the foot of the stairs and he handed her the money without a comment.

Before, when John was still at home, he would sometimes be there when Hubert gave her the money, and then the two of them, she and John, would exchange a look. On her part the look said, "You see the way he treats me." And John's look said, "I see. I see." They agreed that Hubert knew no better than to behave the way he behaved. This knowledge, that Hubert *knew no better,* formed the foundation and framework of the conspiracy between them that made their days so interesting and that gave a warm start to most of their conversations. They were always talking about Hubert. There was no need for Hubert to do anything unusual to get himself talked about—not that he ever did do anything unusual or out of the ordinary. All he had to do was go about in his habitual way, coming in after work and sitting down with the paper and then sitting down to his tea and going to bed and getting up in the morning and doing all the things he always did in his routine that never varied and that at the same time never became monotonous. There was something insistent about Hubert's daily procedure that called attention to itself, as though he was behaving as he did on purpose, and as though at any moment he might drop the charade and turn and show them the face they both suspected him of possessing, his true face, the face of a *villain,* the face of a man of violence, capable of saying and doing the most passionate and awful things, shocking things.

He kept them in a constant state of suspense, and they were always exchanging looks when he was in the house, even when they only heard him walking about upstairs. But Hubert maintained his accustomed countenance, mild, amiable, complacent, burnished with his natural distrust of everyone and of every word anyone said, and held in firm focus by his consciousness of the worth of his own judgment.

Now, with John gone, there was no one for Mrs. Derdon to exchange glances with. There was no one for her to look at, except Hubert, and Hubert could turn into a raving lunatic, frothing and cursing, and there would be no one to see him except herself. There was no one to look at her, and she felt that she had become invisible, and at the same time she felt that in her solitude she followed herself about the house all day, up and down stairs, and she could hardly bear to look in the mirror, because the face she saw there was not the one that was sympathetic to her but her own face, her own strong defenseless face, the face of one whose courage has long ago been petrified into mere endurance in the anguish of truly helpless self-pity. There was no hope for her. That is what she said to herself.

There was no hope for her inside the house. Her entire life was in the house. She only left it to do her shopping or to go to Mass. She went to the early Mass on Sundays (she and John had always gone together), and Hubert went to the late Mass by himself. It had been many years before John left since the three of them had gone for a walk together, and she and Hubert never went anywhere or visited anyone. He never brought anybody from the shop to his house, to spend an evening or to see the garden in the summertime or anything like that. From the time they were married, Hubert had shown that he distrusted her with money—he said she had no head for money—and as the years went by he had come to distrust her presence everywhere except in the house. In moments of nervousness—with the priests at John's school or at occasional gatherings they had attended in the early days of their marriage—Hubert had noticed that his wife turned into a different person. In the presence of strangers, she sometimes took to smiling. One minute she would produce a smile of trembling timidity, as though she had been told she would be beaten unless she looked pleasant, and then again, a minute later, there would be a grimace of absurd condescension on her face. And before anyone knew it, she would be standing or sitting in stony silence, without a word to say, causing everybody to look at her and wonder about her. And if she did speak, she would try to cover her country accent with a genteel enunciation, very precise and thin, that Hubert, from his observation of the world, knew to be vulgar. He felt it was better to leave her where she felt at ease, at home. Somehow she wasn't up to the mark. She wasn't able to learn how things were done or what to say. She had no self-confidence, and then, too, her feelings were very easily hurt. If you tried to tell her anything she took it as an insult. Hubert thought it was very hard for a man in his position to have to be ashamed of his wife, but there it was, he was ashamed of her. And he was sorry for her, because her failure was not her fault. She had been born the way she was. There was nothing to be done about it.

When Mrs. Derdon turned away from the mirror that reflected her hopelessness, she saw the walls of her house, and its furniture, the pictures and chairs and the little rugs and ornaments, and the sight of all these things hurt her, because she had tried hard to keep the house as it had been when John left it, and the house was getting away from her and away from the way it had been when John lived in it, when she and John lived in it together. There seemed to be no way of controlling the change that was taking place in the house. Two of the cups from the good set had slipped out of her hands for no reason at all when she was taking them with the rest of the good china to wash, and now her arrangement of glass and china in the glass-fronted cupboard in the back sitting room looked incomplete. There was a big stain on one of the sofa cushions in the front sitting room and she did not know how it had got there. One of the children from the neighboring houses threw a ball into the front garden and crippled a rose tree that had grown in safety for years there. She herself in a fit of despair removed a little pile of newspapers and magazines and pamphlets that John had left on his desk in his bedroom. She had not thrown them out, they were on the bottom shelf of the cupboard in the kitchen, but even if she carried them back up to his room they would not be exactly as he had left them, and they would never again look just as they had when he had last seen them. And she bitterly regretted pulling out the rusty little wad of newspaper that he had been accustomed to stuff underneath the door of his wardrobe to keep it tightly shut. She had thrown it into the fire and fitted a new bit of newspaper under the door. Nothing would ever be the same.

There were worn patches in the stair carpet that had appeared suddenly after all these years, and the wallpaper around the hall door had begun to peel badly and something would have to be done about it. Even the dust seemed to have found new places to settle, or to be settling in different places, and it seemed to her that in sweeping up the dust, day in and day out, all she was doing was sweeping up the time since John had left—more dust every day, more time every day—and she began to think that all she would do for the rest of her life was sweep up the time since John left. The dust got on her nerves. It made her feel sick to see the way it was there every day, new dust, but looking just as old and dirty as the old dust her mother used to be always sweeping up and throwing away, long ago in the country town where she had been born and brought up. As surely as the clock ticked and had to be wound up again, the dust made its way around the house, and it got on her hands. It got on her hands and on her wrists, and no matter how hard she scrubbed her nails, there always seemed to be some of it left there under her nails. She told herself that she had the hands of a servant. Hubert's hands were soft and neat, but hers were big and rough, as though she were a person who worked with her hands. She had often caught Hubert looking at her hands when she was dealing with the food on her plate and looking at her when she put food into her mouth. She always ate a lot of bread, and she thought he must sometimes wonder how she could eat so much bread or why she ate it so fast. She couldn't help it — she felt there was something shameful about eating so much of bread or of any food, but she wanted it and she ate it quickly and there were times when she felt her face getting red with defiance and longing when she reached for the loaf to cut another slice. One thing, she had stopped putting jam on the table since John left. She and John both loved jam, but Hubert had no taste for it at all. When John was at home, she used to make jam — raspberry, damson, and gooseberry — but what they both liked best was the thick expensive jam that came in jars from England. It was best not to put the jar on the table. Hubert never questioned the expense, but he would sometimes take the jar in his hand and turn it around and read the label very slowly and then put the jar back again. Even if the jar was nearly full he would tip it and look into it. One time he had said, "It's a good idea, having something to read on the table." John had laughed out loud, and she had thought it heartless of him to laugh when he knew that his father was only looking for another way to make little of her.

Every day of the six months that had passed since John left to become a priest, Mrs. Derdon realized that he was gone and that he was not coming back, and every day she thought she was only realizing it for the first time. The realization was alive and it possessed her completely and directed all her actions, one minute telling her to sit down and the next minute telling her to stand up immediately without delay and without reason—except that the power of the realization was reason enough, because it directed her every minute now, and controlled her and kept her going and gave its own mysterious organization to everything she did. If it had not been for this realization, keeping at her all day, she would not have known what to do next and she would have done what she really wanted to do, which was to crawl in under the bed and put her face down on the floor and sleep. She kept wanting to lie down on the floor. The realization that John was gone and would not be back took different shapes inside her, but it always stayed in the same place, just under her chest, in the center, between her ribs. Sometimes it went away altogether and she felt empty, and then, at these moments, she would go and get herself something to eat, but almost always when she had the food before her, the realization would come back again and she would feel sick at the thought of eating. At times the realization would go away altogether, or seem to go away, and she would become terribly excited and run to the front windows knowing that John was coming home, that he was at this exact moment walking along the street carrying his suitcase, and that she would have to wait only a minute or so to get her first sight of him, coming around the corner from the main road. But of course he wasn't coming, and he wouldn't be coming, and the excitement inside her would flatten out and stupefy her with its weight, and her disappointment and humiliation at being made a fool of would be as cruel as though what she had felt had really been hope and not what it was, the delirium of loss.

Out of this recurrent delirium two daydreams had grown, long, peaceful, pleasant dreams, always expanding, always increasing in their progress and in their detail, alike in only two respects—in their soothing monotony and in their endings. Both dreams ended at the moment when John became her own again, only hers.

In the first dream, John came back. In this dream, she was watching for him at the front window, and when he turned the corner she went to open the front door for him, but then she wanted him to have his first glimpse of her framed in the window and she went back and stood in the window (holding the net curtain aside with her hand) until he saw her and smiled. When he got to the low gate that opened backward into her tiny front garden, she hurried into the hall to open the front door wide so that he could walk straight in and put his suitcase down in the hall, to get rid of the weight of it—he had never been very strong. Then they would look at each other and she would say, "I knew you'd be back, John." Or she might put it this way: "I knew you'd come back to me, John." And he would say, "You always knew what was best for me, Mother." They would go down to the kitchen, where she would have the table set and ready, everything he liked on the table. He would eat something, and then he wouldn't be able to hold it in any longer, what was bothering him, and he would say, "But Mother, didn't you mind when I went away? Didn't you miss me at all? You never said one word, not a word." Those words would tell her what she wanted to know—that he had noticed her heroic silence, how she hadn't said a word when she realized he was going off and leaving her, how she had kept back all the reminders and reproaches that she had been longing to let loose at him, and that he understood how brave and unselfish she had been, letting him go off free as she had done. There would be no end to the amount they would have to say to each other, once that point in their reunion had been reached. They would drink an awful lot of tea. She would tell him that she had missed him terribly. She would say that she had been dead lonely, even crying with the need of him (she would remind him that his father wasn't much company), but that she had been only thinking of his own good, and only wanting the same thing that she had always wanted—what was best for him. And that she had never imagined not letting him go in peace, as long as his heart was set on it.

But it was all a dream. He wasn't coming back at all, and she bitterly regretted having let him go as easily as she had done. She had been so sure he would come back that she hadn't said a word, getting her sacrifice ready for him to admire. There were many things she could have said to him, the evening when he finally spoke to her, telling her that it was all settled and that his mind was made up and he was going. At that point, his mind wasn't made up at all. She could have stopped him with a word. She could have reminded him that he was an only child and that his duty was to his father and mother. And he had no faith at all in himself; it was only because of her prayers and encouragement that he had got through his examinations his last year in school. She had carried him all his life, and now he imagined he was going to be able to get along without her. And how did he think he was going to be able to get along in a house full of men—priests and students—all better ready for the priesthood than he was, and all better up on the world than he would ever be. They would look down on him. He would be very glad to get away out of that place and come back to her.

But he wasn't coming back, there was the realization of that stirring in her again, and it would start giving her orders again, taking charge, and she would obey it, getting up and sitting down and walking here and there and never easy anywhere, because the only ease that could come to her would come if she could just get down on the floor and put her face in the corner and let her mind wander away into sleep, but into a different, roomy kind of sleep, very deep and distant, where there was no worry and where her mind would not be confined in dreams but could float and become vague and might even break free and sail off up like a child's balloon, taking her burden of memory with it.

There was not only nothing nice, there was nothing definite at all to remember, only a great many years that had passed along and were now finished, leaving only the remnants of themselves —herself, Hubert, the furniture; even the plants in the garden only seemed to hold their position in order to mark the shabbiness of time. All the things that she had collected together and arranged about the house could blow away, or fall into a pitiful heap, if it were not that the walls of the house were attached on both sides to the walls of the neighboring houses. There was nothing in sight that rested her eyes and nothing in her mind except the realization that John was gone, and the necessity of obeying the dictates of that realization in order to continue, even for a little while longer, her flight from it. The realization badgered her, and she had to obey it and at the same time pretend she didn't notice it. There was only one time of day when she ignored it, when it was weakest and she was strongest, when they first woke up in the morning, she and it, and it barely stirred, and what it told her then was that she should go back to sleep at once and not wake up at all. But she ignored it then, because it was a matter of pride with her to be up and dressed and downstairs before Hubert opened his eyes, and to have his breakfast ready and waiting for him and part of her housework done by the time he came down to the kitchen.

It was terrible having nobody to complain to; not that she had anything actual to complain about, but it was terrible having no one to talk to. John had always been a great confidant, and the Blessed Virgin had been a great consolation to Mrs. Derdon all her life, the One she had always turned to for help and advice and understanding, but she could hardly turn to the Blessed Virgin now, when it was the Blessed Virgin who had taken John away. It was not the Blessed Virgin herself who had taken John away but his own devotion to the Blessed Virgin, but it all amounted to the same thing in the end, and between the two of them she felt she was left out and left behind.

John had always been a very holy little boy. He was always going over his collection of holy pictures and sorting them out and looking at the holy medals he had and strewing his little saints' relics all over the house. He had a habit when he was small of wandering into the kitchen with a holy picture in his hand and standing looking at it until she asked him to tell her what he was thinking, and it was always some holy thought, surprising in such a young child. Sometimes he would prop a holy picture in front of his father's place at tea, prop it against the sugar bowl or the milk jug so that his father would see it when he was sitting down to the table. But Hubert put a stop to that one evening by putting the holy picture — it was of St. Sebastian being tortured — on his bread and smoothing it with his knife as though it were butter and then biting it. He tore off a corner of it, along with some bread, and he sat there chewing it and smiling what he called his happy-family-man smile. John cried, and Hubert pretended he didn't know what he had done wrong, and she said, "Hubert, I'm scandalized at you." Then she cried, too, because Hubert said, "I'm fed up with the two of you."

The second dream she had of John was a very simple one. It was more a vision than a daydream, and all that really happened in it was that she saw his grave. In the second dream, he had not gone away at all, he had died. It had not been his fault, after all. He had not wanted to leave her. In the second dream she visited his grave every day, and sat beside it for hours, and wore black, like a widow. When she cried, everybody sympathized with her, because who has a better right to cry than a woman who has lost her only son. Everyone marveled at her devotion when they saw her going to the grave every day, rain, hail, sleet, or snow, no matter how she felt, bringing flowers and leaves and ferns according to the season of the year. She would mourn John constantly, and even Hubert would hardly have the heart to reproach her for her long face.

This evening, getting the tea for herself and Hubert, she was arranging Christmas holly and ivy on John's grave when she heard Hubert's key in the lock, and then the closing of the front door. Now Hubert would go into the back sitting room and light the fire there and sit beside it until she called him to tea. Sometimes she lighted the fire in the back sitting room and sat there herself. This afternoon she had hardly left the kitchen. They burned coal. They kept the coal and the firewood, together with her garden things, in a small wooden shed that was attached to the back of the house. Every day she carried in two scuttles of coal, one made of iron, for the kitchen stove, and one made of brass, for the sitting room. She sometimes wondered, when she lifted the coal, if Hubert had any idea how heavy it was. Now, crossing the kitchen to turn the gas from low to high under the kettle, she saw the brass scuttle standing alongside the stove, filled and ready. She had carried it in and then forgotten to carry it up to the sitting room. She was irritated with herself for forgetting to bring it up and leave it ready for him when he came in. It was a bad sign —to start to be forgetful, to start forgetting things that ought to be done. Well, she wouldn't give him the chance to come down and ask for it, or to watch her clamber with it up the three steps that led to the hall and the sitting room. He said his heart was bad and that that was why he couldn't do much of anything that would exert him. But it had been the same when he was forty and thirty and younger. He loved to be waited on.

She took the handle of the brass scuttle in both hands and carried it with difficulty across the kitchen and up the stairs and into the back sitting room. She found that Hubert had already put a match to the fire, which she had laid ready with paper and wood and a few bits of coal that she had dotted across the top of it. He was fanning the small blaze with his open newspaper, his evening paper. He turned when she came in, and the newspaper billowed toward the fire and then blazed up. Hubert dropped the newspaper in his fright. Mrs. Derdon ran and got the poker and pushed the newspaper into the grate. Scraps of the blazing newspaper floated out and around the room. While she was stamping them out, Hubert raced off to the kitchen shouting, "That's all right, that's all right. I'll get some water!" and then he came dashing in with the hot kettle that he had snatched off the stove and poured a stream of water all over the fireplace. The fire, already tamed, gave up at once and turned into black soup, which streamed out between the bars of the grate and down onto the tiles of the hearth, where it settled into puddles of various sizes and shapes.

Mrs. Derdon sat down in a chair and began to cry helplessly. She hid her face behind her hands and then she pushed her hands into her hair and pushed her hair about and then she wrapped her arms about herself and rocked in grief. Disorder had finally prevailed against her, and there was nothing further she could do. She could kill herself over this room now and it would never look the same. This was the worst thing Hubert had ever done, and John had not been here to see it, and she would never be able to find the words to describe it to him. She glared at Hubert, who was watching her with dislike and alarm.

"Oh, what will I do!" she cried.

"Oh, for God's sake, pull yourself together," Hubert cried. "What ails you? No harm done."

"What ails me?" she cried. "It's what ails *you* coming in here and setting fire to the grate with nothing in it but paper. You couldn't come down to the kitchen and ask me for the coal. Oh, no, not you. You'll wait till it's brought up to you and burn down the house in the meantime."

"You shut up!" Hubert shouted. "Do you hear me? Shut up before I say something you won't want to hear."

"First you drive my son out of the house and then you try to burn the place down around my ears, around my *ears!*" Mrs. Derdon screamed.

"I suppose I should have tried to burn the place down while he was still in it!" Hubert shouted. "It was you gave me a fright, clumping in here with your Mother of Mercy face and banging the coal down on the floor so that I dropped the paper. It was you did it, with your spite and your bad temper."

She sat forward in her chair and spoke, but Hubert could not catch her words through the storm of hatred that blinded, deafened, and choked her, and that shook her so that when she leaned forward to fling her accusations more heavily toward him, she tumbled out of her chair and onto her hands and knees on the floor. She dragged herself back up into the chair as though she were dragging herself up onto a rock out of the sea, and then she sent Hubert a look of terrified appeal that vanished at once under a witless, imploring, craven smile.

Hubert saw the smile and knew that she was silenced. "Well, now you've made a proper fool of yourself!" he cried, "falling and flopping all over the room and crying over a few spots on the linoleum. Come on now and cheer up and stop making a show of yourself over nothing."

"Over nothing is it!" she cried. "If John was here, he'd tell you.

John would stand up for me. John knew how hard I worked. Working and slaving to keep the place nice and you call it nothing. But what do you care! You never cared about me and you never cared about him and you ended up driving him out of the house." She stopped because Hubert had leaned back in his chair and was smiling at her.

"I'm going to tell you something, Rose," said Hubert. "You won't like it, but I think it's time you learned. Do you know who really drove John out of the house?"

Mrs. Derdon said nothing.

"Answer me," said Hubert.

"I thought you did," Mrs. Derdon said.

"You thought what it suited you to think," Hubert said. "No, I didn't drive John out. We never got along, but that was because you made it your business to see that we didn't get along. You drove him out yourself," Hubert said. "It was to get away from you. That was all he wanted. You wouldn't even let him go to school by himself. He couldn't go on the tram by himself like the other boys until the priests told you to leave him alone. And when he went to work, you were down there at lunchtime half the time, weren't you? He got so that he was ashamed to be seen with you. A month before he left, he told me he was leaving, but he didn't tell you till the very last minute, because he knew you'd find some way to stop him, and he was bound and determined to go. How do you like that? Tell me, how do you like that little piece of information? He told me first."

"If he got ashamed of me he got it from you," Rose said.

"Oh, of course you'd have to say that," said Hubert. "Of course you can't face facts. But I've had to face facts. He was sick of you and I'm sick of you, sick of your long face and your moans and sighs—I wish you'd get out of the room, I wish you'd go, go on, go away. I don't want any tea. All I want is not to have to look at you anymore this evening. Will you go?"

"Oh, I will," Mrs. Derdon said. "I'll go. Indeed I will. Only to get away from you, that's all I ask."

She hurried out into the hall. She felt very free. She felt very independent. In that untrammeled moment she surveyed herself in the hall mirror as she adjusted her hat and stuck her two mother-of-pearl hatpins through her thick, light brown hair. For the first time for many years she saw the color of her own eyes. They were a clouded green, and as she stared at them she saw that they were filling up with tears.

Giving the hatpins a final push, buttoning her coat, taking her key to the front door out of her handbag and throwing it on the hall table, she saw that she was in terrible danger. She was in danger of hurling herself back into the room and throwing herself into the chair alongside Hubert and begging him to forgive her and to comfort her. She listened fearfully for the sound of her own running footsteps and for the sound of his voice, but there was only silence in the house, no sound at all. She had been in danger, but she had not given way, she had not moved. She turned off the light in the hall and also the light that shone over the front door, to show that she expected no welcome back, because she was not coming back, and she left the house. She was astonished; she felt an indulgent astonishment at her former anguish and helplessness and at the importance she had attached to the house and all its little furnishings, when all the time all she had ever really wanted was to run away as far as she could go. It had taken the awful things Hubert had said to make her see the true facts of the case. He had hunted her out of her own house. He must have been mad for a moment there, to say such things. His face had been very red. He had never been so angry before. But he had ordered her out. She had always felt responsible for the house. She had always thought he needed her there to take care of him. There were a lot of little things she did for him — waiting on him and seeing that things were as he liked them to be. He would miss her. But nobody could ever blame her for going, not after tonight. Nobody could ever accuse her of running away from her duty. And she could not blame herself, after what he had said to her, after the terrible things he had said. It showed the sort of man he was, that he would make up things like that. She would never give him away, she would never let out a word of what he had said, even to John. She would never tell anybody. She would try to forget it herself, but it was going to be difficult to forget a shock like that.

She reached the corner of her own street and began to hurry along Sandford Road. She began to consider what she was about to do. She would have to tell Father Carey that Hubert had driven her out of her home for no reason. She would tell him that she was afraid to go back there. What she had in mind was to borrow enough money from Father Carey to pay her way to where John was. She was sure that when the priest heard her story he would give her the money. She didn't know him well, she had only had the one talk with him, when John went away, but she had often attended his Mass and she was sure he would not refuse her. Once she saw John again and talked with him, she would be on sure ground. She would find some kind of work, maybe even in the seminary. Sewing, cooking, minding children, even ordinary housework, she would do anything, and when you came to think of it, there were a lot of things she could do. She had always wanted to be a nurse, when she was young. There might be some work to be found in a hospital. She would expect very little in the way of pay, only enough to keep body and soul together. She would do her work, she would go to Mass, she would pray, and that is all she would ask in exchange for the chance of seeing John once in a while. She would become friendly with all of John's friends. They would come to her with their troubles, and she would be the one who would know best how to talk to them. The priests in charge would wonder how they had ever got along without her. She was surprised that all this had not occurred to her before, and then she remembered that she could never have left the house if Hubert had not thrown her out. Now nobody could attach blame to her. She had done the only thing she could do. Someday she hoped Hubert would be ashamed of himself, but by then it would be too late. It was too late now. As long as she lived she would not be able to forget what he had said, or to remember exactly what it was he had said, only that it was the sort of thing people in their right minds didn't think of.

She was hurrying along Sandford Road in the direction of Eglinton Road, which led to Donnybrook and the church where John had been baptized and where they had all always gone to Mass. Sandford Road was always very busy, a main road out from town. On her side, on the side of the road where she was walking, the noisy trams went by her on their way out from town. The trams were nearly empty; the depot was not far away. The corner of the street where she lived was one of the last stops out from town. On the other side of Sandford Road, the trams passed on their way into town and they, too, were nearly empty. It was dark, except for the light from the street lamps and the occasional dim glare of light from the trams as they passed. It was the time of evening when nearly everybody was at home. A few men passed her, getting home from offices, and a few young girls. Boys and girls whirled by her on bicycles, not in crowds, as they would have been half an hour or an hour earlier, but in ones and twos. It had rained during the afternoon and the air was damp and cold, with a vigorous wind that she was grateful for because it seemed to wash her stiff face. The wind felt clean.

She crossed Sandford Road and stood on the corner where Eglinton Road runs in to Sandford Road. Eglinton Road was very wide, with big stone houses set back from the road and high up with stone steps in front of them. It was a residential road, quite well-to-do. There was no one on Eglinton Road, as far as she could see, and the way looked far and dark that she had to walk. She thought she had better sit down for a minute and collect her thoughts before she saw the priest. She wanted to tell him enough to convince him, but she did not want to tell him too much. She wanted to speak to him clearly and sensibly, so that he would respect her and give her the money. She wanted him to give her the money, but she wanted him to continue to regard her as an upright, dependable woman who had been driven to do what she had done. A few paces from the corner there was a wooden bench set alongside one of the heavy, big-branched trees that marked the length of Eglinton Road. This tree, the one nearest the bench, was so old and secure that some of its root lay coiled and twisted about it above the ground, making a rocky pediment on which John had often climbed when he was small, finding his way around the tree with his small hands against the trunk while she watched him from this bench. Although it could hardly have been the same bench. That was a long time ago.

She sat down and began to try to select and arrange the words that would best describe her plight to Father Carey and win his sympathy. There was what she had to tell him, about Hubert, and what she had to ask him for, the money, and her reason for having to ask for the money, to get to John. She started her appeal to the priest one way, and then she started it another way. She put in more and more details to make her story more persuasive, and then she took out some of the details. She couldn't make up her mind whether to end by asking for the money or to work the money in as she went along. The more she fumbled with the words, the more she became convinced that her story was lame and sounded suspicious. She hadn't the ability to describe the scene that had just taken place between her and Hubert. A person would have had to be there, to have heard it, to believe it, and if a person had been there the scene would not have occurred. She was going to go to Father Carey and make a show of herself, that was plain. He would never believe her. He would think she was making it all up, or that she was making an excuse of some little incident to spite her husband and get to her son. In either case, he would disapprove. He would tell her to go back to her husband. He would say, "Mrs. Derdon, you must return home at once. And you must on no account go near your son. If you interrupt your son's studies now, you may endanger his vocation." She could hear the priest saying the same words over and over again, and she couldn't hear him saying anything else. It was no use. He would never give her the money. She would have to find the money somewhere else, and there was no other place to go. But it would be useless to go to Father Carey. Worse than useless, even. He might get out of his car and take her back to Hubert and make her go into the house. He might side with Hubert against her. It was more than likely that he would.

If John had happened along Eglinton Road at that moment he would have seen on his mother's face the fierce, cruel expression that they had both always thought belonged on his father's face. She looked capable of anything. She looked capable of murder, but she was only suffering what murderers suffer before they strike. But she would never strike. She was afraid. She thought it was pride that held her hand, but it was only fear. Fear and longing struggled for supremacy in her soul, but it was not their struggle against one another and against her that troubled her — it was her lifelong denial of herself, bolstered and fed as it was by fear. She longed to be near to someone, but there was no one who wanted her. She was sure of that. Nobody wanted her; it was her only certainty. It was bad that people turned their backs on her, but what was worse, worst of all, was that she saw no reason why they should not turn their backs on her. She was not surprised at the way her life had gone. She sat bewildered by her own judgment against herself, and unaware of it.

She felt cold. It was foolish to stay out in the air this time of year, this time of night. She put her hands inside the sleeves of her coat. She did not want to move just yet. She kept thinking that something wonderful might happen, and that if she stayed patiently where she was, somehow or another she would be able to get to where John was. If she fainted from the cold and from exposure, an ambulance would have to come and take her to the hospital, and if she was in there, sick in the hospital, surely they would see that there was great necessity for John to come home again.

She must have come this way, around this corner, thousands of times, and she looked curiously about, because she had almost never been here at night before. She looked at Sandford Road, where trams and cars and bicycles and people moved steadily, passing one another, and she gazed down Eglinton Road at all the lighted houses, as far as she could see. She seemed to be saluting what she looked at, but she was no longer thinking of where she was. She was thinking of the place where John was, and of the town where she had been brought up, and of the hospital that was not going to admit her, and she was seeing the future that had once lain before her, full of light, reflecting heaven, that was now opaque and blank like fear and reflected nothing.

She got up and started walking. When she got to the corner of her street she saw that the light over the front door was lighted, and the light in the hall was lighted, too, and all the lights in the front sitting room were on. As she unlatched the gate, the front door opened and Hubert peered out. He opened the door wide and she walked in past him and began taking off her hat and coat. He closed the door and followed her down to the kitchen.

"Rose, listen to me a minute," Hubert said. "I'm awful sorry about what I said to you. I don't know what got into me. I had no right to say what I said."

"It doesn't matter," she said.

"Oh, it does matter," he said. "Forgive and forget."

"I'll forgive you because that's what John would want me to do. John would never want me to hold a grudge, and that's the reason I'll forgive you. But I didn't come back for his sake. I came back because it's my duty to stay here and keep your house."

She was trying to keep her dignity, but her voice trembled and she was wearing the craven smile, but Hubert could not see that, because she was standing at the stove with her back to him, waiting for the kettle to boil.

"Have it your own way," he said. "Maybe someday your precious John'll have his own parish and you can go and keep house for him. Then you'll have him all to yourself. All to yourself. Maybe then you'll be satisfied."

"The tea is ready now," she said.

They had their tea in silence, and when he was finished Hubert left the kitchen and she heard him go along the hall and into the front sitting room. That meant he must have lighted a fire for himself there. She would have two grates to clean in the morning, and the back sitting room to do, if she could do it. She would not look at it until morning. The damage would all be very clear then. She poured herself another cup of tea. It was warm in the kitchen, and there was no hurry about clearing up. She didn't mind the thought of tomorrow as much as she might have. She kept going back to Hubert's remark about her keeping house for John. There was more in that remark than met the eye. Sometimes people said more than they meant to say. She wondered if Hubert had realized what he was saying. He had probably meant it for a sneer at John, at the idea that John would ever be given a parish. But why should John not be given a parish? It was very likely that he would get one, sooner or later. Of course it might be a long time, but she could wait. Her family was long-lived on her mother's side. If anything happened to Hubert, she could sell this house, keeping only enough of the furniture and other things to make John's new home look familiar to him. She would make a new cover for the armchair he always liked, and a new cover for the cushion that had the mysterious stain on it. She would manage his house for him. The first few days would be strange, but after that they would settle down as though they had never been apart. She would become known in his parish as a very holy woman, and everyone would look up to her. His vocation would be her vocation. Everybody would say what a devoted mother she was, an example to all. All the ladies would consider it a privilege to have tea with her, and she would invite some of them. She would wear only black. John and she would have a great deal to say to one another, there would be no end to their conversations. She saw quite clearly now that all this was going to happen. It might be thirty years before John got a parish, but then again it might not take anything like as long as that. Whenever it happened, she would be ready. She would always be ready to go to his side, whenever he needed her. All she had to do was wait. There was no doubt that what she foresaw would happen, and when the day came she would pack up, sell out, and go straight to John, and after that it would be roses for the two of them all the way, roses, roses all the way.

Family Walls

For the fifth day in a row there had been no rain, and in Dublin, even in June, that was unusual. Hubert Derdon, who worked in a men's outfitting shop on Grafton Street in the center of the city, had brought his raincoat with him when he left home in the morning, but when closing time came and he saw the golden evening he thought he might walk all the way home instead of taking that long ride out in the tram. He was a creature of habit. His daily habits were comfortable, but it would do him no harm to miss his tram for once, even if it meant being late for tea. Hubert was always thinking about doing more walking. He knew that for a man in his forties he did not get nearly enough exercise. But there was the raincoat, and having to decide whether to carry it or put it on. If he was going to make a start on walking he did not want to start in his raincoat. And in the back of his mind he had an objection to wasting all that exercise on hard pavements with nothing ahead of him. He thought of mountain paths and tangled woods and narrow roads that ran between green fields. He imagined himself wearing a heavy pullover and walking steadily, but not in the direction of home. All the time he was thinking about walking, he was hurrying to get his place on his usual tram, and in the end he turned his own corner and walked past the neighboring houses to his own front door and turned his key in the lock at the same time as always.

Thinking about doing all that walking had given him a sense of energy and well-being. He felt in good health and good humor, and contented to be coming home after his day's work, and he was smiling as he stepped into the hall. There were red glass panels in the side frames of the front door, and he was always aware of the glass and always closed the door carefully. At the same instant that he was hanging his raincoat on the rack, he looked down the hall and saw the kitchen door close quickly and quietly, but not quickly enough to prevent him from seeing that Rose was down there. Her head was turned away from him as she closed the door.

The entrance hall where Hubert stood was narrow. It was no more than a passage, and the floor was covered with linoleum. At the end of the hall there were stairs going up to the bedrooms and, farther along, the three steps down to the kitchen. The hall was dim although it was still bright outside. The kitchen had been lighted up, the glimpse he had seen of it before the door closed. There had been only a second of time, and hardly more than a line of light that narrowed to a thread and then vanished. He might as well not have seen Rose at all, but he had seen her, and he wondered if it could possibly have been intentional — to shut the door in his face like that. He considered going down to the kitchen and asking some question, saying something, anything at all, but instead he went along the hall and into the back sitting room and walked over to the window, and turned at once from the window and began to stare at the doorway. But of course it was already too late. By this time Rose should have opened the kitchen door and called up, "Is that you, Hubert?" She must have heard him coming down the hall. You could hear everything in this house. He listened, but he could hear no sound at all. That was strange. He should at least have been able to hear some little noise, teacups and saucers or something, the tea being got ready. He might as well have been alone in the house for all the evidence he had of life near him. He felt that he was alone, and he wished there were someone in the room with him who could give him advice, because he wanted to be told to go straight down to the kitchen, or else not to go down there but to sit down at once and ignore the whole matter.

He wished he had someone to talk to. He wanted the impulse he felt — to go down to the kitchen — to be made impossible by a command that he was bound to obey. But no word came to forbid him and so, although he knew it was impossible for him to go down and speak to Rose, he knew also that it was not forbidden, and he did not know what to do. What he could not do was to sit down. He was too angry to sit down. But he was trembling, and he sat down in his chair, which had its back to the window and was beside the fireplace, where it stayed summer and winter, close to the hearth, with Rose's low chair across the hearthrug from him. The hearthrug was a dull, warm red, and it was fringed at the ends.

Hubert wished he hadn't seen the door close. If he had taken that walk home, he would have been very late, and he wouldn't have seen the door close. But when had he ever walked home from work? Never. Rose had closed the door at the exact moment when she had every right to expect him home, and something in her attitude as she closed the door told him that she had seen him letting himself into the house. The more he thought back, the more he was sure he was right. In the glimpse he had had of her, there had been something hasty, he would even say furtive. Unless he was imagining things. But he knew he wasn't imagining anything. She was down there now, wondering if he had seen the kitchen door close, and she was frightened, and he wondered what she was thinking about him. She had no right to behave like this. It was intolerable. The whole thing was intolerable.

Then he heard the kitchen door open and footsteps on the stairs. When Rose appeared in the doorway, Hubert felt such dislike that he smiled. He saw the confusion caused by the smile, and he saw her hand fasten on the doorknob as her hand always fastened on something—the back of a chair or her other hand—before she spoke.

"The tea is ready," she said.

"I don't want any tea," Hubert said.

"What's the matter?" she asked. "Why don't you want your tea?"

She was standing stiffly and her face was pink. It was clear that she knew she was in the wrong.

"I don't want any tea," Hubert said. "That's simple enough, isn't it? And I can guarantee you this—the next time you shut a door in my face like that I'm going to walk out of this house and I won't come back. I mean what I say."

"Hubert, I don't know what you're talking about," she said.

Hubert said nothing.

"Will you let me bring you up a tray?" she asked.

"Never mind about the tray," Hubert said. "I don't want your tray. If you'd only get out of here and leave me alone."

Hubert watched until the door was shut, and then he leaned forward and put his elbows on his knees and began to study the red hearthrug. He began to hum softly:

> "She is far from the land where her
>   young hero sleeps,
> And lovers around her are sighing,
> But—"

He sighed and lay back in his chair and was silent. He wished he had followed his original plan and walked home. Then he would not have seen the door close. If only he had not seen it close — but he had seen it, and having seen it he had to take a stand. It was partly the fault of the house, which was much too small. Any house would have been too small, but this one was much too small. There wasn't a corner in it where you could hide without causing questions — those silent questions that were not questions at all but reproaches.

There was no possible way for Hubert to ignore what went on in the house. He would have liked to be able to shut his eyes. Then he could control his temper. Rose was not ashamed that she had closed the door against him; she was only frightened because she had been caught closing it.

He wished he had had sense enough to go down to the kitchen and have it out with her the minute he saw the door close. He felt he was walking along a path that was separated from another identical path by a glass wall so high that it went out of sight. The path he was following was full of mistakes that he recognized, because they were all his own, but while every mistake was familiar to him, every mistake came as a shock, because of the different intervals of time that elapsed between one mistake and the next. Just when he felt fine and imagined everything to be all right, there was another blunder. There seemed to be no escaping the contentiousness and disagreeableness in this house. And all the time he was making mistakes and tripping over himself, he could see through the glass to that other path that was also his own. On that path there were no mistakes, and he did only the right thing and did it at the right time, and he knew how to deal with everything, and he walked like a man who was in command of himself and his life. Sometimes it seemed that only a trick of light, nothing at all, stood between Hubert and the place where he would know how to conduct life in accordance with its meaning, which he understood perfectly.

Nothing in his life made sense. But once you had said that you had said it all. Hubert could hardly march out of his house and down onto the main road and stop some stranger and say, "I understand nothing." To do a thing like that would be — it would be the action of a madman.

If he had been on his own it wouldn't have been so bad, but a wife makes a man conspicuous, especially if he doesn't amount to much, and at this moment Hubert felt he amounted to nothing at all. Poor Rose, he didn't blame her, but by her presence in his life she showed what he had tried to do and that he had hoped, and by her behavior she showed what his hopes had come to. He was ashamed of her. Without her, who knows what he might have done. And then again he might have gone through life invisible, but anything would have been better than being held up to ridicule in his own house. Anything in the world would have been better than being held up to ridicule to himself. He felt uncomfortable in his chair, and angry. It was not that she was demanding or extravagant. She asked for nothing. The reason he grew irritable when the time came to hand her the housekeeping money every week was that she always took it apologetically, and on the few occasions when he had forgotten it, reminded him timidly. Of course, he grew irritable once in a while with her pretenses, and no one knew how many times he restrained himself when she irritated him nearly beyond endurance. He could not stand the way she ate, or to know the amount of food she ate, which was a good deal more than he ever felt inclined to take. The word "appetite" embarrassed him, and the knowledge he had of her appetite, which was so much greater than his own, made her mysterious to him, but not in a way that aroused his interest or affection. He thought her appetite was something to be ashamed of, and he did not want to think about it. He did not grudge her the food, but he thought she attached too much importance to it. He dreaded to see her eat, because he could not keep his eyes off her, and there had been times when he saw her turn red and swallow quickly when she caught him watching her. He always had his breakfast by himself, and he had his dinner in town in the middle of the day, so there were only teatimes and Sunday dinners to be got through.

Sometimes as they sat at tea Hubert told Rose about incidents that had taken place in the shop during the day. These anecdotes dealt mainly with the customers, and often the point they were working up to was the customer's discomfiture, which Hubert found funny, or the customer's ignorance, which Hubert also found funny. Some of the men who came to the shop were so dense that they did not know they were making fools of themselves or how they were laughed at after they left the place. They were the men who were too tall or too short or too fat or too thin for the patterns they preferred and for the cut and fit they decided upon. Hubert derided the dense customers, not because they looked ridiculous, but because they did not seem to know how ridiculous they were. Hubert could forgive any man for looking like a fool if he played the fool and showed that he could laugh at himself and take a joke, but he had no mercy on people who believed, or pretended to believe, that they looked just like anybody else. Outside the shop Hubert could call attention to people's shortcomings and so test their sense of humor, but at work he naturally had to restrain himself, and it used to drive him nearly mad to see all those posturing fellows get away without knowing they had been observed by a man who had a sharp and humorous eye and a great gift for cutting people down when they got above themselves.

·   ·   ·

Hubert had heard Rose returning to the kitchen, but he had not heard the kitchen door close, although he knew she must have closed it. Now there was no sign from the kitchen. "Well, that's all right," Hubert said, "let her do what she likes." But he couldn't go on sitting in his armchair forever, doing nothing. He couldn't concentrate. He couldn't read. He didn't want to read. He didn't want to do anything. He had made up his mind not to give in to her. Sooner or later somebody was going to have to make a move, but Hubert felt that the decision had been taken out of his hands, and that it was now up to Rose to make some gesture. When he first came home and saw her close the door against him, he had had the choice between going down to the kitchen or not going down there. Now that choice was gone. Instead of making the choice he had asserted himself, and any sign he gave now would mean that he had backed down. She would have to come out of the kitchen sometime. She would want to go out to have a last look at her garden. Bedtime would come. It was only a matter of waiting until the normal routine of the house washed him out of the corner he had been forced into. It would be all the same in a hundred years, but Hubert knew that as long as he lived he would never understand why Rose had closed the door against him like that. He no longer wondered why she had closed the door, he only wished he had not seen it close.

The window behind him was a big oblong, almost a square, a sash window, and it faced the end wall of their garden. At the other side of the wall lay the courts of the tennis club. Hubert and Rose considered the members of the tennis club to be a gay and fashionable set, and Hubert said they were a worthless crowd. On Saturday nights they could hear dance music from the large new addition to the clubhouse. The members called the new addition the Pavilion. The dance music annoyed Hubert, and although Rose had once loved to dance she never protested when he got up and shut the window so that they could have a little peace and quiet in the house. The entrance to the club was on the main road that ran past the end of the terrace of small houses where the Derdons lived. On one side, the club grounds ended at the long end wall that was common to the twenty-six gardens owned by the Derdons and their neighbors all up and down the terrace. The farther boundaries of the club were marked by groves of trees. If Hubert had gone to stand by the window he would have seen the tops of the trees far away beyond the courts, and beyond the trees, coming toward him, the sky. He didn't move. He sat and listened. The window was open at the top and he could hear the quarrelsome old woman next door scolding her middle-aged daughter, who was unmarried and lived at home, doing the housework and cooking and easing her occasional rebellious rages with loud crying fits that could be heard in the Derdons' kitchen and also in the back sitting room. That garden next door was a wilderness of ivy and nettles and neglected cabbage plants. It was a disgraceful household. Hubert hoped the unhappy daughter would not have a crying fit this evening, and he wished both women would be removed to some lunatic asylum and that a single man who was never at home would move in next door. He listened to the old woman's thin, cruel voice, and he thought he heard her daughter's hysterical silence. He heard, faintly, voices from the tennis courts, and he heard the Donovans' big collie crying pitifully as it strained at the chain that held it to the cramped kennel that had been its home from a puppy. The Donovans kept the dog as a protection against burglars. Hubert wished a burglar might climb over the end wall and free the dog, who could then go into the house and kill Tom Donovan and his wife and their three impertinent children, and perhaps have enough to eat for once in its life.

He heard more than he could bear to hear. The back sitting

room was filling up with lives he despised and with people he detested, and he had no defense against any of it. He could have closed the window, but he was sure that the minute he appeared there with his arms up, pushing the sash tight, Rose would open the kitchen door, coming out into the garden, and he did not want to see her. He didn't want to see her because he did not care about her. It was the first true thing he had said in a long time, and he was glad it was out in the open at last. He simply didn't care about her. He cared nothing at all about her, and he couldn't understand why he hadn't realized it a long time ago. He couldn't stand the thought of seeing her and having to speak to her and having to go on living in the same house with her. He could not think of her now without seeing the fluttering dishonesty of her expression, and he wondered if it would ever seem worth his while again to try to speak directly to her. What was the use of trying to talk to her? She never said "Yes" or "No." It was always "Whatever you like," or "I don't mind," or "Maybe, if that's what you want." And then the mute resignation that followed his decision, which, of course, was never what she wanted, although wild horses would not have dragged an objection out of her.

No, he wouldn't bother trying to talk to her. It wasn't worth his while, and it would only distress her for nothing. All the same, although Hubert felt that Rose was of no importance, he knew she was better than a good many people — better than the two women next door and better than the Donovans and better than that loud, good-for-nothing crowd at the tennis club. And he knew she was defenseless, and he felt that his indifference left her exposed, even though she didn't know about it, and he pitied her, because in her own way she did her best, and nobody cared anything at all about her. She was a lost cause, all right, and it was a good thing that only he knew it. It would be terrible for Rose if the rest of the world knew what he knew about her. It was no accident that she had always lagged behind him. She had no sense. She was not able to take care of herself. She had always been the same.

Rose had not always been the same, but there was no one now to tell what she had been or to see her as she had been seen. Once in a while she thought of her father, who died when she was ten. When she remembered him, trying to remember his voice, she looked more than ever like a bird that has found its feet on the ground instead of finding its wings in the air. She looked around her and wondered. She was tame, but the place was strange. Whatever she might have been, laughing, solemn, hopeful, melancholy, serene, unquiet, ambitious, or whatever she might have become, she was now only tame. She had turned tame when her father died, as she might have turned traitor to a cause she had once been ready to give her life for. She had known her father was dead but not that he was gone, and even when she began to know he was gone she refused to believe that he was gone out of sight, and she put the strength of a lifetime into her struggle to keep him in sight until she was sure he was safe. She had forgotten all that was familiar to her in her struggle to stand by the one who had made it all familiar. She knew he would expect it of her. He had said that she was faithful. He had said that she would never let anyone down. Over and over again he had said she was a good child, and that she had no bad in her. He had always defended her to her mother.

Rose's father had thought the world of her, and he had told her and told anyone else who would listen, that she was an unusual child who could do anything she set out to do. Once when she was dancing around their kitchen showing off, he said, "One of these days Rose is going to show us how the birds fly." There was no end to their conversations, and they agreed on everything. After he was dead, when she set about remembering him, she found that she had memorized him, and he was so clear in her mind that, as she listened to her mother and the neighbors talking about him, all she had to do was to look above their heads and she could see him—not as he had been but as he was now, above them all and smiling down on them as he listened to the nice things they were saying about him, although none of them had had much opinion of him when he was alive. She hated them all, but the more she hated them the more she feared them, because she knew that if they found out about her dreams they would laugh at her and call her "Miss Importance." Her mother had always said that she had too good an idea of herself and that she was too fanciful.

Rose knew that she must be a good child, but she never learned that there is more to being a good child than just doing what you are told. She did not know where she was. She wanted to be told what to do, and when she was not told, she imagined she had done something wrong. She had never been able to meet the world on its own terms—she did not measure up—and she had no terms of her own, and had not tried to make any. She had not known she had the power to make terms. She found the world difficult, because, while she knew that life is precious and must be watched night and day or it will vanish without warning, she also knew that in the long run life is of no value at all, because it vanishes without warning. Between these two sharp edges she made her way as well as she could. When Hubert first saw Rose, he thought how light and definite her walk was, and that her expression was resolute. He never learned that the courage she showed came not from natural hope or from natural confidence or from any ignorant, natural source, but from her determination to avoid touching the two madnesses as they guided her, pressing too close to her and narrowing her path into a very thin line. She always walked in straight lines. She went from where she was to the place where she was going, and then back again to the place where she had been. She kept close to the house. She might as well have been in a net, for all the freedom she felt.

In the early days of their marriage Hubert and Rose lived in two rooms at the top of a house on Somerville Street, off Stephen's Green. The first evening they walked in there together was the evening of their wedding day. It was also the occasion of Rose's first journey in a train—from the town of Wexford, where she was born and brought up, to Dublin. A friend of Hubert's named Frank Guiney met them at the station to welcome them and to help carry their parcels and suitcases. Rose was carrying a basket of groceries her mother had packed for her at the last minute. It was all she carried, but Hubert and Frank were burdened down. When they reached the top of the tall building they were all breathless from the long flights of stairs. Hubert dropped everything he was carrying on the landing and put his hand against the wall to support himself, until he could catch his breath.

"What made you stop?" Frank said to him. "We'd have been in heaven in another five minutes."

Rose thought Frank was very funny. Frank had found the rooms for them and he had given Hubert the key at the station. Rose had watched Hubert put the key carefully in his waistcoat pocket, and now she watched him take it out again. He was very self-conscious, and in his eagerness to open their door he stumbled over one of the suitcases he had put down, and he nearly fell through the doorway ahead of Rose, but Frank grabbed him and held him back, and Rose went in first.

"Ladies First!" Frank shouted, loud enough to rouse the whole neighborhood. They were all there laughing. Rose put her basket on the shaky round table that stood in the middle of the room, and she stood there looking around her while Hubert and Frank brought in the luggage. The scrap of thin carpeting under her feet was faded, and it was so worn that most of it was the same straw color as her basket, with traces of red and pink to show how bright it once had been. When everything had been brought in, Frank made a great display of trying to pick Hubert up and carry him around.

"This is a remarkable parcel, Madam," he said to Rose, while Hubert struggled. "It has delusions of grandeur. It thinks it's alive."

Rose had never laughed so hard in her life. She saw Hubert watching her and admiring her, and she knew they were both showing off for her benefit. Then Frank suddenly got serious and took his watch out of his pocket and looked at it and said he had an important appointment, a matter of life and death, and that he was two days and ten minutes late already. He was outside and closing the door after himself while he was still talking, and he wouldn't listen to Hubert's invitation to stay a minute. Then he vanished and they heard him running down the stairs. Rose looked at Hubert.

"Frank's a great man," Hubert said, "but I'm glad he's gone. Aren't you? Aren't you glad, Rose?"

"Yes," Rose said, and then she turned and went quickly to the window, a small, square window that looked across Somerville Street to the tops of the houses beyond.

"It's a lovely sky," she said.

"Take off that old hat," Hubert said. "You're at home now."

She had lifted the flimsy green net curtains that covered the windows while she was looking out, and as she raised her arms to take the pins out of her hat the curtains fell back to the wall and she saw that they were of unequal lengths.

"Look, one of these is too long," she said. "I'll have to even them up."

She took her hands from her hat and lifted the curtains and stepped back, measuring them together at their hems.

"About an inch," she said. "That should be right."

She let the curtains go, and when they dropped back into place she sighed with satisfaction, as though they had passed a test and carried the whole house to victory with them, and now she knew that the curtains and the walls and the long stairs up would stand fast and keep their appointed positions, all true weights to anchor her so that she would never get lost, because she was held safe where she belonged. She turned to Hubert and smiled at him. Then she remembered her hat and she put up her hands and began searching for the pins again.

"I'll do that curtain tomorrow," she said.

"Green curtains for your green eyes," Hubert said, but he knew there was no comparison, because the curtains were a garish green and Rose's eyes were the color of the sea.

When Rose was asleep her face looked solitary, and when she was awake she looked lonely. There was implacability and pride in her solitude, but her loneliness was helpless. Hubert could not reach her solitude, and he could not destroy her loneliness. He thought of the sea and did not know why. When she woke up suddenly, turning over in bed, that implacable solitude shone triumphantly in her eyes for an instant before loneliness shadowed them. Hubert marveled at her. He couldn't understand why she had married him, and at the same time he couldn't understand how she had lived until she married him.

"How did you ever get along before you met me?" he asked her.

"I don't know," she said. "I can't remember."

She was always smiling at him. She only stopped smiling in order to smile again.

One evening after tea he asked her if she had mended his

socks. They were still sitting at the table — the shaky round table in the room with the green net curtains. They were two months married to the day, and Rose had bought a slice of dark fruit cake to celebrate the anniversary. She had cut the cake into fingers, and they had eaten it all except for one small piece, which lay on the plate between them. Hubert knew she wanted the cake but that she also wanted him to have it. He intended to give it to her, but he wanted to tease her. When he asked about the socks he was grinning. He still thought it absurd that Rose should do his mending. Rose had her elbows on the table and she was looking at her hands and admiring the one that wore the wedding ring. When she heard his question she looked at him in astonishment, as though he had deliberately said something he knew would hurt her.

"I forgot them," she said. "I forgot to do your socks. Isn't that just like me, to forget the one thing you asked me to do."

"It's not all that important," Hubert said.

He was still smiling, but he was hurt. She looked at him as though he was turning out to be just like her mother — catching her out in a mistake and then bullying her.

"It doesn't matter," he said impatiently. "Here, look, have this nice piece of cake."

"I don't want it now," she said, and "now" told him he had spoiled everything.

"Oh, all right, so," he said, and he took the piece of cake and crammed it into his mouth and got up from the table and went over to stand by the window.

He pushed the green net curtains aside and looked out. He saw the chimneys of the houses on the other side of the street and the gray streaked sky above. It had been raining on and off all day. As Hubert watched, another shower began, and the raindrops dashed violently against the window. He felt a chill go through him although the windows were closed. Rose still sat at the table where he had left her. He felt ashamed of himself. If he had left her alone she would have eaten the cake and then she would have been happier. He longed to comfort her, but the cake was gone and he could think of no other peace offering. He wished he knew what to say to her. He hoped she would soon get up and start clearing the table, because until she gave some sign he could not turn from the window and he was tired of standing there looking out at the rain and blaming himself. Then he turned without intending to, and she was sitting with her head down and her hands in her lap.

She looked at him piteously and said, "I'm sorry, Hubert."

He said gently, "There's nothing in the world for you to be sorry about."

She gave no sign that she heard him, but she continued to look at him. He felt that she was waiting for him to tell her what to do, and that she would do whatever he said. Her helplessness confounded him. He felt he could deal with *her*—after all, she was Rose, he knew her, she was his wife—but he could not deal with her helplessness. If he had put it into words he might have said, "I married Rose, not her helplessness," as another man might have said, "I married her, not her family." Hubert had seen Rose get that beaten look in her mother's presence, but there was no need for any of that now, and he knew it would be a bad thing to encourage her in these moods. It would be bad for *her*. Her mother had warned him that Rose was inclined to brood over nothing at all. The thing to do was not to take her seriously and not to admit that there was anything wrong. There *was* nothing wrong. Hubert knew that the way to deal with Rose when she was in this frame of mind was not to comfort or coddle her but to distract her, and so instead of putting his arms around her, as he wanted to do, he said, "The shower will be over in a minute.

Why don't we forget about all this and go out for a little walk and talk about the nice house we're going to have all to ourselves one of these days?"

The house they found was the one they lived in now. The linoleum on the floor in the back sitting room where Hubert sat had been there when they moved in, and they had paid extra for it. Before they moved into the house, they came out on the tram from Somerville Street one day and walked around the empty rooms they would soon be living in. One tour of the house was enough for Hubert, but Rose was reluctant to leave, so he sat down on the floor in the back sitting room, with his back to the wall under the window, and told her to look around to her heart's content.

He was not easy in his mind, but the deed was done now—they had the house. He listened to Rose walking about upstairs. There was linoleum in the back bedroom but none in the front. She walked across the bare boards of the front bedroom and then she stopped. She was at the windows upstairs, looking out and wondering about the neighbors. Now she was coming back, and down the stairs. Her step was dulled by the narrow red carpeting on the stairs, and she was coming slowly and being careful to keep to the center of each step. She continued on down to the kitchen. The floor in the kitchen was covered with red tiles. After a minute she left the kitchen and came into the back sitting room, which they then called the dining room.

"I love looking around like this," she said. "I'll never get tired of this house. I wonder how they came to pick out those colors."

She was looking down at the linoleum, which was beige and brown and maroon in a pattern of large and small feathers.

"It's in very good condition," Hubert said gloomily. "I'm afraid we'll have to get used to it."

"Oh, it's not that I don't *like* it," Rose said.

She looked curiously at the linoleum other people had admired and taken care of. If it hadn't already been in the house she would never have owned it. It was like a gift brought from some foreign place. She would never have chosen that pattern or those colors. They were a part of something strange, from someone else's life, souvenirs of a country she did not know at all and where she did not want to be, because she would find herself timid and ill at ease there, and nothing there would ever be as real to her as the linoleum they had left behind was now under her feet. She walked possessively around on it.

"I never want to leave this house," she said.

Hubert got out of his chair and walked to the door. His mind was made up. He would go upstairs and wash his hands as usual, and change from his suit coat into his woolen cardigan, as usual, and then he would come down and let events take their course. His mind was made up, but even so, he hesitated before opening the door. But once the door was open he was up the stairs like a shot and into the bathroom, where he scrubbed his hands vigorously and splashed cold water on his face. He felt better already, knowing he was going to do the right thing. It was all a lot of nonsense, much better to get everything out into the open. Now he would go straight down to the kitchen and have it out with Rose. He would laugh her out of her gloominess. It was only a matter of finding the right thing to say. He would get her to laugh at herself and see what nonsense all this bickering was. He hurried down the stairs and down the three steps that led from the hall to the kitchen as though he were bringing news that could not wait, good news, the best news, but at the kitchen door he hesitated and then, hearing no movement inside, although she must have heard him thundering down the stairs, he beat a loud postman's tattoo on the door and burst into the room to find it empty. The door into the garden was open. She had gone out there, and he could not follow her. All the neighbors would look out through their back windows, and anyone who happened to be out in the neighboring gardens could hear every word he said.

He looked over at the stove to see if by any chance she had left the teapot there, but the top of the stove was as clear as the top of the table and the drainboard by the sink. The kitchen was spotless. She had finished working there. There was to be nothing to eat, then.

He went back up to the sitting room and went in. There on the dining-room table, which they kept folded against the wall opposite the fireplace, she had left a tray. He went over and looked at it. Brown bread and a slice of ham. She had taken the trouble to shape the butter into curly balls. A tomato. Three chocolate biscuits. The teapot was at the fireplace, sitting inside the fender with the cozy over it. He hurried over to the teapot and pulled the cozy off it, and carried it to the table and shakily poured tea into his cup and returned the pot to the hearth. It was too hot to set down on the table. He poured milk into his tea and drank it down quickly. He wanted another cup at once, but this time he carried the cup over to the hearth and filled it there. Then he sat down at the table and began to eat his way through everything on the tray. When everything was gone he felt better, although he thought he could have done without the third chocolate biscuit. He had been hungry, that was all. Famished. He wouldn't mind having his tea from a tray like this every evening. He sat gazing at the ravaged tray and thinking about how she had smuggled it into the room while he was upstairs. It was clever of her. She had wanted him to have his tea but she had not wanted to face him. She had taken a lot of trouble over the tray.

He got up and went to the window. She was there, kneeling sideways to him by the flower bed that ran along the wall where the laburnum tree was. The laburnum had been there when they moved in, together with a yellow rose that was on the opposite side of the garden. Apart from the laburnum and the rose there had been nothing. The place was a wilderness when they first saw it, but Rose had seen immediately that it had the makings of a good garden. Her work in the garden was wonderful. Hubert did not know where she had got her knowledge of flowers. She was kneeling out there now, settling something, some little plant, into its bed. She was intent on placing the plant in its exact place, and she was as anxious at her work as though she had taken the future of the world between her hands and must set it right once and for all because there would be no second chance — no second chance for her, at least — to prove that if it was left to her, all would be well. For this moment the weight of the world was off her shoulders and in her hands.

She finished and sat back on her heels and rubbed her open hands together to get rid of the earth. Then she put her hand on the handle of the watering can and began to get awkwardly to her feet. Hubert looked away from her and down at his own hands. There was no need for him to watch her, to know how she got up. He had seen her often enough, raising herself after doing out the fireplace, by placing her hand on the edge of the coal scuttle. When he looked out again she was standing with her back to him, looking about her as though she was calculating the effect of some improvement she had in mind. She raised one hand to her hair, to smooth a loose strand up off the back of her neck into the thick bun she wore. She was wearing a white blouse with loose sleeves, and as the sleeve fell back, her upraised arm gleamed. Hubert saw her wrist and her elbow, and in that fragment of her he saw all of Rose, as the crescent moon recalls the full moon to anyone who has watched her at the height of her power. Then Rose stooped and lifted the heavy watering can with both hands and began to move slowly away toward the end wall, watering the plants as she went.

The day was almost worn out. The light was thin — fading light that left everything visible. That evening's light was helpless, the day in extremity, without strength enough left to dissemble with sun and shade, with only strength enough left to touch the world as it withdrew forever from the world. The evening light spoke, and what it said was, "There is nothing more to be said." There is nothing more to be said because what remains to be said must not be said. It is too late for Rose.

Hubert was silent. He had nothing to say, and in any case there was no one to hear him.

The Drowned Man

AFTER HIS WIFE DIED, Mr. Derdon was very anxious
to get into her bedroom, to have a look around on his own with
the door closed and with no one there to watch him and wonder
how he was feeling. It was not anxiety or grief or any painful sen-
sation, not longing or yearning or anything like that, that drew
him to the room, but curiosity. He wanted to look at it. The
room, that had hardly existed for him while she was alive, and
that he had seldom entered, although he had occasionally stood
in the doorway or at least paused in the doorway to call something in to her on his way out of the house—the room now
seemed mysterious to him the way an empty house will suddenly
seem mysterious and even frightening to children who never noticed it when it was occupied, and the way a bird's nest lying
empty on the ground after a summer storm will crowd the mind
with thoughts that have nothing to do with wings and food and
warmth and song: thoughts of vacancy, and thoughts of winter,
and of winds that are too violent and nights that are too dark, and
thoughts of stony solitude, endured in silence, and of landscapes
that are too cold and flat and where no one cares to walk. The little nest, cast to the ground, contains an emptiness that is too big
for us to understand. We cannot imagine how it must feel. It is a

limitless emptiness, and beyond us, although we would like to be able to understand it, and examine it from all angles, and mark its limits, and bring it under control, and then put it away in a comfortable place and forget about it. But the nest is nothing, no more than a scrap. The empty nest is only a brazen image of the fear that is so commonplace that we cannot merely walk through it every day pretending we do not notice it but can walk through it and pretend it is not there. As long as the nest is there empty, we look into it, but then it is gone and we think no more about it.

As long as the door of his wife's bedroom, in which she had died, remained closed and the room behind it empty, Mr. Derdon thought of nothing else. The emptiness beyond the door excited him, and he began to dream about it at night, and in his tired mind the door was open to him, and then — mistake — it was not open to him, and it expanded and contracted, being first a very big room and then a very little room, but never its own size, and it developed extra doors, strange doors that frightened him. And after these dreams he awoke in the morning exhausted, as though he suffered nightmares, when all he had done was to dream of his wife's bedroom. His sister, his maiden sister, had come to Dublin to keep house for him, and on the very few occasions when she went out, the woman who cleaned was there fussing around him and looking after him. They felt he should not be left alone at this time. He wondered what did they mean, "at this time." It was not a case of this, that, or the other time. At the moment, it was simply *before* Rose died and *after* Rose died, and when they said to him "at this time," did they mean that he was never to be left a minute to himself for the rest of his life? They bothered him, always hovering around him, and he wondered, in bewilderment, at all the freedom he had had only a month, even ten days, ago, all the freedom he had had and had not valued. Then, before, he had been immeasurably free. He marveled at

could he mourn her, when there was hardly anything he could remember about her apart from the obvious facts that she had been gentle, quiet, uncomplaining, beautiful — or at least more or less beautiful in her youth — things like that. He literally could not remember very much about her. He began to believe that she had been invisible, but when he thought that, he felt that he might cry with fear, because how could he even think that, when *they* were there talking about his dead wife and he knew he had had a wife for more than forty years and they had had a son and the son had vanished into the priesthood, and here he was now and he could hardly remember one solitary thing about her and not really remember seeing her very much. And how could he grieve for what he could not define, or mourn for what had vanished without a trace. That was it — she had made no impression. Somehow or another, however she had done it, she had managed to live with a man, a sensitive, kindhearted man, for more than forty years without making the slightest impression on him. She had always been impossible. Several times, long ago, he had said as much to her. "You are impossible," he had said to her. And she had said *nothing*. She had said nothing and she had given him nothing, nothing to be angry about and nothing to be sad about and nothing to laugh at and nothing to wonder at and nothing at all to remember. She had given him nothing and she had left him nothing, and by leaving him nothing she had taken away from him the one thing that might have been a rock of strength to him now — that rock of grief where he might have rested in blessed isolation, not able to see or hear or speak or think with the sorrow that filled and destroyed him. But that monumental grief would now remain as it was, only a dream of grief that seemed from where he sat to be a dream of peace, because he knew that in that dreadful suffering he would find peace at last, and then he could rest himself, knowing he had done the right and proper thing, and had felt the right and proper emotions, those that represent the just tribute we must pay to death. But it was no use. He felt nothing. He could see and hear and so on, the same as usual, and he even had a little appetite for his food.

If they would only let him stand and watch her garden, he might be able to see her there, she had spent so much time there. If they would only let him stand at the back window and look at her garden, and it was well worth looking at, he might be able to find her there, and then he might be able to begin missing her — it was the least he could do, to miss her. But he didn't miss her, he didn't miss her at all; everything was just the same, he didn't miss her at all, and if he tried to stand by the window looking out into her garden, his sister or the other one would come clucking around, trying to take him out of himself. Then, before, when he had his freedom, he could have stood by that window forever without being interfered with. Then, before, he could have sat all day long in his armchair by the fire, dreaming about nothing, thinking peacefully of nothing at all, immersed in memories so confused and so alike that they were warmth to him; it was like thinking about warmth to sit there like that doing nothing and remembering, really, nothing. Then, when she was alive and he didn't know the freedom he had, he could have sat in his chair for as long as he liked, not holding a book or a newspaper or anything, and no one would have come up talking at him and telling him he mustn't be morbid and that he must keep busy and interested. How could they know that what was in his mind was morbid, when he did not really know himself what was in his mind. They were training him as if he were a dog, a poor unfortunate dog that had to do as he was told and not ask any questions, because he was a *dog* and for no other reason. Poor dog. Poor animal. It made no sense. He had to move briskly or they sighed. He had to talk distinctly and with some vivacity or they gazed at him in worry and surmise. He had to take his walk every day, not in the garden, because that was her garden and so morbid, but out — he had to go out by the front for his walk. They seemed to believe that there was no air at the back of the house anymore, but only in the front, beyond the front door, where the neighbors would come trotting up to him, people he only knew by sight, and say things to him that he hardly understood and did not want to hear, although through some miracle he kept making the correct sorrowful responses to all their sorrowful platitudes. And he felt that every word he said was a lie, and when he returned to the house he returned worn out.

He would have loved to make a clean breast of things to his sister and the others. He would have liked to confess to them — he longed to confess to them — that he felt no grief. He wanted to tell the truth. He wanted them to know what a sham, what a sham he was, or at least show them that they were making him into a sham. But if he told them the truth they would think him a monster, and he would rather know he was a sham than be thought a monster. He was a man who could feel no grief, an empty man. Even so, he would have liked to be let do as he liked, but he hesitated to hurt their feelings. There were plenty of sharp remarks that came into his head, but he did not want to say them unless he was really pushed to the wall. He knew the women meant well. He could tell them to go, of course. They would protest, but they would go, and then he would be alone and then he could be quiet. If he ordered them out, and they saw he meant business, they would have to go. But he could not do that, when they meant so well, and then it was something to keep in mind, that he could be rid of them in a minute, any minute. It was something to look forward to, the minute when he would order them out once and for all, and he did look forward to it. Once he made up his mind, they would go, and no ifs or buts. Once his mind was made up he would take no nonsense from them, but for the time being he let them have their way in the house and he did what they told him to do and he would go on doing as he was told for as long as it suited him and not one minute longer. But it was good to look forward to the moment when he would turn them out. He would let them have their way, he would let them have their head, they would imagine themselves entrenched, and suddenly, all of a sudden, he would turn on them and show them who was master. The moment would come. He was sure of that. They would drive him too far. He was sure of that. He would turn when they least expected it, and he would blast them. He would send them packing. He had to smile, thinking of the sur-prise on their faces, and his sister caught him smiling, and he caught her catching him, with that sympathetic expression on her that meant she imagined he was thinking kind sweet gentle happy thoughts about his dearest departed, and he was so an-noyed he could have hit her, and he turned down the corners of his mouth and began to look gloomy again.

They thought it was a sign of grief that he had ordered them to leave Rose's room as it was, but it was not a sign of grief at all. It had been an impulse that had made him tell them to shut that door and leave it shut. He had simply wanted to assert himself and to give a reasonable order and be obeyed, and they had obeyed him, but it had not been an important matter until all of a sudden, in some mysterious way, the closed door had become ex-tremely important.

He thought that once he got into that empty room by himself with the door closed, he would be able to think more clearly and to know something that he did not now know. Once in there, he might be able to remember more of her than — as she was now in his mind — something humble and busy about the house. Once in there, he might be able to find more to think of than that eternal acquiescence. Even the very last word she had said to him was "Yes." There was nothing strange about that, she had always said yes, but unbroken acquiescence had not been indefinite enough for her; she had always, until that last yes, had to qualify even her yes — "Yes, all right," "Yes, if you want to," "Yes, I don't mind, if you like. If you want to, I suppose so, yes." But that final "Yes," when he asked her should he send for the doctor, stood alone in his mind. He could hear her voice now, saying "Yes," and he recalled that even as troubled as he had been he felt surprised, and maybe even pleased, that she was definite. It had been as though he heard her voice once again after a very long time, when she said "Yes" like that to him.

As he looked forward to the day when he would order his sister and the other woman to leave his house, now he looked forward to the opportunity to slip into the empty room and be alone there, but without anybody knowing he was there. He waited for the chance when they would both be out of the house together. He schemed. He played up to them. He did not sit dreaming in his chair by the fire, but held his book in front of him and read it with attention. He asked them to bring him the evening paper, as though he was interested in what was in it. He did not look out of the back window into her garden. He ate what was put in front of him, and even suggested that if they both thought hard and put all their brains together, they might be able to remember that he liked his eggs just lightly boiled and that he liked them hot, because cold boiled eggs were bad for people, especially first thing in the morning. He grew bolder. He told them that when the conventional period of mourning was past they would all get dressed in their best clothes and go into town in a taxi and see a play or something. At that, they looked at him in astonishment, and then they turned their faces away, like disappointed cats who

see that their prey has ceased to move and who hope that by pretending to remove their attention from it they will trick it into
life again, and into movement again, and so find it still within
their power. Mr. Derdon's sister and the lady who cleaned looked
away, startled, and then they looked back again, but he knew
their ways and he was still smiling. "We're not doing poor Rose
any good, sitting around here with long faces," he said.

A couple of days after that, or it might even have been the very
next day, through some miracle that was carefully explained to
him, while he pretended to listen, he found himself alone in the
house in the afternoon. He hesitated a short time before opening
the door of Rose's room. He walked up and down the hall awhile
as he had longed to do, and he thought about going into the
room. He did not want to go blundering in. After all, once he had
gone in, the emptiness that had been increasing in there since her
death would be destroyed forever, and he was anxious to catch
some impression of it while it still lingered. He walked up and
down a few times, thinking intently and rubbing his hands together, and then without thinking any more about it he turned
the knob and opened the door and went in and closed the door
behind him. There was nothing. There was not even a percepti-
ble emptiness. It was her room, or it had been her room, but she
was not in it anymore. The room said nothing. The emptiness,
what emptiness he felt there, was not particular, and he could not
pretend to himself that he could identify it as a special and indi-
vidual emptiness that she had left and that she and she alone
could have left. It was a general emptiness that filled her place —
he might as well have been looking into a fallen nest to try to discover the nature of what was not. He grew tired trying to press
himself into what was not there and therefore could not or would
not resist him. There was no resistance in the room. There was

nothing he could pit himself against. He felt let down, as he had when he was a child and Christmas was over, and at the same time he felt keyed up, as though he were going to have to face an examination, *take* an examination that he had not been warned about, that he had never known people had to take, that he was not prepared for and could not prepare for, since he had no idea of the nature of the questions that would be asked him or of the tests he might be called upon to perform. He had always felt uneasily that there was something other people knew, something everybody knew and took for granted, but that he did not know. He had sometimes hoped that he might come upon this bit of common knowledge, by luck, as he might come upon a touchstone that would guide him to the secret whose existence he felt, the secret that others had and that remained closed to him. What he had thought out loud in his own mind always was, "There must be more than this to life, there must be more to life than this." Oh, indeed indeed, yes, there must be more than this to it all, he used to think, and then, at such incredulous moments, he used to look into the faces of the people who passed him in the street, to try to read in their faces what he was sure they must know that kept them going every day, because it was not everybody that had his strength, and it was not everybody — there was hardly anybody who could have the fortitude to keep on going day in day out in the bewilderment in which he himself lived. It was not possible that others could go from day to day, as he did, for no real reason, or that others could put up the brave front that he put up, the brave, respectable front that was a front for nothing, and nothing but a front. At such moments, when he felt that he must make one more attempt to discover the secret, he used to glance, just glance, into Rose's face when he felt she would not notice him looking at her. He remembered that at such times, on those evenings, he used to hang his hat and coat in the hall as usual, and put his umbrella in the stand, and walk down the hall to where she sat, and he would sit down opposite to her and open his evening paper, but at such times he would use the evening paper only to camouflage himself as a reader while he watched her, not as a husband, not even as a man, but as a supplicant who hoped she might be able to tell him what had kept them together all these years, or what kept any two people together, or what kept people going and doing as they had been told they ought to do. When had all this obedience begun and who had marked out the appointed way where men and women walked without protest and most of the time without complaining? Most important of all, what reason had been given that guaranteed this obedience and why had the reason not been given to him as well as to everybody else? There was a common secret that he had not been allowed to share, and now it seemed that grief must also remain a secret to him, because even now, sitting in the room in which she had spent a good part of her time, and in which she had slept in her bed, he felt no grief. He was sitting on the straight chair she had kept handy to her sewing machine. The sewing machine was closed and made a flat smooth surface that was faintly marked by whitened circles, where she had kept some of her plants when the machine was not in use. She could have got herself a little plant table. He would not have minded the expense. He would have given her the money for a table, if she had asked him for it, but she had not asked. She had preferred to play the martyr and so, contemptuously and in despair of ever coming to any terms with her, he had ignored her or, as you might put it, let her have her way. She had preferred to clear the top of her chest of drawers when she wanted to do any sewing on the machine. Then to the top of the chest of drawers she would lift the plants, some of them big and heavy, and when they were all safely arranged she would open the sewing machine and go to work, bending very close to

it. And with the work finished, she would go through the whole
laborious process of transferring the plants back to the machine
again. The machine was a makeshift plant table for her, as much
in her life had been makeshift. Take, for example, that arrangement of old chocolate boxes on the blanket chest under the shelf
where she had kept her few books. You would think, to see those
chocolate boxes, and to note the careful order in which they were
arranged, by size and also by shape, a rectangular one set straight
and centered on top of a larger rectangle, the square ones built up
like child's blocks on top of the squares, and the two long equal
ones set apart from the rest, completing the design of even lines
and sharp angles, all of it speaking of neatness and care and of an
overpowering concern with order — you would think, looking at
such an arrangement, that the boxes contained something of interest or of value. And what did they contain? Old bills marked
paid thirty years before. Recipes for dinners she had never
cooked, dinners so elaborate that she must have been dreaming
of a visit from the king and queen of England when she cut the
menus out of the magazines in which she had found them. Directions for making dresses that she would never in her life have
had occasion to wear — there was a whole pamphlet that gave in-
structions, measurements, etc., for the construction of a satin ball
gown. It would have been laughable if it was not so pathetic. One
box contained cards of tailor's samples — bits of tweed, bits of
serge, bits of velvet, bits of suiting and coat materials. He knew
how she had come by those cards. She had never told him, but he
had known her so well that he knew very well how she had come
by those cards. He could see her now, standing in front of the tailor's window, one tailor one time, another tailor another time,
admiring the bolts of cloth in the window and the pictures dis-
played of suits and coats, and imagining to herself that she would
order something, a costume, as she would have called it, and

THE DROWNED MAN · 205

making up her mind how she would like it made and out of what material. He could see her making up her mind, and opening the door of the shop, and going inside with that timid air of consequence that she affected in public and that had nearly driven him mad with irritation. And he could see her approaching the tailor, and speaking in the accents of a lady who may or may not bestow her custom here, and discussing with the tailor the cut and style of this coat or skirt or whatever it was she imagined she was going to buy for herself. And he could see her, in all her seriousness, taking the card of samples from the tailor and bringing it home and sitting down by herself in the afternoon to dream over it, carrying it to the window so that she could look at the scraps of fabric in a better light, and only lifting her eyes from it to look at the flowers in her garden, and all the time dreaming, dreaming, dreaming, always dreaming, and what was it that she had dreamed about, all her life? She had never said. She had never even admitted how she dreamed her time away. If you had asked her what she was "thinking" about, she would have said, "Oh, nothing," and then quickly turned her hands to something to divert attention from herself. Or she might have replied, in answer to any question at all, "There is a bad scratch on the linoleum near the door there. I was wondering what I could do to cover it." She was all indirection.

The contents of the chocolate boxes revealed a mind given over entirely to trivialities and makeshift, always makeshift, making do, making last, putting to use somehow, wasting nothing except her time and her life and his time and his life. Even so, those times when he watched her secretly, he had had hopes that she possessed and would reveal to him the common secret that had been given to everybody except him. She had been weak, and it was simply impossible that she had lived along like that unless she was held by something, some truth, or some belief, some magic word, some comfort that she might have shared with him, if she had been willing to speak and able to speak. But the times grew rarer when he was able to watch her, because as he grew older he grew less and less able to bear the uneasiness that trembled all over her face when she felt his eyes on her. She would be sitting there knitting or sewing or mending or looking through one of the household magazines she loved, her face all intent on what was in her hands, and in the space of an instant she would become aware that he was looking at her, and the change in her expression would be terrible to see. Her face would become destroyed with shame and apprehension. And what it all amounted to, the beginning and the end of it, was that she was afraid of him. Once long ago he had been driven to challenge her. "Am I a monster or something?" he had shouted at her. "What's the matter with you? What's wrong with you? Why are you afraid to look at me? Am I a monster?" But she had trembled so violently that he had left her alone. She was afraid of questions. He left her alone. But it was no use going over all that again, no use thinking about it, better to put it out of his mind.

Still, he could not believe that even a human being as ineffectual as she had been could vanish from life without leaving any trace of herself at all. Any trace would be a sign that might guide him to the grief he wanted to suffer for her. But there was no sign.

He got up from the chair and went and stood by her bed. It was narrow. He stood there as he had stood on her last morning. Of course, looking at her that morning, he had had no idea how bad she was. He had gone into her room when she had not turned up as usual at nine o'clock sharp with his breakfast tray, which he liked to have in his own room, by himself. He went into her room in his dressing gown and slippers, and she was lying there in bed doing nothing, not even looking, although her eyes were open, and he was so surprised to see her, it had been so long since he had seen her lying in bed, that he said, "What are you doing in bed, Rose?" And she said, "Nothing." Her voice had been perfectly normal. He started to make some little joke that would lead him around to reminding her of the breakfast tray, when she said, in the same perfectly normal voice, "I have a terrible pain in my chest." And the minute she had said those words he felt the pain in his own chest, but with him it was not new but too familiar. He had often told her that pain was familiar to him, and here it was now again, his message from that treacherous old heart of his that was going to be the death of him someday, and he put his hand up to his own chest and said, "Will I call the doctor? He can have a look at me too as long as he's here." But Rose had not answered him. Instead, she began looking at him, and her eyes that he had always considered frightened and not direct, even furtive, preoccupied, and worried—those shaded green eyes suddenly seemed to belong to her, as though she had taken command of them for the first time and was asserting her right to see for herself, and to look, and not to look at just anything but to look at everything, and then to choose what she really wanted; not that she would not see all the rest, but that she would look at and possess what responded to her, and if what responded was joy she would look at joy, and if what responded was pain, then she would look at pain, and if what responded was cruelty she would look at cruelty, until cruelty, like pain and joy, turned again and turned again and turned at last to show her what she had chosen to see in the first place, a face that was disposed to smile on her, eyes that seemed to recognize her, a heart that was inclined to value her, and hands that knew her but that wanted her just the same, just as she was, whatever she was.

She had lain there looking at him like that, and still she had not answered his question, and he said again, still stroking his dressing gown over his heart to signify his pain, "Will I call the doctor then, or not? I think I'll call him anyway, for myself. Do you want me to call him?" And Rose had said, "Yes." "Yes," she said, and the one word came out quickly, like a sigh or a laugh, like a sound of recognition and acceptance and mockery. "Yes," she said, but only once, as though she was finally giving in to something and accepting something that she had not wanted to give in to or accept yet.

He had gone then and called the doctor, and he had sat down in the sitting room to wait, and he had wished there were someone to bring him a cup of tea, and of course, when the doctor arrived and went into the room, all there was left to say was that it was over for Rose.

Now, Mr. Derdon thought, there was no use staying in that room any longer. There was nothing to be found there. He opened the door and went out into the hall and he left the door open behind him. His sister and the woman who cleaned could go in there now and do what they liked in the way of tidying up and sorting out her clothes and the rest of it. He didn't care what they did. He went into the kitchen and looked around, and then he left the kitchen and stood in the hall a minute, and then he went into the sitting room and sat down in his chair by the fire. He was too tired to read, and too tired to think, but he could not stop himself thinking. It was all a mystery, where their life together had gone, or why they had come together in the first place. He remembered the night he asked her to marry him. They were standing together on a small stone bridge that overlooked a river outside the town where she lived. He had not intended to ask her that night—he had meant to keep her wondering a little longer, not to let her get too sure of herself—but all of a sudden he turned to her and said, "I thought we might get married." She continued looking down into the flowing water and she did not answer him. He said, "I was wondering if you had thought of me at all." Still she said nothing and had not raised her head. Then he said, "Rose, please, for God's sake, will you marry me?" And she raised her head and looked at him—her eyes were still clear in those days—and she said, "Yes," and that was all she said. "Yes," she had said, in a voice that was definite and that at the same time seemed to have been forced out of her, as though she had wanted to say yes, and expected to say yes, but at the same time would have liked to put off saying yes for just a little while longer, just a little while. Her face, turned up to him that night, had been the face of one who finds herself fallen into the middle of a deep lake, and who does not know how to swim, but would rather hope for help than scream for it. "It was careless of me to fall into this deep water," her face seemed to say, "and I am all to blame for not having learned to swim, but even though I was stupid, not learning to swim, and even though the water is deep, I do not want to drown." And he had put his arms around her and told her he would always take care of her. Sitting by the fire now, thinking of that night, he found he could see her face quite clearly, as she had looked then. He could see her face, and in her face all the promises that her face had shown him, the promises that had not been fulfilled. Her walk, her step, had been brave and free and definite, and it occurred to him now, as it had before, that he had fallen in love with her for the exact qualities that were not hers at all. It was not Rose's fault that he had been mistaken in her. She had shone at a distance, but close to she had ceased to shine. Still, she was gone, she had been good, and he wished he could miss her.

When his sister returned home and found the door of Rose's room standing open, she hurried into the sitting room and confronted Mr. Derdon where he sat before the fire.

"I see the door of the room is open," she said.

"I thought it had been closed long enough," he said. "We can't make a shrine out of her room."

"Did you go into the room?" she asked.

"Yes," he said. "I went in there."

He looked up at her.

"There's nothing in there," he said, and he put his hands up in front of his face and started to cry. His sister started to cry, too, and she went out of the room and was back in a minute with a cup of tea for him. He refused the tea, and when she suggested calling the doctor he refused to see the doctor. He would not take his hands from his face and he would not get up and go into his bedroom and lie down and he would not do anything except cry. The tears hurt him. They hurt his chest and his eyes and they seemed to be tracing sticky wooden lines all over his face and neck and they hurt his brain and made it ache. The tears did not run down his face and away. They poured all over him and stayed on him and encased him, and when he tried to stop crying, because he was afraid he might smother in them, imprisoned in them, they poured out all the more and there seemed to be no end to them. The tears had him in a straitjacket, and he could not speak. Now that he could not speak, he wished he could speak, because he longed now to tell his sister the truth and have the matter cleared up once and for all. The tears hurt him and covered him with a pain that seemed to grow more unbearable every minute, but what hurt most of all was his inability to tell his sister that he was not crying for Rose, because he really and truly felt no grief for Rose, but that he was crying for the lack of grief, because surely poor Rose had deserved more than a casual dismissal from life, and that most of all he was crying simply and solely because he was sad. He was sad and he was crying, and that is all there was to it. But he could not speak to tell his sister that, and she continued to watch him, helpless with tears herself and murmuring about how happy Rose was in Heaven, and he could not speak to her to tell her that it was all only a masquerade and that he was only a sham of a man, and after a long time, when he finally got command of himself, it no longer seemed worthwhile to tell her, and the way it worked out he never told her, and never told anybody.

The Twelfth
Wedding Anniversary

M RS. B AGOT had a very short straight scissors for cutting
all the flowers except the roses. She had a small knife for the
roses. The scissors and the knife were kept together at the end of
the narrow shelf over the kitchen sink, beside the door that led
out into the garden. The door was thick and heavy, of painted
green wood. It often got stuck in its frame, especially at the bottom, but today, in the pleasant June weather, it stood open, showing a small corner of cement yard enclosed by the sharp right angle of two gray walls.

Bennie, the rough-haired white terrier, lay outside the kitchen
doorway with his back firmly pressed against the step. Bennie
was getting old. His legs were stretched stiffly in front of him and
his eyes were closed, but when Mrs. Bagot stepped over him,
stepping from the red tiles of the kitchen floor to the gray cement, his stubby tail began to wag gently and his uppermost eye,
at least, opened and followed her until she reached the grass, a
few feet away. Then he scrambled up and ran after her. The grass
was a neat oblong surrounded on three sides by flower beds. Mrs.
Bagot moved very slowly along at the edge of the grass. She had
only the scissors with her. She wanted a few flowers to brighten
up Martin's room—a few pinks, a few daisies, a few marigolds

to fight with the pinks, no roses, no wallflowers, perhaps a sprig of forget-me-not if it looked strong enough not to droop. She kept her neck bent and looked at the flowers with severity and concern, frowning. She wore a navy blue skirt and a white blouse and an apron of faded blue cotton. She was very thin to be the mother of three children, one of them dead. Every time she paused, or bent to cut a flower, Bennie sat down at her feet.

Where the cement joined the grass, the garden wall that separated Mrs. Bagot from her neighbor dipped suddenly to a height of only five feet, and along this low part Mrs. Bagot had put up a green wooden trellis. She had extended the trellis to about a foot above the wall, and there she trained ivy and something she called "the vine," but for politeness' sake she left an open space where the red-haired lady next door, Mrs. Finn, could peer through and make remarks. Mrs. Finn had something to say about everything, and she never waited to hear whether you agreed with her or not. She was goodhearted, in her way, but she was too loud.

Beyond the wall Mrs. Bagot and Mrs. Finn shared, a row of identical walls stretched off into the distance. All the gardens were attached, like all the houses. A grove of trees, forty diminishing walls away, completed the view to the sky. It was a narrow side street, a dead end, in the suburbs of Dublin. There were shops around the corner, on the main road, but none on the street itself. Schoolteachers, shopkeepers, and minor civil servants lived on the street, and a policeman had recently moved into one of the houses with his family. Because it was a dead end the street was safe for the children to play in, although Mrs. Bagot was not yet willing to let her two daughters outside their front garden, they were so small. Lily was six and Margaret was four. They were in the front garden now, sitting on a rug she had laid down on the patch of grass there. She had looped a piece of chain around the spikes of the gate and the railing so that they could not unlatch the gate and walk out and away.

The end wall of Mrs. Bagot's garden was raised too far beyond its normal height by the back of the big garage that had been built along there to the length of five houses. Mrs. Bagot hated the garage when it was first put up, because it cut off her view of the open fields, but she had got used to the high end wall now and in any case the fields had been made into tennis courts. It was impossible not to admire the orderly appearance of the courts, and the neat way they were cut out, and the care that was given them to keep them exactly right, but she missed the peace and simplicity of the fields. There was a sense now of being shut in. To her right and left there were the neighbors' houses, and their gardens. At her end wall there were the garage and the courts, and in front of the house there was the street, with the row of houses opposite. Sometimes in the evening they heard music — dance music from the tennis clubhouse, which everybody called the Pavilion. There was no music at this hour in the afternoon, but she could hear voices from the courts, and the sound of the game.

Mrs. Finn next door had one boy, Willie, ten years old. She was very particular about him. She had had concrete poured down all over her garden, making a hard gray surface where grass and flowers might have grown, so that Willie could play out there without getting mud on his shoes. Willie never went out there anyway. He preferred study to play. He stayed in his room and read his books and did his homework. He always got good marks in school. Mrs. Bagot had heard a good deal about Willie's eternal industry, and she could have believed it all except that she had often seen him standing at the window of his room staring across at the tennis courts and down into her garden. She thought that perhaps the reason he shut himself up in his room so much was to escape from his talkative, bossy mother. He had the big back bedroom for his own, and his mother said he had his books and his desk and his writing materials and his maps all so neatly arranged that his room looked like a little monk's cell.

There was no sign of Willie at his window today, and Mrs. Bagot thought his absence made the day more quiet. When he was there, she felt his eyes looking down on her, or imagined she did. He looked down at her as well as at everything else, and sometimes she waved up at him, although he never waved back. Once when she waved he put his head on one side, looking at her, and she was so surprised that she dropped her hand and then put it up again to wave at him, but he turned and vanished behind the thin net curtain that veiled his window. A few feet to the right of Willie Finn's window was the window of the bedroom Lily and Margaret Bagot shared. Lily and Margaret slept together in a big brass bed. What sort of bed Willie Finn had Mrs. Bagot did not know, and she had no idea what his room really looked like. Mrs. Bagot had never been in the Finns' house, and Mrs. Finn had never been in hers. Mrs. Finn and Mrs. Bagot held their conversations across the garden wall and that was the extent of their friendship, except for a greeting when they met occasionally outside their houses or down on the main road that ran past the end of the street on its way in to the heart of Dublin.

They were four-room stone houses that jutted out at the back to give space for a kitchen, and above the kitchen a small extra room with a bathroom next to it. Mrs. Bagot's husband, Martin, slept alone in their small extra room, and she had been standing at the window there looking out at the garden when she had the idea of putting a few flowers in his room to brighten it up. Seen from his window, the garden was a deep oblong filled with shadows, light, flowers, grass, the ivy, the vine, and the laburnum tree that stood over to the right by the trellised wall. The sun made dark shadows but seemed to concentrate all its light in the half naked, yellow circle of grass where the big pot of geraniums had stood until recently, near the corner where she had made the rock garden. The grass at that corner was cut back into a crescent to conform with the shape of the rock garden and to give it more space. Mrs. Bagot had worked very hard to get the crescent right. The yellow circle where the pot of geraniums had stood was so close to the edge of the crescent that it seemed to be revolving on it—an exercise in geometry, or in balance.

A few feet below the window of Martin's room, Rupert, the big orange cat, lay sleeping on the slanted, corrugated-tin roof of the shed where she kept her gardening things, empty flowerpots, and the shears and the rake and so on, and the dustbin. Rupert lay on his side, sleeping peacefully. He looked very soft. His front right paw covered his eye and nose. His back paws were crossed and his tail lay neatly alongside them. The corrugated roof was uncomfortable to lie on, but Rupert was so fat that he flowed into it and may even have imagined he was lying on a flat surface. Mrs. Bagot let the curtain fall into place and turned back into the room, which seemed dull and small after the brightness and life and space outside. The room was so dull it reminded her of Mrs. Finn's gray concrete yard, and it was at that moment she decided to run down and find a few flowers to put on Martin's desk.

When Mrs. Bagot had collected the flowers she wanted, she took them into the kitchen and began to arrange them in a small green bowl. Then she changed her mind. She went up to the dining room, to the glass-fronted cabinet there, and got a cut-glass bowl, a treasure of hers. She took the bowl to the kitchen and started all over again, arranging the flowers quite differently. The glass bowl was particularly well suited to the flowers, and she carried it upstairs proudly and set it on the desk by Martin's window. He got home from work very late, long after they were all asleep, and he would be surprised when he put on the light and saw the flowers waiting for him there beside his books. She was used to his coming home late. He didn't want to disturb her or the children, and then he didn't want to be disturbed by them in the morning when they all got up. It had seemed natural enough at the start, when he first said he'd like to be able to lie down in the little room when he came in very late, and she remembered the pleasure it had given her to arrange the room for him and put some of his shirts and things in here to make it more convenient for him. Now he was beginning to collect his books in here. And yet she was certain that at the beginning he had not known any more than she had that he would prefer this room to the big front room where she slept, or that what he really wanted was to be alone. She was certain now that if she had raised some objection at the beginning he would have thought no more about the little room. Or if the little room had never existed, he would never have had the idea of shutting himself away from her. What an alarming truth it was that if they had had a smaller house they might have been happier. And yet, the house was quite small.

When she went down to get the flowers, Mrs. Bagot had left the window open, and now she wanted to shut it. Rupert was too lazy even to attempt the leap from the shed roof to this window-sill, but Minnie, the thin black cat, could do it easily, and Mrs. Bagot did not want to risk Martin's coming home tonight and finding Minnie on his bed. Mrs. Bagot did not know for sure whether it was the animals or Martin's hatred of the animals that caused a good many of the complications in the house. She gave in to him on most things, but she wouldn't give up the animals. The children would miss them terribly, and so would she. She would simply have to go on keeping the animals out of Martin's way, and keeping the children away from his door in the morning when he was sleeping. And in the end, all she was really doing was keeping herself out of his way. She couldn't bear to think about it, because what had started out as a simple arrangement for Martin's comfort had gone all out of hand, and now there seemed to be no way of putting an end to it. The situation in the house was unnatural, with no real consideration going for anybody. She found herself getting very nervous about the children when Martin was in the house, and when they were all together she couldn't stop herself from watching the children, as though Martin were there only to pass judgment on them. She was always keyed up, ready to defend them against him, and ready to take any blame on herself for what they did, and ready to snap at them if they showed signs of doing anything that might irritate him.

They were all much happier when he wasn't in the house, and that wasn't right. She wished she knew what to do. She kept remembering Martin the way he used to be, good-natured and always making jokes. Sometimes even now he was like that, but more often than not he seemed to be trying to control himself, as though seeing them all together and being shut up with them was more than he could bear. And on the weekend he went off for walks by himself, long walks that kept him out for hours. There was a lot of strain in the house. She felt constantly anxious, as though something terrible might happen, or as though she had done something terrible and might be found out. And all because of this little room. She was sure it was all because of this little room. It was bewildering to know that you started out helping somebody, agreeing with somebody about an ordinary private matter—a room to lie down in when he came in late—and you ended up building a wall that went on forever and that would never come to an end, because you made it stronger every day, without wanting to and without being able to stop yourself. She was constantly trying to keep her thoughts from going in this direction, because she became lost in their confusion, so that instead of reaching the words she wanted, and instead of being able to find the words that would explain everything she felt to Martin, she felt herself becoming incoherent, and she felt herself beginning to smother with anger, and then all she wanted was to run away and not make any explanations to anybody, and not listen to anybody's explanations. No, Martin was too clever for her. He was always able to shut her up. And yet it wasn't his words she minded so much as his silence. There were times when she thought Martin's clever silence might drive her out of her mind.

There was no use trying to think things out. Her ability to think was destroyed by strong feelings that stopped her easily because they were so much stronger than she was. Mrs. Bagot's feelings towered like ancestors, like reminders of a past that she could not remember but that she must remember if she was to get control of herself. These huge feelings, which appeared shrouded, triumphant, and ugly, were what she must face up to before she could face up to Martin. There was no use trying to speak to him if she was going to start gibbering. She did not know where to start.

She leaned across the desk and closed the window down to within an inch of the bottom, and then she stretched up and opened it an inch down from the top. Even Minnie could never squeeze herself through such narrow spaces. As she stepped back from the desk she looked at the flowers, and she had a moment of despair for herself because she had gone to the trouble to cut them and arrange them and put them there. But they were beautiful, and they improved the room. She would leave them. She put out her hand to touch the biggest marigold, and she imagined she saw her wedding ring reflected in the sharp edges of the cut glass. It was a plain gold ring, the only one she wore. Today was her wedding anniversary, the twelfth. She had been waiting for this day for weeks.

She had not known until this morning how much she had been counting on this day to somehow break the stillness between herself and Martin, but to break it in a natural way as any anniversary, Christmas or Easter or any feast day, will break into life and bring everything to a stop for the time of its celebration. She had been sure in the morning when she took in the breakfast tray that Martin would say something, but he was sitting on the straight chair beside his desk, reading the paper with such concentration that for a minute she thought he hadn't heard her come into the room. When she put the tray on the desk, he said, "Thanks, honey," and she hesitated, still thinking he would surely say something to her, but he said nothing. He had forgotten. And she walked out of the room and closed the door quietly behind her, not knowing if she was angry with him or with herself. She was shaking with anger. She was so upset that she had to hold onto the banister, going down the stairs.

As she looked at the flowers, she thought, I should have spoken up. It's too late now, but I should have spoken up.

There was nothing more for her to do in the room, but still she lingered, and when she finally went out she went very quickly, and closed the door behind her with relief, not realizing that once again she had substituted a prayer for a decision, and that the prayer was not even for certainty but only for an extension of hope.

She was beginning to wonder about the children. They were very quiet out there. She should have taken a look out at them on her way upstairs with the flowers. She wanted to hurry to them, but Bennie was in her way. She had to push him with her foot, because he had gone to sleep on the landing and the landing was very little bigger than he was. When Bennie was up, she hurried down the stairs and into the front sitting room and looked out through the bow window.

The children were all right. She had forgotten about them for a time, and so endangered them, but they were all right. She continued to look at them without speaking to them. They didn't see her. They didn't seem to have moved from the rug since she left them. They were undressing a small rag doll. When the doll was naked they would dress it again. They sat facing the railings so that they could see whatever went on out there on the quiet, narrow road. Far away at the head of the road some children were playing. Mrs. Bagot could hear their voices from the distance. She was pleased at the way her children looked in their short pink dresses. She was leaning across the table of ferns that crowded the window. One of the taller ferns tickled her chin and she stepped back. The ferns were in good condition. The flowered carpet she stood on was well brushed. It looked very nice under her feet. Her shoes were new. She was breaking them in, wearing them around the house, but she shouldn't have worn them into the garden. Fortunately it was a dry day. The shoes were as clean and shining as when she put them on in the early morning. Bennie was there at her feet, of course, looking up at her. Bennie, too, looked very well today. His nose glistened, and his tiny brown eyes were full of life. His coat was snow white and woolly. She had given him a bath yesterday. He looked like a new dog. He opened his mouth, to catch more of her attention, and Mrs. Bagot remarked that he had the strong white teeth of a very young dog.

Bennie was intelligent. He knew why she was at the window, looking out. She was looking at the children. Bennie gave the children patient devotion at all times, but even when he was asleep he watched Mrs. Bagot for every scrap of affection she had to spare for him. The children would grow up, but Bennie would remain the same—the same size, with the same expression. Years from now, Bennie would appear in Mrs. Bagot's memory exactly as he was this minute. There would never be another dog like him, she thought. He was a very unusual mongrel. Tears came into her eyes as she looked down at him, but she smiled. Then she began to hurry. She hurried across the room and along the hall, and she opened the front door in a hurry. She wanted to get to the children at once. She wanted to speak to Lily, to praise her for having been a good child, and she wanted to pick Margaret up. She wanted to snatch Margaret up off the rug. She couldn't wait to get her arms around Margaret, to pick her up and hurry with her into the house while she was still small and young enough to be carried close like a baby.

Martin Bagot knew perfectly well it was his wedding anniversary, and the thought of it embarrassed and irritated him. Things were going along well enough, and he wanted no sentimental reminders. He wanted no reminders of any kind. He wanted to be left alone. When Delia hesitated after putting down the breakfast tray, he thought he knew what she was going to say, and he felt panic-stricken. Then when she left the room without speaking he was glad—ashamed of himself but glad anyway.

Lately he had the feeling of putting things off. He only had that feeling when he was at home or when he was on his way home, and he would have liked to put off coming home indefinitely. He would have liked to have a rest from himself. When he was in the house he was hateful to himself. The feeling of being hateful to himself grew worse every day. He knew it grew worse, because at times he was able to remember his feelings of six months ago, and the feelings that had seemed so painful then were nothing compared with what he felt today.

He wanted time to think. He wanted a chance to separate the

hateful picture he had of himself from his real self, so that he could stand back and decide what to do. There was a phrase that kept coming into his mind that filled his eyes with tears of shame: "a wife and family around his neck." That was the phrase, and it kept torturing him. "He has a wife and family around his neck now." It was a common enough phrase, and he couldn't understand why it kept haunting him, because it didn't describe his case and didn't describe his attitude to Delia and the children. That was not how he felt about them. His life was not so small that it could be dismissed in a cheap phrase like that. His life had not come to that, because he was not the sort of man who could be reduced like that. He was not an ordinary man. He, Martin Bagot, might be described as having a wife and family "in the background" but never "around his neck." That's why he wanted time to think, so that he could free himself once and for all from the hateful self who behaved like a poor wretch with a wife and family around his neck. He detested the house when he felt like this, because he felt the house transformed him. When he was away from home he was all right, and able to convince himself that Delia was all right. After all, she had the house and the children, and what more did she want. She had a life of her own. That is what he told himself. But then the minute he got home he felt harassed and pursued, as though the house were full of people all waiting for him to say the one word that would make them all happy.

She seemed to have no resources of her own. When she looked at him, the expression in her eyes put him on edge. He was always afraid she would say something that would bring the house down around his ears before he had time to decide what he was going to do. And now, on the morning of their anniversary, when she left the room after that significant hesitation, he had a sudden feeling of fondness for her, and of gratitude that she had said nothing to make him uncomfortable. Perhaps, after all, she understood. He didn't pause to wonder about what she understood, what it might be, or anything like that. With her silence still glowing about him he felt relieved and happy, and he felt justified, as though he had held a course with difficulty and at great cost to himself, and had gained a victory that was well deserved, although he had never dared hope for it. He felt better than he had felt for a long time, and he ate his breakfast with appetite.

He was still lighthearted that night when he came home. He let himself into the dim hall and hurried up the stairs without touching the banister, which creaked loudly in the silence of the night as it had done on the first day he and Delia walked into the house, when it was empty and full of hollow sounds. He was tired, and anxious for sleep. He was so sleepy that his mind was already sinking comfortably into the quiet, dark hours that waited for him. His thoughts floated drowsily ahead of him, drawing him into the room where he would rest, but when he opened the door and switched on the light he became wide awake. He looked at Delia's flowers, and he felt betrayed and shocked, as though she had set a trap for him. Whether she spoke or not and whether she was in the room or not she still managed to reproach him. There was no escaping her. And there was no contending with her. There was no way to deal with her. He had come to believe that she really did not know why she did the things she did. He thought of her standing in the room, and putting the flowers on the desk, and looking around her and walking out again, closing the door behind her so that the animals could not get in and annoy him, and all the time imagining that she was being "good." She never understood why she did anything, and she never admitted even to herself why she did anything. She didn't know, that was the real trouble. Where the rest of the world was concerned, all she seemed able to understand was the necessity for obedience. She always did what she was told, and then she waited to be told what to do. She had no will of her own. Even to think about her irritated him. She was a great burden. It wasn't that she was lazy. She was always on the go, always doing something around the house or in the garden, and if she sat down even for a minute she had her knitting or her sewing or her mending in her hands. But the house and the garden and even the children were only a camouflage, and when all camouflage was gone and they were alone together Martin could not endure the sight of her passive face and passive hands, and her passive body. All he wanted was to get away from her. When they were alone together she seemed lifeless, and if there was a name for the expression on her face it was shame. Her shame irritated him, because he felt it was artificial, and he thought she could have chosen another expression if she had wanted to—a more cheerful expression.

Now here were these flowers, put here to remind him, *too late,* of the wedding anniversary. And their beauty and innocence also called his angry attention to all the care she gave him. The room he was standing in spoke only of love. And it was her care for him that was driving him to despair—the ceaseless care that he understood, and could not return, and did not want, and could not avoid. He picked up the bowl of flowers so carelessly that some of the water splashed out, and he had to put his other hand to it to steady it. He would take the flowers downstairs and leave them somewhere, and in the morning he would not speak to her about them. And if she mentioned them he would simply say that he did not like flowers in the room. He had no choice. He had to get the flowers out of the room. They made him feel sick. As he turned from the desk the flowers all slipped sideways, and when he tried to right them, the bowl fell from his hand to the floor and broke into large pieces, making very little noise on the rug. He bent and picked up two of the pieces and fitted them together, and then he bent again and collected all the pieces and the flowers and put the whole lot on top of the desk. Then he sat down on the chair and put his face in his hands. He wouldn't have had that happen for the world. He wouldn't for the world deprive her of anything, or hurt her. The poor thing, she had meant no harm. He could have left the flowers. It wouldn't have killed him, to have left them in the room for the one night.

He knew that what he had intended to do was far worse than what he had actually done. He was frightened now at the thought of what he had meant to do. He was more than frightened. He was terrified. What he had intended—to all intents and purposes he had done it. The breaking of the bowl had awakened him from a prophetic nightmare, and he knew that for the rest of his life he would be stealing down the stairs in this sleeping house with the bowl of flowers in his hands. Oh, yes, he would do it. Over and over again he would do it. He knew that. The temptation would always be too strong, the temptation or the provocation or whatever it was. His disappointment in her would always master him. He stood up. He was going to have to go downstairs now anyway to get a glass or something to put the flowers in, because without water they would be dead before morning.

Out on the landing he looked up the short flight of stairs, five steps, that led to the two bedrooms. The doors were closed, and behind them Delia and the children lay sleeping, dreaming, far away in themselves, not thinking of him. Their sound sleep turned the house into a refuge, and Martin thought, If this night could only last a week, or two weeks, I might have time to get everything straightened out in my head, and then I would know what to do... If they would only sleep happily like that for a long time, he might find himself able to think again. But the coming of day, a few hours off, rose up in his mind like a towering wave that was all the more awful because it would be succeeded after twenty-four hours by another wave, and then by another. There was no end to the days ahead, and the ones farthest off, years from now, were gathering power while he stood waiting on the landing. It was a merciless prospect. There was no way out of this house, which now seemed to contain all of his future as well as a good part of his past.

And Delia knew nothing of this. She could never understand his suffering, even if he tried to speak to her about it. He was a lonely man. He had always been a lonely figure, more or less, but he was lonelier now than he had ever been. He was proud of his loneliness, and he understood it. He knew it was what set him apart. He was a solitary man, not an ordinary family man, not at all a domesticated sort of person. He believed his loneliness came from a deep source in his nature, and that it made him more sensitive than other men, and at the same time stronger — a visionary of a kind. He was hard to live with, perhaps, but Delia's trouble was not that he was hard to live with but that she did not appreciate him. Delia had no understanding whatever of him, and never would have. He had given up hoping for under- standing from her. On she went, on and on, "improving" the house and working in the garden and saving for a new piece of linoleum or a new set of curtains, wasting her time for the most part, and yet at this moment, standing on the landing, Martin felt more like himself than he had for a long time, and he felt not only patience for Delia but pity, because she was so blind and so weak, living along like a little mole, with no idea of what life might be like beyond these four flimsy, commonplace walls.

He started down the stairs. Tomorrow morning was not going to be so difficult after all. When she came in with the tray he would show her the broken pieces and tell her he had only taken the flowers up to admire them when they fell from his hand. He would show her how he had saved the flowers for her in a glass of water, and he would promise to buy her a new cut-glass bowl. He would bring the new bowl home with him tomorrow night, and if it didn't cost too much he might even get her a smaller bowl of the same pattern as well. She liked things that matched. She wouldn't question him about what had really happened. She would be very pleased to hear he was going to go to the trouble of getting her a new bowl. She would tell him not to bother, but he would insist. She wouldn't mention the anniversary. There would be no awkwardness. Martin knew Delia was no more anxious for a scene than he was, and in any case they both had the children to consider.

The Carpet with the
Big Pink Roses on It

THE BEIGE CARPET with the big pink roses on it had been taken up off the floor of the front sitting room and dragged through the hall and through the kitchen and out into the garden and laid on the grass, where it was now being beaten and brushed by a small woman whose face wore an unbecoming expression of severity. That was Mrs. Bagot. She thought it was funny that her two children, who ought to be getting fresh air, were in the house, while the carpet was out in the garden getting fresh air. The carpet owed its airing to the long dry spell. There had been no rain for almost two weeks, and the grass was very dry. It needed water, and it would need it more than ever after having been crushed by the carpet. But because the grass was dry, the carpet was safe—there would be no damp spots on it. The carpet was safe, and the grass would be saved, although saved was too strong a word—there was no danger of the grass withering. The grass would be refreshed. And in the meantime the carpet looked beautiful, as though the true foundations of the garden had been uncovered and found to be full of pink roses.

Lily Bagot, who was seven, had the day off from school because one of the nuns had died. Lily wanted to come out into the garden and sit on the carpet and go away somewhere, but Mrs.

Bagot had said no. The carpet was in the garden to be beaten, not to be sat on or made into a playground. But to sit on the carpet and go away somewhere — Mrs. Bagot would have liked that, although she did not admit to Lily that she agreed with her. To get the two children and Bennie, the dog, settled on the carpet and then to vanish and go away somewhere, even if it was only for the afternoon, or part of the afternoon. To disappear for a little while would do no harm to anyone, and it would be very restful to get away from the house without having to go out by the front door and endure the ceremony of walking down the street, where everybody could see you.

But all this dreaming was not getting the work done. It was a shame for Lily to be shut up in the house, but it couldn't be helped. As soon as the carpet was back on its floor again, Lily could come out, and in the meantime she was well occupied up in the bedroom with Margaret. Margaret, who was five, was in bed with a cold. Margaret had an inclination to get lonely when she was left by herself, and when she was lonely she screamed. She would not have a chance to scream with Lily there chattering and bullying her.

At Mrs. Bagot's back the laburnum tree was in perfect bloom. You would think, to look at it, that yellow was the only true color. Something — an overweight bee or an interfering insect — caused one of the yellow blossoms to fall, and it floated uncertainly down to the carpet, where it rested on the worn green stem of one of the central roses. Mrs. Bagot put her hand out to save the little victim from the dust and from her own violence. But then, instead, she stood up to rest her back. Oh, it was very gratifying to feel the pull on her back as she straightened up. She was tired. She knew it by the way her back felt. She was not imagining things. She might imagine things, but her back would tell the truth, and what her back said was that she was tired. It was very gratifying to feel her muscles sorting themselves out and trying to find their own shapes again, and she paid attention to their complaints and pitied them vaguely. What she needed was a good stretch. She would like to stretch herself, stretch her arms up, stretch all the weariness out of her body, but she could hardly start stretching herself here in the garden. Mrs. Finn next door would think there was something the matter with her, and she would come to the wall that separated their gardens and start talking in a loud voice about illnesses and bad symptoms.

Mrs. Bagot knew that the thing to do was to go into the kitchen and sit down for a minute and then come straight back out and quickly finish with the carpet. But still she remained standing in the mild sunlight, with the laburnum making a dusky yellow shadow behind her head. The thought of stretching and resting had cleared her mind of all but the one word, sleep. Sleep—her mind was full of it, it was evaporating inside her head, clouding her thoughts, and she wondered how the one word, sleep, could be so distinct and at the same time so indistinct, like writing in the sky.

She went toward the house, only a few steps away. The cement patch between the grass and the stone wall of the house looked very swept and clean—she had done that herself, dragging the carpet across it. She hurried through the kitchen and straight through the hall. The children had been quiet too long. She was starting upstairs when she heard a sound from the front sitting room—Lily, of course, who would not do as she was told. Lily was lying face down on the bare wooden floor of the front sitting room. She was trying to see between the boards, focusing first with one eye and then with the other, and also trying to focus with her hands, which were bent into blinkers at each side of her face. She looked up at her mother, and her eyes showed that she was ready for the battle.

"Lily, I thought I left you upstairs," Mrs. Bagot said, and then she stopped. After all, it was not often Lily got a day off from school. "Never mind, Lily. I'm not angry, I'm not anything. It's only that I don't like you to be in here by yourself. And why are you trying to see through the floor?"

It was a very short story, quickly told. Lily had been given two pennies, which had been left in safety far out of her reach, on the mantelpiece in the back sitting room, but she had managed to reach them, and she had taken one of them and fitted it between the boards, and it had slipped, and was gone. And all she had been trying to do, all she wanted, was to see whether the penny would fit between the boards.

"I suppose it's my fault," Mrs. Bagot said. "I should have let you keep one of them in your hand. Then you wouldn't have been so curious. Well, you'll never see that penny again. It's gone for good. Never mind. It's happened before, and it will happen again. We were hardly in this house when I lost a sixpence. It fell out of my hand and rolled over there. I nearly had it and then it was gone, down under the house. The foundations of this house must be made of money."

"When will we get it?" Lily asked.

"Oh, how do I know? They would have to tear up the floor-boards. You ask too many questions. Now, are you going to stay here, or will you come upstairs with me?"

"You ask too many questions," Lily said. "I'll come upstairs with you."

The window of the back bedroom, where Margaret was, looked out over the garden, and beyond the garden at the courts of the tennis club, and beyond that, but too far away to see, lay the Dublin hills. The carpet did a lot for the garden, Mrs. Bagot thought. The carpet and the laburnum together made a picture. She was sleepy again. It was really very silly. They might not have another day like this for a long time, and she could think only of wasting it in sleep. The carpet looked so inviting down there on the grass. It would be just right, to lie there in the open air and dream, not sleep. She envied people who felt free to do as they liked, without feeling self-conscious or ashamed of themselves. There were a lot of women who would lie down on that grass, or on that carpet, and never think the less of themselves, and never wonder what other people thought of them. Mrs. Bagot wished she could be like that. They were lucky, those people.

She pulled down the blind, and the bright room became dim —a dim blue—and then she went back to the big brass bed that Lily and Margaret shared. The bed was covered by a red-white-and-pink patchwork quilt that hung down to the floor on each side. Margaret was sitting up, propped by pillows, and, alongside her, two cats, one orange and one black, had entrenched themselves in comfort. At her feet, the rough-haired white terrier, Bennie, lay on his side. Bennie prudently kept his arm over his eye, but he wagged his tail hopefully. The cats, open-eyed and wary, did not move. The big orange one, Rupert, purred loudly and methodically. It was his only skill, and he was proud of it. He never stopped purring. He purred at friends, strangers, and furniture. Earlier in the day, he had draped himself, purring, along one of the thin branches of the laburnum and he had continued to purr even when he lost his balance and was left hanging, like a fool, by his front paws, while he wondered whether to drop to the grass or try to scramble back to his perch. He purred for his life, and nobody knew whether he was truly stupid or truly amiable. Margaret had her hand on his ribs, where she could feel the purr working. Her other hand was on Minnie's thin black ribs. Minnie's purr was muted and premeditated. She only purred when she was happy. She was purring now, but only Margaret could be sure of that.

"Let them stay," Margaret said to her mother. "They are very good today."

"They can stay," Mrs. Bagot said. "If I put them downstairs, they'll go out and tear the roses off the carpet. And Bennie can stay, too. If he sees the carpet out there, he'll try to drag it back into the house. But you have to lie down and sleep now. You have to shut your eyes."

Lily laughed. "It would be worth anything to see Bennie bringing the carpet into the house," she said.

Margaret slept on the left-hand side of the bed. Lily's place was on the right, nearest the door. When Mrs. Bagot slipped the extra pillow from behind Margaret, she bent and kissed her, and then she kissed her again. Margaret stared up at her as though they were saying goodbye to each other. Margaret always fought sleep at the last minute, and she fought it in whispers, whispering her fears and longings, as though she hoped sleep would hear her and spare her because she was so interesting to listen to. She whispered now, and her voice barely rose above Rupert's industrious purr. "Stay with me," she whispered. "Don't go away. Stay here with me."

Mrs. Bagot smiled at her, and then she looked up and smiled at Lily.

"Oh, she is full of tricks," Lily said. "Full of tricks, that's what she is."

"Margaret, I can't stay," Mrs. Bagot said. "I've got to get back down and finish the carpet." She walked around the bed and stood at the other side, near the open door. "Now, you will go to sleep," she said, "won't you?"

"Stay with me," Margaret whispered, "just for a minute, only a minute. Stay with me. Don't go away. Just a minute, stay with me. Then I'll go to sleep."

"Oh, Margaret," Mrs. Bagot said, and she leaned across the bed and smoothed the hair back from Margaret's forehead. Then she began to yawn, and she turned from the child and buried her face in Lily's pillow until the yawn was finished. The pillow was soft. She pressed her face into it and drew her legs up on the bed and lay there. "Oh, this is very nice," she said, and she pushed off her shoes, first one and then the other. "Lift my shoes down onto the floor, Lily," she said, "and I'll just lie here for a minute, just until Margaret goes to sleep."

Lily took the shoes and put them on the floor, and then she stood looking down at her mother. "You're very flat in the bed," she said.

"Don't let me fall asleep, Lily," Mrs. Bagot said.

"Mother, could I ask you one more question?"

"What is it, Lily?"

"If the house blew up, then would we get the money?"

"What money? What are you talking about?"

"The money that's under the floor downstairs."

"The house isn't going to blow up. You shouldn't think things like that."

"But it might blow up, mightn't it? It might blow up."

"It might, but it can't. Will you stop talking and let Margaret go to sleep."

"Why can't it?"

"It — the house can't blow up because we are living in it. Now, stop it, Lily. I want Margaret to sleep."

"I have another question for when we go downstairs," Lily said.

Mrs. Bagot felt her arms and legs sinking down into the bed, as though they would hold her there, sinking slowly into soft ease, and then she felt her back sinking down, and then her shoulders began to rest, but she could not settle her head. Her hair was in the way, and she lifted her arm from across her eyes and pulled out the pins and pulled her hair over onto the pillow where it loosened out, tumbling sleepily to its full length.

"Oh, I hope nobody comes to the door," Mrs. Bagot said. "They will think I am a madwoman, with my hair down in the middle of the day."

"Maybe nobody will come," Lily said.

"Let me know when Margaret drops off," Mrs. Bagot said, "and then I'll get up. Don't let me go to sleep now, Lily."

Margaret had already dropped off. Margaret was fast asleep, and then Mrs. Bagot slept suddenly. Before she knew it, she was asleep. Margaret slept with her right arm lying alongside her orange favorite. Bennie slept. Minnie, sensing something unusual, crept across the bed and settled blissfully into Mrs. Bagot's long brown hair, the best nest she would ever know. They all slept safely. There wasn't a sound in the house. Nobody came to the door. Nobody saw them. There on the bed they might all have been invisible, or enchanted, or, as they were for that time, forgotten.

Down in the garden Lily sat on the carpet and traveled without delay to Paris. From Paris she went to Spain, where she hesitated, floating high in the air, trying to remember the name of Spain's capital city. The effort of remembering caused her to lie down, and as she lay there with her eyes closed the carpet turned around and sailed home, back to the garden, where it lay flat on the grass, looking again exactly as it had looked when the thought of sleep drew Mrs. Bagot gently into the house that might blow up but that would never blow up. Never, never. That house never blew up.

The Shadow of
Kindness

Mrs. Bagot missed the children. They had been gone twenty-four hours. It was exactly that length of time since she had put them on the train, in the care of the guard, and sent them off to her sister and brother in the country, where they were going to spend a month. She wished the month were over. She didn't know what to do with herself when they were away. Without them the house had neither substance nor meaning. The house was lonely, that is what it amounted to, and Mrs. Bagot felt the house was making her lonely. But the house was going to look very nice when the children came back. She was already planning what she would do to welcome them. She was going to put flowers all around — she would cut all the flowers in the garden. And she was going to bake a cake and put both their names on it in icing: "Lily," "Margaret." And then there were other things she was going to do, but these preparations, which she had already memorized and timed to the minute, still left her with nothing to do for a month but look *forward,* and she knew a grown woman should have more life of her own. Even if she had children, a woman should have a life of her own that would stand up when the children were out of the house for any length of time. She knew that. It was not right to let yourself get so lost in your children that you could find no trace of yourself when they were gone. What would she do when they grew up? Of course, it was silly to think of it; not silly — morbid. She was letting her imagination run away with her. She would make herself a cup of tea and cheer herself up. The tea would cheer her up. Still, she did not move. She continued to stand by the big window looking out into her garden.

The big window was the window in the dining room. It was very big, a sash window, and almost square, and at the moment it was very bare, because she had taken the curtains down for washing. The garden was almost out of sight behind the rain. The yellow rosebush seemed far away, a steady blur of brightness, like a street lamp in the fog. And the other flowers, not as intimately massed around one center as the roses were, and not so strongly defined, seemed to be moving about by themselves, swimming slowly about in the wet gray air and arranging themselves in different patterns from the ones she had imagined and seen come to life as the summer wore on. This was the heaviest rain they had had for a long time and she was glad to see it — it was needed. And she was glad it had come today and not yesterday. The children would not have liked traveling in the rain. They had been looking forward to the view from the train windows. And then there would have been all that worry about damp feet and damp heads. Yes, it was fortunate the rain had held off until now.

Earlier in the day, in the morning, when she saw the rain getting heavier, she went out and cut all the full-blown and half-blown roses. She cut the white, the pink, and the red — all but the yellow. The yellow rosebush had been in the garden when she and Martin moved here, and she had a particular affection for it, because she felt it had encouraged her to set to work and make the lovely garden she had out there now. She seldom cut a yellow rose, and this year, as they bloomed, the roses on that bush had arranged themselves so marvelously that it was as though a great artist had made them grow in that certain way to match a picture he had in his mind. And so this morning she had left all the yellow roses to survive or fall together. As well as she could see, they were holding up, in a round shape that tapered slightly toward the top—a dense, delicate ball of yellow that was like a Christmas tree ornament or an Oriental roof. It was accidental, that grouping. It might never occur again. She was glad she had not disturbed them.

The white roses, and all the pinks and all the reds, made quite a big bunch. She had put them around in this room and in the front room and in the hall, and then, foolishly, she had put a small bunch in the children's room to make it seem less deserted. When she wrote to Lily and Margaret tonight she would tell them there were flowers waiting for them in their room, beside their window, on the little table that was all marked and stained with chalk and ink and putty and plasticine. The window in the children's room corresponded with this window where she stood —they had the back bedroom. The paper on the walls of that room was cream-colored and covered with miniature garlands of small blue flowers. The flowers were faded and as indistinct as the real flowers in her garden were today in the rain. It was old wallpaper and, like the yellow rosebush, it had been here when she and Martin moved in, years ago.

All the windows in the house were closed tight against the rain, but the damp had crept in anyway. Mrs. Bagot turned from the window. Her feet and legs were cold—that was how people got rheumatism. On a day as bad as this, if the children were here, she would have lighted the fire hours ago, even if it was an extravagance. There was no use risking colds and coughs. She took the box of matches from the mantelpiece and knelt down on the hearthrug. It was between two and three weeks since they had needed a fire, and the coals were nearly hidden under a litter of tiny balls of paper, thrown in there, she knew, by Lily. She hated to burn them up. She took one ball and smoothed it out and, as she expected, it was a code. Lily was always hoping to discover a code that would be easy to write and impossible for anybody except herself to understand. Mrs. Bagot thought of taking the others out, just to look at them, but then she thought better of it. If she continued to think like this about the children she would bring bad luck on them. She struck the match impatiently and touched it here and there to the newspaper at the bottom of the grate. There were tears in her eyes. She wanted the children to enjoy themselves, but she wondered if they thought of her at all when they were away from her. They would be falling in love with their aunt and with their uncles. They would come back at the end of the month pining for the farm and the animals and all the freedom they had down there. Well, it couldn't be helped. Maybe it was all for the best.

She started to stand up, when a warm body touched her leg. It was Bennie, the white terrier, who had come out of his sleep on the rug beside the folding doors to hear a match being struck and a fire beginning. He looked up at her. He had small brown poverty-stricken eyes and limp ears, but the line from his black nose to his chin was fine and square, and she often told the children Bennie had very good blood in him. She put her arm around him and felt how close his bones were to the flat white coils of his fur. She wondered how old he was. You never could tell with a stray, and poor Bennie had been on his last legs when she found him on the street one morning on her way from Mass and took him home. She might have been able to walk past him, but some young boys were tormenting him, and she knew she would never be able to look herself in the face again if she abandoned him to their cruelty. He had been in the house five years now. Sometimes he seemed like a puppy and sometimes he was a very thoughtful, grown-up dog. He was very faithful. He had never once snapped at the children. He had never even snapped at the cats, although Rupert, the big orange one, was very greedy and often put his face into Bennie's food dish in the hope of finding a morsel there he might fancy for himself. "Good Bennie," Mrs. Bagot said, and pressed him closer to her side, and he stretched his neck up to her, and the storm of devotion in his eyes could never have found expression in speech. His silence burned with devotion, and so it would as long as he was alive.

She rubbed his shoulder and smiled at him and then she stood up. She moved easily, rising from her knees to stand with no effort, but when she was on her feet she felt dizzy. It was her own fault. She had not bothered to eat anything at breakfast time. She had had a cup of tea when she got up, and then, in the middle of the day, more tea, and that was all. She had felt angry with the children at breakfast time, because while she could feel angry she believed she did not miss them, and then, in the middle of the day, when her false anger, her pretense, had faded, she felt shame at the picture of herself going to trouble over food that the children would not be there to share.

Now then, she was going to have to stop thinking like that. She should know better by this time than to let herself fall into this train of thought. In the beginning, at the beginning of their marriage, Martin had warned her often enough against thinking, because thinking led to self-pity and there was enough of that in this world. What he had really told her was that she must stop forcing herself, stop *trying* to think, because her intelligence was not high and she must not put too much of a strain on it or she would make herself unhappy. "I don't want you to make yourself unhappy," he had said, and she remembered the nice tone his

would have to give it to Martin — he would be sure to ask if there was a letter from Lily, so that he could take it along to the office to show his friends what a clever daughter he had. And then ten chances to one she would never see it again. It would stay there in the office and get mixed up in the papers on his desk and maybe be thrown out, unless someone took it. She would ask Martin to bring it back, and he would promise to bring it to her, but he would forget, and she might ask him the second time but not the third time — it was too much like nagging. And all this brought home to her how little she meant to anyone in the world except the children. And Bennie and the cats. Martin objected to the animals, and he had told her to get rid of them, but she refused to get rid of them. She had stood up to him there. Anyway, he hardly saw them. He woke up late, naturally enough, considering how late at night he had to work, and she brought him up his breakfast on a tray, and then he dressed himself and went off and came back in the early hours of the morning. He did not like her to wait up for him, and besides she couldn't and still get enough sleep to be able to give proper attention to the children. But she would always wait up for him if she thought that was what he wanted. But the times she had been up, when he got home at eleven o'clock, for example, instead of at one or two — at those times he had come in and hung his coat and hat in the hall and gone straight upstairs to his room without even saying good night to her. There were times when it seemed that he could not control his dislike of her, and yet she knew very well he did not dislike her. One night, not so very long ago, he had come into the front bedroom where she slept and waked her and asked her to heat up some milk for him, and when she brought him the milk he thanked her and told her he did not know what he would do without her. She had gone back to her own bed and lain there in an ecstasy of gratitude — a gratitude she did not understand and did not question. She knew positively that everything was going to be all right, and she was so sure of that—that everything was going to be all right—that she did not even wonder what she meant, or who or what it was she was thinking about. She only knew that her memory had lighted up and that all she remembered were times so happy that they must surely cast their radiance far into the future, over years so far ahead that she could not even dream of them.

Once, shortly after she and Martin were married, shortly after they moved to Dublin, she had wanted to get material for curtains for the back bedroom, which was still unfurnished then, because there were only the two of them in the house. Martin said he had heard of a good shop, and he volunteered to go with her, and he said, she remembered very well, that he would take her there and see that she had someone to wait on her but that then he would have to leave her, because he had an appointment. But when they got to the shop, he didn't leave her. He stayed and watched while the man behind the counter showed her what they had in the way of cretonne. The man behind the counter gave Mrs. Bagot a chair, but Martin refused to sit down. "I feel like a bull in a china shop," he said, "but at least I needn't be a sitting bull." They all laughed, and a woman standing nearby waiting for her parcel to be wrapped laughed and smiled at Mrs. Bagot, and the man behind the counter winked at Mrs. Bagot and said, "That is a witty man you have there, Mrs...." And she had said "Mrs. Bagot," in such a high voice that Martin burst out laughing and said to the man behind the counter, "She's still surprised at her new name." And then Martin said, "We're only four months married," and he spoke so proudly that even she could see his pride, and she couldn't take her eyes off him—she looked at him, she gave him the same devoted, desperate look that Bennie always gave to her.

Yes, that day had been wonderful. After they left the shop the day did not end; they did not part. She was certain when they walked out onto the street that he would hurry away, and she was ready for that—to turn and go her own way home alone—but Martin said, looking up and down the crowded, busy street, "I could stand a cup of tea. What about you, Delia? After all this exertion you'd like a nice cup of tea, wouldn't you?" He was grinning at her, and then he said in a false, funny voice, "A nice cup of tea for the lady of the house?" Two or three times over the years, she had gone back to that tearoom, but the tables were always full, and so she had never gone in there again. The tea had been very good, and the cakes, and the girl had given them special attention, just as the man in the shop had done. And after tea they had gone for a walk, strolling around, looking in the shop windows, and when she reminded him of his appointment he said, "They can wait, I can see them anytime. But when will I get another chance to show you off like this?" It was strange that at the start of that long-ago day, when she got out of bed in the morning, she had not had a hint that she was seeing the beginning of a day that would never cease to unfold in her memory and that would always be waiting there, undimmed and undamaged, providing her with a place where her mind could rest and find courage.

Martin had given up sleeping in the big front bedroom, because she and the children got up early and disturbed him, moving about, and now he slept in the small room next to the bathroom, on the landing halfway up the stairs. Lately she had been hoping he would say something to her that would give them both a chance of a talk, but he had said nothing. She knew things were not as they should be between them, but while the children were at home she did not want to say anything for fear of a row that might frighten the children, and now that the children were away she found she was afraid to speak for fear of disturbing a silence that might, if broken, reveal any number of things that she did not want to see and that she was sure he did not want to see. Or perhaps he saw them and kept silent out of charity, or out of despair, or out of a hope that they would vanish if no one paid any attention to them.

But here she was now, doing herself no good—it was only storing up trouble to let herself get weak with hunger simply because she longed for a *real* reason to feel sorry for herself. She would make the toast and have tea with it. But before she did anything she would open the folding doors into the front sitting room and let some of the warmth of the fire steal in there. The room where she stood was less a dining room than a back sitting room, because she and the children spent their time there when they weren't in the kitchen. The leaves of the big table had been let down, and it stood flat against the wall, with a bowl of her roses on it from this morning. The floor was covered in linoleum, but the rug Bennie had been sleeping on before he crossed to lie in the warmth of the fire fitted very neatly under the folding doors, very much as though it had been specially made, and it gave the room a nice, well-furnished appearance. She opened the doors back carefully. The front room was dim. The curtains were still up on the windows in this room—long French windows that curved out into a bow—and the gray houses across the street were dark in the falling rain. Her own house, she supposed, looked dark to her neighbors over there. She saw that some of them had their lights on, although it was only five o'clock. There was an upright piano against the wall opposite the fireplace in this room. She had put a bowl of pink roses on the piano earlier in the day, and a small vase of them on the mantelpiece. She thought that what light there was in the room came from the roses and from the shining wood of the piano. Also, the fragrance of the roses was stronger in this room than in the back room where she had been standing for so long. Standing doing nothing, she thought. But instead of reproaching herself she went to the windows and looked out into the street, which was narrow and had two facing rows of houses, all identical with her own. She liked to watch people going up and down the street, and she sometimes came in here to attend to her collection of ferns so that she could watch what was going on outside without seeming curious.

The ferns, all of them tall and feathery and all in the same bright shade of green — bright moss green, grass green — were arranged on a table that stood inside the bow window. She had to leave a space between the two middle pots so that Minnie, the small black cat, could sleep there. Minnie's favorite spot was in the center of the table between the ferns, and if a suitable place was not left for her she would make one, squeezing herself in until the pots rattled dangerously. Minnie was there now, half asleep, and Mrs. Bagot stroked her and watched the street. The street was safe for the children to play in. It was a dead end, and there were no garages, and in any case very few of the people had cars. The milkman came early in the morning and the bread man at eleven, but otherwise Mrs. Bagot hardly ever had to open the front door, except for the children when they came home from school at half past three. At noon every day she walked to the school with the children's lunch.

The school was not far away — a short walk along the main road and then a longer walk down a side street that was wider and busier than this one, with much bigger houses, except at the end, where the houses were suddenly very small and close together. The school was across from the small houses, behind a high cement wall with a narrow iron gate in its center. The gate opened into a cement yard, where the children played at lunchtime, and the school building, gray and high, with a few large, oblong, institutional windows, fitted and matched the yard exactly, as though a child had drawn and colored it. The yard was completely closed in by high cement walls, and to the right, looking from the gate, there was a very long, low wooden bench where the smallest children sometimes sat in a row and did their lessons. There were children in the school who were no more than three years old, and some of them, Mrs. Bagot suspected, were only two. But they were able to walk—that was all the school required—and Mrs. Bagot would not have admitted to anyone that one of her reasons for going to the trouble of bringing Lily and Margaret their lunch every day was so that she could see the little boys and girls who were just able to walk. The little ones were let out to play before the rest of the school, and by the time she got to the gate they were generally running around, stumbling like moths from one side of the yard to the other and beating at the air with their hands, and looking up at their teacher as though they imagined she produced the light by which they played. There was no one to question Mrs. Bagot's right to stand and watch the children. If anyone questioned her she would simply say she had to bring Lily and Margaret their lunch. Well, there would be no bringing lunch for a while. It would be more than five weeks before they had to go back to school.

Mrs. Bagot turned from the street and from Minnie and from the ferns, and was surprised to see how like a mirror the big naked window in the back room was, but like a mirror that you could see through, a mirror that went both ways and showed both sides. It was like a painting. She saw the wet, reluctant daylight air out there in the garden, and the rain was falling so strong and straight that she was sure she could make out every separate driving line of it. Beyond and through the rain, as in a dream, there were the indistinct colors of the garden, and then, coming back through the glass to herself, she could see herself, with the folded-back door to her right, and behind her the wavering green heads of her ferns, and behind the ferns the starched white net curtains making a ghostly and final wall. She knew that what she saw was beautiful, and at the same moment she knew that she did not want to look anymore at the window or the garden or the ferns or anything. She was tired. She hurried out of the room and down to the kitchen, where she filled the kettle and put it on to boil for her tea. While the kettle was boiling she would wash her face and hands and straighten her hair. The cold water on her face would wake her up—she felt that she had been sleeping for hours, and not sleeping happily. She hurried upstairs. The narrow stairs from the hall had a wine-red runner that was held in place at each step by thin brass rods that she pulled out and polished every Monday. The rods shone more steadily in this evening's dimness than they ever shone on a sunny day, and the wooden banister glowed with the same warm and reverberating depth, as though the dying light called up sources of strength that went unnoticed in the self-sufficient daytime. The house was full of secret light that she never noticed when the children were at home.

After washing her hands, she hurried up the five top steps to the upper landing, where there were two doors opening into the front bedroom and into the smaller back room where the children slept. Both doors were closed, and instead of going into her own room, where her brush and comb were, she turned into the children's room and went across and looked into the small framed mirror that stood on their chest of drawers. She began to smooth her hair with her hands, but her reflection was so lost and pale that it frightened her, and she put on the light to reassure herself. She bent forward to the mirror again and carefully pushed a loose strand into the neat bun at the back of her head, but as she moved, something moved with her, something much larger and even more silent than she was. Her shadow was on the wall to the side of the mirror and it was following her, and now it was bending with her, bending toward her, and she stared at it. The light in her own bedroom gave her no shadow that she had ever noticed. She paused and the shadow paused also, waiting for her as she waited for it. She looked closer and at that moment, as it bent its head, she knew what she was looking at. That was her mother's shadow there on the wall. There was no mistake about it; that was her mother.

Mrs. Bagot could not understand it. She and her mother had not looked alike. But there it was, her mother's shadow as she had often seen it — the thin line of the cheek, the indentation at the eye, the high curve of the forehead, and, above all, the little straying hairs that always escaped the brush to wave independently at the sides of her mother's forehead and at the back of her neck. The little stray hairs were never more than the length of a straight pin, and there were only a few of them. Mrs. Bagot thought she recognized every one of them, there in the shadow. She thought that if she put out her hand she would surely feel that hair again. She put out the light and then put it on again at once. There again was the neat, bent head, with the thin hairs making a frail pattern on the wall, a frail pattern that was more real at this moment than the pattern on the wallpaper, as the penciled rain in a Chinese watercolor is more real than the strong and enduring landscape that lies beyond. It is my mother, Mrs. Bagot thought; there she is, how patient she is.

She sighed once and smiled at herself without looking at herself, and then she put out the light and went down to the kitchen, where she found the kettle boiling furiously.

The tea was soon made and so was the toast. She took down Martin's breakfast tray and set it carefully for herself, even putting a clean white cloth on it, but when everything was arranged, instead of carrying the tray up to the fireside, she pulled a chair up to the kitchen table and sat down and poured herself a cup of tea. She was too hungry and too thirsty. She could stand no further delay; she must have something to eat at once. She thought about the shadow that had been waiting for her up there in the children's room all these years and that had remained hidden from her until tonight. She had never seen it in any other room in the house and she did not think it was to be seen in any other room of the house.

She looked around her, but the shadow was not in the kitchen. Bennie was sitting on the tiled floor at her feet, and she broke off a piece of toast and gave it to him. Rupert and Minnie had suddenly appeared and were sitting thoughtfully beside their milk saucer near the door that led out into the garden. She got up and poured milk for the cats, and then she went back to the table and poured herself another cup of tea. She decided to make more toast, and to eat some of the chicken that was left over from the special dinner she had made for the children yesterday. She felt all different—not sad, not tired anymore. She felt very hopeful all of a sudden. It was wonderful how seeing that shadow had raised her spirits. It was wonderful knowing that shadow was upstairs and that it would never go away. It was almost like having somebody in the house.

The Sofa

T HE NEW SOFA was to be delivered today, Tuesday, but "sometime during the day"; no set time had been given by the people in the shop. Mrs. Bagot had been so pleased when they told her she would have the sofa for sure on Tuesday that she hadn't thought to ask if she should expect it in the morning or in the afternoon. She should have asked them to set a definite time, or at least to say whether the sofa would arrive in the early part of the day or later. As it was, she had spent the whole morning in waiting and it was now two o'clock in the afternoon. She had wasted the better part of the day wandering about the house and not doing much of anything, and yet you could hardly say wasted when she had really been waiting, and waiting for something worthwhile. The downstairs part of the house was going to be completely furnished at last. The sofa was going to make all the difference.

She was sitting on a low chair beside the fireplace in the back sitting room, where she and the children spent most of their time. The fire was laid — paper, sticks of wood, lumps of coal, all in neat bumpy layers, ready to blaze up and spit sparks at the touch of a match. The small hearth, of pale greenish tiles, was washed and shone with a dull, clean glow. The hearthrug, thin and fringed, was woven in a dark Oriental pattern of red and green lines, circles, curlicues, and unfinished curves, and all it had in common with the linoleum that covered the floor was that both rug and linoleum were well taken care of. Rug and linoleum looked their best. The rug had been brushed until its worn spots looked hardly less rich than the rich design, and the diligently domestic red-green-and-brown fleur-de-lis pattern in the linoleum was clear as glass. And what it said was "I am a plain, inoffensive piece of linoleum, ready to last for years, even in a house where there are children." To the right of the fireplace, shelves fitted into a shallow alcove held Mr. Bagot's library, which included books by Sidney and Beatrice Webb, Darwin, Shakespeare, Turgenev, Edgar Wallace, Wolfe Tone, W. B. Yeats, James Joyce, Chekhov, Ibsen, Molière, Edgar Allan Poe, and others. The books were old for the most part, and well worn, but they were tidy, and at the moment they were nearly hidden from sight by the folding doors that opened the front sitting room and the back sitting room into one quite large room.

Mrs. Bagot had opened the doors back as far as they would go so that she could get an idea of how the front room was when it was empty, and it was nearly empty now, with the old piano gone that had taken up so much space and the sofa still to come. The sofa would be wonderful in that room. She had made a good choice. The carpet on the floor in there was beige with big pink roses on it, and the sofa was fat and beige and had room enough for almost four people. The sofa would face the fireplace. The fireplace in there was the same as the one in the back room except that the tiles in the hearth were golden brown and the brass bars in the fender were flat instead of being round and had a panel of filigreed brass in between, so that the panel of brass ran all around the hearth, just as the Greek frieze ran all around the top of the wallpaper, just under the ceiling. It was clever of whoever

had decorated the house to put that frieze around to break the
hard line that might have showed where the painted ceiling
joined the papered wall. The wallpaper was no longer in the best
of shape. After all, it had been on the walls at least fifteen years,
maybe longer. But even so, the room looked very nice. And what
made Mrs. Bagot wonder was that the room looked quite furnished enough with just the carpet on the floor and the table of
ferns there filling the bow window that looked out onto her small
front garden and beyond the garden to the narrow Dublin street.
The room looked very carefree with no furniture in it. The children had walked around in there this morning as though they
had found themselves in a new house. They said they never saw a
room with no furniture in it before. They walked on all the part
of the carpet that had been hidden by the piano, and on all the
part that would be hidden by the new sofa.

There were only two children — Lily, who was nine, and Margaret, who was seven. When they grew tired of walking around
on the carpet they sat on it, and then they lay down. They were
dressed for school and they had very little time to spare, but Mrs.
Bagot could not bear to hurry them. By the time they came home
from school in the afternoon, a good part of the carpet would be
covered up by the sofa and they would never be able to play in the
room like that again. She thought she had never seen them so
completely before, except of course out in the open — in the garden, or on the street, somewhere like that. They were lying on
the floor with their heads toward the windows and their feet toward where she was in the back sitting room, which they often
called the dining room. They were on the carpet, and she was
standing on the shiny linoleum that covered the dining-room
floor. She could see the soles of their shoes, their knees, the hems
of their dresses and of the coats that covered their dresses, and the
palms of their hands — their hands were flung out, and she could

see the insides of all their fingers. She could hardly bear it. They were just as they always were, but she put her hands together as though she were going to applaud them. She wanted to laugh out loud. She felt weak and silly with pride, with surprise and a joy that held no taint of fear. The children were safe. There was no one near to cut them down, or to put them in their place, or to look at them with the ugly eyes of suspicion and tell them they were too sure of themselves. There was no one to tell them to *stop*. Mrs. Bagot thought that the worst thing in the world was to be told to stop when you had no intention of doing anything and did not know that you had been doing something you should stop doing.

There was a solid bar of molding nailed across the floor under the folding doors. One of the doors could be bolted into the molding, and then when the doors were fastened together they stood firm as a wall, and both the front and back rooms were sealed against drafts. Now that the doors were wide open, Mrs. Bagot could see how the edge of the rose-covered carpet lay neatly parallel with the molding and about two inches away from it. It needed only a row of footlights on this side of the molding to turn the carpet into a stage. It *was* a stage. She could see the children as though they were on a stage. The soles of their shoes, their knees, the palms of their hands, their necks and chins, their nostrils, their foreheads, and their straight hair—which spread out around their heads as though it were flying in the wind or with their movement, although they were motionless and there was no wind. They were watching her, looking at her and smiling. Their eyes were shining. They were waiting for her to tell them that they would be late for school, and she thought they might have been far above her on an important stage, dancing some wild, slow dance—something they made up as they went along. Bennie, the white terrier, brushed Mrs. Bagot's legs on his way into the room to investigate the children. There was plenty of space between the doors, and Mrs. Bagot was a very small woman, but Bennie must brush against her. Bennie must brush against her every chance he got, and he must put his nose against her hand when she sat in her chair, and he must follow her anxiously to the front door and stand anxiously wagging his tail while she talked to whoever was there, and all it was was that he must at all times know that she was still herself. Verification, ascertainment, recognition, and silence—Bennie lived in the blazing humility of perfect love. And Mrs. Bagot wanted to lie down on the floor with the children and embrace them both and press them *with her hands* into her memory so that she might always have them before her as she had them now—alive and confident in their independence, and seeing her. They saw her. She knew they did. Their smiles were happy and secretive. They were testing her. They were waiting for her to speak. She did not speak and she did not move. She kept smiling and she almost laughed with pleasure. She pressed her dry palms together and then she clasped her hands and let them fall down to arm's length in a gesture that seemed to say, "So this is the way it is." Bennie smelled each child's face and then he sat down between them. As soon as Bennie sat down, Lily jumped up.

"That's enough of this nonsense," Lily said. "We are going to be late for school."

"Nonsense yourself," Margaret said. But she jumped up, too, and pushed past Lily so as to get to the hall first. Bennie ran past both of them and began smelling their schoolbags, which were lying on the chair in the hall. The bags were particularly interesting to Bennie because each bag contained a wrapped lunch. Mrs. Bagot would not be bringing the children their lunch to school today. Today she had to stay close to the house and wait for the sofa. The children knew all about the sofa, and they were looking forward to its arrival just as much as she was. It was an important day in the house, and its importance had grown overnight, while they slept. Yesterday seemed a long way in the past, gone, quite gone. And tomorrow had a long way to travel before it would reach them. Tomorrow was still far away in the distant future. Mrs. Bagot could not think of tomorrow. In fact, she could not think of anything—the sofa kept getting in the way, and it was restless, as though it longed to be in the house and settled down so that ordinary life could begin again and everybody could go about their business as usual.

It was two o'clock and then it was past two. When Mrs. Bagot sat down and began watching the clock, she said to herself that when the hands marked two she would get up and find some little job to occupy her—something she could leave at a minute's notice. But two o'clock came and then one minute past two, and on, and still she sat, calmly doing nothing. That big clock was most dependable. It always kept perfect time. All the other clocks in the house were set by it, and it had ruled Mrs. Bagot's days and nights during all of her married life. Through the years she had watched it; she had looked at it in anxiety, excitement, apprehension, satisfaction, relief, and anticipation, and in disappointment, and in annoyance, and now she simply sat and looked at it as though she dared it to tell her to stand up and do something. But the clock, which had been so domineering all these years, had no power over her today, and as one wasted minute after another turned and vanished before her eyes she began to smile. She did not know she was giving the clock the same smile she used to give the children when they were babies and slept past their time and she smiled at them as though to say, "Sleep on, you will be awake soon enough." It was a secret smile, amused, absent, and speculative. When Mrs. Bagot smiled like that her eyes reflected something she did not know about herself. She was in touch then with a spirit she did not know she possessed, and when she smiled, her face was lighted by the faint and faraway glimmer of an assurance that was truly hers, but truly buried, buried deep down under the sound, useful earth of her thirty-five years of unquestioning, obedient life. She thought the clock was beginning to look quite friendly, and she also thought it had calmed down and was taking its time, just as she was.

She did not sleep, she did not even doze, but she must have been hypnotized by the clock's big innocent face, because when she heard the knock at the door she was terribly startled. She ran along the narrow hall to the front door, and as she ran she kept thinking that it was too soon; she was not quite ready for the sofa yet. But when she opened the door and saw the deliveryman actually standing there, she said, "Did you bring the sofa? I hope they sent the right one. I hope nobody has made a mistake." The man looked at her in surprise and said, "I just want to see how wide the hall is." He peered in past her and said, "We'll manage all right." And then he went down the tiled path to the miniature iron gate, which he had left standing open, and around to the back of the van, where two other men had opened the doors and were waiting for him without enthusiasm. Mrs. Bagot flew after him and around to the back of the van and looked in. Yes, it was her sofa.

The big man who had come to the door had already climbed into the van and was beginning to move the sofa out. She saw that he was grinning cheerfully at her, and she turned away in confusion and hurried back to stand at her front door. She felt she had made a fool of herself and shown herself to have no dignity, and she thought the men must be laughing at her for her eagerness. She made up her mind to look severely at the big man when he came into the house.

The sofa began to emerge, timidly, from the van, and as it did,

Lily and Margaret came into view, running up the street. Some other children from the houses around appeared and stood watching curiously. Lily and Margaret were quick to disassociate themselves from these unfortunate children who were not getting a new sofa, and they raced up the tiled path and stood beside their mother at the front door. She looked so serious and worried that they became serious, too, and worried. Getting a new sofa was not the simple matter they had imagined. The sofa was not just going to float into the house and take its place in the front sitting room. There might be difficulties. The sofa was all the way out of the van now, and it looked huge and helpless, high and dry and stranded on the shoulders of two of the men, who did not seem to enjoy carrying it. "The legs on it are very small," Margaret said.

They were all afraid the men would drop the sofa and break its legs.

"I hope they don't drag it across the top of the railing and tear the underneath part," Mrs. Bagot said. She was trembling. "Listen to me," she said to the children. "We have to be very careful not to get in the men's way. When the sofa starts coming through the gate, you two run back and sit on the stairs, and I'll go back and stand at the head of the kitchen stairs. That way we'll leave the hall free and clear and there won't be any damage and the men will have room to move around. Now, are you listening to me — when they get it to the gate, we'll all go back."

With this strategy planned and agreed upon, they were able to give their full attention to the sofa again. "They'll never get it through that little gate without destroying it," Mrs. Bagot said. But when the men got to the gate they lifted the sofa high in the air and carried it triumphantly and arrived so quickly at the front door that Mrs. Bagot and the children barely had time to rush back and take up their positions by the stairs. The sofa filled the hall for a minute and then it began to sidle into the front sitting room. Mrs. Bagot hurried into the back sitting room and stood where she had stood watching the children that morning. "Facing the fireplace, please," she said, which was unnecessary because there was no other way for the sofa to face.

The sofa looked very well in the room—much better even than she had expected. "It looks as though you had it made specially," the big man said, and she forgot to look at him severely.

She saw the men to the front door, and she watched the van drive off, and then she went back to join Lily and Margaret in contemplating the sofa. They walked all around it, sat on it, stroked its back and sides, and said everything they could think of about it, and they continued to talk about it all through dinner, which they had in the kitchen as usual.

The Eldest
Child

M<small>RS.</small> B<small>AGOT</small> had lived in the house for fifteen years, ever
since her marriage. Her three children had been born there, in
the upstairs front bedroom, and she was glad of that, because her
first child, her son, was dead, and it comforted her to think that
she was still familiar with what had been his one glimpse of earth
—he had died at three days. At the time he died she said to herself that she would never get used to it, and what she meant by
that was that as long as she lived she would never accept what
had happened in the mechanical subdued way that the rest of
them accepted it. They carried on, they talked and moved about
her room as though when they tidied the baby away they had
really tidied him away, and it seemed to her that more than anything else they expressed the hope that nothing more would be
said about him. They behaved as though what had happened was
finished, as though some ordinary event had taken place and
come to an end in a natural way. There had not been an ordinary
event, and it had not come to an end.

Lying in her bed, Mrs. Bagot thought her husband and the rest
of them seemed very strange, or else, she thought fearfully, perhaps it was she herself who was strange, delirious, or even a bit
unbalanced. If she was unbalanced she wasn't going to let them

know about it—not even Martin, who kept looking at her with frightened eyes and telling her she must try to rest. It might be better not to talk, yet she was very anxious to explain how she felt. Words did no good. Either they did not want to hear her, or they were not able to hear her. What she was trying to tell them seemed very simple to her. What had happened could not come to an end, that was all. It could not come to an end. Without a memory, how was the baby going to find his way? Mrs. Bagot would have liked to ask that question, but she wanted to express it properly, and she thought if she could just be left alone for a while she would be able to find the right words, so that she could make herself clearly understood—but they wouldn't leave her alone. They kept trying to rouse her, and yet when she spoke for any length of time they always silenced her by telling her it was God's will. She had accepted God's will all her life without argument, and she was not arguing now, but she knew that what had happened was not finished, and she was sure it was not God's will that she be left in this bewilderment. All she wanted was to say how she felt, but they mentioned God's will as though they were slamming a door between her and some territory that was forbidden to her. But only to her; everybody else knew all about it. She alone must lie quiet and silent under this semblance of ignorance that they wrapped about her like a shroud. They wanted her to be silent and not speak of this knowledge she had now, the knowledge that made her afraid. It was the same knowledge they all had, of course, but they did not want it spoken of. Everything about her seemed false, and Mrs. Bagot was tired of everything. She was tired of being told that she must do this for her own good and that she must do that for her own good, and it annoyed her when they said she was being brave—she was being what she had to be, she had no alternative. She felt very uncomfortable and out of place, and as though she had failed, but she did not know whether to push her failure away or comfort it, and in any case it seemed to have drifted out of reach.

She was not making sense. She could not get her thoughts sorted out. Something was drifting away — that was as far as she could go in her mind. No wonder she couldn't talk properly. What she wanted to say was really quite simple. Two things. First, there was the failure that had emptied and darkened her mind until nothing remained now but a black wash. Second, there was something that drifted and dwindled, always dwindling, until it was now no more than a small shape, very small, not to be identified except as something lost. Mrs. Bagot thought she was the only one who could still identify that shape, and she was afraid to take her eyes off it, because it became constantly smaller, showing as it diminished the new horizons it was reaching, although it drifted so gently it seemed not to move at all. Mrs. Bagot would never have dreamed her mind could stretch so far, or that her thoughts could follow so faithfully, or that she could watch so steadily, without tears or sleep.

The fierce demands that had been made on her body and on her attention were finished. She could have met all those demands, and more. She could have moved mountains. She had found that the more the child demanded of her, the more she had to give. Her strength came up in waves that had their source in a sea of calm and unconquerable devotion. The child's holy trust made her open her eyes, and she took stock of herself and found that everything was all right, and that she could meet what challenges arose and meet them well, and that she had nothing to apologize for — on the contrary, she had every reason to rejoice. Her days took on an orderliness that introduced her to a sense of ease and confidence she had never been told about. The house became a kingdom, significant, private, and safe. She smiled often, a smile of innocent importance.

Perhaps she had let herself get too proud. She had seen at once that the child was unique. She had been thankful, but perhaps not thankful enough. The first minute she had held him in her arms, immediately after he was born, she had seen his friendliness. He was fine. There was nothing in the world the matter with him. She had remarked to herself that his tiny face had a very humorous expression, as though he already knew exactly what was going on. And he was determined to live. He was full of fight. She had felt him fight toward life with all her strength, and then again, with all his strength. In a little while, he would have recognized her.

What she watched now made no demands on anyone. There was no impatience there, and no impatience in her, either. She lay on her side, and her hand beat gently on the pillow in obedience to words, an old tune, that had been sounding in her head for some time, and that she now began to listen to. It was an old song, very slow, a tenor voice from long ago and far away. She listened idly.

> *Oft in the stilly night,*
> *Ere slumber's chain hath bound me,*
> *Fond memory brings the light*
> *Of other days around me.*

Over and over and over again, the same words, the same kind, simple words. Mrs. Bagot thought she must have heard that song a hundred times or more.

> *Oft in the stilly night,*
> *Ere slumber's chain hath bound me,*
> *Fond memory brings the light*
> *Of other days around me.*
> *The smiles, the tears,*

Of boyhood's years,
The words of love then spoken,
The eyes that shone
Now dimmed and gone,
The cheerful hearts now broken.

It was a very kind song. She had never noticed the words before, even though she knew them well. Loving words, loving eyes, loving hearts. The faraway voice she listened to was joined by others, as the first bird of dawn is joined by other birds, all telling the same story, telling it over and over again, because it is the only story they know.

There was the song, and then there was the small shape that drifted uncomplainingly from distant horizon to still more distant horizon. Mrs. Bagot closed her eyes. She felt herself being beckoned to a place where she could hide, for the time being.

For the past day or so, she had turned from everyone, even from Martin. He no longer attempted to touch her. He had not even touched her hand since the evening he knelt down beside the bed and tried to put his arms around her. She struggled so fiercely against him that he had to let her go, and he stood up and stepped away from her. It really seemed she might injure herself, fighting against him, and that she would rather injure herself than lie quietly against him, even for a minute. He could not understand her. It was his loss as much as hers, but she behaved as though it had to do only with her. She pushed him away, and then when she was free of him she turned her face away from him and began crying in a way that pleaded for attention and consolation from someone, but not from him — that was plain. But before that, when she was pushing him away, he had seen her face, and the expression on it was of hatred. She might have been a wild animal, for all the control he had over her then, but if so she was a wild animal in a trap, because she was too weak to go very far. He pitied her, and the thought sped through his mind that if she could get up and run, or fly, he would let her go as far as she wished, and hope she would come back to him in her own time, when her anger and grief were spent. But he forgot that thought immediately in his panic at her distress, and he called down to the woman who had come in to help around the house, and asked her to come up at once. She had heard the noise and was on her way up anyway, and she was in the room almost as soon as he called — Mrs. Knox, a small, red-faced, gray-haired woman who enjoyed the illusion that life had nothing to teach her.

"Oh, I've been afraid of this all day," she said confidently, and she began to lift Mrs. Bagot up so that she could straighten the pillows and prop her up for her tea. But Mrs. Bagot struck out at the woman and began crying, "Oh, leave me alone, leave me alone. Why can't the two of you leave me alone." Then she wailed, "Oh, leave me alone," in a high strange voice, an artificial voice, and at that moment Mr. Bagot became convinced that she was acting, and that the best thing to do was walk off and leave her there, whether that was what she really wanted or not. Oh, but he loved her. He stared at her, and said to himself that it would have given him the greatest joy to see her lying there with the baby in her arms, but although that was true, the reverse was not true — to see her lying there as she was did not cause him terrible grief or anything like it. He felt ashamed and lonely and impatient, and he longed to say to her, "Delia, stop all this nonsense and let me talk to you." He wanted to appear masterful and kind and understanding, but she drowned him out with her wails, and he made up his mind she was acting, because if she was not acting, and if the grief she felt was real, then it was excessive grief, and perhaps incurable. She was getting stronger every day, the doctor had said so, and she had better learn to control herself or she would be a nervous wreck. And it wasn't a bit like her, to have no thought for him, or for what he might be suffering. It wasn't like her at all. She was always kind. He began to fear she would never be the same. He would have liked to kneel down beside the bed and talk to her in a very quiet voice, and make her understand that he knew what she was going through, and that he was going through much the same thing himself, and to ask her not to shut him away from her. But he felt afraid of her, and in any case Mrs. Knox was in the room. He was helpless. He was trying to think of something to say, not to walk out in silence, when Mrs. Knox came around the end of the bed and touched his arm familiarly, as though they were conspirators.

"The poor child is upset," she said. "We'll leave her by herself awhile, and then I'll bring her up something to eat. Now, you go along down. I have your own tea all ready."

Delia turned her head on the pillow and looked at him. "Martin," she said, "I am not angry with you."

He would have gone to her then, but Mrs. Knox spoke at once. "We know you're not angry, Mrs. Bagot," she said. "Now, you rest yourself, and I'll be back in a minute with your tray." She gave Martin a little push to start him out of the room, and since Delia was already turning her face away, he walked out and down the stairs.

There seemed to be no end to the damage—even the house looked bleak and the furniture looked poor and cheap. It was only a year since they had moved into the house, and it had all seemed lovely then. Only a year. He was beginning to fear that Delia had turned against him. He had visions of awful scenes and strains in the future, a miserable life. He wished they could go back to the beginning and start all over again, but the place where they had stood together, where they had been happy, was all trampled over and so spoiled that it seemed impossible ever to make it smooth again. And how could they even begin to make it smooth with this one memory, which they should have shared, standing like an enemy between them and making enemies out of them. He would not let himself think of the baby. He might never be able to forget the shape of the poor little defeated bundle he had carried out of the bedroom in his arms, and that he had cried over down here in the hall, but he was not going to let his mind dwell on it, not for one minute. He wanted Delia as she used to be. He wanted the girl who would never have struck out at him or spoken roughly to him. He was beginning to see there were things about her that he had never guessed at and that he did not want to know about. He thought, Better let her rest, and let this fit work itself out. Maybe tomorrow she'll be herself again. He had a fancy that when he next approached Delia it would be on tiptoe, going very quietly, hardly breathing, moving into her presence without a sound that might startle her, or surprise her, or even wake her up, so that he might find her again as she had been the first time he saw her, quiet, untroubled, hardly speaking, alone, altogether alone and all his.

Mrs. Bagot was telling the truth when she told Martin she was not angry with him. It irritated her that he thought all he had to do was put his arms around her and all her sorrow would go away, but she wasn't really angry with him. What it was—he held her so tightly that she was afraid she might lose sight of the baby, and the fear made her frantic. The baby must not drift out of sight, that was her only thought, and that is why she struck out at Martin and begged to be left alone. As he walked out of the room, she turned her face away so that he would not see the tears beginning to pour down her face again. Then she slept. When Martin came up to the room next time, she was asleep, and not, as he suspected, pretending to be asleep, but he was grateful for the pretense, if that is what it was, and he crept away, back downstairs to his book.

Mrs. Bagot slept for a long time. When she woke up, the room was dark and the house was silent. Outside was silent too; she could hear nothing. This was the front bedroom, where she and Martin slept together, and she lay in their big bed. The room was made irregular by its windows—a bow window, and then, in the flat section of wall that faced the door, French windows. The French windows were partly open, and the long white net curtains that covered them moved gently in a breeze Mrs. Bagot could not feel. She had washed all the curtains last week, and starched them, getting the room ready for the baby. In the dim light of the street lamp, she could see the dark roof line of the row of houses across the street, and beyond the houses a very soft blackness, the sky. She was much calmer than she had been, and she no longer feared that she would lose sight of the small shape that had drifted, she noticed, much farther away while she slept. He was traveling a long way, but she would watch him. She was his mother, and it was all she could do for him now. She could do it. She was weak, and the world was very shaky, but the light of other days shone steadily and showed the truth. She was no longer bewildered, and the next time Martin came to stand hopefully beside her bed she smiled at him and spoke to him in her ordinary voice.

Stories
of Africa

A RETIRED BISHOP of the South African Missions was coming for tea, and Mrs. Bagot and her two little girls were very busy getting ready for him. He was coming at four. The children weren't home from school until after three o'clock, and Mrs. Bagot had to get them to eat the sketchy dinner she had waiting for them, and then they had to get out of their school clothes and into their good dresses. Then she had to brush their hair and put on their new hair ribbons—wide ribbons of pale blue satin. She dressed them alike, as though they were twins, although there was nearly three years between them. Lily was going on ten, and Margaret was seven. She had told them they were all going to hear great stories of Africa—strange tales of ostrich feathers, and monkeys, and cannibals, and big wild birds, and lions, and a sun so hot that people ran to get out of it.

"Is there no rain there, Mother?" Lily asked, and then she said, "When I'm a bit bigger I'll be able to look into your mirror while you brush my hair."

She was standing by the chest of drawers, which held a small standing mirror with the brushes and combs and ribbons arranged in front of it.

"When you're a bit bigger you'll brush your own hair," Margaret said quickly.

Margaret was sitting on the edge of her mother's big bed, waiting her turn. She was getting impatient. The Bishop would be
here any minute. Lily and Mrs. Bagot were both silent after she
spoke. Mrs. Bagot was silent because she was anxiously tying
Lily's hair into the new ribbon, and trying to get it balanced so
that each loop of the bow would be exactly the same size and
would sit at exactly the same angle. And Lily was silent because
she was always surprised when Margaret said anything that
showed a capacity for thought. Margaret's words usually expressed desire, or protest, or affection. And Lily had another reason for silence. She could feel her mother's fingers struggling
with the bow, and she knew that her whole appearance depended
on the next minute or so, because if the bow went wrong the first
time it would have to be untied and taken off, and the ribbon
would be wrinkled, and there was no time to run the iron over it,
and the chances of it going right the second time would be small.
One word from her now might cause her mother's hand to slip,
and so she was silent and tried to hold her breath.

They were in the front bedroom. The big brass bedstead was
placed with its head against the wall. The end of the bed made a
bright railing between Margaret and her mother and sister. She
was sitting kicking her heels on the far side of the bed from
where they stood, and watching herself in the long mirrored door
of the wardrobe. The bed was covered from top to bottom with a
patchwork quilt so large that it hung almost down to the floor on
both sides. The quilt was very old, and it was precious to Mrs.
Bagot, and she usually kept it folded away out of sight, but she
had put it out today in honor of the Bishop's visit, and to satisfy
the children, who had been pestering her to let them see it all
spread out on a bed where they could really get a good look at the
different patterns and colors. The Bishop would never see the
quilt, of course, but it made the whole house better and richer

just by being on the bed for the day. It was forbidden to sit on the quilt, and Margaret sat on it very lightly, hoping her mother wouldn't notice her. In the mirror she could see her own hands wandering around, touching the hard lines where the separate pieces, scraps of ancient dresses, were joined together in small, precise octagonals. This was disobedience, and she knew she would have to tell about it in confession. She had only lately made her first confession, and she thought her sins were like plums—bad plums that she plucked out of the air, which had formerly been clear and empty. Formerly, before she reached seven, the age of reason. And then, at the end of the week, she gave all the bad plums to the priest in the confession box. Always, at the last minute before she got into the box, she felt frightened, wondering what he might say to her, but he never said anything and always gave her a small penance. Now she sat on the quilt and looked at herself, sitting in sin. She watched herself thinking about confession and sin, and she felt she was in control of the situation and well able to manage for herself.

The chest of drawers was so tall and bulky that it spoiled the look of the bow window where it stood, but there was no place else in the room to put it. It nearly hid the middle part of the window but through the right-hand side pane Lily could see the narrow Dublin street outside, and the row of houses opposite, all exactly like her own. At the end of the street she saw the main road. A tram went by, coming out from town, and she hoped the Bishop had not been on it. There was still Margaret's hair to be done, and they would all want to be downstairs and ready before he knocked on the door. Then she felt a final, definite tug at her hair, and her mother stood straight and stepped back, away from her.

"That's as good as I can get it," Mrs. Bagot said. "Turn around now till I take a look at you. And Margaret, get down off that quilt and come over here till I do your hair. It'll be a miracle if we're ready for the Bishop."

Margaret slid off the bed and came over to stand beside her mother. Her mother had known all the time that she was sitting on the quilt, and she had said nothing, because she wanted peace in the house when the Bishop arrived. Margaret would have liked to squeal with annoyance. Her mother had made a fool of her again. And Lily, who was standing rigid while her mother gave a final combing to the ends of her hair — Lily was watching her sideways to see if she would say something. She would have liked to push Lily, but more than that she wanted to say something to show her mother she was not a baby anymore. They treated her like a baby, letting her do wrong things and not saying anything, because they were afraid she'd make a scene. She wasn't going to make a scene with the Bishop coming. They didn't trust her any more than they would trust a tiny baby. Margaret wished she could say something clever that would put both of them in their place, but she could think of nothing. No words came to her, and if they had come there would have been no room for them, because her head was full of tears that rushed forward, searching for her eyes. She was going to disgrace herself. She shut her eyes tightly, but the tears burst out and she felt them beginning to pour down her face. She sobbed loudly. The first sob came out angrily, because she had tried to hold it back, and it left her helpless to resist the smaller sobs that drove up from her chest and straight into her brain, so that each time she opened her eyes to look at her mother she had to shut her eyes quickly again until the sob released her and left her longing not to make any more noise. The sound of the ugly sobs made her ashamed and made her feel dirty and sleepy. But she was helpless, and able only to stare at her mother with terrified eyes. She was adrift, tossing up and down on the awful tiny-baby fury that always seemed to be catching up with her, even out on the street in front of people. And the Bishop was coming. Margaret opened her mouth and screamed.

At the sound of the first sob, Mrs. Bagot lifted the comb from Lily's hair and hesitated before turning to look at Margaret. She could not face it this time. Margaret was having one of her crying fits, and Mrs. Bagot could not face it, not with the Bishop coming. She felt she was very tired, and she thought resentfully that the Bishop could have chosen another day for his visit. It was always hard, dealing with these fits of Margaret's. It wasn't so much that it was hard as that it took time, first to calm her down and then to get her into bed so that she could sleep until her exhaustion lifted and she began to look like her normal self again, her normal pretty little self that everyone admired. Strangers in the street always glanced at Margaret, and when Mrs. Bagot took the children into town on the tram, the people sitting across from them always nodded and smiled at Margaret — at her pretty, anxious little face. Margaret had been a delicate baby and she was still delicate. She was born very thin and weak, and there had been doubt whether she would live until her first birthday. And now here she was sobbing her heart out in a fit of nerves that came only from her precarious health. School was a great strain for Margaret. She was always missing days at school, always having colds and coughs, and then she had a struggle catching up with the other children. And her balance was bad — she was always falling down and hurting herself. She was very small and light, not solid on the ground like Lily. This present outburst was the result of too much worry over the Bishop's visit. The thought of seeing a real bishop and speaking to him was too much for Margaret. Mrs. Bagot realized, too late, that she should have kept Margaret home from school today. Too late. But of course that is what she should have done. She should have kept Margaret at home and avoided all this last-minute rushing and fussing with their hair. In an instant of sickening panic Mrs. Bagot saw all the mistakes of her life rush together to congeal into the one fatal mistake that had made everything go wrong from the beginning. But the instant passed and with it her glimpse of that original mistake, the fatal one, which she could have named if it had only stayed before her eyes long enough to give her a chance to get a good look at it, so that she could see it and recognize it and call it by its name and know at last, once and for all, what it was she had done that separated her from the wisdom she knew other people possessed. She could not deal with anything, and in particular she could not deal with Margaret's crying fits. Well, the Bishop would be along any minute and there was nothing to be done now but reason with Margaret. By reasoning Mrs. Bagot meant that she would have to promise Margaret something, a treat. Mrs. Bagot knew perfectly well that it is wrong to bribe a child, but there was no time for anything now except a bribe. She would promise Margaret a day off from school tomorrow. Yes, she would keep her at home tomorrow and make a little bit of a fuss over her.

Then Margaret screamed. Mrs. Bagot bent quickly to put her arm around her. She was still holding the comb, and Margaret slapped it out of her hand. Lily cried out and bent to pick up the comb, but Mrs. Bagot gave her a little push and said, "Lily, run downstairs and go into the front room and stand at the window and watch for the Bishop. Call up to me when you see him coming, and then open the front door and leave it open, and go out and stand at the gate, and open the gate for him. Go on now this minute and call me when you see him."

As she went downstairs Lily heard her mother begin to speak in a very quiet voice that Lily associated with seriousness, and sadness, and patience, and weariness, as though she were trying to explain something that she could never explain, because it was beyond words.

Much earlier in the day, Mrs. Bagot had carried the alarm clock down from her bedroom, and she now had clocks going in the kitchen, where there was always a clock, and in the back sitting room, where her best clock, the wedding-present one, had lived for years on the mantelpiece, *and* in the hall, on the hall table, where a clock had never been seen before. She had been watching one clock or another all day, and all day she had felt she was losing time, but as she came downstairs now, holding Margaret's hand and moving carefully so that they took each step together, which was difficult because the stairs were narrow and Margaret was hesitant — as she came slowly and gratefully down the stairs she saw that the clock on the hall table said five minutes to four. After all, there was plenty of time.

The front sitting room was usually kept closed. Mrs. Bagot went in there every day to attend to her collection of ferns, which she kept on a table in the window. This morning she had cleared the table of its ferns, and it stood transformed now, with a white lace-edged cloth covering it, and the white china tea things shining in the light from the fire. The fire made the room very cozy. It was late May, a temperate day, but Mrs. Bagot knew that priests returning to Ireland from South Africa felt the change in the climate very much, and besides, the Bishop was a very old man. The Bishop and Mrs. Bagot's father had been the same age, and they had gone to school and grown up together on neighboring farms in Wexford. Mrs. Bagot's father had died when she was two years old, and she always felt her childhood had ended then, before it began. As far back as she could remember, she and her older sister and her brothers had been like little men and women, citizens of a republic where her mother was the stern, distant, and all-seeing head. It was said that Mrs. Kelly, Mrs. Bagot's mother, had never got over her husband's death. She was a silent, unsmiling widow, and the mantle of grief she drew about herself and her children became a substitute for the protection they had lost at his death, and, after that, it became a symbol of his will. Mrs. Kelly's children always did as they were told.

Mrs. Bagot wanted to ask the Bishop about her father. She wanted to hear someone tell her once again that she had been her father's favorite. She had heard it often enough, from her mother, and from her sister and her brothers. Mrs. Bagot had been told what a favorite she *used to be* all during the time when she was a child and when she was growing up, and she had got tired of hearing it, but all of a sudden she wanted to hear it said again. She hoped the Bishop would remember she had been her father's favorite, and that he would say so. But the Bishop was very old. He might have begun to forget.

She had bought a white iced cake for the tea, not trusting her own confectionery, and she had made bread, brown and white, and scones. And she had jam, and honey in the comb. She wished he would come. She was getting nervous waiting for him.

Lily turned from her vigil at the window when her mother and Margaret opened the door and peered in. The door had to be kept closed against the cats, to keep them away from the tea table, but Bennie, the old white terrier, lay on his side on the hearthrug pretending to be asleep but with his eyes wide open, waiting for the cake to be cut. Lily saw that her mother was smiling hopefully, as she did when everything had gone wrong and was now on the mend, and that Margaret's face was shiny but calm.

"We're going to go down to the kitchen and get the kettle going," Mrs. Bagot said. "And you're not to take your eye off that window, do you hear me now, Lily?" As though it were Lily who had driven her mother to the limit of her patience. "Do you hear me now, Lily?" she said again, "I want to know the minute you see the Bishop."

Mrs. Bagot was no longer smiling, and as Lily looked at her small face, pinched into severity and appeal, she felt a rush of impatience and misery. One way or another the day was sure to be spoiled. But there was no chance of saying anything because the two faces, Mrs. Bagot's and Margaret's, vanished, and the door closed. The little room was crowded, with the sofa and the chairs and the tea table and all the plants, and Lily could see nothing of Bennie except his back legs and his stubby tail, which now began to bang steadily against the hearthrug. Bennie had heard Mrs. Bagot's altered tone, and he was taking no chances. Good fortune had brought cake to the tea table, and Bennie wanted to be sure he would be allowed to stay in the same room with it.

"Cake, Bennie," Lily said, and the tail hesitated a minute and then began again, gently beating.

The front sitting room was smaller than the bedroom above it by the width of the hall that led to the front door, and the window where Lily stood watching for the Bishop corresponded with the window upstairs where she had stood while her mother combed her hair. There was no one coming up the street, no tall old man striding like a prophet toward the gate. The Bishop was late.

Just below the window was the curved flower bed Mrs. Bagot had cut out of the grass patch that was the front garden. The flower bed clung to the bow-window wall like a collar of daffodils, crocuses, and snowdrops. The grass, a tiny plot, was bright green and very trim. Mrs. Bagot had clipped it the night before, and this morning she had washed down the narrow red-tiled path that led to the front gate. The front garden was about the same size as the front sitting room, the red-tiled path was about the same width as the front hall and its hat-and-coat rack and its table, where the clock now stood at ten minutes past four.

The Bishop did not come hurrying around the corner from the main road and he did not come striding up the street. He arrived in a car, a big black car that rolled slowly up the street until it stopped before the house. It was a very important-looking car. Lily ran shrieking for her mother, and after that everything was all right. She got the front door open and was down the front path and had the gate open exactly at the moment when the chauffeur opened the rear door of the car and began helping out a large old man who was dressed all in black and wore a black hat. Lily had never been so close to a chauffeur before, and she admired his puttees. Margaret pushed past her into the street and stood stiffly with her back pressed against the garden railing and her little face radiant with excitement. Mrs. Bagot stepped forward to offer her hand in help, although holy awe and superstition made her unwilling to touch the consecrated Bishop. She had been taught, and she had taught Lily and Margaret, that you never shake hands with a priest, and now, with the chauffeur's firm hands under his arm, the Bishop got out of the car and stood almost upright, leaning on his two sticks. He was a very shabby old man. Even Mrs. Bagot, standing in helpless veneration, could see that, and she also saw that his blue eyes were vague and distant, as though they had seen enough and could accept no more impressions, and were no longer inclined to make the effort to separate faces he had seen before from the faces of strangers. He put his sticks together and held out his hand to Mrs. Bagot with a humble and ministering forgiveness that was too calm to hold pity and too proud to hold reproach.

The captive monkey, reduced by grief and age to the lowest and farthest corner of her cage at the zoo, watches the crowd that stares at her with an acceptance so profound it shines like sympathy. All struggle had vanished from the old Bishop's eyes, and Mrs. Bagot saw that he was close to death. She lifted her hands and gave him a smile of tremulous indignation, showing him how, one morning, she would face her own death.

"We have the tea all ready for you, Your Grace," she said.

"God bless you," he said, "but never mind 'Your Grace.' I'm a very plain priest. 'Father,' or 'Father Tom,' whichever you like. Delia, is it? Am I right? You're the image of your grandmother, Delia."

Mrs. Bagot was amazed by the Bishop's voice. She had expected smooth, sanctified tones, the voice of an ecclesiastical dignitary, and instead she heard the rough, warm, monotonous accents of home. Mrs. Bagot thought, He sounds like one of my own brothers. She moved alongside him, keeping step with the chauffeur, who was on his other side, and together they guided him onto the narrow red path that had been washed twice that day, first by Mrs. Bagot and then by a soft shower of rain that still glistened in the grass and over the yellows, whites, and mauves in the flower bed.

The Bishop steadied himself against the railing that separated Mrs. Bagot's tiled path from her neighbor's.

"I'll be all right now," he said to the chauffeur. "Thanks very much."

"Mother, there's a lady in the car," Lily whispered.

"That's Mrs. Sheffield Smith," the Bishop said. "A very good woman. If it hadn't been for her I never would have managed to get here today."

Mrs. Bagot had never heard of her, and she began to think anxiously that she should run back and invite the stranger in for tea along with the Bishop, but she was busy guiding him into the house and into the sitting room and into the chair she had ready for him.

Mrs. Bagot did not doubt that Mrs. Sheffield Smith was a very good woman, but she thought she must be a very strange woman, and very self-important, that she did not even bother to look out at Margaret, who still stood with her back pressed against the railing, staring at the car. Mrs. Sheffield Smith must be very rich. The house she lived in must be very large, and no doubt there was a great deal that was beneath her notice. She had done them all a kindness by giving the Bishop a lift over, but it was a pity she couldn't have taken a minute to admire Margaret standing there in her best dress.

But when Mrs. Bagot had seen the Bishop into his chair, she glanced out and saw to her surprise that the car was still outside, and at the same moment the chauffeur appeared in the doorway of the sitting room.

"I beg your pardon, Madam," he said, "but Mrs. Sheffield Smith wants to know if she can take the two children for a drive. We are going for a drive until it is time to call back for His Lordship."

Mrs. Bagot stared at him. Lily and Margaret were standing behind him. They were silent with longing.

"Oh, Mrs. Bagot," the chauffeur said, "I hope you'll let them come. It would be a great treat for Mrs. Sheffield Smith, and for me, too. She's not able to get out of the car, but she's waving at you, if you will just go to the window."

"Let the little ones go for the drive in the big car, Delia," the Bishop said.

"Yes," Mrs. Bagot said. "Yes, they can go. Get your coats, Lily."

She went to the window and looked and waved and smiled and nodded at the gray-gloved hand and the scrap of veiled face that appeared for a moment and then vanished as Mrs. Sheffield Smith sank back into her corner. The front door closed, and the chauffeur and the two children hurried down the path and to the car. He lifted Margaret into the back, and then helped Lily scramble up into the front seat. The children had been silent as they put their coats on in the hall, and silent going out to the car. It was one of their ways of being good.

"They're gone," Mrs. Bagot said to the Bishop, or to herself, and she turned away from the window and took the chair opposite him.

"I can't get over how like your grandmother you are," the Bishop said. "You're the image of her. I knew I did the right thing to come here today. I'm glad to see you. Your grandmother was a sprite, like you. She was that supple"—the Bishop said "soople"—"that light on her feet, and small, but she was a very hard worker. And you take after her. I can see, just by looking around this room. It's a lovely place you have here."

He looked at Mrs. Bagot, at her plain navy blue skirt and her plain white blouse and her smooth brown hair, and he looked curiously around the small crowded sitting room, and rested his hands on the arms of his chair while he made a careful survey of the ceiling, and of the Greek frieze that ran all around the top edge of the wallpaper to make an ornamental border. He looked at the folding doors that closed off the back sitting room. Mrs. Bagot considered the back sitting room very ordinary, with its linoleum-covered floor and its gas fire and its big table where the children did their homework and where they all had their dinner on Sundays. The Bishop was very anxious to see what lay beyond the folding doors. He was full of curiosity about Mrs. Bagot. She had been born at Poulbwee, the farm he loved more than any other place on earth. His own family had all died out. There was not one left belonging to him around there, but he could still be sure of Poulbwee. He glanced from the folding doors to Mrs. Bagot and back to the folding doors again before he asked his first question.

"I suppose you have another room in there," he said reluctantly.

"Oh, the back sitting room," Mrs. Bagot said. "Or if you like you can call it the dining room. It's quite different from this room. The children do their lessons, their homework, on the big table in there, and I have the sewing machine, and we all have dinner in there on Sundays. Sometimes I open the folding doors back. I am keeping them closed today because of the draft. I don't want you catching a cold, Father."

The Bishop said nothing.

"Would you like to see in there?" she asked in surprise, smiling at him.

"I wouldn't mind the draft," the Bishop said. "Anyway it's very sheltered here, beside the fire."

She stood up and opened the doors. She had cleaned the whole house in honor of the Bishop's visit, and now she was very glad she had polished this room. The smell of the wax and polish came to her, and the room seemed dim and rested in contrast with the commotion in the front room, where there was the tea table and the ferns and the big Bishop. The Bishop leaned sideways in his armchair to try to see everything, and then he got to his feet and came very slowly over to where she stood, helping himself on the way with his hand on the back of the chair where she had been sitting. When he reached the edge of the linoleum floor he stood and supported himself with his hand against the folded door. Mrs. Bagot lifted one of the dining-room chairs over, and he put both hands on the back of it and leaned on it as though it were a railing.

"Now I have a grandstand seat," he said, and from the slow, intent movement of his head and the delighted interest in his eyes you would have thought there were goldfishes swimming about in the air and in and out of the corners under the ceiling, or little birds flying busily around, some of them singing. "Oh, it's great!" he said. "You have a great sense of order, Delia. So did she, God rest her soul."

Mrs. Bagot understood that the Bishop was talking about her grandmother, Mrs. Kelly of Poulbwee. She had never known her grandmother.

"You have a gas fire in here," he said. "That's very handy. And that's your garden out there. I see a lot of yellow."

"That's the laburnum tree," Mrs. Bagot said. "And the side wall is covered with nasturtiums."

"And you have flowers there on the table. Your grandmother always kept the spring and summer flowers on the big round table in the parlor, even though nobody ever went in there. She had that Waterford glass flower bowl that she was very proud of."

"Oh, the Waterford glass for flowers," Mrs. Bagot said. "It's still there at Poulbwee. It's like a fountain."

"Yes, a fountain," the Bishop said. "And it made a fountain out of the roses. They looked as though they had leaped up out of the glass. I never saw such colors. And they used to be reflected in the wood of the table the same way your flowers are reflected here in this table. I can see the yellow laburnum out there in the garden about as well as I can see the reflection in the table. My eyes are that bad."

He turned around and made his slow journey back to his place beside the fire, and Mrs. Bagot lifted the dining-room chair he had been leaning on back into its place at the table and came to sit opposite to him. She left the folding doors open behind her.

"Lately, more and more, I have been noticing what I can see and what I can't see," the Bishop said. "It's like going in and out of a dream, the way things, rooms, and faces fall away if I only take a few steps this way or that way. It is true that we walk this way only once. It is true. It is true. It is the truth. Indeed it is. It is the very truth. And the other truth is that all is vanity. Yes... Those flowers you have in there on the table now, they are blurred to me as though they were only reflections of themselves. And the whole room in there is dim, very indistinct, but I know what it looks like, thanks to you... I am very glad I managed to get over here today. If it had not been for Mrs. Sheffield Smith I never would have been able to come. They told me they had got a car to bring me and there she was. They are sending me to Parknasilla tomorrow or the next day. The Order has a house there for old fellows like me." Since his return from the missions, the Bishop had been staying in a rest home at Clontarf. Parknasilla, in Kerry, in the west of Ireland, is a little pocket in the countryside where through some mysterious whim of nature the climate is semitropical, with warm, balmy air and plants and flowers, palm trees and bamboo and so on, that are not usual in other parts of Ireland. "They say the climate is like Spain, or the Riviera," the Bishop went on. "The Riviera! What do you think of that? They tell me about it as if they were sending me to Heaven."

He looked at Mrs. Bagot as though he had surprised himself by making a joke and wanted to be sure she had noticed.

"As though they were sending me to Heaven," he repeated.

But Mrs. Bagot did not want to see the Bishop's joke. She looked stern, and jumped up to take away his half-empty cup, and then she poured him a cup of hot tea and sat down again.

"I have been hearing of Parknasilla all my life," Mrs. Bagot said. "It's only a little place, but they have wonderful plants and flowers there."

"So they tell me," the Bishop said, but he had already lost interest in Parknasilla. "Well now, you have these two rooms here, and of course you have a kitchen."

Mrs. Bagot laughed. "Of course I have a kitchen," she said. "It is a very good little house, very well built. The kitchen is at the end of the hall outside where you came in. You go three steps down to the kitchen. Then there are the two rooms upstairs, over these two rooms, and partway up the stairs there is a half landing, with the bathroom, and next to the bathroom a very small room. We call it the boxroom. It has a nice window looking out on the garden."

Mrs. Bagot's husband slept alone in the boxroom, but she wasn't going to tell that to the Bishop or to anybody else. The Bishop nodded at her, and then he asked the question he had been waiting to ask ever since he walked into the house. "You have the whole house to yourselves then?" he said, meaning that Mrs. Bagot was not obliged to share her house with lodgers.

"Oh, yes," she said, and then she said quickly, "We own the house outright. We have enough."

"It's what I thought," the Bishop said, "but I'm glad you tell me. You have a good man then, a good protector."

And having established that Mrs. Bagot's husband was able to provide for her and her children, and that they had, as she put it, enough, he proceeded to ask her a lot of questions, and she answered each question as easily and as proudly as though she were conducting him around her garden, or walking with him along a street in a country that was strange to him, although it had long been familiar to her. He asked her about her life, and as they spoke she had the feeling she was talking about someone who was very well known to her although they had never met. She was talking about herself, and she was amazed to find how much there was to be said about this person, herself, who had come into the conversation from nowhere and who was now becoming more real, although still invisible, with every word that was spoken. In response to the Bishop's trust in her she spoke as though in Braille, feeling her way eagerly and with confidence along a path that she found she knew by heart, every inch of it, even in the dark. And as she spoke, that path, her life, became visible — a natural path that was in harmony with the surrounding country-side. She saw that although she had walked the path without as-surance, she had kept to her appointed direction, and she had not trespassed, and she had made no undue demands, and she had not spoiled anything along the way. Or at least this person, her-self, who had come into being without warning and who was now so real in the room, this person, still unknown and yet well known, at least to the Bishop, who was so curious about her and so interested in her—this person, Mrs. Bagot saw, had done nothing without good reason. Not only that, but this person the Bishop admired had done nothing wrong. In fact, it was all very interesting. Mrs. Bagot sighed deeply and then she looked horri-fied. She had forgotten herself before the Bishop. The Bishop was gazing at her with a timid smile, as though he had followed her thought. His smile was a crescent in his big oval face, which was very white, as though he had lost his color all at once, through ill-ness. His lower lip was thick, and his upper lip was sharply pointed in the center so that it looked like a beak. They were lips that would have made a very resolute mouth when he was a young man. Mrs. Bagot looked devotedly at the old, ascetic, fleshy face, at the hooked nose, and at the faded blue eyes that watched her hopefully from far away, from Africa. The Bishop seemed to know that she was thinking of him now, because he began to speak again.

"You have the two little girls," he said, "lovely children. And what other children have you, Delia?"

"The eldest was a boy," she said. "The only boy. He would have been thirteen. He died at three days."

"Delia," the Bishop said. "My dear child. But it won't be long now. I'll see your son. I'll know him the minute I see him. We will have long talks. I will tell him all about this afternoon—all about his little sisters, and the old dog here, and all. By the grace of God, he is thirteen years ahead of me up there. Was he born in this house, Delia?"

Mrs. Bagot nodded *yes,* and then she said, "He was born and died in the front bedroom upstairs."

"In the front bedroom upstairs," the Bishop said, repeating her words carefully, as though he had been given information he had never hoped to get. "Oh, Delia, I am very fortunate that I came here today. I didn't know about your son. I came here to find you, and now I find him, too. He will show me the ropes. I hope I am able to walk better there than I am here. Please God I will. But I will see your son first thing. And perhaps, even before that, he will help me, at the last minute."

Mrs. Bagot smiled weakly, as though she were trying to show she appreciated a remark she did not really understand.

"At the last minute," she said, echoing his words but not his thought. Then she said, "There are a lot of last minutes."

"One for each of us," the Bishop said quickly. "Oh, it is another of the blessings Our Great Lord gives us, a last minute in addition to all the other minutes. A last minute. It fills me, the thought of it fills me with fear, and also with joy."

"Fear, Father?"

"My body is afraid, Delia, but my soul is filled with joy, and at this minute, when I am sitting here looking at you, and thinking of you and also of your grandmother, whose true daughter you are, I am all gratitude. I think of the days when I used to walk down the lane from the village of Oylegate to Poulbwee. It is a mile walk. You know it as well as I do. You must have walked that lane thousands of times. Oh, I can see you on that lane, walking along, admiring the scenery, missing nothing. That is why my soul is full of joy, when I think of the last minute that makes all the other minutes blaze up, and up, in praise of Almighty God and in recognition of ourselves and the way we are always reaching up, always being better than we are able to be. Your father and I used to walk along that lane from school every day, and then I would cut off across the fields to our place, Cooldearg. Cooldearg is gone; even the house is gone, torn down, and there is not one of my family left. But Poulbwee is still there the way it always was. Your father and I used to have great times. We were the best of friends from the time we were infants. We used to have great talks. I often think, if we could only call back into our minds the words we said when we were children we would know a good deal about ourselves, and what we would know would be the best of ourselves. I used to watch the children out there in the mission — little small black children, very mysterious, very friendly and open. I used to watch them talking among themselves, and when I walked up to them they stopped talking, or if they went on talking it was with me in mind, and what they said was not the same. And it was the same with your father and me when we were children. Even with your grandmother, we watched ourselves. What we said when we were by ourselves was very different from what we said when there was a member of the older generation at hand. And so there is never anybody to remember what the children say, because the children vanish. Nobody ever knows what the children say."

"It seems a very long time from those days to now," Mrs. Bagot said, "and yet the lane is exactly the same. It's a full mile from the village of Oylegate to Poulbwee, and yet it never seemed like a mile. The lane is so nice, the way it turns around to suit the fields and then goes straight between the hedges when it gets a chance. And I used to like opening and shutting the gates as I went along. I never climbed over them. I always opened the gates and then shut them after me. And the last big turn you make, that brings you in sight of the house, the lane widens out and gets wider as you get nearer the house, and there are very high trees on each side along that last stretch. There was a place along there where I used to find white ivy."

Poulbwee is a very long two-story farmhouse with a deep thatched roof. The house is whitewashed and the front door is painted green. The front door stands open on a square hall that is only large enough to step into. To the right is the door leading into the parlor. That door is always kept closed. To the left is the kitchen with the door always open. The inside wall facing you has a very small window in it so that anybody sitting at the kitchen hearth can peer out and see who is coming along the lane.

"Your grandmother used to watch for me," the Bishop said, "and the minute I came around the last turn she would appear out at the door and stand there waiting for me. I could feel her smiling as I came along down the lane. God bless her kind heart, she was never ashamed to show you that you were welcome, never ashamed, never afraid. She was very gentle. I could see that people with no sense and who did not know her very well might think little of her... My first leave home from the missions—my first and my last, because I never came home after that until now —I used to say Mass in the chapel in Oylegate every morning, and then I would walk down the lane to Poulbwee, and your grandmother would have breakfast waiting for me. I had been out of Ireland fourteen years. I went out to the missions after I was ordained and I didn't see Ireland again for fourteen years. My mother was dead and there was only my brother at home. He never married, and I suppose the loneliness got in on his mind. He lost heart. All the time I was there he kept talking about how he was going to sell up the place and go to America. He had already sold off all the stock and all the furniture out of the parlor, furniture that had belonged to our great-grandmother, and before that. I tried to persuade him to get a hold of himself, and he said it was easy for me. I was always considered to be the scholar in the family, and he minded that. He said I was the favorite with my mother, and he may have been right, but she always intended the farm for him, although he was the younger. He was in a terrible way, catching a rabbit now and again for his dinner. He slept most of the day and most of the night. He was ashamed of sleeping so much and he didn't like anybody coming near the place, and gradually they all began to stay away. I never knew a place could go down as fast as Cooldearg had gone down the last time I saw it. I had no warning. After the fourteen years away I made for Cooldearg as fast as my legs could carry me, and it was a great shock, to see it. A great shock and a great lesson to me, to curb my vanity that I did not know I had. The Devil is always waiting to catch us in our weak moments. My brother came out of the house, and it was all I could do to keep myself from knocking him down. And yet the day I left he walked as far as Oylegate with me, where I got a lift into Wexford, and when we said goodbye I turned around and walked a bit back down the lane with him, and we shook hands and said goodbye again, and the tears were running down his face, and down my face, too. I watched him go. He never turned around until he reached the first turn and then he turned and lifted up his arm to me and then he was gone. I never saw him again. He sold up the place as he said he would and went to America. I never heard from him. But while I was there, that last time, I said Mass in Oylegate every morning and then I walked down the lane to have breakfast at Poulbwee. I could draw a map of that lane for you. I used to play a game with the children at the mission. 'Going to Poulbwee,' we called it. They got to know the lane nearly as well as I did, and every field along the way, and they were never tired of hearing about the house."

There was a time when the Bishop had looked on that lane from Oylegate to Poulbwee as the only path he knew through a maze that had no center and no form and no secret—worst of all, no secret. There was nothing secret and hidden that he could ferret out and destroy and punish himself for and do penance for. There was nothing. There was only the maze. As a young man, the Bishop had not understood that when he became a missionary priest he also became an exile, and the two words, "priest" and "exile," did not seem to him to be in accord, and he felt it was unsuitable and dangerous for a priest to know himself to be an exile. He felt his homesickness to be self-indulgence, but he was homesick all the same. He had doubts about his own worth but no doubt about the authority of his vocation. His only desire was to serve. To have faith and a chance to show it. The Bishop thanked God in deep humility for the chance that had been given to him. He had found, after leaving Oylegate, that he was not as great a scholar as they considered him to be at home. He felt himself to be a big clumsy fellow, more at home on the farm than he would ever be away from it, and yet when he put on his robes to say Mass he felt like a soldier in uniform on his way to fight for what he believed in. Even in his youth the Bishop never aspired to sainthood or martyrdom. To become, someday, a truly good and faithful servant of the One he loved—that was his highest hope.

When he was thirty-six years old, still plain Father Tom and nowhere near being a bishop, he reminded himself that we on earth are all exiles, exiled from the Presence of Almighty God. But the kind of exile he felt, living inside his own body and dragging along while the priest within him strode proudly, that was an entirely different kind of exile—somebody inconsolable and stubborn who was not intelligent enough to understand the earthly sameness between his own and other countries and who therefore in bewilderment tormented himself about the *difference*. Or you could say that an exile was a person who knew of a country that made all other countries seem strange. In that sense, the exile inside the priest, or living with the priest, hanging onto him, might be a helpful being, enabling the priest to dream sometimes and find a little respite in the tranquillity of memory and of familiar places. The Bishop, thirty-six years old, kneeling in meditation before his altar, arranged a sentence in his mind: *The strong resolute priest finds respite in the tranquil recollection of familiar places and in that respite gains the grace to be more humble and more watchful in his care of his flock*... And then he ground his hands together in the impatience he had forbidden himself, the impatience that expressed a distress he feared because he understood it. What was he doing inventing and polishing and making phrases that said nothing at all? Anyone listening to him would imagine he thought Ireland to be a pretty little oasis of some kind or another, a kind of family paradise. He thought of his country, where terrible pride and terrible humility stand together, two noble creatures enslaved, enthralled, by what defines them, the bitter Irish appetite for humiliation. No, there was no complacency there, no complacency and no chance of any. He thought of his country and sighed in admiration, and grinned, although he knew he was being guilty of self-satisfaction. Then he took hold of his thoughts. He was barking up the wrong tree. What was bothering him and causing him all this weak misery was that he felt ill at ease, and clumsy, and confused, as though he moved through a maze that was formless until he made a mistake, and then in his mistake he touched something that made him draw back. Or, to put it another way, in his mistake he touched something strong enough to prevent him from moving forward, something implacable. How could he have the temerity to expect to be able to help save the souls of the people around him when he had left his own brother to perish in a wasteland of bitterness?

·   ·   ·

Lily and Margaret were very much surprised that they had to ring the bell in order to be let into their own house. They thought surely their mother would have been waiting impatiently for their return, and perhaps a little angry with them for staying out so late. Mrs. Sheffield Smith had told them the Bishop would be late for his supper and that she would be blamed, but she smiled and they knew she was making a joke. They waited, looking up at the door as though their mother's face, when she appeared in answer to their ring, would be at least a foot higher than usual. They could not remember how tall she was, and they looked far up, like Bennie, bending their necks back. They each carried a very large box of chocolates with a picture on the lid of children in old-fashioned clothes.

When the door was opened, Bennie ran out excitedly and the children ran into the sitting room where the Bishop was standing up and arranging his sticks for his journey out to the car. Mrs. Bagot presented the children to the Bishop and then hurried out to greet Mrs. Sheffield Smith and thank her for taking the children driving.

Mrs. Bagot said, "It was a great occasion for them."

Mrs. Sheffield Smith said, "And for us, too, a great occasion. I hope you have no objection to chocolates. One at a time, I told them. They are charming little girls. At first they would not speak, and then they talked a good deal. You must be very proud of them."

"Oh, yes," Mrs. Bagot said. "And Mrs. Sheffield Smith, thank you for bringing the Bishop here today. It meant everything in the world to us, to have him in the house."

When Mrs. Bagot returned to the sitting room, the Bishop smiled at her before he spoke.

"Two great talkers you have here," he said. "I told them that on Mondays I saw more lions than monkeys, and on Thursdays I saw only giraffes."

Then he straightened himself and moved his sticks into his left hand. "And now," he said, "I will give you my blessing."

Mrs. Bagot and the children knelt down, and Mrs. Bagot began to cry. The Bishop raised his right hand and raised his face, and blessed them, and then he looked down at them, and offered each of them his ring to kiss. He started across the room as they were getting to their feet, and they followed him out to the front door where the chauffeur stood waiting. The chauffeur and the old man went slowly down the red path, and when they reached the gate Mrs. Bagot and the children walked after them and stood in a row outside the railing while the Bishop was helped into the back seat. He sank back out of sight at once. The chauffeur turned and saluted smartly, with a wink for Margaret, before he climbed into his own place and the car started off up the street to where it would turn at the dead end. Mrs. Bagot and the children remained where they were, waiting for the car to come back. It came rolling down the street and slowed as it approached them, and then it stopped and the Bishop leaned forward and looked at them once again, and they looked at him. They waved and he nodded at them, and then the car started off again and went on down the street and around the corner. The Bishop was gone.

Mrs. Bagot and the children went back into the sitting room and there was an argument about the chocolates, but finally both boxes were opened and Mrs. Bagot had first choice out of each box. Mrs. Bagot put her chocolates on the mantelpiece to save for later, but the children ate three each and Bennie got cake.

Christmas Eve

THE FIREPLACE in the children's bedroom had to be swept out and dusted so that Father Christmas would have a place to put his feet when he came down the chimney. Lily and Margaret Bagot watched their mother, who knelt close in to the grate, brushing the last few flecks of ash out of the corners. Lily was eight and Margaret was six, and the long white nightgowns they wore fell in a rumpled line to their ankles. They wore no dressing gowns although the room was cold — they would be getting into bed in a minute. It was a square room, the back bedroom, with faded garlanded wallpaper in blue and pink and green, and it was lighted by a single bulb that hung from the middle of the ceiling. One large window looked out onto the garden and the adjoining gardens. Mrs. Bagot had pulled the blind down all the way to the sill. She wanted the children to have their privacy and, beyond that, she wanted them to be safe. She didn't really know what she meant by safe — respectable, maybe, or successful in some way that she had no vision of. She wanted the world for them, or else she wanted them to have the kind of place that was represented to her by lawyers and doctors and people like that. She wanted them to go on believing in Father Christmas and, more than that, she wanted to go on believing in Father Christmas herself. She would have liked to think there was someone big and kind outside the house who knew about the children, someone who knew their names and their ages, and that Lily might go out into the world and make something of herself, because she was always reading, but Margaret was very defenseless and unsure of herself. Lily was maybe a bit too sure of herself, but at the same time she was very soft, very nice to people who maybe wouldn't understand that it was her nature and that she wasn't the fool she seemed to be. Father Christmas knew that Lily was clever, always getting good marks at school. No matter where the presents came from, Father Christmas came down the chimney, Mrs. Bagot was sure of that. He was probably hovering over Dublin now, seeing how the city had changed since last year. The children were all older, that was the great change. It was always the great change, every day, not just once a year. She placed her dusting brush across the paper in the scuttle and stood up.

"Now Father Christmas will have a place to put his feet," Lily said.

"He wears big red boots," Margaret whispered.

"Time to go to bed now," Mrs. Bagot said. "Come on now, into bed, both of you. Margaret is nearly asleep as it is." She had left them up long past their usual bedtime, and Margaret was drooping. Lily was as wide awake as ever; she'd be awake all night if this kept up. But it was Christmas Eve, and Martin was home early from work. He was downstairs now, reading the paper and waiting to come up and say good night to them. Because Martin was home, the two cats and Bennie, the dog, were all shut up in the kitchen. He hated to see the animals around the house, and the animals seemed to know it—they had all settled themselves very comfortably around the stove the minute she told them to stay. They were all stray animals that had found their way to the house at one time or another, and they had never lost their watchfulness. They knew where their welcome was. Bennie was Mrs. Bagot's special pet. He was a rough-haired white terrier. Mrs. Bagot had rescued him years before from a gang of small boys who were tormenting him, and since then she had seldom been out of his sight. He slept on her bed at night. Martin Bagot didn't know that. Martin had his own room at the back of the house. He generally got home from work very late, after Mrs. Bagot and the children and Bennie and the cats were all asleep. He didn't like to have Mrs. Bagot wait up for him, she had to get up so early in the morning to get the children off to school. He thought the animals all slept in the little woodshed behind the house.

Minnie, the thin black cat, belonged to Lily, but Rupert was Margaret's. Rupert was a fat orange cat who was so good-natured that he purred even the time his tail was caught in the kitchen door. Martin knew the names of the animals and sometimes he asked the children, "How is Minnie?" or "How is Rupert?" but he liked them kept out of the house. He half believed the animals carried disease and that the children would suffer from having them around.

Downstairs in the front sitting room Martin was watching the flames in the grate. He had thrown the evening paper aside. There was nothing in it. He was thinking it was nice to be home at the time other men got home at night. Nice for once, anyway. He wouldn't want to have to get home on time every night the way other men did, walking into a squalling household, with the children trying to do their homework on the same table where their mother was trying to set the tea. But, of course, he was different from other men. He wasn't the least bit domesticated. Nobody could call him a domestic animal. How many other men in Dublin had their own room with their own books in it, and their own routine going in the house—an unbreakable, independent routine that was perfectly justified because it depended on his job and his job depended on it. Delia had her house and the children, and he had his own life and yet they were all together. They were a united family all right. Nobody could deny that. Delia was a very good mother. He had nothing to worry about on that score. Ordinary men might want to be lord and master in the house, always throwing their weight around, but not Martin. A bit more money would have come in handy, but you couldn't have everything.

The room was decorated for Christmas. He and the children had worked all afternoon on it, with Delia running up and down from the kitchen to see how they were getting along. They had all had a great time. Even Margaret had come out of herself and made suggestions. There were swags of red and green paper chain across the ceiling, and he had put a sprig of holly behind every picture. The mistletoe was over the door going out into the hall. At one point Delia had come hurrying up to say they must save a bit of holly to stick in the Christmas pudding, and he had caught her under the mistletoe and given her a kiss. Her skin was very soft. She looked like her old self as she put her hand up against his chest and pretended to push him away. Then the children came running over and wanted to be kissed too. First he kissed them and then Delia kissed them. They were all bundled together for a minute and then the children began screaming, "Daddy, kiss Mummy again! Daddy, kiss Mummy again!" and Delia said, "Oh, I have to get back to the kitchen. All this play-acting isn't going to get my work done." Lily said, "Women's work is never done." Lily was always coming out with something like that. You never knew what she'd say next. Margaret said, "I want to kiss little Jesus," and she went over to the window where the crèche was all set up, with imitation snow around it and on its roof.

The window was quite big, a bow window that bulged out

bit cold after the warmth of the sitting room. But he felt very comfortable, very content. All of a sudden he felt at peace with the world and with the future. It was as though the weight of the world had fallen from his shoulders, and he hadn't known the weight of the world was on his shoulders, or even that he was worried. In a few years he would be making a bit more money, and then things would be easier. He had no desire to know what Delia was saying, or to go up there and join in. That was all between her and the children. He would only upset her if he went up there now — he would wait till she called him. It was dark in the hall except for the faint light filtering through the glass panels in the front door from the street lamp outside. He listened to Delia's voice, so quiet and authoritative, and he had the feeling he was spying on them. Well, what if he was. He didn't often have the chance to watch them like this, in the gloaming, as it were. How big this little house was, that it could contain them all separately. He might have been a thousand miles away, for all they knew of him. They thought he was in there in the room reading the evening paper, when in fact he was a thousand miles above them, watching them and watching over them. Where would they all be if it weren't for him. Ah, but they held him to earth. He had to laugh when he thought of the might-have-been. He might have traveled. There was very little chance now that he would see the capitals of the world. He never knew for sure whether Delia and the children were his anchor or his burden, and at the moment he didn't much care. He had seldom felt as much at peace with himself as he did now. It would be nice to fall asleep like this, happy like this, and then wake up in the morning to find that the world was easy. He had often thought the house cramped, and imagined it held him down, but tonight he knew that he could stretch his arms up through this hall ceiling and on up through the roof and do no damage and that no one would re-dreaming that rested her, and she was forced back on herself, so that instead of rearranging things she had to face them. The past led to the present—that was the trouble. She couldn't see any connection at all between herself as she used to be and herself as she was now, and she couldn't understand how with a husband and two children in the house she was lonely and afraid. She stood there talking to the children about what a lovely day they were all going to have tomorrow, and she was well aware that she was falling into a morbid frame of mind. And there was no excuse for her. She had nothing to worry about, not tonight anyway. There wasn't even any wind, although it had rained earlier and would probably rain again before morning. There was really nothing to worry about at the moment, except, of course, how to get Bennie up out of the kitchen and into her room without Martin knowing about it. It would be terrible, awful, if Martin found out that Bennie slept every night on her bed, but she couldn't leave him out in the shed in the cold. The cats always slept on the children's bed, but they'd be all right in the shed for the one night. She had a basket out there for them. They could curl up together. But Bennie couldn't go out there—she'd miss him too much. She wished she could talk to Martin and explain to him that Bennie was important, but she knew there was no use hoping for that. It was time now to go down and call him to come up and say good night to Lily and Margaret, but when she walked out on the landing she saw him standing in the hall below.

The hall was quite narrow and was covered with linoleum, and it served its purpose very well, both as an entrance to the house and as a vantage point from which the house could be viewed and seen for what it was—a small, plain, family place that had a compartmented look now in winter because of all the doors being closed to keep whatever heat there was inside the rooms. In the hall there was a rack with hooks on it for coats, and there was an umbrella stand, and a chair nobody ever sat on. Nobody ever sat on the chair and nobody ever stood long in the hall. It was a passageway—not to fame and not to fortune but only to the common practices of family life, those practices, habits, and ordinary customs that are the only true realities most of us ever know, and that in some of us form a memory strong enough to give us something to hold on to to the end of our days. It is a matter of love, and whether the love finds daily, hourly expression in warm embraces and in the instinctive kind of attentiveness animals give to their young or whether it is largely unexpressed, as it was among the Bagots, does not really matter very much in the very long run. It is the solid existence of love that gives life and strength to memory, and if, in some cases, childhood memories lack the soft and tender colors given by demonstrativeness, the child grown old and in the dark knows only that what is under his hand is a rock that will never give way.

In the big bed in the back room upstairs, Lily Bagot lay sleeping beside her sister, and if they dreamed nobody knew about it, because they never remembered their dreams in the morning. On the morning of Christmas Day they woke very early, much earlier than usual, and it was as though the parcels piled beside their bed sent out a magic breath to bring them out of their sleep while the world was still dark. They moved very slowly at first, putting their hands down beside the bed and down at the end of the bed to feel what was there, to feel what had been left for them. They went over each parcel with their hands, getting the outline and trying to make out from the shape what was inside. Then they couldn't wait any longer, and Lily got out of bed and put on the light so that they could see what they had been given.

The Springs of Affection

DELIA BAGOT died suddenly and quietly, alone in her bed, with the door shut, and six years later, after eight months of being bedridden, Martin, her husband, died, attended by a nursing nun and his eighty-seven-year-old twin sister, Min. And at last Min was released from the duty she had imposed on herself, to remain with him as long as he needed her. She could go home now, back to her flat in Wexford, and settle into the peace and quiet she had enjoyed before Delia's death summoned her to the suburbs of Dublin. To the suburbs of Dublin and the freedom of that house where she had wandered so often in her fancy. For fifty years she had wandered in their private lives, ever since Delia appeared out of the blue and fascinated Martin, the born bachelor, into marrying her. Min wasn't likely to forget that wedding day, the misery of it, the anguish of it, the abomination of deprivation as she and her mother stood together and looked at him, the happy bridegroom, standing there grinning his head off as though he had ascended into Heaven. She and her mother and her two sisters, all three of them gone now, and Martin, too, gone. Min thought of the neat graves, one by one—a sister's grave, a sister's grave, a mother's grave, a brother's grave—all gone, all present, like medals on the earth. And she thought it was fitting that she should be the one to remain alive, because out of them all she was the one who was always faithful to the family. She was the only one of the lot of them who hadn't gone off and got married. She had never wanted to assert herself like that, never needed to. She had wondered at their lack of shame as they exhibited themselves, Clare and Polly with their husbands, and Martin with poor Delia, the poor thing. They didn't seem to care what anybody thought of them when they got caught up in that excitement, like animals. It was disgusting, and they seemed to know it, the way they pretended their only concern was with the new clothes they'd have and the flowers they'd grow in their very own gardens. And now it was over for them, and they might just as well have controlled themselves, for all the good they had of it. And she, standing alone as always, had lived to sum them all up. It was a great satisfaction to see finality rising up like the sun. Min thought not many people knew that satisfaction. To watch the end of all was not much different from watching the beginning of things, and if you weren't ever going to take part anyway, then to watch the end was far and away better. You could be jealous of people who were starting out, but you could hardly be jealous of the dead.

Not that I was ever jealous, Min thought. God forbid that I should encourage small thoughts in myself, but I couldn't help but despise Delia that day, the way she stood looking up at Martin as though she was ready to fall down on her knees before him. She made a show of herself that day. We were late getting out for the wedding. We were late getting started, and then we were all late getting there and they were all waiting for us. And after it was over and they were married and we were all in the garden, she came running up to my mother and she said, "Oh, I was afraid you weren't coming. I began to imagine Martin had changed his mind about me. I thought I would burst with impatience and longing. I had such a longing to see his face, and then, when I saw you driving up, I still had a great fear something might come between us. I'll never forget how impatient I was — I see it would be easy to go mad with love." She said that to my mother. "Mad with love," she said. My mother just looked at her, and when she flew off, all full of herself as she was that day, my mother turned and looked at me, and said to me, "Min, I am an old woman, but never in my life have I spoken like that. Never in my life have I said the like of that. All the years I've lived, and I've never, never allowed myself to feel like that about anybody, let alone be that open about it. That girl has something the matter with her. My heart goes out to Martin, I can tell you. There's something lacking in her."

Min remembered that Martin's wedding day was a very long day, with many different views and scenes, country roads, country lanes, gardens and orchards and fields and streams, and a house with rooms that multiplied in recollection, because she visited them only that one time, and they attracted her very much — dim, old rooms that maintained an air of simple, implacable formality. She envied the way the rooms were able to remain unknown even when you were standing in them. It was the same with the people out there in the country — even when they were most friendly and open they kept a lot of themselves hidden. Min thought they were like a strange tribe that only shows up in force on festival days.

The days before the wedding were a great strain, and Min always said she never understood how they got themselves out of the house the morning of the wedding. If it had not been that Markey was standing outside with the horse and car they had hired, they might all have stayed in the house and let Martin find his way out to Oylegate as best he could. He might have changed his mind then, and remained at home where he belonged. Driv-

ing out of the town of Wexford, they crossed the bridge at Ferrycarrig, and there was the Slaney pouring away under them,
flowing straight for the harbor as unconcernedly as though it
were any old day. And then the long drive out to Oylegate. And
when they got to Oylegate the chapel yard was waiting for them,
looking more like an arena than a religious place. And the chapel
itself, all solemn and hedged in with flowers so full in bloom that
they seemed to be overflowing their petals, color flowing freely
through the air. Min drew deep breaths, filling her lungs with
fright. The fright built up inside her chest — she could feel it beginning to smother her. There was no air in the place. She said to
her mother later, "I nearly got a headache in the chapel. I thought
I might have to walk outside. It was too close in there. I began to
feel weak. I thought we'd never get away out of the place." Polly
was listening. Polly always seemed to be listening in time to turn
your own words against you.

Polly said, "You always tell everybody you never had a
headache in your life. You always say you never had time to have
a headache. You leave the headaches to the rest of us. Clare and
Polly have time for all that kind of nonsense, imagining themselves to be delicate — that's what you always say. And then in the
next breath, every time anything goes against you, you tell us you
almost got a headache. If you almost got a headache it would
show on your face. You're overcome by your own bad humor —
that's all that's the matter with you."

"In the name of God," their mother said, "this is not the time
for the two of you to start fighting. Do you want to make a show
of us all, have them all laughing at us more than they're laughing
already?"

They were walking through the chapel yard after the wedding, and Min went ahead, looking hurried, as though she had
left something outside in the road and wanted to look for it. In

Polly's voice she heard the enmity that had been oppressing her all day, enmity that came at her out of the streets of the town as they started to drive out here, distant, incomprehensible enmity that rose up at her from the bridge at Ferrycarrig, and from the road itself, and from the fields and trees and cottages they passed, and even from the sky itself, blue and white and summery though it was. Even the faraway sky looked satisfied to see her in the condition she was in. Min didn't know what condition she was in. She knew that she couldn't say a word without being misunderstood. She knew that something had happened that deprived her of an approbation so natural that she had always taken it for granted. She only noticed it now that she missed it — it was as though the whole world had turned against her. Polly must have rehearsed that speech — Polly was very spiteful. But where had Polly found that tone of voice, so hard and condescending? She's very sure of herself all of a sudden, Min thought. I must have given myself away, somehow. But what was there to give away — Min knew she had done nothing to earn that tone of contempt from a younger sister. She had an awful feeling of being in disgrace with somebody she had never seen and who had never liked her very much, never, not even when she was a little mite trying to help her mother with the younger children. No, wherever it came from, this impersonal dislike had been lying in wait for her all her life. And it was clear from the way people were looking at her that everybody knew about it. She couldn't even say a word to her mother about a headache without being attacked as though she were a scoundrel. All the good marks she had won at school were forgotten. Nothing was known about her now except that she had presumed to a place far above her station in life. She had believed she could fly sky-high, with her brains for wings. Nobody notices me as I am, Min thought; all they can see is the failure. I was done out of my right, but they'd rather say,

She got too big for her boots, and Pride must have a fall. She had to face up to it. There was nothing she could say in her own defense, and she condemned herself if she remained silent. It is impossible to prove you are not a disappointed old maid.

Min remembered Martin's wedding day as the day when everything changed in their lives at home. My mother was never the same after Martin married, she thought, and it was then, too, that Clare and Polly became restless and hard to get along with, and stopped joining in the conversation we always had about the family fortunes and talked instead about what they were going to do with their own lives. *Their* lives—and what about sticking together as a family, as we had been brought up to do? They got very selfish all of a sudden, and the house seemed very empty, as though Martin had died. After the wedding he never came back again except as a visitor. They lived only around the corner, but it wasn't the same, knowing he was not sleeping in his own bed.

There was eight years between Delia and Martin, and then, since he lived six years after her, there was fourteen years between them, and now that they were both gone, none of it mattered at all. They might have been born hundreds of years apart, Min thought with satisfaction. But it was not likely that Martin would ever have belonged to any family except his own, or that he would ever have had sisters who were not Min and Clare and Polly, or that he would ever have had another woman for his mother than their own mother, who had sacrificed everything for them and asked in return only that they stick together as a family, and build themselves up, and make a wall around themselves that nobody could see through, let alone climb. What she had in mind was a fort, a fortress, where they could build themselves up in private and strengthen their hold on the earth, because in the long run that is what matters—a firm foothold and a roof over your head. But all that hope ended and all their hard work was mocked when Delia Kelly walked into their lives. She smashed us up, Min thought, and got us all out into the open where blood didn't count anymore, and where blood wasn't thicker than water, and where the only mystery was, what did he see in her. It was like the end of the world, knowing he was at the mercy of somebody outside the family. A farmer's daughter is all she was, even if she had attended the Loreto convent and owned certificates to show what a good education she had.

Min sat beside her own gas fire in her own flat in Wexford and considered life and crime and punishment according to the laws of arithmetic. She counted up and down the years, and added and subtracted the questions and answers, and found that she came out with a very tidy balance in her favor. She glanced over to the old brown chest that now held those certificates, still in the big brown paper envelope that Delia had kept them in. Min intended to do away with the certificates, but not yet. She liked looking at them — especially at the one given for violin playing. It was strange that in spite of her good memory she had quite forgotten that Delia had a little reputation as a musician when she first met Martin. A very little reputation, and she had come by it easily, because she had been given every chance. All the chances in Min's own family had gone to Martin, because he was the boy, and he took all their chances with him when he left. And spoiled his own chances for good, because he did nothing for the rest of his life, tied down as he was, slaving to support a wife and children, turning himself into a nobody. After all that promise and all that talk and all those plans, he made nothing of himself. A few pounds in the bank, a few sticks of furniture, a few books, and a garden that still bloomed although it had gone untended for six years — that was the sum of his life, all he had to show for himself. He would have done better to think of his mother, and

316 · THE SPRINGS OF AFFECTION

ing. By that time they were all out working—Polly in the knitting factory, Clare in the news agent's, Martin in the county surveyor's office, and Min in the dressmaking business. She was a dressmaker from the beginning, through no choice of her own, and she made a good job of it. Everybody said she was very reliable and that she had good style. As soon as she could manage it she moved the sewing machine out of her mother's front parlor and into the rooms on the Main Street, where she now lived. One way and another, she had had a title to these rooms for almost sixty years. The house changed owners, but Min remained on. She had no intention of giving up her flat, especially since her rent included the three little atticky rooms on the third floor, the top floor of the house. She showed great foresight when she had those top-floor rooms included in her original arrangement, all those many years ago. Now she had made the top floor into a little flat, makeshift but very nice. She found young couples liked it for the first years or so of their married lives. And she still had the lease of the little house at the corner of Georges Street and Oliver Plunkett Street, where her mother had taken them all to live when they were still babies. That little house Min had turned, in her informal way, into two flats, and she had the rent from them. And she had her old-age pension, and something in the bank—nobody knew how much, although there were many guesses. Some said she was too clever, too sharp altogether. The butcher downstairs under her flat hated her. She didn't care. She had the last laugh. He could stand in the doorway of his shop and watch her coming up the street, and give her all the black looks he liked—she didn't care. She couldn't help laughing when she thought of how sure he was when he bought the house that he would be able to get rid of her simply by telling her she wasn't wanted, and that he needed the whole house for his growing family. She wasn't going to die to suit him and she didn't care whether he wanted her or not. It was presumptuous of him to imagine she would care whether he wanted her there or didn't want her there. He even had the impertinence to tell her that he and his wife had the greatest respect for her. Min didn't know the wife but she knew the people the wife came from. No need to see people of that class to know what they were, and what their "respect" was worth. She told the butcher to his face that he might as well leave her alone. She wasn't going to budge. Of course, it would be very nice and convenient for him only to have to walk upstairs to his tea at night after he shut up the shop, but he was going to have to wait for his convenience. A narrow gate alongside his shop entrance led into a covered passage, and there was her downstairs front door at the side of the house, as private as you please. She was very well off there. The place was nicely fixed up. She liked being there in the flat alone, with the downstairs door locked and the door of her flat locked and the fire going and the electric reading lamp at her shoulder and an interesting book to read and the day's paper to hand, in case she felt like going over it again. And she had Delia's little footstool to keep her feet off the floor. She thought it was like a miracle the way things had evened out in the end. She had gone around and around and up and down for all those years, doing her duty and observing the rules of life as far as she knew them, and her feet had stopped walking on the exact spot where her road ended — here in this room, with everything gathered around her, and everything in its right place. Her mother had always said that Min was the one who would keep the flag flying no matter what. Min had never in her life been content to sit down and do nothing, but now she was quite content to sit idle. What she saw about her in the room was a job well done. She had not known until now that a job well done creates an eminence that you can rest on.

The room where she sat beside the fire, and where she spent

nearly all of her time, had been her workroom in the old days. It was the front room, running the whole width of the narrow old house, and it had a high ceiling and three tall windows. The windows were curtained in thin blue stuff that showed gaps of darkness outside when she pulled them together at night. Min didn't care. Often she didn't bother to pull them but just left them open. The house opposite was all given over to offices, dead at night, and in any case, she told herself, she had nothing to hide... It was only a manner of speaking with her, that she had nothing to hide: she meant that she wasn't afraid to be alone at night with the windows wide open to the night.

There were three doors in the wall that faced the three windows. Two of the doors led into the two smaller rooms of the flat, and the middle door led out into the hall. One of the smaller rooms used to be her fitting room, and the tall gilt mirror was still attached to the wall there. It was Min's bedroom now, although more and more she slept on the narrow studio couch against the wall in her big room. The gas fire was on so much, the big room was always warm. She craved the warmth. She believed the climate in Wexford to be warmer than in Dublin, and she blamed the six years she had spent living with her brother for the colds that plagued her life now. She wore two cardigans and sometimes a shawl as well, over her woolen pullover. She buttoned only the top button of the outer cardigan. The inner cardigan she buttoned from top to bottom. Her pullover had long sleeves, and so she appeared with thick stuffed arms that ended at the wrist in three worn edges—green of the pullover, beige of the inner cardigan, and mottled brown of the outer cardigan, which was of very heavy wool, an Aran knit, Min called it. Her hands were mottled too, brown on pink, and she had very small yellow nails that were always cut short. She was very small and thin, and only a little stooped, and in the street she walked quickly, with no hesitation. She went out every day to buy a newspaper, and she bought food. Bread, milk, sometimes a slice of cooked ham or a tomato. She liked hard-boiled eggs. She nodded to very few people as she went along, and very few people spoke to her. She was a tiny old woman, dressed in black, wearing a scrap of a hat that she had made herself and decorated with an eye veil.

She read a good deal, leaning attentively back toward the weak light given by the lamp she had taken from Delia's bedside table. Before getting the lamp she had relied on a naked bulb screwed into a socket in the middle of the ceiling. She was very saving in her ways — she had never lost the habit of rigid economy, and in fact she enjoyed pinching her pennies. She hadn't amassed a great fortune, but it was the amassing she enjoyed as she watched her wealth grow. She looked at people with calculation not for what she might get from them but for what they might rake from her if she gave them their chance. She wasn't inclined to gossip. She admitted to disliking or hating people only to the degree in which they reminded her of a certain type or class. "Oh, I *hate* that class of person," she would say, or "Oh, that's not a nice class of person at all." Grimaces, winks, nods, and gestures indicating mock alarm, mock shyness, mock anger, and mock piety were her repertoire, together with a collection of sarcastic or humorous phrases she had found useful in her youth. But she saw few people.

In the days when this was her workroom, the furniture had been sewing machines, ironing boards, storage shelves, and, down the center of the room, the huge cutting table that was always having to be cleared of its litter of fashion books and paper patterns, and cups of tea, and scissors, and scraps and ribbons of cloth. Underfoot there was always a field of thread and straight pins. Mountains of color and acres of texture were submerged in that room under the flat, tideless peace of Min's old age. The gas fire glowed red and orange—it was her only extravagance. On the floor was a flowered carpet that had once been the pride of Delia's front sitting room in Dublin, and the room was furnished with Min's souvenirs—Delia's books, Martin's books, Delia's low chair, Martin's armchair. She had Delia's sewing basket and Martin's framed map of Dublin. On the fourth finger of her left hand she wore Martin's wedding ring. She had slipped it from his dead hand. She told herself she wanted to save it from grave robbers.

If she lifted her eyes from her book she could see, down a length of narrow side street, the sky over the harbor, and if she stood up and walked to the window she could see the water. Below her windows there was the Main Street. The streets in Wexford are very narrow, and crooked rather than winding. At some points the Main Street is only wide enough to allow one car to pass, and the side path for pedestrians shrinks to the width of a plank. There are always children bobbing along with one foot in the street and one on the path, and children dodging and running, making intricacies among the slowly moving bicycles and cars. It is a small, worn, angular town with plain unmatched houses that are dried into color by the sun and washed into color by the rain. There is nothing dark about Wexford. The sun comes up very close to the town and sometimes seems to be rising from among the houses. The wind scatters seeds against the walls and along the edges of the roofs, so that you can look up and see marigolds blooming between you and the sky.

Min's father had been a good deal older than her mother, Bridget, and he could neither read nor write. He was silent with his vivacious, quick-tempered wife, who read Dickens and Scott and Maria Edgeworth with her children, and he worked at odd jobs, when he could get them. It was the dream of his life to make money exporting pigs to the English market, and to everyone's surprise he succeeded on one occasion in getting hold of enough money to buy a few pigs and rent a pen to keep them in. He discovered at once that possession of the pigs brought him automatically into the company of a little crowd of amateurs like himself, who gathered together in serious discussion of their animals, their ambitions, their hopes, and their chances. The pigs were young and trim and pink and healthy, and they were very greedy. He found he very much enjoyed giving them their food and that he didn't mind cleaning up after them. He began talking about how clean they were, and how well mannered, and how friendly. He marveled at the way they opened and shut their mouths, and he thought their big round nostrils were very natural-looking, not piglike at all. He liked to see them lift their heads and look up at him with their tiny, blind-looking eyes. He said a lot of lies had been told about pigs. He interpreted their grunts and squeals as words of affection for him, and after a day or two Bridget told the children their father had gone off to live with the pigs. "He likes the pigs better than he likes his own children," she said. He did like the pigs. He liked having a place of his own to go to, outside the house. He liked being a man of affairs. He began smiling around at his children, as though he were keeping a little secret from them. Martin kept his accounts for him, writing down the number of pigs, the price he had paid for them, and the price he expected to get for them. Once Martin visited the pen and saw the pigs. He was forbidden to go a second time. Bridget said that one lunatic in the family was enough. Martin cried and said he wanted a dog of his own. He knew better than that. There was never a dog or a cat in that house. Bridget said she had enough to do, keeping their own mouths fed.

The great day dawned when the pigs were to be sold. Their father was gone before any of them were awake, and he didn't come home until long after the hour when they were supposed to be in bed. They weren't in bed. They all waited up for him. When he came in they were all sitting around the stove in the kitchen waiting for him. They heard him coming along the passage from the door at the Georges Street side of the house and, as their mother had instructed them to do, they remained very quiet, so that he thought there was nobody up. At the doorway he saw them all, and he looked surprised and not very pleased. Then he put his hand in his top pocket and took out the money, which he had wrapped in brown paper, and he walked over to the kitchen table and put it down.

"There's the money," he said to Bridget. "Blood money."

He looked very cold, but instead of getting near the stove to warm himself he sat down at the table and put his elbows on the table and his head in his hands.

"What sort of acting is this?" Bridget asked. "What ails you now, talking about blood money in front of the children. Will you answer me?"

"I'm no better than a murderer," he said. "I'll never forget the look in their eyes till the day I die. I shouldn't have sold them. I lay awake all last night thinking of ways to keep them, and all day today after I sold them I kept thinking of ways I could have kept them in hiding someplace where nobody would know about them—I got that fond of them. They knew me when they saw me."

Bridget stood up and walked to the table and picked up the money and put it into her apron pocket. She was a very small, stout, vigorous woman with round blue eyes and straight black hair, and she was proud of the reputation she had for speaking her mind. She was proud, cunning, suspicious, and resourceful, and where her slow, stumbling husband was concerned she was pitiless. She didn't want the children to grow up to be like him. She didn't want them to be seen with him. She told them she didn't want them dragging around after him. She had long ago grown tired of trying to understand what it was that was holding him back, and so impeding them all. But tonight, for once, it was clear to her that he was going to make an excuse of the pigs for doing nothing at all about anything for weeks or even months to come. It would be laughable if it weren't for the bad effect his laziness might have on the children. But he was useful to her around the house, as a bad example. The children were half afraid of him, because they were afraid of being drawn into his bad luck. They were ashamed of him. Min thought anybody could tell by the way her father spoke that he couldn't read or write. Maybe that was the great attraction between him and the pigs. He always seemed to be begging for time until his speech could catch up with his memory, and he never seemed to have come to any kind of an understanding with himself. He always seemed to be looking around as though somebody might arrange that understanding for him, and tell him about it.

On the night he came back so late after having sold the pigs, he was so distressed that he forgot to take off his hat. It was a hat he had worn as long as any of the children could remember, and Bridget told them he had been wearing it the first time she ever set eyes on him. She said she was so impressed by the hat that she hardly noticed him at first. It was a big, wide-brimmed black hat, a very distinguished-looking hat, although it was conspicuous now for its shabbiness. It was green with age, and the greenness showed up very much in the lamplight that night as he sat by the table with his face in his hands, grieving for his pigs. He never went out without first putting his hat on. He was never without it. He depended on it, and the children depended on being able to spot it in time to avoid meeting him outside on the street some-place. When the money was safe in Bridget's deep pocket she reached out and snatched the hat off her husband's head.

"Haven't I told you never to wear that hat in the house?" she said.

He looked up at her in bewilderment and then he stood up and reached out his hand for the hat. "Give me back my hat," he said, looking at her as though he were ready to smile.

Min hated her father's weak, foolish smile. Sometimes Martin smiled like that, when he was trying to prove he understood something he couldn't understand. She thought Martin and her father were both like cowards alongside her mother. She wished her mother would throw the hat in her father's face and make him go away. She wished everything could be different—no pigs, no old hat, no struggling and scheming. She wished her mother hadn't snatched the hat off her father's head. She didn't like it when her mother started fighting, and sometimes it seemed she was always fighting. She even went out of the house sometimes and went into the house of somebody who had annoyed her and started fighting there. Then she would come home and tell the children what she'd said and what had been said to her.

One time Bridget's sister Mary came storming into the house. Bridget and Mary hated each other. They began fighting, and then they began hitting each other. Bridget hit the hardest, and Mary ran out of the house with her children screaming at her heels. Martin and Min saw it all, and they told their mother she was very brave, but they were frightened. Afterward, when Bridget told the story of the battle, she always ended by saying, "And there was my sister Mary with her precious blood running down her face." Min despised her father, but she hoped her mother wouldn't hit him. She didn't want to see his precious blood running down his face. She began to cry, and when Clare and Polly saw their formidable older sister crying they began crying along with her. Martin stood up and begged, "Give him the hat, Mam, give him his hat!" And then he began crying and lifting his feet up and down as though he was getting ready to run a race.

"You'll frighten the wits out of the children," their father said, and for once in his life he sounded as though he knew what he was saying. "Give me that hat this minute. I'm going out. I'm getting out of here." And he made a grab for the hat, which Bridget was holding behind her back.

She struck out at him. "Don't defy me, I'm warning you!" she screamed. But he dodged her hand and reached behind her to snatch the hat away, and then he hurried out of the kitchen, and they heard the Georges Street door bang after him.

He didn't come home again that night, but he was there in the morning, sitting at the kitchen table, and Bridget gave him his tea as usual. The children looked around for the hat. It was in its usual place, where he always left it, on top of a cupboard that stood to one side of the door that led out into the yard. He used to lift the hat from his head and toss it up on top of the cupboard in one gesture. Always, when he walked in from outside, he threw the hat up, as though he were saluting the wall of the house. And when he was going out, in one gesture he lifted his arm to reach the hat and put it on his head, often without even looking at it. One afternoon, when they were all in the kitchen after school, Bridget decided to play a little trick on their father, a joke. She said he needed a new hat anyway, and that a cap would suit him better. A cap would be better for keeping out the rain—a nice dark blue or dark gray cap. He looked a sketch in the old hat, and it was time he got rid of it. Once he was rid of it, he would be glad, and he would thank them all, but there was no use trying to persuade him to get rid of it himself—he would only say no. He could feel loyalty for anything, even an old hat. Look at the way he had gone on about those pigs. He wasn't able to deal with his own feelings, that was his weakness. There are only certain things a person can be true to, but he didn't know that. Once the hat was gone he'd soon forget about it, and it was a shame to see him going around with that monstrosity on his head. She had an idea. They would take the hat down and cut the crown away from the brim and then put the whole hat back on the top of the cupboard and see what happened when he lifted it down the next time he was going out. They got the hat down and Bridget cut the brim away, but she left a thin strip of the velours—hardly more than a thread—to hold the two parts of the hat together when their father lifted it down onto his head. It all happened just as they expected—the brim tumbled down around their father's face and hung around his neck. He put his hands up and felt around his face and neck to see what had happened, and then he took the hat off and looked at it.

"Which of you did this?" he said.

"We all did it," Bridget said.

He held the hat up and looked at it. "It's done for," he said, but he didn't seem angry—just puzzled. Then he went out, carrying the hat in his hand, and they heard no more about it.

Not long after that, Bridget went to see a man she knew who worked in Vernon's on the Main Street, and he arranged for her to buy a sewing machine on the installment plan, and she set about teaching herself to make dresses. Min was the one who helped her mother, so Min was sentenced to a lifetime of sewing, when she had her heart set on going to a college and becoming a teacher. Min wanted to teach. She wanted to have a dignified position in the town, to be appointed secretary to different committees, to meet important people who came to Wexford, and to have numbers of mothers and fathers deferring to her because she had their children under her thumb. But she learned to cut a pattern and run a sewing machine, and the only committee she ever sat on was the Committee of One she established in her own place on the Main Street. She always thought if her father had gone ahead with the pigs, and learned to control his feelings, and if he had cared anything about her, she would have had a better chance. But all the chances in the family had to go to Martin, because he was the boy, and because he had the best brains, and because he was the only hope they had of struggling up out of the poverty they lived in. He was doing very well and turning out to have a good business head when he threw it all away to get married. The best part of their lives ended the day Martin met Delia. Min remembered the nights they all used to sit around talking, sometimes till past midnight. They were happy in those years, when they were all out working, and at night they had so much to talk about that they didn't know where to start or when to stop. Clare used to bring all the new books and papers and weeklies home from the news agent's on the sly for them to read. Polly and Martin had joined the Amateur Dramatics, and they were always off at rehearsals and recitations, and they began to talk knowledgeably about scenery and costumes and dialogue and backgrounds. They talked about nothing but plays and acting, and they knew everything that was going to happen — they had all the information about concerts and performances and competitions that were coming off, not merely in Wexford but in Dublin. Min thought the future was much more interesting when you knew at least a few of the things that were going to happen. There was something going on every minute, and it was really very nice being in the swim. People went out of their way to say hello to the Bagots in the street. They had a piano now, secondhand but very good. It was the same shape as their tiny parlor and it took up half the space there. They took turns picking out tunes, but Clare had the advantage over all, because she had had a few lessons from the daughter of a German family that

in, Min?" And he would stand outside making jokes while all the women scurried about pretending to be alarmed and making themselves decent. The women used to tease her about having such a handsome brother, and ask her if she wasn't afraid some girl would steal him away. And Min always replied that Martin thought far too much of his mother ever to leave home.

"He's devoted to my mother," she always said, lowering her eyes to her work in a way that showed Martin's devotion to be of such magnitude that it was almost sacred, so that the mere mention of it made her want silence in the room. Silence or an end to that kind of careless meddlesome talk.

"Martin has no time to spend gadding around," she said to a customer who teased her too pointedly.

"Oh, Min, you're a real old maid," the customer said. "Martin's going to surprise you all one of these days. Some girl will come along and sweep him off his feet. Wait and see."

Min told her mother about that remark. "Pay no attention to her, Min," Bridget said. "Martin's no fool. He knows when he's well off. He's too comfortable ever to want to leave home. He's as set in his ways as a man of forty. Martin's a born bachelor."

And of course, the next thing they knew, Martin was married and gone. And then Polly ran off with the commercial traveler, a Protestant, and it turned out he was tired of traveling and wanted to settle down. Being settled didn't suit him either; he was never able to make a go of anything. And Clare married another Protestant, an old fellow who made a sort of living catching rabbits, and he used to walk into the house as if he owned it, with the rabbits hanging from his hand, dripping blood all over Bridget's clean floor.

Min never understood how things could come to an end so fast and so quietly. It was as though a bad trick had been played on them all. There was an end to order and thrift and books and singing, and the house seemed to fill up with detestable confusion and noise. Everywhere you turned, there was Clare's husband or Polly's children, he with his dead rabbits and his smelly pipe and the children always wanting a bag of sweets or wanting to go to the lavatory or falling down and having to be picked up screaming. She couldn't stick any of them, couldn't stand the sight of them. And then Martin moved off to Dublin in anger, telling them that his mother wouldn't let Delia have a minute's peace, that Delia had no life at all in this place, and that there was no future in Wexford anyway. Bridget always said that Delia had ruined Martin's life, and Min agreed with her, except that Min said Delia ruined all their lives. They were a good team before Delia arrived on the scene. The saying was that when a couple got married they went off by themselves and closed the door on the world, but Min thought that in her family what they did was to get married and let the whole world into the house so that there wasn't a quiet minute or a sensible thought left in this life for anybody. Such a din those marriages made, such racket and confusion and expense and quarreling. She thought it was awful that brothers and sisters could shape your whole life with doings that had nothing at all to do with you. She felt they were all tugging at her, and that her mother was on their side.

When Min got back to Wexford after Martin's death, and got her flat all cleared out and arranged with her new acquisitions—Delia's things, Martin's things, their set of wedding furniture, and their books and pictures and lamps—she suddenly realized that she was at home for good. There was nobody left who mattered to her, nobody to disturb her. The family circle was closed. She was the only one left of them. She could only think of them as the crowd in the kitchen at home long ago, and she felt it was they who had finally died, not the men and women they had turned into, who had been such an aggravation to her. She dismissed Delia. Delia was just a long interlude that had separated Martin from his twin, but the twins were joined at the end as they had been at the beginning. Min was Martin's family now.

It was hard to believe that only nine years had elapsed between her father's death and Martin's marriage. Those were the best years. She remembered the day her father died, giving them all a great fright. None of them really missed him. It was a relief not to have to worry about him—an old man not able to write his name, going around looking for work, or pretending to look for work. He couldn't stay in the house. He was gone before any of them got up in the morning, but he was always there to spoil their dinnertime, and to spoil their teatime. And often in the evening he was there listening to them, although they all knew he couldn't understand a word they said. What was most annoying to Min was that he took it for granted he had a right to come in and join them and sit down in the corner and settle himself as though he had something to offer. He had nothing to offer except his restlessness. He always seemed to be on the point of leaving. He even interrupted their conversations to describe long journeys he might take, but he never went anywhere in particular. He just wandered. The restlessness that brought him to Wexford afflicted him till the day he died.

Maybe if he'd learned to read he would have been more content. He could have learned if he'd wanted to. Bridget would have taught him to read when they were first married, but he said no, he'd wait till the children were big enough and then learn when they were learning. But the children weren't pleased to have him sit down with them when they were doing their homework, and he said himself that he felt in the way. Bridget felt that he was indeed in the way, and that he was depriving the children of a part of something they needed a good deal more than he needed it. Bridget was surprised at how strongly she felt that he should not look into their books. She was afraid he might hold the children back. She despised him, the way he went on talking about his dream of being a sailor, when everybody knew he was afraid of water. Oh, he was a great trial to them all, and toward the end of his life people got to be a bit fearful of him, and even the children seemed to know there was something not quite right about him.

It was probably the same restlessness that made their father queer that drove Martin to go off and get married on impulse the way he did. He made up his mind in two seconds, and there was no arguing with him. Min would never forget that wedding day, the struggle they had to get Bridget dressed. She was dressed in black from head to toe, as though she were going to a funeral. She generally wore black, very suitable for a middle-aged woman who was a widow, but that day the black seemed blacker than usual. Min made her a new bonnet for the wedding, of black satin with jet beads, and a shoulder cape of black satin, with jet beads around the neck. It made a very fetching outfit, but Bridget spoiled the effect by carrying her old prayer book stuffed with holy pictures and leaflets and memory cards, and she wound her black rosary beads around the prayer book so that the big metal crucifix dangled free. She looked very smart, quite the Parisienne, until she got the prayer book in her hand. Her iron gray hair was pulled up into a tight knot on top of her head, the same as every day, and the bonnet, skewered with long hatpins, crowned the knot and gave her a few more inches extra height. Min and her sisters wore stiff-brimmed white hats and white blouses with their gray costumes, and Min felt they gave the country wedding a cosmopolitan touch. But of course Clare had to spoil it all by saying to anybody who would listen to her, "We're Martin's sisters. We have the name of being short on beauty but long on brains." Clare always said the wrong thing at the wrong time. It was her way of trying to get on the right side of people. It didn't matter whether she liked a person or not, Clare had to curry favor. She couldn't help herself. You could trust her to make a fool not only of herself but of you. And Polly got fed up and said, "Oh, it's well known that Martin's the beauty of the family." And naturally there was no one at the wedding but friends and relatives of Delia and her family; Bridget invited nobody, because it wasn't at all certain, she said, that Martin would go through with it.

It was true that Martin, with his glossy black curls and his bright blue eyes, was the beauty of the family. On him the features that were angular in Clare and lumpy in Polly and pinched in Min became regular and harmonious. Before he got married, when they all used to go around together, the three girls took luster from Martin's face, and that was fair enough, because their faces reflected his so faithfully that one could say, "He shows what they really look like." But after he left them, the likeness between them became one they did not want attention for. Instead of being reflections of Martin they became copies of one another, or three not very fortunate copies of a face that was gone. It was as though Martin was the family silver. They all went down in value when he went out of their lives.

Martin's wedding day always opened up in Min's memory as though it had started as an explosion. It was because they had been so full of dread driving out in the car they'd hired, and then, when they arrived in Oylegate, there was everybody ready and waiting, the priests and all the strangers, and candles and flowers, and the terrible sense of being caught up in the ceremony and of having to go on and on and on, knowing all the time that you had no voice in the matter and that it didn't matter what you did now. That was a terrible drive out to Oylegate that day. When they finally succeeded in getting their mother out of the house and into the car, she closed her eyes and kept them closed until she got out at the chapel gates. Up to the last minute she had been hoping Martin would change his mind.

"Martin, I'm asking you for your own good," she said. "Couldn't you put it off till tomorrow? I'll never get used to losing my little son, but I might feel stronger tomorrow." She even offered Martin the fare to go to Dublin and start up on his own, away from all of them, at least until any fuss there was blew over.

"Ah, what's the use of this, Mother?" Min said. "Come on now, and we'll all go out together with big smiles on our faces, not to let everybody in the town know how cut up you are."

Min was angling for a grateful look from Martin, and she got it. She thought how easily swayed he was, for all his brains. Oh, she could have kept him and given me his chances, she thought. But Min could not really have been accused of holding a grudge against Martin. She could be angry with him, but she couldn't hate him or even dislike him. He was her twin. There should have been only one of us, she thought, in despair, and saw Delia Kelly making free with a part of Min Bagot, who had known more about hard work when she was ten years old than Delia Kelly could ever know. She wondered what Delia really saw when she looked at Martin. She wondered what Delia saw and how much she noticed with those queer, cloud green eyes. All the Bagots had bright blue eyes, very keen eyes, and they all had coal black hair, but only Martin's was curly. The Kellys were much fairer in coloring; they didn't look Irish at all, Bridget said. And except for Delia they were all bigger than the Bagots, big and strong-looking, country people. Min felt defeated by them, and she didn't know why. She felt that what mattered to her could never matter a bit to them, and she didn't know what mattered to them. They were friendly enough, and why wouldn't they be, with Martin taking one of the girls off their hands. They're not our sort at all, she thought. East is East and West is West. In a way, it was worse than if Martin had married a girl from a foreign country.

On the way out to the wedding Bridget made Markey go slow. They jogged along, and they were late already; they were late leaving the house. The horse kept flicking his tail as though he were impatient with them. Markey was irritated, because he'd had such a long wait outside the house, but he tried to put a good face on it with philosophical chat about weddings and marriages and young men, and on and on. Bridget lost patience with him and asked him whether he charged extra for the conversational accompaniment. Markey was so insulted he started to stand up, which shook the car and made the horse try to turn his head to look back at them, and Polly squealed with fear and asked her mother if she was out to have them all killed with a runaway horse. Bridget replied, "I wouldn't mind."

It was an inside car, and they sat three on each seat, Markey and Clare on one side with Min in between, and, facing them, Bridget and Polly with Martin in the middle. Markey looked at Polly when she spoke, and then he winked at her and sat down without saying a word, and they continued on at the same slow rate until they got to the chapel gate.

Entering Oylegate, they passed the top of the lane that led with ups and downs and various curves to the house where Delia lived. The lane was on their left, and on their right there was a prosperous-looking grocery with a public house attached to it. There was a gap between the grocery and a row of whitewashed cottages with thatched roofs. Outside one of these an old white-haired woman sat crouched on a short wooden bench. The narrow door of her cottage stood open behind her, showing how much darkness can gather in a small room on a bright day in

June. She had a piece of sacking tied around her waist for an apron, and on her head she wore a man's cloth cap. She smoked a clay pipe and regarded the carful of Bagots with an amusement that was as empty of malice as it was of innocence. Markey touched his hat to her and said, "Fine day, Ma'am." The others didn't notice her — their eyes were ahead to the little knot of people at the chapel gate. Min knew Delia must be waiting, and she thought, One good thing, we've given her a few anxious minutes. Martin looked as if he had felt a twinge of doubt about what he was doing. He said, "I feel like a great stranger all of a sudden."

"There's time yet, Martin," Min said. "We can hurry the horse and go on past them all and go to Enniscorthy and take the train back to Wexford and never see any of them again."

Bridget turned her head and opened her eyes and looked at Martin. "Come on home with us, darling," she said, "and you'll never hear another word about it."

Markey pulled the horse up and said to Martin, "Here you are, now."

Martin stood up, making the little car suddenly flimsy, and he pushed his way between their skirts and jumped out onto the road. It was at that moment, when she heard his feet land on the ground, that the day began whirling in Min's memory. She had known perfectly well that the day would be hateful, but she had not known that it would all be so unnatural, or that she herself would feel worn and dry and unable to manage, because the only thing she wanted was to escape from it all, and she couldn't leave her mother's side. Min had never felt trapped before that day. She felt like a prisoner. She longed to be back in her workroom, where she was monarch of all she surveyed. She didn't like the voices of the people out here in the country. They were hard to understand. She knew they were discussing her behind her back, and she tried to let them know she was on to them by the knowing way she looked at them. Martin behaved as though he had forgotten she was alive. She thought it was strange that the world lit up in moments of joy, but that everything remained exactly the same when disaster struck. Martin turned into a different person when he jumped out of the car at the chapel gate. From now on there would be nothing more between her and him than running into each other in the street once in a while.

After the wedding ceremony was over, they all drove out a very long way along the road to Enniscorthy, and then off that road onto a rough country road that took them to the Slaney River. Delia's mother's family, her old brother and her three old sisters, lived by the Slaney in a very big farmhouse, whitewashed, with a towering thatched roof. The size of the house and the prosperous appearance of the place impressed Min. Delia's aunts and her uncle were all unmarried, and they had all been born here. Min heard the house was very old, and that the family had been in this lovely spot beside the Slaney for centuries. She and her mother were amazed by the furniture they saw in the parlor and in the rooms beyond the parlor. It was grandeur to have furniture like this.

"This house must have a great upstairs," Bridget whispered to Min, and Min felt very sorry for her mother. The best her mother had been able to do was to struggle out of a district where the people were down and out and into a street where the poor lived —self-respecting people, but poor. And here they were, at Martin's wedding, surrounded by women who were mistresses of farms, some of them owning more than one house, all of them in possession of so many acres, and even the least of them with a firm hold on the house she lived in, even if it was only a cottage, or even a half acre.

Min glanced about. These people out here in the country all belonged to one another, and they were related to one another from the distant past. These families went a long way back in time, and they remembered marriages that had taken place a hundred years before. They didn't talk, as Min understood talk. Here in the country they wove webs with names and dates and places. The dead were mentioned in the same voice with the living, so that fathers and sisters and cousins who had been gone for decades could have trooped through the house and through the orchards and gardens and found themselves at home, the same as always, and they could even have counted on finding their own names and their own faces registered faithfully somewhere among the generations that had succeeded them. Min thought of all the dead who had been familiar here, and she wished her name could have been woven into talk somehow. She noticed there were no children in sight—they must have been sent off to play by themselves. There was plenty of room for children here —the farm was big, a hundred acres.

She thought many acres seemed to have been given to the orchard—there was no end to it, and from where she stood, the view was more like a forest than like a field of fruit trees, which is what she understood an orchard to be. The ground was uneven, for one thing, slanting this way and that. In her reading, she had always imagined an orchard to be a geometrical place, square or oblong, with the trees spaced evenly. This orchard was wild and looked unknown, as though it had been laid out and cultivated long ago and then forgotten until this wedding day. Min thought of the town of Wexford, of the trees and houses and shops, and she thought of the harbor. Even in the dead of night when people were asleep, the town remained alive and occupied, waiting to be reclaimed in the morning, and the harbor was always restless. The town was always the same, very old and always on the go, with people around every corner, and no matter who they were, you knew you had as much right there as they had. Min knew every inch of Wexford and every lift of the water in the harbor, and she thought that even if everybody belonging to her was dead and gone she would never feel lost or out of place as long as she could walk about in the streets she had known all her life. Out here in the country, things were different. You had to own your place—not merely the house but some of the land. And the houses were miles apart from one another, and the families lived according to laws of succession that were known only to them, and people had to depend for recognition on a loose web of relationships, a complicated genealogy that they kept in their heads and reinforced by repetition on days like today when they were all gathered together. Min thought it would be pleasant to walk around the orchard once in a while when the weather was fine, but for a nice interesting walk she would take the streets of Wexford any time.

Min stood on a narrow path that led from the orchard's entrance to nowhere—it seemed to pause and fade under grass somewhere among the trees. There were rounded grassy banks on either side of the path, but they disappeared into high ground beyond the point where the path gave out. Near the edge of the bank, which was not very high, Min's mother sat talking with two of Delia's aunts—Aunt Mag and Aunt Annie. Some of the lads had carried out three kitchen chairs so that the ladies could rest themselves while they looked at the orchard. The ladies talked comfortably, all of them glad to have something to divert them from the marriage that had brought them together. Bridget lost something of her edginess and made complimentary remarks about the house, and said it was a treat to get out into the country on a day like this. The day grew in beauty, coming in like the tide, minute by minute. There were a lot of butterflies. Min saw a bronze-and-gold one she would have liked for a dress, except that she was not likely to have occasion to wear such colors, and it would be hard to find a design like that anyway, even in the best silk.

"Oh, Min has good sense. She is a born old maid. I can always depend on Min," she heard her mother say, but she kept her eyes on the ground as though she were deep in thought. She didn't care what they said, and she wasn't going to be drawn into their talk. She thought of wandering off toward the garden. Most of the younger people were there, and she supposed Martin was there too, with Delia at his side. She wondered when Martin and Delia would be leaving for the station. They were taking the train to Dublin. They were going to a hotel there. Well, she wasn't going to the station to see them off. She would get out of that little demonstration, even if it meant she had to walk back to Wexford. She would go on toward the garden now, not to have to listen to her mother talking nonsense to these strangers. There were times when her mother was as bad as Clare.

There was a stone wall around the garden, and inside the wall a rich green box hedge that grew very tall and was clipped into a round arch over the narrow gate at the garden entrance. A similar green box arch showed the way into the orchard, but the orchard had no gate. When Min and her mother walked into the orchard earlier, Min had the impression, just for a second, that she was coming out of a dark tunnel, the green box was so thick at her sides and over her head—so dense, you might say—and that they were walking into an unfamiliar, brilliantly illuminated place full of shadows and green caves and a floor of broken sunlight that seemed to undulate before their dazzled eyes. The boys who carried the chairs out from the kitchen were going to put them in an open space where the ground dipped—a very suitable-looking grassy sward, Min thought it. But Delia's Aunt Mag wanted to sit close to a particular tree she said was her favorite, and that is where her chair was placed, with the two other chairs nearby. The boys couldn't get the chair close enough to the tree to suit Delia's Aunt Mag, and when she sat down she moved her body sideways in a very adroit quick way, and then she put her arm around the tree and her face up against the trunk as though she were cuddling it. "I love my old tree," she said. She looked up into the tree, stretching her head back, and she began laughing. "The best parts of the sky show through this tree. Now you know my secret." Min thought she was a bit queer.

She told them the tree bore cooking apples that were as big as your head and too sour to eat. Delia's Aunt Mag and her three sisters, including Delia's mother, all wore long-sleeved, high-necked black dresses cut to show the rigidity of their busts and waists, and the straightness of their backs. They were big women, and the sweeping motion of their long heavy skirts gave them the appearance of nuns. Yes, they looked like women belonging to a religious order. Min thought them very forbidding, all four of them, and she was surprised at the change in Aunt Mag once she got her arm around the tree. Her face got much younger and she looked a bit mischievous. She was a strange, wayward old woman, and Min wondered if Delia took after her. There was something dreamy about Delia that Min didn't really trust.

Thirty years later, when Min was obliged to have Clare locked up in the Enniscorthy lunatic asylum, she remembered Delia's Aunt Mag, and she wondered how many people were abroad in the world who should by rights be locked up out of harm's way. By then, of course, Bridget was dead. Bridget had always said that their father would have ended up in the poorhouse if he had been left to himself. Min thought he might have been very well off in the poorhouse. Maybe that was where his place was. There were people who couldn't manage in the world. But Bridget would never have let Clare go into the lunatic asylum. She always said, "Poor Clare, she takes after her father." Min couldn't see that at all. Their father had been very silent. But Clare never shut up, and all she did was pray for them all. It got on Min's nerves to hear the rosary going day and night. Clare's rabbit-chasing husband was no help at all. He just laughed, probably pleased in his heart to hear the prayers mocked. Min finally lost patience when she found out that Clare had given away every piece but one of the blue-and-white German china their mother had treasured. Only the soup tureen remained, with its heavy lid. Min never got over the loss of that china. She would have gone and demanded it back, but Clare wouldn't tell her who had it. It was gone for good, no hope of ever seeing it again. Clare claimed the china was hers, and that where it went was none of Min's business. Min knew otherwise. Clare didn't live many years after being shut up, and Min brought her body back to Wexford and buried her there where they would all be buried. All but Martin. Martin and Delia were buried together in St. Jerome's in Dublin.

During the years she lived with him after Delia died, Min found Martin very changed. Fifty years with Delia had left their mark on him. He wasn't the brother she remembered. She had seen other men like that — so buried in habit that their lives were worth nothing to them when the wife was gone. Martin would begin to read, and then his hand would sink down, with the book in it, and he would stare over to the side of his chair, as though he were trying to remember something. More likely he was trying to understand something, Min thought. He had had a habit like that when he was young, of staring away at the wall, or at nothing, when things were going against him. He didn't want her in the house with him — that was obvious — but he had to put up with her. She didn't care. She was being loyal to their mother, that was the main thing. He continued to take his walk every day till his legs gave out. He never went out in the garden, never, but every once in a while he would go to the big window that looked out on the garden and he would stand there staring and always turn away saying, "The garden misses her."

Min got tired of that, and one day she burst out, "Oh, she was a good gardener. That is what she had a talent for. She was good at gardening." He turned from the window and he said to her, "What did you say? What was that you said?" She repeated what she had said. She wasn't afraid of him. "I said, she was a good gardener. That is what she was good at, I said." Min was shocked at what he said to her then. "And what were you ever good at, may we ask?" he said. Martin of all people ought to know she had always been good at anything she chose to put her hand to. All the times she came here to visit them, he used to hold her up as an example to Delia. He used to tell Delia that Min could have done wonders if she hadn't been tied to the sewing machine. Martin ought to be ashamed of himself, but she said nothing to defend herself now. He was an old man, wandering in his mind like their father.

Martin was restless too, and the more feeble he became, the less he wanted to stay in the house. He said he wanted to see the water again. He wanted to go to the sea. He wanted to walk on the strand. He even talked about paying a last visit to the west of Ireland. He wanted to walk by the Atlantic Ocean once again. He said the air there would put new life into him. Once he began talking about Connemara and Kerry, there was no stopping him. He liked to recall the adventures he'd had on the holidays he used to take by himself in Connemara and Kerry long ago. He used to go on long walking tours by himself. He'd stay away for a week at a time. He liked to recall those days when he was on his own. He seemed proud of having gone off on his own, away from this house and from Delia and the children, away from all he knew. He sounded like a conjurer describing some magical rope trick when he talked about how he left the house at such and such an hour, and what So-and-So had said to him on the train, and how he carried nothing with him but his knapsack and his blackthorn stick. Min didn't like hearing about it. She knew his adventures, and she had no sympathy with him. If he was all that anxious to have a change from Delia—and nobody could blame him for that—why hadn't he come to Wexford to see his mother, and to see his sisters, and to go about the town and have a word with all the old crowd? Most of them were still there at that time.

He could have taken a walk about the town with me, Min thought. It would have set me up, in those days, to be seen with him, show off a bit. Many a time he could have come down to see us, but no, he was off to Connemara, or to Kerry, to enjoy another holiday by himself with the Atlantic Ocean. The Irish Sea wasn't good enough for him anymore, and Wexford Harbor was nothing compared with the beauties of Galway Bay. He talked about the wild Mayo coast as though wildness were a sort of virtue, and one you didn't find in the scenery in Wexford. She reminded him that he had once been in love with their own strand at Rosslare, and she described to him how he used to spend half his life out there, riding out on his bicycle every chance he got. Every free minute he could get he spent at Rosslare. He listened to her, but as though he was being patient with her. "I'd be very glad to see Rosslare again," he said when she had finished talking.

Then he gave up talking about Connemara and Kerry, and he began to wish for a day out at Dun Laoghaire. And he said he'd like to have a day at Greystones. And he wanted to go out to Killiney for a day. Which would Min like best? Maybe they could manage it. Min didn't see how they were going to manage it. A whole day out of the house, and no guarantee of what the weather might be like. They might not be able to find shelter so easily in case of a sudden shower. If he got his feet wet there'd be the devil to pay. They had no car, even if they could drive, and it was an awful drag out to Killiney and back on the bus, or on the train, if they took the train. It would be foolish to go to the expense of hiring a car. She didn't see how they were going to do it.

He seemed to let go of the idea, and then one day he said, "Min, do you remember the lovely view of the Slaney from the garden that day? Do you remember how the Slaney looked that day, flowing past us into Wexford? And we all stood looking at it? I thought of the passage of time. I stood there, and I thought for a minute that the garden was moving along with the river. And then later on when Delia and I were at Edermine station waiting for the train to Dublin, there were all the flowers in the station, and the stationmaster laughing at us and talking to us, and the white stones spelling out the name of the station. Delia said an expert gardener must have planted the bed of flowers beside the station house, and the stationmaster said he'd done it all himself, getting the place ready for her. But the garden they had there by the Slaney — that was magnificent. Wasn't it, Min?"

Min remembered standing in the garden, surrounded by roses with big heavy heads, and hearing her mother say that she would like very much to have a bunch of flowers to take back to Wexford with her. They all got bunches of flowers to take home. And there was a bunch of flowers for Markey to take to his wife. The car was filled with flowers, and still the garden looked as though it hadn't been touched.

"That was a grand place they had there," Min said, and she was glad to know that the garden was in ruins now, and that the house stood empty with the roof falling in and that the door there stood open to display the vacant rooms and the cold hearth in the kitchen. "It's all gone now," she said.

"It was a marvelous day," Martin said. "I never forgot what Delia's Aunt Mag said to me. Do you remember — she said the air was like mother o' pearl. Wasn't that a funny thing for an old country woman to say? I wonder what put a thought like that in her head. 'The air is like mother o' pearl today,' she said, looking at me as though we were the same age and had known each other all our lives."

"She didn't look at me that way," Min said. "But I remember her saying that. She was a bit affected, I think — inclined to talk above herself. I didn't care for her. Something about her made me very uneasy."

"Ah, no," Martin said. "Delia was very fond of her."

"Oh, Delia," Min said impatiently. "Delia said the first thing that came into her head. You told her so often enough, to her face, with me sitting here in this room listening to you barging at her. She couldn't open her mouth to suit you. There was no harm in Delia, but she never knew what she said. Half the time she made no sense. There was nothing to Delia."

The minute she finished speaking, she was sorry. She didn't want to start a row. But Martin was silent, and then he said, "Nothing to Delia. That's true. I never thought that. But as Shakespeare says, It's true. It's true, it's a pity, and pity 'tis it's true. Nothing to Delia. Shakespeare was right that time."

"Shakespeare didn't say it. I said it," Min cried furiously.

"You or Shakespeare, what matter now. It's true, there was nothing to Delia. Wasn't she a lovely girl, though."

"Are you going to make a song out of it?" Min said. "What's got into you, Martin?"

She looked at him sitting across the hearth from her. His snow white curls floated on his head. His narrow face was the same shape as her own face. His blue eyes watched her through his rimless spectacles, and he smiled easily, as though they were discussing something pleasant from the past. She thought of Clare singing "You stick to the boats, lads…" that morning when she was being driven off in the car that took her to the asylum. They told Min later that Clare stopped singing quick enough when she saw where she was going. Min wondered if the queer strain that was in Clare had touched Martin, and she was glad that she herself was free of it. Martin seemed to follow her thoughts.

"You put poor Clare into the asylum," he said gently.

"She was off her head, driving us all to distraction, trying to give the house away!" Min said indignantly. "What help were you, up here in Dublin, away from all the unpleasantness?"

"Clare was mad," Martin said. "There was nothing to Delia. That's a weight off my mind. I know where I am now. I always knew where I was with her, even though I didn't know what she was, and now I still don't know what she was, and God knows I don't know where I am without her. But there was nothing to her."

"My mother said Delia didn't amount to much," Min said spitefully. "Right from the beginning, she said that."

"Nothing to her. You said it yourself," Martin said. "I'll show you a picture of her, taken when she was sixteen years old."

He pulled himself slowly to his feet, and made his way across the room to the cupboard, which had glass doors on top and solid wooden doors underneath. Behind the glass doors Delia's Waterford glass bowls and her Waterford glass jug shimmered dimly. They had a shelf to themselves. Another shelf held her good Arklow china. Martin bent painfully to open the lower doors, and when they were open wide he reached in and took out a large brown envelope. He pushed the doors shut and made his way back to where Min sat in Delia's chair on Delia's side of the fire. He unfastened the envelope and slid the photograph out carefully, holding it as though it were thin glass. His hands are trembling more these days, Min thought. When the photograph was free, he held it up for Min to see.

"There she is," he said. "That's what she looked like. Look at the hair she had. Who ever had hair like that, that color? Nobody else in that family had hair like that. They said she took after her father. He died young. Look at that, Min."

"That photograph glorifies her," Min said.

"She was very good," Martin said. "I remember that day we got married, I was standing off to myself, looking at the Slaney. I was lost in admiration. I was looking through a gap in the hedge —one of the children had pulled open a place there, to look through. The river seemed very close up to the garden, under my feet. It was very close. Even then the water was eating in under the garden, and the little strand they told me they had there at one time was gone, or nearly gone. I remember I was there by myself—the water was dazzling. I didn't know where I was. I was inside a dream, and everything was safe, I know. The Slaney was very broad that day, and powerful, sure and strong—you know the way it used to be. An Irish river of great importance, the inspector said the day he visited the school. But I felt grand, looking at the Slaney that day. To know it was my own native river and was so, long before I was born. I was standing there like that, when Delia's Aunt Mag came up alongside me. 'I was looking for you,' she said. My God, how well I remember her voice, as if it was five minutes ago. We might still be there. 'I was looking for you,' she said. She saw the break in the hedge. 'Ah, you found a spy hole,' she said. And do you know what she did? She put her arm around my shoulders. She was taller than me—they were big women in that family—and she stuck her face out past me so that she could see what I was looking at. I started to move to the side, to give her room, but she held on to me. 'Stay where you are,' she said. I said, 'I'm in your way.' 'You're not in my way, child,' she said. 'Haven't you more right to stand here than anybody? I only want to have a little look before Willie comes along and finds this hole and starts to patch it up. "The lads have been up to mischief again" — that's what Willie will say. He says they're tearing down the hedge, helping the garden into the river. The river is eating up the garden, you know — if it wasn't for Willie always on guard, we'd be swallowed up.' I said, 'It's great to see the Slaney like this.' 'I have a great fondness for the water,' she said. 'I couldn't be content any place but here where I was born and brought up. I've never spent a night away from this house in my life, do you know that? It's a blessing the day turned out so grand. And nobody was sick or anything. Everybody was able to come see Delia married. The Slaney is in full flood, and the springs of affection are rising around us.' She spoke the truth. The Slaney was in full flood that day."

"That's sheer nonsense," Min said. "How could the Slaney be in full flood on a fine day in June? The Slaney was the same as any other day."

Martin went to his own chair and sat down. "My legs aren't getting any better," he said. "I can't stand on my own feet these days."

"You've tired yourself out making speeches," Min said.

Martin still held the photograph of Delia. He lifted it to see it better. He's trembling too much, Min thought. She wondered if she could get him to go to his room and lie down. "You're wearing yourself out," she said.

Martin gazed at the shaking photograph. "It's very like her," he said. Then he fitted it back into its envelope, pressing his lips together and frowning, like a foolish old man making an effort to do something that was beyond him.

"I'll do that for you," she said, getting ready to stand up and go over to him.

"You stay where you are," he said, and when he had the photograph safe he placed the envelope on the low shelf under his table. "I shouldn't have stood up so long," he said, and then he took his book from the table and began reading, but after a minute he got up and went out of the room, carrying the book with him. "I'm going to my room," he said without looking at her. "I might lie down for a bit."

Min was glad to see him go. There would be peace now, for a while. She didn't like to see him getting into these states where he talked so much. All that raking up of the past was a bad sign. She would have asked the priest to come in and talk to him, but she knew Martin would fight the priest's coming until he could fight no more. Martin didn't want the priest in the house. His mind was made up to that, and there was no use arguing with him. Min only hoped she would be able to get the priest in time, when the time came. She didn't want her brother dying without the Last Sacraments. She didn't understand Martin's bitter attitude toward the Church. Polly went very much the same way, of course. Min would never forget Polly's blasphemous language when the third-eldest child died, the little one they called Mary. Min was trying to comfort Polly by telling her the baby would be well taken care of in Heaven, when Polly burst out laughing and crying and saying she could take care of her own child better than God and His Blessed Mother and all the saints and angels put together. "They might have left poor little Mary with her own Mammy!" Polly said. "They must have seen the way she was holding on to my hand, wanting to stay with me. They have very hard hearts up there, if you ask me." Martin had never gone that far in his talk against the Church. At least, as far as Min knew he'd never gone that far, but she knew she was going to have to do a bit of scheming to get the priest into the house. "The springs of affection are rising." She didn't like to hear him talking like that. What Min remembered of that day in the garden by the Slaney was that she felt worn out and dried up, and trapped, crushed in by people who were determined to see only the bright surface of the occasion. They could call it a wedding or anything they liked, but she knew it was a holocaust and that she was the victim, although nobody would ever admit that.

She thought they were all very clumsy. It wasn't that she wanted to be noticed. But she knew that any notice she got was pity, or derision. Nothing she could say was right. She was out of it, and nothing could convince those people that she wanted to be out of it. She would ten times rather have been back in Wexford working as usual, but she had to go to the wedding or cause a scandal. Now here they were. Bridget was giving every evidence of enjoying herself, and so were Polly and Clare, and in Min's opinion they were letting the side down. She had been dragged out here like a victim of war at the back of a chariot, and all to bolster Martin up, and he didn't need bolstering up.

She stood outside the garden gate. The children had all vanished, and she imagined they had gone to play somewhere by themselves, but suddenly the place was full of children running around, and she thought they must have been having their dinner. Children always had to be fed, no matter what. These children were a healthy-looking lot, fair-haired or red-headed, most of them. Min remembered how black she and Martin had been as children, Martin with his black curls and she with her straight black plait. They were a skinny pair, very different from these children. A little boy ran up to her so suddenly that she thought he was going to crash into her, but he stopped just in time and stared up at her. He was about five years old, a very solid-looking little fellow. His eyes were so blue that it was like two flowers looking at you, and he had a very short nose, and there was sweat on his forehead. His hair was nearly white. He wore a little suit of clothes, a little coat and trousers and a white shirt, and black stockings pulled up on his legs under the trousers. He opened his mouth, but he said nothing, just stared at her. Min gave him no encouragement. She didn't dislike children, but she had no great fondness for them, and she didn't want a whole crowd of them trooping along after him and asking her questions and making her conspicuous. He turned red, and he threw his arm up over his eyes, and peered up at her from under his sleeve, and began to smile. She smiled at him. He was a nice little fellow. She ought to say something to him.

"Are you a good boy?" she asked him. He turned and ran off, flapping his arms at his sides like a farmyard bird, and when he was a little distance away he turned and looked back to see if she was watching him. Then he ran off out of the garden. She didn't see him again.

The next thing she remembered was a moment of terrible unhappiness—it gave her a shock. What happened was that Martin and one of Delia's brothers and a woman she didn't even know came up to her and began talking about the train. They kept saying that it wouldn't do for Delia and Martin to miss the train. Min never knew the woman's name, but she remembered that she made a great fuss, as though she imagined that the day depended on her. There were always people like that everywhere, trying to boss things. She wanted to tell that woman to mind her own business. All these strangers were taking Martin over. They thought they owned him now.

"The springs of affection are rising." It would be those people who would say a thing like that, including everybody in their inspirations, everybody, even people who didn't want to be included. Min thought of that garden. She thought of the green box hedge and the monkey-puzzle tree and the pink and white roses and all the big dark and white star-shaped flowers, and she thought of Delia's Aunt Mag on the kitchen chair under the cooking-apple tree, and she remembered Delia's brothers and sis-

ter and Delia's mother, and the white-haired child. She had forgotten nothing of that glittering day, and she saw it all enclosed
in a radiant fountain that rushed up through a rain of sunlight to
meet with and rejoice with whatever was up there—Heaven,
God the Father, the Good Shepherd, everything everybody ever
wanted, wonderful prizes, happiness.

Min knew it was only the transfiguration of memory. She was
no fool, and she was not likely to mistake herself for a visionary.
The lovely fountain was like a mirage, except that in a mirage
people saw what they wanted and were starving for, and in the
fountain Min saw what she did not want and never had wanted.
Why was it nobody ever believed her when she told them she
wanted nothing to do with all that hullabaloo? The fortunes of
war condemned her to a silence that misrepresented her as thor-
oughly as the words she was too proud to speak would have
done, and she knew all that. Martin's lightmindedness had
changed the course of her life, and there wasn't one single thing
she could do about it. He turned all their lives around. He cared
no more about his mother and sisters and what happened to them
than if he had been a stranger passing through the house on his
way to a far better place, where the people were more interesting.

He made his mother cry. For a wedding present, Bridget
wanted to give Martin the good dining-room set that she had
paid for penny by penny at a time when she couldn't afford it. A
big round mahogany table and four matching chairs that must
have had pride of place in some great house at one time. She kept
that furniture up to the nines, polished and waxed till you could
see to do your hair in it. But Martin turned up his nose at it. No
secondhand stuff for him and Delia, and the mahogany was too
big and heavy anyway. He didn't want it. He and Delia went and
ordered furniture made just for them; new furniture, all walnut
—a bed, a chest of drawers, a wardrobe, a washstand, and two

sitting-room chairs so that Delia could hold court in style when they had visitors. Those were Martin's very words. "Now Delia can hold court in style," he said, and never noticed the look on his mother's face. Min noticed the bed had vanished out of the house in Dublin, and she was never able to find out what happened to it. But the other things were still there. Above all, the two sitting-room chairs were still there—Martin sat in his own, and she sat in Delia's. She would take the whole lot back to Wexford when the time came. She would bring the furniture back where it belonged. It was never too late to make things right.

In Wexford, in her own flat, she sat in Delia's chair, and sometimes for a change sat propped up with pillows in Martin's big chair, his armchair. It was nice to have the two chairs. The wardrobe and the chest of drawers went into her bedroom, and the washstand into the room she used for a kitchen. Delia's old sitting-room carpet was threadbare, but the colors held up well, and it looked nice on the floor, almost like an antique carpet. And the hearthrug from the house in Dublin looked very suitable in front of Min's old fireplace, where so many girls and ladies had warmed themselves when they came in to be measured for a dress, or to have a fitting.

Against the end wall, facing down the room to the fireplace, Delia's bookshelves were ranged along, filled with Delia's books, and with some of Martin's books. Some of Martin's books Min wouldn't have in the house, and she had sold them. She was glad now that she had never spent money on books; these had been waiting for her. The room looked very distinguished, very literary. It was what she should always have had. She wished they could all see it. There was room for them, and a welcome. There was even a deep, dim corner there between the end wall and the far window where her father could steal in and sit down and listen to them with his silence, as he used to do. There was a place here for all of them—a place for Polly, a place for poor Clare. A place in the middle for Bridget. A place for Martin in his own chair. They could come in anytime and feel right at home although the room was warmer and the furniture a bit better than anything they had been used to in the old days.

NOTE

All of these stories appeared originally in *The New Yorker*, except "The Poor Men and Women," which appeared in *Harper's Bazaar*. They are listed below in the order of publication.

"The Poor Men and Women," April 1952
"The Morning after the Big Fire," February 7, 1953
"The Clever One," May 30, 1953
"The Lie," October 3, 1953
"The Day We Got Our Own Back," October 24, 1953
"The Barrel of Rumors," February 27, 1954
"The Devil in Us," July 3, 1954
"The Old Man of the Sea," January 15, 1955
"An Attack of Hunger," January 6, 1962
"A Young Girl Can Spoil Her Chances," September 8, 1962
"The Drowned Man," July 27, 1963
"The Carpet with the Big Pink Roses on It," May 23, 1964
"A Free Choice," July 11, 1964
"The Shadow of Kindness," August 14, 1965
"The Twelfth Wedding Anniversary," September 24, 1966
"The Sofa," March 2, 1968
"The Eldest Child," June 29, 1968

"Stories of Africa," August 10, 1968
"The Springs of Affection," March 18, 1972
"Christmas Eve," December 23, 1972
"Family Walls," March 10, 1973